CLEAR WATER

Will Ashon runs the record company Big Dada Records.
Clear Water is his first novel.

WILL ASHON

Clear Water

faber and faber

First published in 2006
by Faber and Faber Limited
3 Queen Square London WC1N 3AU
This paperback edition published in 2007

Typeset by Faber and Faber
Printed in the UK by CPI Bookmarque, Croydon, CR0 4TD

A CIP record for this book
is available from the British Library

ISBN 978-0-571-23102-7

2 4 6 8 10 9 7 5 3 1

To Mum and Dad for getting me started
And Leila for keeping me going

Unless we change our ways and our direction, our greatness as a nation will soon be a footnote in the history books, a distant memory of an offshore island, lost in the mists of time like Camelot, remembered kindly for its noble past.

Margaret Thatcher

Shudder not. but Write, & the hand of God will assist you! Therefore I write Albions last words. Hope is banish'd from me.

William Blake

Before

'Are you sure all this is entirely necessary?'

Widening as it nears the floor, so muscularly, industrially functional it seems affected, this staircase is made to be grandly descended. And so it is. The door at its head peels back with a sigh of complicity to reveal two columns of three women who immediately march forward, the snap of the heels on their shining black boots perfect, unitary. The theme established by their footwear is re-emphasized in the black trousers they wear, reinforced by the contrast between black shirt and powdered, milky chest, finally hammered home by the black silk scarf loosely knotted round each luminous neck. They walk with an exaggerated swagger, a perfectly drilled gang of principal boys. The smile on every red-lipped face is the same, the tilt of the head, forward and to the right, identical.

'What we're doing or how we're doing it?'
    'Both, really. I suppose both.'
    'Feeling extra scrupulous today?'
    'Ha ha. You can honestly say you've no misgivings at all about this?'
    'Honestly.'
    'I mean, purely budgetary . . .'
    'None.'

It's their hair, though, that holds the attention. Even on these monitors, which Procurement seem to have scrimped on, even with the pixellation and the fish-eyeing towards the edge of the screen, even with the slightly washed-out colours, it is resplendent. If it wasn't

I

for the anachronistic cut – the light perm, the subtle feathering, the way every last strand from the top of the left ear to the right temple is swept up and away from the face – if it wasn't for this the witnesses could be watching a shampoo commercial. The lustre, the bounce, the shine. The brightness, a perfect and unnatural glow or haloing, even with such substandard reproduction.

'I mean, is it clear why we're doing it? What purpose it serves?'

'There always is a purpose. So I guess we have a pretty good idea what that purpose is.'

'Not us personally, obviously.'

'Obviously.'

'I mean, when I say "we" I mean the company.'

'I know.'

'Rather than just us.'

They have reached the bottom of the stairs and started across the room, the two lines of three appearing to be parallel but actually diverging, each step making this incrementally more apparent. So that as they pass the bank of computer screens and keyboards in the middle of the room there is an extra foot between them, the lights echoing faintly between brushed metal surfaces. As the camera's pan follows them past the wide door next to this equipment, the gap has widened to four foot. And as the woman at the front of each line reaches her respective side of the doorway in the far wall, the space between them has reached ten foot.

'How far down did you say they were?'

'Four hundred metres below sea level.'

'Don't your ears go funny or something? Isn't the pressure all weird?'

'Obviously not. Don't you think we'd have thought of that?'

'I guess so.'

The girl to the right of the door presses a square, round-cornered button which looks like it should summon an elevator. Instead, it slides the door back to reveal a machine, artfully lit so that from top to tail it glints a glamorous kind of menace. Black, polished to a high sheen, it appears to be a miniature space shuttle, its wings fisted stubs, its nose cone obscenely protuberant, three small portholes studding each side of its trunk, its windscreen the mouth of an out-of-work clown, even its three wheels more muscular than could possibly be necessary. It is dragged into the room by six pairs of black-gloved hands, the girls turning on their heels as the tip passes them and moving back into the room without disrupting its new-found momentum, so that first becomes last and last first.

'I know it's probably a stupid question, but what's it doing down there?'

'Primarily to defend the shopping centre from attack. But the whole Thames estuary and London, too. It's a Private Finance Initiative thing.' The phrase uttered airily, without any real conviction.

The witnesses, a man and a woman, are younger than they had first seemed, their badly cut suits offering them thin protection. They sit adjacent to one another, the constant readjustment of their posture – the crossing and uncrossing of limbs, the placing and re-placing of posteriors – indicating a certain nervousness. Or merely the quality of their office furniture.

'So we're running defence, too?'

'I wouldn't say running. Not all of it. Just a couple of contracts. Not what you expected when you left the building society, is it?'

'Not exactly. And when I said "we". . .'

'Yeah, I know.'

The shuttle has been pulled over in front of the other door, another square button has been pressed, the door has effaced itself to reveal only blackness behind, a deep, impenetrable wall of darkness. Most of the witnesses' attention, though, is devoted to the image air-brushed up almost the entire length of the machine's body in a detailed, hyper-realist style. It shows a woman in a sheer, white ball-gown, strapless and cutting into the flesh beneath her arms. She is painted in such a way that she appears to be clinging on to the trunk of the shuttle, her hands and her feet presumably meeting on its underside, her buttocks, with the use of a clever perspectival trick, slightly raised. Her head is pulled back and turned to the left so that it is painted in profile, mouth open, a sliver of pink tongue showing between the red lips, the look on her face somewhere between shock and ecstasy. Her hair is exactly the same as that of the women fussing around her and the machine. Running alongside her image in italicized cursive, white with red shadows, the words *A BARNUMS PRODUCTION*.

'What on earth's that?'

'It's a painting.'

'But what's it doing there?'

A shrug. 'Why not?'

'Yeah, but why?'

'Well, I guess we . . .'

' . . . meaning the company . . .'

' . . . exactly, we meaning the company don't get to do it very often.'

'So?'

'So we may as well make an event of it. Besides, the commissioning of art for the purpose of its destruction is tax deductible.'

'Don't you think the whole thing looks a little bit like a Madonna video?'

'A little bit, yeah. Is that a problem?'

'Well, it's just . . . I guess not.'

'And if this is some kind of demonstration – and I'm not saying it is – we may as well *demonstrate*.'

With minute care, the six women unpeel headsets across their identical hairstyles so that the effect stays uniform. Three sit at the keyboards and begin typing; three stand behind them looking at the screens and talking into their microphones. All of them, despite the evident concentration required, continue to smile their broad, tooth-loaded smiles, their hair, as ever, value-added.

'Do you think it'll be much longer? I'm busting for a pee.'

'Not too much. You'll just have to hold it for now.'

'What do they need us for anyway?'

'Dunno. Dunno really. I guess it's for legal reasons or something. So we're witnesses.'

'But we're actuaries.'

'Well, today we're witnesses.'

Occasionally the seated trio have to refer to something on a second screen. To get there, all three grasp the edge of the unit in front of them and pull sharply, using an arcane combination of timing, force and counter-force, so that they spin out anti-clockwise as the runners on their chairs move them to the right, three hundred and sixty degrees being completed just as they've travelled the requisite distance. The standing trio step back as one to let the spinners pass and then, with a subtle bump of their hips, shimmy forward into the gap created. There is no sound of it on the monitor, but no observer could shake the conviction that the team is working to music.

'We're nearly there. They just need to plot the co-ordinates.'

'Of the target?'

'Uh, yeah? What else would they be plotting the co-ordinates of?'

'Ah. Good point. And you think it's a demonstration then, do you?'

'It could be. It's very hard to tell. It's not like we'd come out and say, "This is just a demonstration", is it? Even if it is. It has to be done under real conditions.'

Still they work, fingers flickering back and forth, heads tilted sympathetically, eyes unblinking with concentration, mouths pulled just as wide as ever – air hostesses running the Manhattan Project. Until, with no discernible signal between them, nothing to dent the fantasy of the choreography, without sound or obvious reason, the three sitters rise, the three standers hunch and all six huddle into a perfect circle, their heads concealed beneath the geometry of their shoulders, a black bud ready to bloom.

There is a moment of complete stillness then, one by one, their right hands appear from the centre, a piece of straw held between thumb and forefinger, raised up to arm's reach, face following, body turning at the apex of the arc so that each one is in motion away from the huddle at the moment the next straw rises and theirs begins to fall. The long straw girls fall into line, the short straws head for the shuttle, their column formed with the quick, crisp precision of accountancy.

'If it is a demonstration, don't you think it's, well, a bit of a waste?'
  'Why?'
  'Well, I mean, how much must it have all cost?'
  'The machine?'
  'All of it.'
  'Millions, I would've thought.'
  'Well, there you go then.'
  'But we don't waste money. We make money. So if we're launching an attack – whether it's a real attack or a demonstration attack – there must be a good reason. Everything we do makes sense.'

The doors on the shuttle click upward like a beetle's shell before flight, the painted lady momentarily reconfigured, her head exploding in on itself. The short straws march forward, the first moving to the right, the second the left, the third the right, each nonchalantly throwing her scrap of dried grass away as she bends and squeezes herself into her place in the tiny cockpit. Until, as quick as that, they are in a row, one behind the other, their smiling faces profiled in their respective windows, the doors gliding down again, the shuttle starting to move toward the dark.

'What is the target? Do you even know?'
  'Of course.'
  'So . . .?'
  'So I'm not supposed to say.'
  'Oh.'
  'What do you mean, "Oh"?'
  'Nothing. Just, "Oh". Are you sure you know . . .?'
  '*Yes.*'
  'Well?'
  'It's just some old army fort out in the sea.'

'A fort?'

'Yes.'

'In the sea?'

'Yes.'

'With the army on it?'

'No . . . derelict, isn't it?'

'Is it?'

'Well, we'd hardly be blowing it up if it wasn't, would we?'

'We're going to blow it up?'

'What else would we do . . .?'

'Even if it's a demonstration?'

'Well, it wouldn't be much of a demonstration otherwise, would it?'

In the windows, as the darkness claims the tip of their transport, the three heads turn back to the camera, the line of their sight followed by the three left behind. All six raise their right hands, their thumbs and index fingers making a series of perfect circles, their other three digits exclamations or plumes above them, their left eyes closing for a second, careful, understated, nothing being allowed to disturb the smoothness of their skin, to stretch those perfect smiles into leers.

'Right, we're on. Once we've got this out the way we can go and get a coffee.'

The first witness reaches across and presses a button on the intercom.

'Ma'am? We're ready to begin.'

I am the Word and the Word is God.

I find writing this sort of thing increasingly taxing. You may think it strange in a recipient of a classical education, but My grasp of matters religious – not so much the nitty-gritty as the vocabulary and very rhythm of the sermon – is somewhat shaky. What can I say? Between the ages of eleven and fifteen, when I left, so I believed, for the army, I spent most of my time in RE dreaming of being rogered senseless by the master, the twitchy and nervous but pallidly delicious Mr Tarmigan, which did little for my concentration. And My knowledge of religions beyond English-public-school Christianity renders that small stock positively encyclopaedic.

I am the first to admit this as a weakness, particularly in a Messiah. However, I console Myself with the notion that it is somehow in the nature of a Chosen One to make it up as He goes along, so perhaps My ignorance positively adds to My allure.

In certain dark moments I ponder the possibility of abducting a graduate in Comparative Religions to act as My personal St Paul. Or was it Peter? However, in My mind I see such graduates as jumpy creatures (the influence of Mr Tarmigan with Me to this day!) and abduction can be a messy business even at the best of times. Not to mention the additional upkeep costs of an onsite Apostle. So I struggle through.

I am the One and I am the Light and all shall bow before My phosphorescent aura. That sort of thing.

My website has been established for over three years and has weathered the ups and downs of the market very well, though this is in main due to the fact that it does not rely on advertising revenue or, indeed, any commercial imperative. Which is not to say that the site is unpopular. Visitors flock to it, as is evidenced by the quantity of the often unsettling messages left on My forum. I am fully aware that not everyone who visits takes our content entirely seriously. If being a Messiah was easy, everyone would do it.

On the other hand, the worm we leave upon each hard drive sends Me a constantly growing flood of data regarding the poor lost souls' surfing preferences, email habits, credit-card details – everything in fact. And they are kind enough to pass it on to their friends and business associates, an act of unconscious charity, this particular digital bug being the most self-effacing of guests.

Nevertheless, I tire of these novelty-seekers. I refuse to play games, to perform. I tell you now that I will mislead you, as My life is a life of lies, and habits, by their very nature, are hard to break. But I will try to minimize My dishonesty. I am a Messiah, not an entertainer.

Nor am I deluded. I am not the Son of God. It is, however, important, important for us all, that I am genuinely believed to be so. I hope that by the time we reach the conclusion of My disquisition, you will not only understand why this is necessary but actually believe the very proposition I have just denied. If not, no matter. What will come to pass will come to pass, regardless of anyone's beliefs but My own.

For I am the Light and the Life &c &c . . .

I suppose that what I am writing here is to be My Testament, My theology and philosophy set out in full. Not for the unwashed, television-doped cattle who come to My site looking for diversion. For the true initiates, My inner circle, the Apostles. And as you are reading, I say (verily un)to you: welcome, greetings, congratulations.

Like all the best testaments, what I intend to offer will not be some tightly argued treatise, but rather an expansive, rumbustious story, the story of My Life, from boy to man to Messiah and Founding Father (more of which later). A story that will illustrate and illuminate. That will catch you in your guts as well as in your mind. That will win from you the conviction you will need in the hard days ahead so that, when the time comes, your every sinew, your every living cell will sing *To Vernaland and Empire! To our Divine King James!*

I am trying to picture you, every last one of you. Completely individual, utterly yourself. I want to see you, strong of brow, clean of countenance, sharp eyed, intelligent, raven haired, large breasted or well muscled. But all My mind conjures up is a querulous, self-effacing little place-man dressed in a badly fitting grey serge suit, bespectacled, a zero. It is in the nature of founding a new religion, a new belief system, a new nation, that one is entering uncharted territory. One must try, again and again, to clear one's mind of the archetypes of the past. Particularly the vicars.

Enough. First, identity. I am currently known by the appellation King James of Vernaland. Other names I have taken over the years include James King, Bertie Mannering, Peter Trout, Oliver Turpington-Turpington and David Archipeligo. Unlikely names, I know, but that is their point. The unaccustomed identity-changer picks a dour name such as John Smith – a name so commonplace it seems almost unlikely. The true connoisseur of disinformation chooses a name of such outrageous unlikeliness that no one would believe it had been made up in order to deceive them. And it is this that gives it its grace. You are likely to be remembered, but only as a man of unquestionable integrity and honour. Anonymity is useless if it feels dishonest.

Sometimes, of course, whether through necessity or ignorance, one finds oneself having to adopt an identity not of one's choosing. A new life is thrust upon you – you are made afresh without the luxury of choosing the exact nature of that freshness, or even if one is fresh at all.

Thus it was – to My shame – that the first identity I ever adopted was under the distinctly lacklustre name of Derek Brown. Let Me explain.

I had considerably less fervour for war in 1940 than I do now. But I was stuck in a dilapidated fake castle in the middle of the Fens at an institution that barely passed muster, even then, as a proud part of England's great and good public school system. Everything about the place (including Mr Tarmigan, who was both beautiful and distant) depressed me. Bleak indeed was the view from my dormitory window on a sun-touched morning, when the sky would loom turquoise from almost behind me to the flatly distant, yellow-brown horizon, the whole leaving my eyes sore and my stomach dropping at the sheer impossibility of escape. Bleaker still was the refusal of any boy in that large and ugly, decaying sandstone building to indulge me in any way. Whilst I could barely sleep for the rustle of sheets and the inadequately suppressed groans of the boys about me fellating, masturbating and pleasuring each other in a panoply of interesting ways, not one of those selfsame sex-blasted young men would touch me. Not even when playing rugby football (where, as a direct result, I quickly became my House's leading scorer; though obviously never one carried shoulder high – or at any other height – from the pitch).

I have never adequately established why this should have been – whether these children were scared or repulsed, or were merely indulging in a particularly elaborate form of the kind of mental torture for which such schools rightly possess a worldwide reputation of excellence. At the time it made very little difference: I was miserable, plain and simple.

So the war presented an escape route. I had no desire to die heroically, but death seemed preferable, in a vague, self-pitying way which nowadays we take for granted in the adolescent, to another night serving drinks at the orgy, so to speak.

The decision was made easier still when the Military Police took Mr Tarmigan away. The sickly youth (as he must have been) had tried to avoid the call-up by fleeing a promising career as a theologian at Cambridge to hide out at our school. The plan certainly made some sense – many of us did not leave even for the holidays, the school was hardly in the top rank of such institutions and few of the pupils ever received a parental visit. Few of us, in fact, had parents. We existed in a perfectly sealed vacuum. To call it living, even, would be misleading.

The fault with Mr Tarmigan's plan was his mother, who ratted on him after listening to a particularly rousing speech from old Winnie on her wireless. He was led through morning assembly in tears, the water gushing so copiously his collar went grey, the sudden silence of the room scraped apart by the steady build of two hundred and thirty-seven boys hissing.

Getting away would not be easy. I not only had no fellow escapees but knew that any of the other two hundred and thirty-six bastards would happily shop me given the chance. And it was not possible just to walk out, first because of the immense, flat distances surrounding us and second because of Poole's dogs.

Poole was the caretaker and odd-jobs man around the school. He had been one of the institution's finest alumni – one of the very few to make it to Oxford and certainly the only to walk away with a Double First and Blues in rowing and cricket. Unfortunately, the Great War had intervened and he had returned with a gangrenous leg (amputated) and a piece of shrapnel the size of a farm labourer's fist embedded deep in his skull. Somehow, by what circuitous route no one seemed to know, he had ended up back at his Alma Mater, hammering things and breeding dogs of a legendary viciousness.

The most famous tale told of these hounds concerned one Adrian Fortescue, who had fled the school after hearing the distressing news that his father had run off with the help and that his mother had died of grief – actually, malaria – on the return journey to England, all the information forthcoming in a short missive from errant Papa, saying that he intended to stay in Hong Kong with said maid and her four children and disown and disinherit the young Fortescue. This in itself would perhaps have been bearable if Fortescue had not fagged for Arthur Wilkes, who, on hearing the news, composed a series of lewd limericks on the topic and read them to the school in Latin. Anyway, Fortescue took off and the Head – a weak man whose name I forget but whose single eye rolling in its socket, the colour of an old cue ball, will stay with Me in My nightmares for all Eternity – panicked and instructed Coddle to release the dogs. Fortescue never returned to the school and though he was not killed, it was widely held that he had lost both his testicles.

True, any of it? These are the stories that institutions run on and their truth is of very little importance. The British Empire was built on the tales told at schools like this. Frightened children can conquer the world. Suffice to say, I felt that I had to be at least thirty miles from the school before anyone was likely to notice in order to feel safe. The only way to attain this goal was in some sort of vehicle. And the only vehicles that came to the school with any level of predictability were those of the tradesmen who delivered the sub-standard goods which would be further degraded and diluted by our ever-diligent staff before being inflicted upon us, the student body.

Bribery would have been the obvious solution were my resources not so limited. And one word from a chippy delivery man would have been enough to see me running the cross-country course in clothes expressly soaked in ice water at six every morning for the next three months. So, logically, the only real option was to decide which delivery vehicle provided the best opportunity for stowing away.

I finally gritted my teeth and decided on the butcher's offal lorry. The smell it emitted as its lone driver pumped the slurried innards into our Meat Tank kept away the prying eyes of our school's most hallowed exports, snoops and stool-pigeons. But in addition to this, the lorry was the only one that not only delivered but also took away. It was a radical concept at the time and our local butcher, Bertrand Bowles, rightly takes the credit as a pioneer of recycling. All the food we failed to eat was given back to Bowles who then sold the slop on to local pig farmers for a few pence per gallon. With a nerve I find admirable looking back at My callow younger self, I elected to escape submerged in the scraps bin.

(Young Robert seems in an even worse mood than usual – I must get him that extra cabling before he becomes so sulky his bottom lip starts getting his keyboard wet. I watch him on Camera 57 and feel a keen sense of disappointment that My only Apostle should be so materially obsessed. And I am sorry to interrupt the flow of My tale but I think it offers a salutary lesson. The life of a Messiah is not all miracles – sometimes man-management must take precedence.)

I acted fast, before my nerve shattered. The Friday after the plan came to me, I slid into the still-warm mixture of rotting mince, mashed potatoes, gravy, custard, spotted dick and liver purée (a school speciality). I was dressed only in my underpants, a package of clothes wrapped in waxed paper under one arm, a bamboo flute with the finger holes blocked in the other. As I sunk beneath the surface, I began to suck for air from the flute, the darkness total.

I am sure you would like Me to say that the experience, in current parlance, *scarred* Me. Nothing could be further from the truth. As I felt the sway of the lorry moving away I found that the sensation of being sunk in waste product was rather pleasant – the closest I had come to contact with a living being in a long, long time. I was momentarily tempted by the idea of letting the flute slip from my mouth, sucking in and sinking further, losing myself there for ever. I resisted this urge, but certainly stayed beneath the surface longer than was necessary and, when I finally pulled myself over the rim, my underpants stretched forward and up like a marquee, albeit a marquee full of school dinner on the turn.

I disembarked from the lorry at a level-crossing ten or so miles from the school, skipped behind a bush, scraped what food I could from my person and dressed. Unfortunately, the waxed paper had been only half equal to the job and I was not my usual dapper self. I was, however, free and felt an elation that could not be dimmed by a few smears of grease. With a real sense that I was becoming a new person, I marched into the village station and boarded the 12.10 to London. I would imagine that the toilet I locked myself in for the journey was redolent of the odour of school dinners until the carriage was decommissioned.

A small aside. I realize that all the above, the tales of My time at school, of My eventual escape, seem far-fetched, laughable. That is sometimes how a life can be, or at least how a life can start. Do not, for one moment, entertain the notion that I am some sort of clown, wheeled out for your amusement. I could have you killed if I wished, and perhaps will. Try to be impressed, then, by My honesty.

From: 100001@hotmail.com
To: mandyhart200@hotmail.com

mand - sorry not 2 say goodbye. keep the disc safe. & let me know u got this. ill be in touch. ur bro rob

(Converted from the ASCII)

2

You enter Clearwater in descent. You drive your car (the only way to get on site is in a car or other motor vehicle) through what Clearwater's in-house publicity material describes as an 'Aztec ziggurat arch'. Above you, the profiled figures ascend to a cash desk offering up coins, notes and, towards the apex, all major credit cards, Visa having apparently paid to achieve ascendancy over Mastercard, all rendered in remarkably realistic – if that is an appropriate term here – polyresin, sand-brown 'stone'. From here you spiral downward and downward, not into darkness but into intense phosphorescent light, the revolutionary *Sunlite Ambient Glare©™* Clearwater literature always makes so much of. Level after level slips by, your car being guided by clear, cheerful and somewhat over-familiar instructions flashed from state-of-the-art consoles on the ceiling ('Hey, Peter, why not speed up just a little and keep going down one more floor to the special spot we've got ready for ya!' – one of the giant, corneacopic eyes winking). Once you have parked in the very place that has been set aside just for you, number-plate recognition and access to the national DVLR database doing wonders for familiarity, you and your family can enter one of the high-speed lifts which will whisk you straight down to any of the four themed, underground floors of shopping which lie deeper still, beneath the parking. Now before you stretches out the possibility of day upon day of consumption over a site with an area of 15.786 square miles and . . .

With Gus utilizing his talking Winnie-the-Pooh to repeatedly hit Poppy over the head while she in turn screams for intervention, with Martha shouting, 'Left! Left! Can't you see the fucking sign?', with the sign itself reading, 'Left, Peter, Left! Don't let us down here!'; with this host of distractions Peter Jones finds himself losing the thread of the introduction to his projected twelve-pages-with-photos colour-supplement lead story on the apotheosis of shopping culture. His hands are red and dusty, gripped tight on the wheel, seemingly unconnected to him. His eyes have lost their focus and no amount of blinking can fix it. He swerves left, the kids, having removed their seatbelts and safety harnesses during a fast-lane episode on the motorway, piling up against the right door and momentarily falling silent.

Some have described Clearwater as a temple to shopping. But is it, just possibly, the tomb of late-twentieth-century consumer culture? Pete would like to roll these sentences round his tongue, mouth them and restate them, tighten to Collected Journalism sharpness. Unfortunately he has parked and can no longer pretend to be concentrating on the road. He knows and understands that interaction is expected of him, so he will have to attempt to interact without interacting, which might seem facile if it weren't a problem that has exercised his imagination for over seven years. All he needs is a little time.

Out of the car and ambling towards the lift, Gus continues his one-word monologue:

' . . . fuck fuck fuck fuck fuck fuck fuck fuck . . .'

Martha heaves out a sigh.

'You're not even going to ask him to stop?'

'I thought we said we wouldn't discuss it in front of him.'

'We're not discussing it. Asking him to stop isn't discussing it.'

' . . . fuck fuck fuck fuck fuck . . .'

'I thought we were meant to ignore it.'

'That was the counsellor.'

'So?'

'So the speech therapist said it was important to confront it.'

' . . . fuck fuck fuck fuck fuck . . .'

'And that's the approach we've opted for, is it?'

'You know it is.'

' . . . fuck fuck fuck . . .'

'Gus, will you please shut up?'

Aggressively semi-compliant, the wet-lipped boy moderates the mantra to a hissed stage whisper.

Pete Jones knows that this isn't how it's supposed to be. At thirty-nine he remains sure, repeats it almost as often as his son repeats 'fuck', that he is the premier lifestyle journalist of his generation and that, in his generation, this makes him the premier journalist of his generation bar none. And if that sentence contains too many generations, then fuck fuck fuck fuck that's what a little time and peace to polish or, failing that, a sub-editor is for. His spine feels corkscrewed, his nails are bitten back, the red stumps of his fingers both inhuman and vaguely pornographic.

The lift, he has to admit, is impressive – impressive in an age where he hadn't really thought there was room to make lifts more impressive. It's not that anything is particularly new or innovative, it's just that everything is so well put together. Instead of looking tired, the brushed chromium effect looks *classic*. The piped music is being played at exactly the right volume, just loud enough for you to know that it's there, not so loud you have to listen and, rather than being Muzak, appears to be Chet Baker in his ravaged-crooner mode. Moreover the motion of the lift is amazing – it doesn't try to disguise that you're plummeting down at speeds approaching freefall, but the acceleration and deceleration is handled with consummate class. Pete imagines it must be similar to the sensation of driving a Mercedes off a cliff. He tries to ignore the tug at his leg but is finally forced to look down at the puddle growing symmetrically from Poppy's feet. Its shape is perfect, indicating a floor that is both very flat and very clean. He has never seen anything like it. The doors open and – the parents with a guilty backward glance – Peter Jones and family step out into the Medieval Zone of their nascent Shopping Experience.

He had started off by writing about the deliberately badly dressed people he knew who allowed him to believe he was their friend. The articles appeared in a succession of magazines already, in the surprisingly easy transition from photocopied 'edge' to W. H. Smith (the journey being considerably shorter than the protagonists had liked to imagine). He had graduated to writing about books, films, music, garden furniture, food and the semiotics of whatever everyday object caught his attention (he never actually used the word 'semiotics' in the articles but he knew what he was doing and was quite happy to describe his work that way over drinks or at dinner parties). These pieces moved from the glossies where he had started out to the ever-growing supplements of the quality papers who paid better (and often printed a picture of you at the top).

Pete's claim to individuality amongst his peers was that he had always wanted to be a journalist. Most – like Martha – had drifted into it as 'stylists' (people who knew 'designers' and hence could get free 'clothes', none of the terms seeming entirely apposite descriptions), or had started out selling adverts or were simply self-publicists without the imagination to think of a better plan for becoming famous. When Peter was still at school, on the other hand, he had dreamt of being a war correspondent. At college, however, he had been asked to cover a student demonstration that had drifted into violence. The horse charges had proved too much for him and most of his report was pieced together from TV pictures on the news later that night. And, anyway, this was not the Age of War, but the Age of Expensive Shoes With Fantastic Hand-Crafted Appliqué and a journalist's job was to report, not create, the world around him.

Careful not to show any distaste, he wrings out the soaked knickers and chucks them in the GAP bag on top of the socks and leggings now replaced with newer, brighter, more attractive versions of themselves.

'All right, lovey?'

Poppy nods without looking up, dry tears marking her face with the stains of the family excursion. Pete has made the first purchases of his Shopping Experience and still doesn't feel any better.

He knows, of course, and has known for a long time, that his justification for his work is bogus. He also knows that much of his language – everyday as well as written – is soaked through with his subject matter. This used to amuse him; now it makes him nervous.

He has a second line of defence that has carried him through this far. He doesn't write about the horror of life – of death and dismemberment and rape and torture and massacre – because he is a genius, or as close as you get these days, whose fragile equilibrium in the world is maintained only by the neurotic marshalling of things and people into familiar routines. He has to do this to protect his sanity, but the torture of life shows through in every word he writes. Banality is – by its very nature – infused with horror and is, in fact, the Age's unique expression of horror.

Recently, though, he has started to wonder if, rather than being the Kafka of the Designer Pepperpot, he is in fact perfectly well adjusted and just doesn't care about people being raped or tortured or massacred as long as they're not doing it in his postcode. Or even, in fact, if they are.

Disappointingly, the shops in the Medieval Zone are in no way Medieval. He had hoped for at least a paragraph of humorous observation on wenches selling the knuckle bones of the Saints. Instead, although the stores may not all be high-street familiar, every one of them fits into what he may decide to describe as the Standard Mall Paradigm, even if they're housed in units made to look like rooms in a Gothic castle. Even in the great banqueting hall, the only franchise to cater specifically to the keen medievalist is McDonald's, who sell a McKnight Kebab, skewered with a minia-ture lance (and he can't be sure they're not selling them everywhere). Nevertheless, he is determined to search carefully for ways in which the environment affects those within it. The shop assistant in Gap, looking at the damp little girl meaningfully, asks if he would 'be wanting a bag' which has an olden ring to it. But he knows this is wishful.

Martha – who thinks it's time to grow up and just fucking get on with shit – steers the Swinton-Jones group toward Habitat. Pete goes to object but gets the look that means that this discussion has already been closed, the look that says that if he had wanted to be shopping somewhere better – i.e. more exclusive – by the time he was thirty-nine then he should have come up with a more effective way of making money than writing self-serving little squibs which don't even dare state that they're about the semiotics of everyday objects. He limits his response to a very long blink, which, though she has never commented on it, he knows Martha finds infuriating.

In Habitat, he adopts the look of distaste of the true aesthete. The effect is amplified by his tow-load – his son mouthing fuck and his daughter weeping quietly. Catching sight of himself on a security TV, though, he sees not the person he knows he is, but a tired, sour, middle-aged man with a collapsing face and dark-rimmed eyes in clothes and with a haircut that make him look at best optimistic regarding his age, at worst slightly – still just slightly – ridiculous. And, secretly, he likes a whole load of the semiotically dubious everyday things he is looking at. That chair he *really* likes.

What worries him most is the cliché of catching sight of yourself and not recognising what you see. He finds himself hoping that, whatever else he may be, he isn't just another stereotype. Then Gus bites his hand.

His third and final line of defence is that war correspondents are self-important buffoons who mistake whatever ridge they're on for the moral high ground. This, like all aggressive defences, is by far the most satisfying.

The Swinton-Jones' Shopping Experience is beginning to swing. They exit Habitat with the chair to be delivered next week and a bagful of bowls that qualify as a passable imitation of Neurkle's (but at roughly one-tenth of the price). Peter is thinking of painting 'Not Neurkle' on the bottom of each as a playful and aggrandizing gesture of self-disdain. Except he knows he'll never get round to it. Anyway, he feels better, Poppy is smiling and trying to do her ballet steps and Gus is limiting himself to the occasional blast of expletive.

Pete decides to increase the peace by purchasing sweets for both children at the TREATS store. He emerges with chocolate for the kids and a bag of miniature marshmallows shaped into philosophers' heads for himself. Popping A. J. Ayer and Kant into his mouth, he allows Martha to steer the party into Uniqlo – Martha loves basics.

Of course, the very superfluity of the theming to the actual shopping experience is its point, Peter decides. It doesn't distract or detract from the purpose of your visit. It tints it at the edges. This would be an interesting line of attack, he thinks, but right now he has to decide which colour to get his new sweatshirt in. And nothing, absolutely nothing, wrong with that.

Every time he leaves a shop unit, another bag hanging from him, he's confronted by the next electronic sign, its colours as bright and warm as summer, and every time it's advertising something he wants. He finds himself seduced, dragged onward by these hints. He wouldn't want to say it out loud, but he had expected Clearwater to be tacky, to be for *other people*. But now he sees it's designed for shoppers just like him. No, more, designed for him alone.

The family are bingeing and they're not even sure why. It's less to do with the place they're in, he knows, than a whole fun pack of factors which have come together today in dolls, model cars, miniature hairbrush sets, plastic guns, sweatshirts, leggings, jeans, trainers, glasses, bowls, chairs, sweets, CDs, DVDs, Gameboy cartridges, espresso machines, stationery – whatever is placed in front of them. Martha leads them calmly into ever more intense transactions. The kids have glazed over at the sheer weight of purchase, look cheerily sick and vacant. Pete knows they can't afford it, that the credit card is screaming through the machines, but he just giggles, doesn't even giggle, just thinks a giggle.

Pete has been seeing Martha for twelve years, has lived with her for eleven years, has been married for eight years, a parent for seven years, a parent of two for five years, a haemorrhoids sufferer for three years, sex-free (in both senses, he almost believes) for two years. He piles those separate numbers up like a pyramid of ever-decreasing possibility.

Martha knows that, despite their protestations to the contrary, the seeming esteem and respect they have always shown him, the apparently genuine friendliness that has grown between the three of them, the scrapbook they keep of his articles, that her parents feel she could have done better than Pete. She knows it even though she has confronted her mother and had her suspicions strenuously denied. Knows it even without a shred of evidence. It irks her but she still craves her parents' approval. And now, although they won't admit it's an issue, she thinks they may be right.

Poppy can't understand why Mummy and Daddy give so much attention to Gus when all he does is say that word and when she tried to say it she got in trouble. And she's lovely and he's horrid.

Gus allows no psychological reading. He is the weather. Fuck fuck fuck.

Each is bathed equally in the uniform brightness, each is treated with gentle solicitousness wherever they step, each feels blessed.

Time stops, or moves too quickly, or ceases to matter. There are no clocks in Clearwater. Just smiling faces, plastic rocks and continual promise, these gentle hints of something better. Blasted, utterly exhilarated by their abandon, the Swinton-Jones Unit staggers into the Village Cantina on the Aztec floor, needing now just to eat, to rediscover their bodies. They each make their special choice from a different stand, the children cupping their hands around polystyrene, four vapour trails of microwave steam threading behind them to their chosen table. And, as he picks at the chicken fajita with sour cream, home-made guacamole and blue-corn nachos he has purchased from the seemingly genuine Amazonian Indian with the little organic snack counter in the corner (just for him?), Pete feels it all drain away. He feels like just another family man out shopping. He can see nothing unique in their experience, nothing to render it transcendent. Or even interesting.

'Back in a minute.'

His food is perfect. He pushes its solidifying mass from him and rises.

'Where you going?'

'Toilet.'

He isn't, of course. He's looking for something that will make the trip worthwhile on his terms instead of Clearwater's. He's looking for his angle. Eyes flickering across frontage he searches for the tackiest, shittiest shop, the easiest target in this fucking hell-hole. He can't get the grease from his mouth. His neck feels like it's moulded from solid gristle.

Peter knows that as a freelance writer your career is either on the up or you're sinking. There's no such thing as ticking over. You learn that even before you learn who to suck up to. (His eyes aren't actually being forced from his skull – it's just how it seems.) It is an objective truth that his earnings have been dwindling for over a year now and that there are a succession of twenty-two-year-old novelists who can write about exactly what he writes about with the kind of studied, harsh self-satisfaction that comes only from having been born in 1979. He, conversely, is old, he is tired – this is his subtext, inescapably generated whenever he touches a keyboard.

As the memory of hope drains from him he raises his eyes to the light and sees it – salvation. Pleasence & Greene, despite the fragrance of its name, is a card shop, also selling badly made teddy bears, T-shirts with your picture on the front, postcards emblazoned with cartoon breasts, personalized key-rings, personalized key-rings emblazoned with cartoon breasts, the works. Pete stands looking into the bright, cheap interior, wondering how they afford the rent. A smile splurts across his face, unforced and uncontrolled. Pure pleasure.

He goes in, trying to look interested, trying not to laugh. Flicks through the birthday cards, the section for eighteen-year-old boys packed with images of generic footballers, generic racing cars, generic yachts – the kind of greeting he hasn't received since his grandmother died. For a moment he feels a guilty tug of affection for them, but knows she didn't pick them anyway. One of the nurses must have bought job lots and then sold them on to the rocking, swaying old ladies.

He makes his way towards the back where the cash desk is located, which seems bizarre to him in terms of shop security until he thinks of all the cameras he has seen and how hard it would be to steal from Clearwater. This way you have to pass everything they're trying to sell in order to make a purchase.

It's while fiddling through a box of Taiwanese rubber bath toys which seem to have come into only passing contact with a mould that he finally sees her. That's to say, he's seen her before this moment, noted that the cash desk is staffed even if not exactly ringing to the sound of unbridled consumption. But it is at this instant, as he looks away from the messy slather of the St George's Cross emblazoning each gonk's white head, that he takes note, casts his professional eye over the everyday object before him.

Let's be clear from the start, utterly clear about Pete's motivations and reactions. Let's lay them out with pins, scientifically. The woman is not beautiful, although this, he feels, may be a direct result of the foundation and blusher caulking her face, the slathers of green eyeshadow, the heavily mascara'd eyelashes and cherryade lips. She is wearing one of the Clearwater Aztec uniforms which the non-chain shops seem to favour. Its design is quite clear – almost embarrassingly brutalist – in its intention of pushing her breasts up and forward, but Pete has seen maybe fifty women wearing this particular number today and it works better for her than for all the others. This is not, though, his motivation. If you were to say it were, he would point angrily to her bleach-highlighted, tightly pulled back hair, a style that he abhors. '*Style???*' he would be liable to explode. 'That, my friend, is a fucking abortion.' (Sometimes Pete makes out that things like haircuts mean more to him than they actually do.) No, his motivation is purely journalistic and his attention has been caught by nothing other than the look on her face. Although as a description this rather misses the point.

The woman – she may, more accurately, as accuracy is important to us, be described as a girl – stands leaning forward on to the beautifully sculpted synthetic masonry of the cash desk's top, her arms pulled in tight at her sides, fingers all running parallel forward, thumbs hidden from view. Her head tilts slightly to one side, an uncomfortable, cricked-neck posture. None of this is important, either. Pete is walking toward her, a bath blob still in one hand, his mouth gaping, in danger of disgorging chilli-tinted spittle, because of her face.

It's blank. Not blank as in distant, unemotional, bored, stroke-afflicted, though a little like all of these. Not blank like an unwritten cheque, not blank like Blank or Blankety Blank, not blank like a shell without a bullet, though like all of these, too. The muscles are in repose. The eyes are open but don't seem to see. But there is no slackness nor any dreaminess. The face seems empty. Utterly empty. It is, Pete thinks, as he finally gets his breath and stops his advance toward the excessively made-up black hole in front of him, the perfect image for the shop he has found it in. It is the perfect image for the whole place. It is, it goes without saying, the perfect guiding metaphor for Pete's piece, which suddenly and beautifully seems like a book and TV series and whole collection of Sunday-supplement articles *about him*. He feels quite teary as he stares into her nothingness and feels posterity beckoning. It's true; Peter is guilty of getting a little carried away. But he is sinking, the bony talons of all the writers he took work from clawing and pulling at his shins. He has been repeatedly struck by – beaten by, almost – the fact that even lifestyle semioticians now need some sort of celebrity to keep their career going. A TV series. A regular slot on those 'Greatest 100 . . .' shows. A book, even. So yes, he grabs on to a lifebelt. No, he doesn't check it for punctures.

How to proceed? Obviously he needs more than just this, than just an image, especially more than a non-image, one that can be described only by what it's not. It's only now that he starts to try to think of ways to render the startling absence he sees in front of him in words and the more he looks the more he becomes aware of the need for background. Background, he thinks, gulping, will be everything here. Background will not be a failure to engage with what he sees in front of him, a loss of nerve. Background will be a responsible journalistic response to a startling natural phenomenon.

As he runs through this a new horror descends on him. Why a *natural* phenomenon? He has spent maybe four hours in Clearwater and nothing in here has been natural. Nothing has even pretended to be natural. That's been the charm. He twists round expecting to find a couple of uniformed goons blocking his exit. There's nothing. He searches for security cameras. There are, of course, three within view, which proves nothing.

It's clear to him, though, that there's no point blundering in here and fucking up or, even worse, making himself look like a credulous twat. He has no idea who might be watching or what the purpose of their watching is. Suddenly his best chance to be a genius, to really be a genius, looks like being difficult, fraught with decisions and judgements. Possibly even a waste of his incredibly limited time. He stops to look down at a bargain bin full of aerosol streamers – only 99p a tin – while he assesses the possibilities. A TV show? A complex sting by the owners of Clearwater where he ends up buying the shop and spends the rest of his life in Aztec uniform by that very till while she swans through editorial meetings and book launches eating the air and light around her? Then he looks up again at the absence and pulls himself together. *I'm going in.* Just play it a little cautious.

He takes the last few steps and lowers the bath toy and a canister of foam on to the desk. Cringes at the choices he's made, wonders how it would be possible to make a good impression through purchases in this particular shop. Notices that she has spoken to him and he hasn't even heard what she said. Pushes his face into a dumb question.

'How much it say it was?' Indicating the gonk thing. Her voice deeper than he'd expected.

'I . . . let me go and check.'

Blundering round in a loose arc, sweating now, definitely feeling the sweat, wondering how bad it smells as he heads back to the tub containing the thing's brothers, a huddled mass.

'Says one forty-nine.' Walking back.

'Two pound forty-eight.'

He reaches into his jacket pocket, hand squirming through receipts, keys, and the more generalized, indefinable detritus that accumulates around his person.

'Been working here since it opened?'

'Here?'

'Clearwater.'

'Yeah.'

He holds the money out but her hands stay exactly where they are. He places it on the counter, from where she sweeps it into her palm and chucks it in the till, taking out the change and placing it back in the space created.

'Like it?'

'Sorry?'

'Working. Here.'

A pause. A pause just long enough for him to realize she's not thinking about the question but the motivation of the questioner.

'S'alright.'

He takes the change. Doesn't want her to think he's chatting her up. Unless it helps? Anyway, can't meet her eye to eye while conversing.

'Thanks then. Bye.'

28

'Bye.'

Peter Jones staggers from the shop, actually staggers round the corner and leans against the thin segment of fake rock that separates one unit from the next. He takes a moment catching his breath, really wishing he hadn't done the staggering thing. He's going to have to go back and what if she thought he was a drunk or a smackhead or just nuts? He breathes again, realizes the last is closest to the truth and splutters a snigger, admitting he's actually enjoyed the whole episode. That was . . . fun. Fun. Ugly, banal-sounding little word. Fun. He walks away, an adolescent swing to his sudden swagger.

The sign opposite, this once, stays blank.

From: 100001@hotmail.com
To: mandyhart200@hotmail.com

mand - not heard from u. dont be mad at me. u know i had 2 go.
hows dad? he noticed ive gone? rob

(Converted from the ASCII)

3

But I forget Myself. My first new identity is what we are trying to deal with here. Though I must admit that this business of telling My Life Story is already beginning to bore Me. I am tempted to treat you solely to My Philosophy, but understand from My inextensive reading on the subject that people need the practical example or they grow restless. And restless readers are inattentive readers. So I am afraid, thanks to Jesus, it's biography and parable all the way.

But enough moaning. (I fully expect that the early Apostles will edit – much easier with a computer than with parchment or, God forbid, tablets of stone. Go ahead. It's almost too tempting. Do your worst.)

There was a boy at our school – an ugly, dribbly little squit with a face that looked like it had been smeared by its careless creator – who had heard only two days earlier that his brother had been killed in the war effort. The elder Derek Brown – for yes, these imaginative parents had christened both of their dear boys with the exact same name – had never actually had a chance to drive the Hun from the door. Presumably equally unlovely, Brown Major was killed on the very first night he joined his squadron in a particularly brutal hazing incident involving a whisky bottle, his anus and massive loss of blood. (I apologize for the use of the Americanism 'hazing'. I blame too much access to the internet, which I fear has degraded My vocabulary.) The Browns' loss was my gain. I was too young to join the army and if I had turned up at a recruitment office with my correct name and date of birth, I would have found myself back at St-George's-on-the-Fen by the following morning. Instead, I squelched my way to the Public Records Office, obtained a copy of the dead man's birth certificate, even then with aesthetic reservations concerning the name forced upon me, and enlisted in the infantry. I marched out Private Derek Brown.

The deception lasted just over a week. One afternoon, as I sat trying to shine my boots with a hot spoon, I was summoned to the CO's office. A couple of my fellow recruits smirked at me less than charitably as I made the long walk between drab bunks to drab door (which I only mention as they were unlucky enough to live to regret their childish behaviour; thou shalt not smirk at Me). I exited the dormitory and left my new identity behind.

I was not met by a soldier in any traditional sense. The man with his feet up on the desk was dressed in pinstripes, tapping the ash from his cigar on to our Commander's scale model of the 44th Foot in a square at Waterloo. He directed at me quite the most insincere smile I have ever seen, leant back further in his chair and signalled with a slight readjustment of his right eyebrow that I should sit in the small chair in front of him. I broke from my imperfect attempt at attention and crumpled down on the seat, a scared child.

He wasted no time. Not only did he know that I was not Derek Brown, he knew my real identity and seemed to be tapping his hand on the large dossier of my small life. His tone was harsh but amused, as if he was enjoying the spectacle of my insubstantial frame shrinking ever further. On occasion, he twitched toward me and I became obsessed by my attempts not to flinch, desperately trying to limit myself to outbreaks of blinking. The not-flinching and the blinking became so important that I barely took in what he was saying, but he spent a not inconsiderable amount of time outlining in minute detail my crimes under the Military Service Act of 1916, before going on to point out that if he had not been able to provide the details of who I was, I would most likely have been shot as a spy. Particular poetic effort was expended on the description of how I would have befouled my underwear as I stood, shaking and coughing, a cheap brand of last cigarette shoved between my lips. None of which was true, of course, but it was many years before I found that out.

The man looked down at me from his great height, his face fake-stern, what it masked seeming even worse.

'Do you have anything to say for yourself?'

Bizarrely, in the circumstances, only one possibility really worried me and it was not being led in front of a firing squad.

'Will I have to go back to school?'

'Good heavens, no. Absolute hell-hole. No, young fellow, you're coming to work with me. And you had better work hard. Or I will personally dump your corpse in the Thames.'

This was My Angel, the man who would awaken Me to My potential. Victor Victor – Poet, Prophet, Inquisitor, Murderer By Appointment To His Majesty, Big Spook, Chairman of The Board, Satrap of Sadism, Killjoy McGonagal, Great Leader, Fucktrap, his self-created appellations numerous and ever-changing, a source of constant pleasure to him and those around him. Or at least I believe so. I never had much contact with anyone else around him. He was like a father to me and I will always regret the fact that I eventually had to slaughter him. Such is life, particularly in the industry we worked in.

British Intelligence during the Second World War was not, as it is often presented, a hierarchical monolith leading directly down from the mighty PM to a bunch of spies. In fact, every Ministry had its own spooks, as did every branch of the Armed Forces. Even Whitehall was secretly running its own agents, although the paper-work was, by all accounts, crippling. Many of these men and women served their country by keeping tabs on what the others were doing, which may seem wasteful, but is essential in times of war, where resources are likely to be shifted at the drop of a hat or, in Winnie's case, the bottom of a bottle. All the real twits were Classified. We were beyond that. If nothing you do is Classified then it is unlikely to turn up as headline news in the Sunday papers fifty years later. And in the fifties we were to move beyond even *a*classi-fication to a whole new level of cleanliness. But to explain how we did this would be to introduce a character before her grand entrance, which I do not believe she would thank me for.

I have never established with any certainty who it was, exactly, that Victor Victor worked for and certainly have no idea who he answered to (although I suspect that the solution to the latter puz-zle was: no one but himself and the feather weight of his conscience). But he did good work, valuable work, that no doubt aided the War Effort in many indirect and even some direct ways. One thing is certain: his pull was second to none. He led me from that office, handed the damp stub of his spent cigar to my Major and bundled me into a very large, very clean, black car. This machine floated me from Aldershot back to London, where diabolical, beautiful Victor bought me a couple of capacious pinstripe suits and lodged me with a terrifyingly young and vivacious landlady, Mrs Hobbs. The next day he furnished me with papers which I quickly learnt afforded me access wherever I pleased to go and which reduced any of the petty, officious little shits who asked to see them to pained, arse-kissing forelock-tuggers. Oh, and Victor also allowed me to choose my new name, advising me only to make it as outlandish as possible. Hence, Selwyn Barrington-Bond.

As Barrington-Bond, my immediate task was simple and yet offered scope for initiative and imagination. It was the perfect job for a noviciate and showed Victor's flair with personnel. The brief was simple. I was to work through a long list of conscientious objectors, making their lives as unpleasant as possible. Victor hated conchies and would probably have paid to have them haunted solely for his own pleasure, but I think the wider idea was to generate a stigma around these principled young men, to obscure any ideology they might have espoused behind a cloud of superstition. The basic idea: conchies always have bad luck.

I proved remarkably adept at the task, quite the evil sprite. Victor claimed it was my 'rat-like cunning', bless him. Some of my success was due to my appearance. I looked young for my fifteen years, with the rosy, bulging cheeks of a baby sated on his mother's milk. I combined this with a Brylcreemed cowlick and one of my pinstripes to fashion for myself a presence that I can only describe as diabolic. On a couple of occasions my visitations alone caused nervous breakdowns (interestingly, both Quakers). In most cases, more was needed. Ration books gone astray, transportation messed with (the effect of a daily flat tyre on the reluctant cyclist should never be underestimated), dog dirt left in new and interesting locations, whispering campaigns started or intensified amongst the neighbours, these were the bread and butter of a normal day's work.

With tougher cases, I developed favoured techniques of my own – a photograph of wife or sweetheart receiving it roughly from a member of the armed forces became something of a calling card.

But there were cases that needed a still more personal touch. I remain proud to this day of the work I did with Walter Beagle, a pacifist painter with bohemian and anarchist leanings and a lamb-to-the-slaughter saintliness that came damned close to vapidness. I spent over two months working through all the techniques I had mastered to no avail. He maintained his equanimity and refused to fray. I even went as far as burning down his studio with his life's work in it. He barely flinched.

And I doubted myself. Walter Beagle's unforced good nature began to eat at me. I dreamt of his beatific, distant smile. And after a week of disturbed sleep I began to fear that it was he following me as I stalked him to and from his work as a hospital orderly. Eventually – exhausted, mind emptied – I resolved to place myself back under the control of Victor and tell him of my failure. And that was when I had my epiphany.

Everybody needs to love. This was my revelation. Perhaps not so very remarkable, except that I was fifteen and had spent all my sentient life in institutions. This explained my nausea and sweats, my constant pacing, the vertigo that gripped me. It was not the fear of failure, but fear that Victor would withdraw his graces because of that failure. And I loved Victor, needed him for more than my lodgings, food and clothing. I needed to feel his hand on my shoulder as he congratulated and insulted me in the same foul-smelling breath. I needed him to want to have me around, to call me 'Rat', to remember that my favourite food was cold tapioca pudding.

I also knew that all this depended solely on my ability to get results, to find my way out of whatever maze Victor placed me in. And I came to realize that what made Walter Beagle's calm, centred life unique was a lack of love. I had to give him something before I could take it away.

I considered Mrs Hobbs, who had found me to be a terrible disappointment, but settled on a kitten. My decision was inspired, blind instinct leading me to Beagle's weakness. He resisted the charms of the Blue Persian I visited upon him for over a week, during which time I made sure that the beast – dropped by myself through any open window or door at all times of the day and night – became thinner and scruffier, increasingly desperate in appearance. Beagle's agitation grew, throwing the cat out with ever greater violence, bursting into the village's public house demanding to know who was playing tricks on him. For a while I thought that my job would be even easier than I had dared imagine – perhaps he was phobic about our feline friends, or superstitious, or my previous efforts had finally worked their spell?

Then suddenly he relented, welcomed the creature in, collapsed before its indifferent, over-bred nose. From that point on, the cat owned Beagle. He starved himself to feed her, compromised himself to buy her luxuries on the black market, abandoned his previous hard-edged abstract style to create ever more anodyne portraits of Her Majesty (for so had he christened her). The cat grew fat and increasingly ugly as he grew thin and increasingly ugly. He began to make clothes for her – a jacket first, then suits, hats, matching boots. His obsession was complete when, in a fit of jealous rage, he confined her to the house.

I could have left it there, been satisfied that I had more than adequately fiddled with the man's mind. I could have just killed the cat and left its entrails spread over every room of his house. I could have abducted the animal and left his imagination to do the rest. But I felt an intense, vindictive hatred for Walter Beagle and decided instead on a particularly nasty variant of my signature trick.

So it was that late one night, having broken in and drugged Beagle while he slept, I dressed Her Majesty in the full Nazi uniform I had commissioned for the occasion, stripped Beagle, coated his genitals in thick layers of fish paste and stood back to let nature and my camera crew do their work.

When he received the film a week later, Beagle throttled the cat and then threw himself under a train. I am led to believe that he is highly rated by the art world today as an early video installationist and that copies of my film (credited to him, of course) now change hands for six-figure sums.

The moral of all this, since I know that as an Apostle you are a seeker after moral truth? Never trust an art dealer. That will do you for now. You are desperate and weak and far, far too close in to see what I am building. It is as if you are seated in a small room with no windows staring intently at a picture on the wall, while outside I create a whole kingdom. How can you be expected to understand it all just because I have left a scrap of paper on the table saying, 'I am making Paradise beyond these walls'? Bear with Me as I attempt to lead you out of the room.

When Victor was apprised of my work in the Beagle case I could tell that I had exceeded his expectations. For the first time since I had met him he hesitated before speaking, less than a beat but enough for me to register. And when he did speak, his voice quavered as if he was struggling to contain his paternal pride.

'Well, you worthless little shit, you certainly possess a unique talent for unpleasantness. Daddy Vile salutes you. I think you are ready to move on from psychic debt collection. You are ready for the bigger stage, for Grand Guignol, my pig-faced son.'

From: 100001@hotmail.com
To: mandyhart200@hotmail.com

mand - if ur getting this mail me back. ur only bro rob

(Converted from the ASCII)

4

When he awakes it seems as if he feels the wetness on his face before he even realises daylight has reclaimed him. He lies there on his back, as still as he can be, trying to pretend it hasn't happened. Trying to pretend it hasn't happened again. But stillness in a body like his is just another form of movement. It hurts. Behind his ears, the cushion grows wetter.

He elects to move. Can't move. Almost tries again. Almost succeeds. Nothing wrong with the body. Nothing wrong as such. But brain refuses today, this morning, right now, to talk to it.

It hurts. Not the body or the brain. It hurts. Worse than hurt. Hurt would be bearable. Hurt would be easy.

Right now, he is beyond hating the morning or despairing of the day, or being sickened by his life. He is just another animal, unremarkable. He tries to block it with blankness but blankness won't come. The more he considers this dream of blankness, the further it is from him and the worse it gets. So he stops trying. Even for that.

He has not been able to cry in front of anyone else since he was eleven. He can cry. He often has. These days he does so incessantly. But only in an empty room with its door firmly shut, all the others – the other weepers and gnashers and wailers, the sobbers, the snufflers, the shoulder-shakers – locked out. He used to think this was a talent honed to a skill, a character trait to be proud of, one of the strengths that made him him. Now he finds every empty room with the door shut an irresistible invitation, his face aching from contortion, his cheeks chapped raw by the tracings from his eyes, his chest convulsing. Or sometimes, some times like now, just a steady stream of salted water dripping out, a whimper trapped in his throat. The only way he has found to stop it is to imagine cameras in the room, unwashed men with mugs of tea watching him from a van down the road. So he continues to lie, caught between movement and no movement, resisting the day without having the energy left to resist.

Eventually it is the other pain, the more specific one emanating from his shoulder, that forces him up. Not so much the pain, in fact, as the physical memory of when that pain could be isolated and made a sensation less than itself. Habit. Habit finally reconnects brain and body deep down somewhere. Habit and he stands.

Across the room to his painkillers. If he had the energy or the inclination he would laugh. Painkillers. Not a pretty laugh, admittedly. If he had the energy. His hand shakes an accidental samba with the bottle as he tries to shift two into his palm. He takes three. It could as easily be one or four. Stands holding them, appearing to examine the picture on the wall, but not examining it, not even seeing it.

Then, with pills sticking to cradled fingers, back to couch. Nothing has changed in his absence and nothing will ever change. He knows this. But still nothing will dull. He craves dull. Foot gently taps an unemptied bottle, his tenderest motion. Hand moves floorward and grasps it gently where body slides into neck. The pills go down with the first drink of the day. Used to be the best. Now just the first.

He sits and surveys his creation in all its manifold and manifest forms. Breakfast television chitters quietly in the corner, cans and bottles clot the coffee table, sideboard, TV top, floor. Scattered between, a few plates with bean smears, a few more foil containers with the glutinous remnants of Chinese, the occasional flapped open, cardboard mantrap of a pizza box with plasticated crusts. All garnished with broke-backed, black-smeared, dead cigarettes. A cigarettes' graveyard – bursting out of bottles, heaped wherever they can find a corner to huddle together. Someone has even stubbed cigarettes out on his carpet, leaving the butts sticking from the melted holes, each one a miniature disaster. No one comes to his parties except him. And they are not, however you look at it, parties.

Now that he's sat again, torpor closes back round him, a blanket soaked in cold water, uncomfortable and heavy. He stares at the flickering faces on the screen, trying to make out the words. The mouths move in familiar patterns but the noises are mysterious, sound without meaning. With complete concentration he manages to get the bottle to his lips again without spilling it, dropping it or chipping his teeth. Its taste meets the taste of itself a few hours old in a metallic swill. Then the alcohol cuts through. Placing the bottle back in his lap, he taps at his pockets, absently at first, then with increasing purpose until he finds the packet and pulls one free. Repeats the process searching for his lighter. Flicks the flint through its clicks, listens to the crackle as he pulls the smoke deep down inside him.

Back on the screen, three people crouch forward on pastel sofas doing something strange with their faces. They keep doing it, occasionally relaxing and then returning to it, this odd, awkward-looking grimace while they babble out the noises and nod at each other like birds. He knows the look, just can't place the word. *Smile*. Fucking smile.

With that, their words slip back into focus and he knows where he is. England. This England. This is England.

'So what you're saying in effect is you can tell what people will buy by what they've bought before?'

'In effect, yes.'

The cigarette gone already, one last half-intake to filter. He looks slowly about him, holding the remains upright, the two centimetres of ash poised. Almost searches – habit again – then rolls shoulders down and flicks it forward to join others on the carpet. The ash explodes out, flickers down on his lap. Shoeless, he casts his head around as the still-burning butt engages with carpet's acrylic fibres. Then he drives the bottle down on top of it, crushing and smothering.

The last time he had thought about anything, properly thought about it, he had thought about habit. About how little he thought. The routines, the endless routines, that carried him from waking to sleep again. The maps of repetition stretching across the town and beyond, lines deepening into troughs. The more he analysed his day, the more he felt like a sleepwalker, unable to change anything or alter his course, driven on by private compulsions. Hidden even from him. At that time he had elected to break his habits. To step out of the ditch. To do something different. Just to try it. Look where it got him. To here, always to here. Now, habit is the only thing that moves him forward through the light.

Habit forces him into the bathroom. His piss is forked at source, one dribble pattering left of toilet bowl, the other hitting the floor. Shrunken penis retrousered, he grabs the mouthwash, removes the lid – less gently than any of his actions with the last bottle – and pours a slug of the electric blue liquid into his mouth. Rolls it round, feeling discomfort build but still holds it there. Splatters it into sink. Splashes cold water on his face and wipes his beard down in the mirror.

Heading back, he clumsily undoes the buttons of his shirt, struggling with each one, his fingers fat and nerveless. Goes into the darkness of another room and re-emerges holding a slightly less soiled shirt and a too wide, badly made, navy-blue, crested tie. Pulls shirt over head, undoes his trousers and smooths crumpled cotton down over off-white y-fronts before rebuckling. Checks the trousers for stains and ash smears. Ties the tie.

Then, having looked at the door, sits down again, sucked out by his efforts, sweat already blooming on the new shirt. Another cigarette, smoked like a chore.

Is it the door causing his delay, rather than what lies beyond? When Jimmy was a young man, back before England, his father became obsessed, for a brief time, with security. Had extra locks fitted and then more locks, windows barred, strips of iron attached across doors. Spent time carefully checking them, allowing his obsession to blossom until, if the rest of the family were truthful with themselves – though, being a family, of course they never were – they would have admitted that this was all he did. Patrol round the house in just his socks, a shirt and underpants, rattling padlocks, attempting to turn keys, resting his weight against the doors. To the point where it was unclear whether the problem was inside or outside or whether, in some insidious way, the keys and locks and strengthened doors and bars had become the problem themselves.

There's the door over there and there he is on the sofa, smoking another cigarette, pretending to watch a news bulletin delivered by another smiler. He stands up suddenly, reeling forward, marches over to it, but too close, far too close, really, to be thinking of opening it. Stands with his nose an inch from the wood, seems to focus on the grain, then turns round, walks back to the couch, stopping above it, this time really looking – or really appearing to look – at the picture behind it.

It's a monochrome photo of his younger self. The man is dressed all in white, the tint of his skin and the blackness of his hair contrasting with the glare of his slightly-too-short trousers and tight shirt, two top buttons undone and revealing a flash of silver. His sockless feet in scuffed and stained but still-white shoes.

He is caught in motion, his face glazed with a kind of empty concentration, his left knee raised, foot pointing daintily down, right leg straight, stretching out slightly behind him from his toes, the curve following through into the whip of his back and then up into his straight right arm. The whole curving even further back to terminate in long fingers gripping a ball in a complex configuration, the torsion obvious in the ridges of sinew on the back of his hand. The stumps are there, too, of course, and chalk lines over polished ground hinting at infinity.

He continues to stare, his expression as flat as the image, as though he is trying to remember something – though not something of the utmost importance. Then, eventually, when he has left it quite long enough, in fact a little longer, he heads to the door.

Stops, pulls his shoulders back, drags his face into the familiar shape of the TV grimace and holds it there. *Fucking smile.* Opens the door and steps through.

Jimmy Patel is ready for work.

From: 100001@hotmail.com
To: mandyhart200@hotmail.com

mand. sis. i know ur pissed off but mail me back. please. rob

(Converted from the ASCII)

5

One week on and Peter Jones has an extensive stock of goods from Pleasence & Greene lying in a number of thin plastic bags in the boot of his car.

There are the postcards, six or seven of them, mostly cartoons with sexual innuendo drawn in a hurry by over-worked draughts-men, but one a photo of Marilyn Monroe pouting, her skirt rising from her thighs like a ghost. There are greetings cards. He has so far purchased for weddings, wedding anniversaries, a birthday, a bereavement and a new baby (the last has a luridly pink lamb on the front, and all feature liberal use of gold embossment). There are the key-rings, the pick of which plays a monophonic version of 'Jerusalem' when you clap your hands. There are a couple of gonks which seem to have been rescued from a fire-damaged warehouse. There is the Tinee Teddee™ manufactured in a sweatshop in Korea and containing a long, sharp metallic spine of some sort that can already be felt pressing through the fabric of the bear's arse. There is the 'Brabie Doll with REAL HAIR' which genuinely scares him. Last, there is the laminated poster of River Phoenix looking slightly chubby with no shirt on. For the life of him, Pete can't work out how the owners managed to wangle a unit in Clearwater.

He has also learnt a little about the girl. By eavesdropping, he has discovered her first name – Amanda, he presumes, though they all call her Mandy. He has learnt that she doesn't work Wednesdays. He has learnt that she does smile, though not at him. He has learnt that when she smiles, her face somehow looks as if it hasn't changed. He has learnt that her basic arithmetic is pretty good – Wednesday's girl had used the till to calculate change and then given him the wrong amount anyway. He has learnt she applies extra hair lacquer when she is hung over (though this is more hunch than knowledge it's in his notebook and so takes on the status of knowledge). He has learnt that she doesn't like making small talk with customers or, at least, with him. He has learnt that she is not held in great esteem by her co-workers and has, in fact, heard another member of staff refer to her beneath her breath as a 'snotty bitch'. He has learnt that she disappears to somewhere out the back of the shop for her breaks. He has learnt she smokes B&H. He has learnt that she can lean on the counter and stay staring without focus, adding nothingness to blankness, for considerable periods of time. Every day has had its revelations, however small.

In the deficit column: the look on Martha's face when he had given Gus a can of foam streamers and Poppy a badly moulded rubber bath toy. The ongoing dispute between him and the aforementioned over car-use rights and, in particular, why he suddenly needs wheels every day when his *essential* and over-priced *design classic* computer is upstairs in his very own also *essential* work room and she has to get the kids to nursery and school by bus. The increasingly irate messages being left on his mobile by the Lifestyle Editor of the *Sunday Abstruser* concerning an unfinished piece on juicers. The electricity bill buried on his desk just payable with the as-yet-non-existent cheque from the juicer article. His continuing failure to clear his ongoing visits with the company that Clearwater uses for PR. Peter has never gone undercover before and he's not sure he likes it.

So it is that this Saturday Pete pulls into his parking bay knowing that he needs results. He hunches forward over the wheel, imagines a cigarette drooping from between his lips.

'Good to see you again so soon, Peter. We love customers who love us. Enjoy your shopping experience,' flickers the message board in front of his windscreen.

He follows the now-familiar path into lift, down to Aztec floor, out and through the mid-morning wash of Saturday customers toward his target.

He is aware, perhaps too aware, although deliberately made too aware, he feels, by the ominous message boards, that his car is logged in and out every day and that it is probably unusual for anyone but staff to visit so frequently. He wonders to what degree information concerning his visits is merely registered and to what extent it is actively interpreted. He wonders, in the event of interpretation, what interpretation will be placed on him. So he runs through his usual subterfuges – looking in shop windows, stopping to try on a pair of shoes, examining the quality of the glassware at a kitchen shop – as he closes in on Pleasence & Greene by today's individually customized route.

When he gets near Peter takes a moment to compose himself, brushing down his clothes, patting at his hair, getting ready for the moment – a constant since adolescence – when his arms start to flail. The unit doesn't have a doorway or windows. At one point you are outside the store and at some other certainly in it. As he approaches this zone he takes another moment, this one to ascertain her presence or absence. A third to watch her, the same queasy mixture as every time he sees her. Dread, excitement and something he won't admit to yet. He breathes again and goes forward.

He is just past the new stock of sub-Pokemon swap cards when she looks up and sees him. Without blinking and certainly without smiling, she turns and walks to the door at the back, pulls the handle and leans in, her right forearm and hand flat across the wall, right foot off the floor and angled back toward him. She stays like that a second and then a second more, he frozen, eyes stuck on the point of her heel. Then the arm flexes and she's turning and coming back to the till, her face, of course, giving away nothing and he fumbling for a new focus, scared.

Scared? Stupid, he knows, but he doesn't have permission to be here and she had seen him and then gone, told someone something, returned. Though, to rationalize, she is close to impossible to read and may have remembered something, looked up without registering him and then gone to relay that something to the someone out the back. *My break, bitch.* All the same, he keeps watching the door there, surreptitiously of course, for any sign that ajar might become open.

And it does, of course, just as he has learnt that 'every pack of DRORKEMON contains FIVE CARDS depicting one of a range of

200 UNIQUE and COLLECTIBLE creatures with SPECIAL POWERS and a range of attributes for YOU to COLLECT and SWAP or FIGHT for with your friends'. From through the door comes a small man, thin hair swept horizontally across his scalp, tie askew, shirt popping over belly, top of trousers diverging underneath belt. His skin is beautiful – a warm, yellow-brown – and he is smiling enthusiastically. He signals toward Pete, eyebrows raised, and she nods.

'Hello, my friend.'

'Ur . . . hello . . . Mr Pleasence? Greene?'

'Ah, if only. It's Mr Patel, Hinesh Patel. Merely the manager. And you are?'

'Jones . . . Peter Jones . . . is there some . . . sort of problem?'

'Problem? No, no problem. You, my friend, Peter, may I call you Peter? You, Peter my friend are a valued customer.'

' . . . I . . .'

'And I like to meet my valued customers. I am old-fashioned, I suppose. The personal touch. The friendly face. This is what builds a business. This is what made this country great. Don't you think, Peter?'

'Well, I, yes, that's . . . admirable.'

'Admirable. Oh, thank you, Peter. Peter, that is too kind. And you don't mind that I call you Peter?'

'No. Not . . . No, I don't mind.'

'I'm told, Peter, that we've had the pleasure of your company every day this week. Every day, Peter, buying this or that, contributing to your family's happiness through our cards and novelty items and trinkets. Peter, I hope I'm not being presumptuous in thinking you have a family and that you're here for them? I hope, Peter?'

'No . . . quite right. The family.'

'Good. Good. Family is so important. So you see anything you like today? Anything catch your fancy?'

Pete glances round, desperate. Waves the Drorkemon cards.

'These are . . . great. These are . . .'

'So you have a boy, yes, Peter? Boys, they love these cards, they love to collect. I'll tell you what I'm going to do. Every pack of these you buy, I'll give you another free, yes?' He turns to her and raises his voice. 'Every pack he buys of these, you give him one free. Not just now. For ever, OK? And you tell the other girls. Yes?'

'That's, that's really really kind of you. Thanks.'

'You're one of us, though, yes?'

'Sorry?'

'You're with me, Peter, right? A P&G man?'

They stand for a moment, smile to smile, mutually uncomprehending.

'P&G . . .? I . . . I, er, you. Sorry . . .?'

'Ah, you're good, Peter. Or "Peter"? You're good, my friend. I knew head office wouldn't send a novice. You are from our head office, aren't you, "Peter"?'

It's only now that Pete sees that this little man is as scared by the encounter as he is. They seem linked, lost, neither daring to break from the other's eyes.

'I'm . . . just a shopper, Mr Patel . . .'

'Hinesh, "Peter", friend, but then you know this.' His eyes filling. 'I understand. I am not trying to make your life difficult. You are just obeying orders. But this spying. Always this spying. The centre already sends the tapes to be reviewed. This presence here. Here in my shop. You are a good man. But this is a harassment? To check up on me so openly?'

'No, really. I came in last weekend and I have to go past for work so I just keep coming through for . . .'

Mr Patel examines his feet and the floor around them. Moves an imaginary blemish with the tip of his toe. Slowly inflates his chest, a new resolve reached.

'Well, Peter, that's probably true, isn't it? Yes, of course, I understand my friend. You are not, no, from head office. You are just a shopper. You're not here to check up on me and my, how did he put it, hare-brained fucking stupid scheme. You're just here to shop and buy cards. A good product, my friend. I don't blame you. It's a good product.'

'Ah. Yes. Very good.'

They both spend a quiet moment looking down at the packet. Peter turns it slowly over in his fingers, half looks up and down again. Looks up.

'Very good.'

Hinesh rallies himself.

'Yes, a very good product. An excellent product. A shop full of excellent products and high-quality novelty items, each chosen for its unique charms and qualities. A shop to be proud of. A shop, my friend, on the very edge of success.'

'Certainly. Yes. An excellent shop. With excellent products. A really good shop of . . . novelties. An infallible enterprise of, er, vision and. Real innovation.'

Hinesh looks like his eyes will burst their banks, but he holds, pulling his shoulders back, growing in stature, happy now, so happy.

'You are always welcome here, Peter. Always. Anything I can do for you or for your family, for your boys, tell me. An excellent shop. As you will not tell anyone at head office when you don't go there. No mention of vision. I thank you, my friend.'

He winks a beautifully executed Hollywood wink which finally forces a little liquid down his cheek, turns and walks back to his office, a clean square of handkerchief muddled from pocket to face.

'Carry on, carry on.'

Peter is left alone again, just another middle-aged man with a handful of worthless swap cards. Maybe not such a great journalist. Just another lost little man with no idea, no real idea about what he's doing, what he's trying to achieve or why. Cut back and cut back and the world grows bigger and bigger around him, every few square feet full of the next one of him. His life dwindling, his chances dwindling, a . . .

'Sorry about that.'

He looks up and she's standing in front of him.

'Lotta pressure on him, innit? Difficult time.'

'Oh. Yes, of course. No. That's fine. It's not a problem. He seemed . . . nice.'

'He's all right. Considering.'

'Yes. Considering.'

He knows now that this is it. He can terminate the conversation and walk away. He can let her terminate the conversation and walk away. Or he can take his one chance. He gathers a few more packs of cards from the basket.

'So you say difficult times . . .?'

'Why *are* you here every day?'

From: 100001@hotmail.com
To: mandyhart200@hotmail.com

mand - just mail me back. everything ok? u got the disc? stupid
question in it? if u aint got the disc u cant read this. if u dint find the
disc this is just double d gook. but i need us 2 speak. i know u think
it aint speaking but really emails more real than speaking. its in a
hard drive some where 4ever. it lasts 4ever. unless some 1 wipes it
of course. some1 who really knows how 2 wipe it. speak 2 me. rob

(Converted from the ASCII)

6

Young people today understand *Love* only as an appetite to be satisfied, a desire to be gratified. My experiments with fatherhood, both biological and in My role as mentor, have taught Me this. I provide Robert with food, clothing, shelter, all the computer equipment he could ever dream of and a stable moral framework, which was quite clearly lacking in his previous environment. Yet despite My best efforts, Robert does not love Me. In fact, he acts as if I have imprisoned him out here. Which is not only a misrepresentation of the situation, but a rather vulgar one at that. I saved him when I brought him here, saved him from himself and from the forces of law and order. And, although those forces were not actively pursuing him, they would have been as soon as I tipped them off.

Robert, you see, is a hacker. He will bore you, given half a chance, with his explanation of how 'hacker' within his *community* (we all have a community these days) means 'computer virtuoso'. If it conjures up in your mind the picture of a social pariah in his late teens using a computer to interfere with information that is not his own, then you are considerably nearer the truth. Robert is, indeed, a computer virtuoso but of the *idiot savant* variety. If I had left him where he was he would undoubtedly be in prison by now, or working for Microsoft. It is hard to be sure which is worse. Instead, I have given him direction, a proper project to keep his mind occupied. What better use could there be for his anti-social, essentially negative skills than bringing about the spiritual, cultural and moral rejuvenation of the very society he has chosen to reject? He is the sword in My Hand and the violence we wreak will be terrible.

My son was – is, I suppose – even more lost. An unengaged and unengaging child, he seemed to spend his time in a perpetual state of avoidance. He would have been classified a veritable Houdini of psychological escape were he not so utterly blank as to render almost any description an exaggeration. He drifted through my early fifties, a wan reproach, all large watery eyes and giraffe knees. At first I envisioned him as an empty vessel ready to be carefully filled by me with notions of duty, respect, love of God and Country. In fact he was a tube, no receptacle at all, all my efforts splashing round his feet like urine.

I have confronted the thought that My own lack of education in the matter of fathering may have played a part in this. Pater died before I was two years old, the marble which I accidentally dropped into his mouth as he snored lodging tight in the entrance to his trachea and quickly rendering him an infinite absentee. But Victor more than made good this potential deficit in my character.

And, anyway, My son and Robert are not exceptional. All youth today is the same – living lives without love or meaning and hence individually and collectively incapable of generating love or meaning. Expecting anything else is like believing that four battery hens will get together, form a barbershop group and end up on television. It is not just the cages that hold them; it is not in their nature. And let us be frank here, feelings of duty and love are difficult to muster for such a shabby God, Queen and Country.

I suppose my doubts concerning the English Trinity stemmed from the first day I saw Verna Landor on a newsreel at a cinema in Streatham in late 1940. She was pictured standing on a small stage, little more than packing crates, at the front of a sweep of cross-legged soldiers. Her blond hair was truly platinum in the film's monochrome, her head tilted back and up, describing a trajectory far above the squaddies' leering bonces. Her mouth moved with a slack sensuousness that moaned fellatio. And the sound! The song, 'No Man Is An Island', was standard for the time – a stoic and optimistic riff on love and nation. From her, though, it was something else again. It is hard to describe exactly what did it – her reading of the tune was almost laughably stilted, as was the style in England at the time, her diction too perfect, her delivery so on the beat it actually sounded wrong. Yet from somewhere she summoned a raw, unsated, almost tangibly damp sexiness. The auditorium filled with a mist of desire and I became lost in it, gulping for air, tugging clumsily at my collar. Here was a true Queen, one hundred times more regal, three thousand times more worthy of worship, than the dumpy Consort with the ugly smile. When I left the theatre I could barely remember who I was, let alone that we were at war. All of it was washed away, everything washed away.

If Victor had shown me how to love a father, Verna showed me something altogether more singular. I had never loved a woman before, far less lusted after one. But Verna did not awaken in me what would no doubt be called my heterosexual side. She awakened in me love and lust for her and her alone, a distant longing, a terrible desire to serve. To this day Verna Landor remains the only woman I can truly claim to have loved. Or even liked very much.

But innocence. Oh, innocence. She was guest of honour at the Admiralty party to which Victor dispatched me to make the acquaintance of Ralph Titfer. Titfer was one of the crackpot inventors who spent their war bothering whoever would listen with their latest scheme to defeat the Nazis solely by mass-producing, at great expense to the nation, arsenic bouncy balls, electronic pocket bomb socks, martial arts pogo-sticks, large holes in the earth's crust, and so on and so forth, a litany of ingenious stupidity. The projects all shared one common trait – the more outlandish and ridiculous it was, the more important it was perceived by its creator to be for the survival *of our very way of life,* the phrase always uttered with eyes popping, face up close to yours, the stench of another's breath fogging your judgement, the tickle of spittle demanding only submission and retreat.

It must be admitted that Ralph Titfer was one of the least objectionable of his type and, judged by history, some of his schemes were not so ridiculous. One, at least, was inspired, though not for the reasons one might originally think. It was this one that Victor, always a good half-century ahead of the game, had charged me with expediting.

Not that any of this concerned me on the night in question. Titfer kept himself busy with his mad scientist act, skipping from group to group, twitching with excitement and rubbing at his hair as he launched into another explanation of how he would win the war.

Which left me ample room to keep myself busy by stalking Verna.

I had not known she would be attending. If I had, I would have made more of an effort. She entered a few minutes after me, accompanied by an Admiral who was obviously fucking her, a fact made clear even to a naïf like me by the way his hand appeared to be glued to her behind. Not that she even seemed to notice. She came in and immediately charged across the room to greet another man, the hand riding her two independent, undulant buttocks, the Admiral barely managing to stay attached at the other end. I, meanwhile, spilt a goodly portion of my drink over the shoes of the man next to me.

The pattern of the night was quickly established. Miss Landor worked the room like the professional she was, chaperoned by her Admiral and an ever growing retinue of admirers. I followed close behind, trying to move in as near as I could, straining to hear her every word without attracting either her attention or that of those surrounding her. This I achieved admirably, learning in the process that she had been a chorus girl in the West End when war was declared, that she loved orchids, that she found men in uniform 'irresistible', that she would do everything she could for the War Effort (the Admiral's smirk at this point was distasteful even to someone in my line of work). She seemed young and shallow but somehow steely, all of which added to my worship.

It must be admitted, though, that the decisive factor in my growing obsession was the dress she wore. It hung round her and left her essentially naked, the slightest movement setting off fleshy echoes beneath the fabric. I studied these ripples with just the necessary detachment to prevent my body from embarrassing me, trying not to miss anything while simultaneously striving to set each moment firmly in my memory. The process was painstaking, requiring absolute concentration and control.

Eventually it had to give. As the evening began to crack apart, guests receiving their coats from orderlies, the last of the drinks drunk, it suddenly came to me that my tactics were fatally flawed and that while I had been shadowing and studying, numerous young men not half my calibre had been making this young lady's acquaintance. I was sixteen but considered myself a man of the world – imagined myself a rakish forty – and yet I had stood by while youths with clotted complexions and only a uniform to disguise them had got a leap on me. I was too angered with my own cautiousness to listen to it at that moment. I set my jaw, pulled my head back and stepped out toward Fate.

Ralph Titfer blocked my path, in fact staggered into it, drunk both on the sherry he had consumed and the constant exposition of his scheme.

'So, Victor's filled you in on my plans, old man? What do you think?'

Though I had been introduced to him earlier I had no idea who he was. My reasons for being at the party were rendered obscure, lost, so it seemed, in a fog of longing. Over his shoulder I could see Verna Landor's stole being draped around her shoulders, her leave being taken of her most persistent suitors and her way being made to the exit. I tried to step past Titfer one, two, three, four times, but he seemed to think this was a game we were playing and blocked my move each time. Eventually I pushed past, not roughly enough in my eyes, but with the necessary force to tip his drunken, unbalanced body over and hence direct his upper lip on to the edge of a nearby table.

'Steady on,' was all he could manage through the blood. And she was gone.

So, my memory returning and mindful of the esteem in which Victor appeared to hold this sorry specimen, I turned again, drew a handkerchief from my pocket and helped Titfer to his feet.

I have often wondered how different the arc of My life might have been had I evaded Titfer with greater alacrity and spoken to the Goddess before me. To the extent that I consider Myself Chosen then perhaps not that much. But I suppose it is also possible to be Chosen and to achieve One's calling in different ways. Perhaps I would have gained My Queen and lost My Country. I remain convinced that the final outcome would have been – will be – the same. There is a certain inevitability to matters of divinity. But I get ahead of Myself.

Titfer was not a man to hold grudges, at least not with one of Victor's men, and soon we were heading out together on to the dark streets, my handkerchief blackening with the blood from his swollen mouth. I got the driver to take us to the club Victor had enrolled me in and there we sat cradling brandy glasses while he spat and slurred his way through his grand scheme.

The details did not matter to me. Victor had told me to make sure it happened and that was what I would do. While Titfer raved about the properties of reinforced concrete and twin pontoons and catamaran hulls, I tried to extract from him who exactly was blocking him at the Admiralty. Ever the *ingenue*, it did not appear even to have occurred to him that he was being blocked. From then on I pitied him.

But I did find out. It was simple, really. It was the man he considered to be his champion. It nearly always is. His name was Admiral Crockenbury and he had been at the party that night. With a young lady?

'Yes, with the singer, what's her name?'

'Verna Landor?' I said it almost too fast and I could feel the crack in my newly broken voice.

'Yes. You know her then?'

'Only from the newsreels.'

'Funny girl. But very interested in floating pontoons.'

'Very interested in everything, I'm sure.'

'Yes, I'm sure.'

'Well, I expect if I have a chat with Admiral Crockenbury, we can work something out between us,' I said, feigning feigned nonchalance. I drank up. It was time to get rid of the prof and get down to business.

On 21st March 1941, Titfer's plans were approved in full and the money and manpower necessary to achieve them were put at his disposal. It was, of course, a perfect job for me, combining as it did business, pleasure and my calling card. The photographs of the Admiral and Verna were some of the most explicit I had ever taken and when I threatened to show them to his wife – also the source of his considerable fortune and expansive country estate – he quickly caved on his objections to the project. My memories of those craven images remain the chief inspiration for a Divine Member which is now in its eighth decade. Victor took the prints and negatives from me. Which was most certainly a Sign, although one that evaded my attention at the time.

And Verna. As you know, My dear disciple, she is more than just another lady. She is our hot and wet Virgin Mary. My admiration for her grew with each move she made. Unceremoniously cut adrift by her Admiral she reacted in the very best way, by taking up with his immediate superior. She was soon to turn her back on the sea, of course, which is where all our problems began.

From: 100001@hotmail.com
To: mandyhart200@hotmail.com

mand - maybe u dont understand how difficult it is 4 me 2 get this 2 u? maybe u think im just having a larf. maybe ur thinking o haha its another of robs games hell be back tommorow. maybe ur pissed off with me 4 going. i had 2 go. u r not a idiot. rob

(Converted from the ASCII)

7

The bowler uses his fingers to impart maximum lateral spin to the cricket ball as it leaves his hand. His arm propels the ball forward; his hand sets it turning. The ball travels through the air in imitation of a leisurely loop, so that, when it lands at the feet of the waiting batsman, it is as if it has dropped flat out of the sky and the remaining forward momentum is combined with sudden sideways movement generated when the revolving seam of the ball bites into dirt.

But this isn't the essence of spin bowling, Jimmy has always maintained, merely its mechanics. Perhaps for the first season that anyone ever deliberately spun a ball, batsmen stood there dumbly, shouldering their bat, while a blur of rotating leather sent bails dancing. But now, even a pub cricketer knows that if a right arm bowler ambles up to the far wicket, he is going to try to turn the ball from a seemingly safe position back into the batsman's stumps. And very many people can learn this skill, even fairly talentless people, if they spend enough time on it. All living people breathe, but breathing isn't the essence of human life.

The skill of spin bowling seems, then, to be deception. The batsman has to be unsure of how much the ball will spin, if it will spin at all, or even if it will move the other way. The bowler has to learn not only to vary the amount of spin, but disguise the grips and wrist movements that generate different amounts of spin. Or bowl the ball with the same degree of spin, but harder and flatter, so that it pushes through more quickly but turns less. The bowler has to learn all this and then learn how to use it, learn the general rules of deception and then unlearn them and focus solely on deceiving just the batsman in front of him.

And this leads to the most important factor of all, which is, Jimmy believes, nerve. To get batsmen out you have to tempt them to hit the ball. To do this you have to make the ball look inviting to hit. Which means, however good you are, that sometimes it can be hit. Which means you will get hit. Most spin bowlers in England push through fast on a flat trajectory and concentrate on landing the ball accurately just outside the stumps. They say that is the way they have to bowl because English pitches offer little in the way of bounce or turn. Jaimin – when he still bothered to maintain anything – maintained that these were excuses. They bowl like this because they lack nerve. And they lack nerve because, collectively, their lives are too easy. In this way, spin bowling becomes the sling shot of the underdogs, though maybe just for him, maybe just in his head. Which is strange, because his father had been a lawyer and he attended one of the best schools in Uganda and it was only when he came to England – someone else's country, however he looked at it – that he ceased to be the colonizer and became the colonized. Which, in turn, was an irony of sorts, though not an amusing one, as every third person he met in England seemed to think that it was him invading them.

But if you do this, you get hit. You have bad days where the ball will not land quite where and how you want it. You have other days where a giant with a heavy bat just seems to read or guess everything you do. You have some days where both happen and sixes seem to be heaved back over your head ball after ball after ball and your team mates look down when you try to meet their eye and your captain takes you off with a resigned, disappointed smile. And at those moments, all you have is the week before or the month before or the year before when you took 5 for 65 or 7 for 32 or all 10 for 102. And you know your team mates have forgotten all that and you know that they are fucking cunts, 'one and all', and that you are playing on your own.

And then one day your nerve breaks. The nerve none of the rest of them ever had snaps inside you and the sweat on your brow is no longer honest and you speed up your run and lose your rhythm and toss it in too flat and and and. And from that moment it's finished.

Jimmy Patel remembers exactly when it happened to him, the

moment he stopped being a cricketer. He had done it before when he was younger but had checked himself, pulled back from it. But this time the crowd had cheered. Perhaps sarcastically at first, as the scorer entered the first dot against his name for longer than he cared to admit. Then with more vigour when he did it again. And the last one even more. A couple of his team even patted him on the back as he collected his cap and he walked back to the boundary, looking straight up into the bright grey sky, trying to pretend this wasn't happening. But it was and his captain called him straight back and he concentrated solely on not conceding any more runs and the crowd seemed to love him for it. And the ten years there where he had tried to attack using just deception and nerve – to entertain them, to entertain *them* – crumbled away.

He should have retired that September with an injured shoulder, which was in fact injured and so was the perfect alibi. He had given nothing away and had still taken wickets, though not as many as before. But now it was all wrong. The air smelt metallic, people's faces seemed empty. He hated the batsmen he got out. *How could you be so fucking stupid?* he shouted to them inside himself. How could they care so little? And why had he previously expended so much effort and thought and cunning on them when they simply weren't worth it? Of everyone, he was sickest with himself. *I am sickest with myself.*

But despite all that he carried on. Though they should have been, when he still regretted, those were not the years he regretted. They were the years when he did some stupid things that seemed clever. He was blinded by cynicism which, like all cynicism, was just damaged naivety, or so O told him. They were the years when he made some money, which was not unrelated to the stupidity or indeed to O, who seemed to enjoy lecturing him on his stupidity while persuading him to act with increasing stupidity. Which showed how well O knew him. Better than most, anyway.

Then, having acquired the money stupidly, he spent it stupidly. The red Porsche is battered now, the dirt that cakes it eating it, one mirror missing, the windscreen cracked where the kid from the estate threw a fist-sized stone as he drove past, the left wing scraped and dented due to the ensuing swerve into a bollard. And yes, he had been drinking. He doesn't really notice any of this any more than he notices the thump of Mud from the speakers, backed by a high whine whose pitch slips up as he accelerates, the perfect noise, if you were inclined to believe in such things, for transmitting subliminal messages. The tape has played back and forth for roughly two years, a replacement for the same, itself a replacement for the same and so on back and back to when he bought the car. Its sound is as familiar as the pain in his shoulder and, through familiarity, as lacking in significance.

He had loved the music that summer after he came to England, the music and the people making it. Nineteen seventy-three, when anything could still have happened to him or been chosen by him. He had sat in the small front room of the small flat he shared with his mother, his grandmother and his younger brother and watched these men stomp round on the black-and-white television dressed as . . . dressed as what? He still didn't know. They were from another planet, but still more here than him. They smiled like idiot children and, watching, so did he.

'Please, Jaimin, I will ask you again. Turn it off?'

'In a moment.'

'It's rubbish. It is giving your grandmother a headache. Turn it off.'

'It's nearly finished.'

'What would your father think?'

'Father is dead.'

The perfect response, cruel and elegant, Jaimin's favourite. His mother began to cry, quietly, features curling up on themselves. He, refusing to move his eyes from the men in the platform shoes, unaware.

Somewhere he has a photo of himself at the club dance, his debut season for the county, out on the floor, the first time he ever danced to it in public. He's twisted over, body tensed around an imaginary guitar, head flipped up on chicken neck, legs two right-angles at right-angles, half a swastika. At the flash's edge, a circle of sunburnt men and their heavily made-up women clapping, cheering, whistling. As Tom Brooker put it to him years and years later, of that night of triumphant strut and acclaim, 'We'd never seen a Paki dance before.'

Just as he doesn't notice the music, nor does he notice his route. A succession of nondescript houses, shops and lock-ups rolls by, some boarded up, some slathered in graffiti and an eczema of peeling posters, all dowdy, dirty and small, as if viewed with a squint. He takes a right through the bricked, plastered, patched and thrice-painted gateway into Coppernail Industrial Estate. Barely slowing, he heads diagonally across the largely empty car-park, aiming directly for a wall emblazoned with a large plastic sign, marbled by a mixture of exhaust fumes and rain, reading 'PLEASENCE & GREENE LTD'. He brings his vehicle to a sudden halt just inches from the wall and the painted, slightly smudgy words 'J. PATEL, RETAIL DIRECTOR, SOUTH-EAST'.

He stops the engine and, with it, the music, the silence releasing tones in his ears. He looks at the sign, more carefully than he should, tracing the cracks and chips in the paint with his eyes, noting, as he always does, the shadow of the erased name underneath. He looks down at his lap and when his head comes back up, the smile is in place.

As he steps from the car he pulls another fag from his packet and lights it as he ambles, beaming emptily, to the door.

From: 100001@hotmail.com
To: mandyhart200@hotmail.com

mand - u know i had 2 go coz u know what i was doing. u know why
the bills was so low. it wasnt coz we wasnt using any leccy was it! u
was using ur hair drier 2 heat ur fucking room! till it melted. remember
the day it melted? didnt think itd smoke that much did u? happy
days eh. remember me? little bro. the 1 who got u a new 1? the 1
sorting out the bills? things u can do with a internet conection in it?
hackerrrr;-) happy days eh. rob

(Converted from the ASCII)

8

Peter doesn't get much from her this first time, beyond the stuff about how all staff sign papers for the centre's holding company as well as for their employers. And he doesn't even understand this. But it's a start, as well as the cause of his problems.

'If you've got time for a coffee I could tell you.'

'Usually have a smoke on my breaks.' Hesitates. 'Complicated, then?'

'Well . . .' Desperate for something vague to say which doesn't sound suggestive.

'Go on. Why not? I'm off in', checking her watch, 'ten minutes.'

'I'll wait.'

'You'll have him out again. I'll meet you at Medici's. I'll have a Choco-Deluxe, extra sugar, extra marshmallows.'

So now he sits, sipping nervously at the foam on his large double latte watching miniature marshmallows slip one by one through aerated can cream and disappear into the deep brown below. More than ten minutes have passed and he's already deep into the anxiety of the potentially stood up. Which is ridiculous, he reminds himself, as this is not a date, but understandable as he sits here with two drinks, under the unblinking eye of the girl who served him and seemed to snigger when he asked for the Choco-Deluxe. Perhaps this is where all potential suitors are sent, the second drink a code between counter girls. Surely she couldn't see him in that way, though? His interest in the idea unnerving him.

And then she's there, a winter coat in a gratuitously unfashionable cut covering but not hiding her uniform. From the market he thinks, a knock-off of C&A styling circa 1985 and so utterly, singularly disgusting he forgets for a moment what he's here for. She slides into her bucket seat, leans forward and picks the remaining sweets from the cream, popping them into her mouth one by one, gently and with complete concentration.

'Good?' he says, realizing at once, definitively, that he is deficient at small talk.

'Mmm,' she nods.

'So. What's the problem with the shop?'

'You see where we are?'

'I, er, I can't say I did.'

'Sports shops? Both sides. JD and Footlocker. I say sports shops, I mean trainer shops.'

'So?'

'Well, what's Pleasence & Greene?'

'A card shop?'

'Ours is, yeah, but the chain does sporting goods.' And so, lips clotted with cream, she tells the sorry story of mismanagement and complacency that has led a traditional sporting-goods retail chain to remain a traditional sporting-goods retail chain, selling cricket bats and football boots, running spikes and tennis rackets, javelins and vaulting poles, all the paraphernalia of all the sports no one plays any more plus many more that few, if any, ever played. She tells him of the management's attempt to reinvent itself with a flag-ship outfit at the soon to open, impossible to ignore, subterranean shopping powerhouse, Clearwater (then, before extensive market research and brand testing had determined a name, known simply as Project X). The depressing tale of how leaner, fitter sports/fashionwear chains had learnt of P&G's plans and just done it – bought up the units either side, signed ultra-exclusive deals with the leading brand manufacturers in exchange for selling off their most hideous new designs at grotesquely high prices, and made the pitifully unprepared P&G's position untenable before the centre even opened. How, in a desperate face-saving effort, the shop's manager, Mr Patel, had dreamt up the idea of opening a novelty and greetings-card shop so that high command could sell it to the press and their owners as diversification rather than a humiliating climb-down. How Mr Patel's plan was foundering on his and Pleasence & Greene's inability to source any goods of a novelty or greetings-card nature which were actually worth buying. The concomitant stress, heartache, woe, torment and so on.

'It sounds terrible. It must be hard for you, too. All the agitation. Worrying about losing your job.'

'You know I don't fancy you, don't you?'

The sharp turn leaves him breathless, sick.

'Well, I, er . . .'

'No offence or anything. I mean you're nice looking and everything. You're just a bit . . . you're just not my type.' Old for me. She was going to say, *you're just a bit old for me.*

He should just laugh casually, smile a wry smile, utter something charming which hints – playfully, mind – that she, a mere child, is more than a little up herself to think that a man as sophisticated and discerning as him would be interested in her. Lovely, he might add patronizingly, though she obviously is. Instead, he blurts, 'I'm a journalist.'

'Fuck.'

In a crackle of polyester she is up and gone, the remains of her Choco-Deluxe tilted forward beyond a retrievable equilibrium and washing toward him, melted mallow remnants lumping up from the gloop, his cover blown in an instant, warm wet drops of brown pattering into his lap. At last he follows, legs flapping like his knees are loose, stomach slackening. He begins to skip after her through the Saturday crowds, trying not to make a scene but suddenly drawn into collision after collision, bags knocked from shoulders, kids tripped on, chest meeting chest, his progress, such as it is, a succession of over-the-shoulder apologies, each one leading to his next encounter. All the same, somehow he draws level.

'Fuck off' – without looking at him or turning her head. Deliberately not looking at him.

'If I could just explain . . . It's nothing sinister. Nothing serious.'

'Nothing serious? I'll lose my job.'

'I really don't see how anything you've done could cost you your job. I don't mean to belittle . . .'

'What, you've read my fucking contract have you?'

'Pleasence & Greene have a clause about journalists?'

'Oh yeah,' the sarcasm gushing from her now, 'yeah, you've

really done your homework.' She looks round at him in spite of herself. Continues as if to a child, 'All staff at Clearwater are contracted to Clearwater as well as their employers. And if you don't fuck off now you're going to cost me my job. So. Fuck. Off.'

He stops, a river of disapproving shoppers flowing back past him to his left and to his right.

It's three by the time he gets back into London, four by the time he gets home. Martha doesn't return his wavering, already-failed upbeat greeting, but Gus comes charging out of the lounge carrying his biggest toy gun. Pete picks up the child and carries him through to the kitchen, the rhythmic thud of plastic armaments on his head strangely comforting. Martha is sitting at the table, staring up at the clock, her jaw clenched.

'Hi.'

'Said you'd be a couple of hours.'

'Sorry. Meant to call. Really sorry. Everything been all right?'

'What do you think?'

'I am genuinely sorry. I wouldn't have been late if it wasn't . . .'

' . . . important. Yeah, I know.'

'Yeah. Important.'

'Maybe you could bear to spend some time with your children now.'

'I'd love to. I'd love to as soon as . . .'

'What?'

'Nothing. I'd love to.'

'As soon as what?'

'Nothing. Right now. Let's not discuss this now. Right now, eh, Gussy? Where's Pops?'

Four hours later the children are both in bed and Martha decides to speak to him again, her anger compacted and refined during her lengthy silence.

'You've remembered we're going to John and Aggie's tonight, haven't you?' The tone making the question's underlying assumption clear. Correctly.

'Yeah, of course. What time?'

'The babysitter's due here at half eight, we've got to be there by nine. Being as you're so used to the car, you can drive.'

'As soon as that?'

'What?'

'We've got to leave as soon as that?'

'No, we're eating at three in the fucking morning . . .'

'It's just that I've got some work that I've got to get done.'

'Oh yes, your work. Your work. Would that be the work that I had Donald McCracken screaming down the phone at me about?'

'What?'

'The juicer piece you haven't done. That's meant to be in tomorrow's paper. That three hundred quid you decided we didn't need.'

'Ah.'

'Ah? Pete, what's going on?'

'Listen, I'm sorry, the ideas are just coming together and I don't want to talk about it until it's all clear, but I'm working on something really big. A book. A TV series, maybe. This is the one, though, I'm sure.'

'Do you have any idea how pathetic that sounds?'

'Oh. Oh thanks. No really, thanks for the support. That's fucking. That's great.'

'Are you coming tonight?'

'I need to do this bit of work.'

'So I'll cancel the babysitter then, shall I?'

'It's important.'

'I'll go on my own then?'

'Mart, it's important.'

'Don't even fucking call me that.'

So now he sits at his desk, his features washed clean by the glow from his screen, trying to seduce not his wife but the girl, trying to find the way to persuade her to talk to him, openly, without inhibition, as if it were as important to her as it is to him.

Firstly, I am so sorry that I risked you losing your job.

A very bad start. Delete.

My apologies for what happened today

Delete

  on Saturday. I never meant to cause you any distress or difficulties
and it certainly was not my intention to put your job at risk.

Better . . .

I should have told you I was a journalist straight away, then perhaps
I could have had the opportunity to tell you what kind of journalist
(yes, there is more than one kind). I am not a tabloid hack. I am a
freelancer working for a Sunday broadsheet, the *Abstruser*. I am not
even an investigative reporter. I am a 'lifestyle' writer – my pieces
are concerned with what colour you should decorate your bathroom,
not with sharp business practice or corporate fraud. To be honest
with you, those kind of subjects bore me. I'm more interested in the
décor.

I want to write a piece about Clearwater. In fact, I want to write a
book about Clearwater. I have hopes, with my contacts in television,
that there will also be a BBC series to coincide with the publication
of the book, plus serialization in a paper such as the *Abstruser*.
Plus, you may not know, but non-fiction is 'hot' in Hollywood right
now and I would not rule out a feature film coming out of all this.

All I want to do is look at how people shop and how other people
help them shop. None of this has been cleared with the Clearwater
PR department yet, but once I have enough material to give them an
idea of what I am trying to achieve, it most certainly will be and I
think they will like where my work is coming from. Which is not to
say that it will be a puff piece – I want the book (and TV series, etc.)
to be unflinchingly honest and this is where you (hopefully) come in.
I needed a focus for my work, a 'way in' and somehow I settled first
on Pleasence & Greene and then on you.

In many ways I want this to be a collaboration. Not me exploiting
you, but us building something together. Yes, there will be risks
for you, but also great benefits. Perhaps a career in journalism, or
modelling, or television presenting, or film. You strike me as a very

interesting and intelligent young woman and I would hope that this project will open a world of opportunities to you. Stranger things have happened – the world I inhabit is one defined by contacts and I pride myself on my ability to navigate that world. Tell me how I can help you as you help me and I will strive to make it happen.

How ever I put this proposition to you it sounds like, well, a proposition, with all the connotations that word implies. But I guess the most important thing I can offer you is the experience – of creating, of collaborating, in an intellectual and yet grounded exercise, of expressing yourself in a whole new arena. I can't even guarantee that it won't cost you your job, but I can guarantee that if it does you will be compensated for that loss, and not just financially.

And that's really all I can say to persuade you. My mobile number is 07997 203307. Please ring me, day or night, if you are interested. Check out my work in the papers, have a think, ring me and ask me further questions but please do not dismiss this out of hand.

Thank you for reading this.
Yours in good faith,

Peter Jones

He leans back as the printer begins to hum and hum and hum and hum.

From: 100001@hotmail.com
To: mandyhart200@hotmail.com

mand - r u there? all right. it wasnt just the bills. i got my self in trouble. i went 2 far. always went 2 far in it? just needed 2 disapear for a bit. let things settle down. my bad. rob

(Converted from the ASCII)

9

Of all the most overrated foundations on which to build a community, none is more deserving of contempt than friendship, or, for that matter, *fellowship*. What are these people thinking of? Fear and awe really is the only way. Look at the history of the Christian Church. When they dealt in fear and awe they were all-powerful. As they moved toward *fellowship* they slumped into a continuous decline. Sometimes I find myself wondering what Jesus thought he was playing at. Who on earth would want to worship a lamb? I have never had any time for friends or they for Me. Fuck every last one of you.

Whatever Verna and I were to one another, we were never friends. Victor made sure of that from the very moment we met.

It should have been a routine visit to receive instructions. He summoned me at least once a week, often daily. But as soon as I pushed at the door and smelt perfume rushing out to meet me I knew something was wrong, though not yet how very wrong.

She was perched there on the edge of his vast desk, her dress riding up above her knees, her breasts pushed forward by the artful positioning of her arms, as if it were the most natural place for her to be, as if I were the intruder there, her eyes never leaving his face.

'This is Miss Landor. I would be much obliged if you would refrain from addressing her directly. Understood?'

She wrinkled her nose for him, just for him. My face filled with all the blood deserting my cock, capillaries stinging under the pressure. Head rotating, my chin flapped as if my face were buried deep between her legs. Her tongue toyed with her lip, glistening pink against the red of her lipstick.

'. . . H– how . . .?'

'Oh dear. Do you imagine you are the only one to go to parties? Miss Landor and I share a common interest in the theatre. And defeating Jerry, of course. It was only a matter of time. Now, are you waiting for something . . .?'

My mind, I found, had emptied, unable to locate the blueprint even for the basic motor functions of speech. Who was I? Who were these people? What was I doing in this room? I turned and fled, her laugh like a dropped tray of glasses. Still I could not stop myself from turning at the door, her head right back so that her long, pale throat pointed the way to her open mouth, her whole body shuddering as if in ecstasy, her teeth, like the rest of her, perfect.

I knew that Victor was testing me again, but I did not know why. At first I was sure that this was all there was to it. But the more I saw them together, the more I became convinced that he was rather taken with Verna. And I only ever saw them together. Whereas I was an operative, Verna was his muse. His lover. I would like to say she was a trophy. I would be lying. At best, I could say she was the golden tart, which is childish. I felt childish, with that nauseous hatred children find so easy to muster.

At the time I was forced to live the majority of my life in Gravesend, the site of Titfer's precious project. Day after day I awoke to the peculiar grey of that place, as if the sky and the land had somehow fused during the night, the utter mediocrity of both a meeting of mindless minds. I would pick my way through the vomit of last night's shore-leave sailors, between the gaggles of foul-mouthed children who should long ago have been evacuated to a quiet mass grave, around the boilersuited women, their make-up seemingly applied with the same tools they employed during their shifts building tanks. I headed down to the wharf where the boffin and his team were creating the first four of the forts, a huddle of furtive, sexually charged engineer-speak. There I would spend the day seeing to Titfer's needs – in effect, making sure that no one, from the most junior lady docker to the head of the Admiralty, dared cross him. It goes without saying that I was excellent at it, but also that it was beneath me, an insult to my imagination. In the evening I would return to my damp lodgings and spend the night listening to bombers trundling overhead, waiting for them to dump their load on me, a titanic game of Russian roulette which offered me my only release from the muggy hollowness of the day. It is hard for you to envisage just how depressing a place Britain at war was. Blitz spirit? I would quite happily have flattened the lot myself.

On the few occasions Victor summoned me to London it was invariably to one of the private clubs I missed so much, where I would find Verna perched on a cushion sipping gin and tonic while I stood, my latest report tersely requested. To say my feelings for her changed is to understate the case quite magnificently. The little cunt just sat there, smirking and sipping, smirking and sipping. And yet my loins would not allow my eyes to move from her lips, liquid sparkling on them, the urge to suck and lap at them exquisitely painful.

Which is not to say that the job was completely without pleasures. Concrete was still new then, a substance free of connotation, a remarkable gift from science. I would watch them pour the thick, lumpy liquid into their wood-made moulds, then return the following morning, embarrassed by my excitement at seeing the huge, smooth elephant's legs appear. I suppose I was in actuality still a child and if this only expressed itself in a feeling of wonder at the dawning of the Towerblock Age, I ask you to remember that in those days we made our entertainment where we found it.

I am obliged to try to describe these structures for you but what I remember most clearly is that sense of awe, the conviction that what stood before me was too new, beyond words. The first models were designed for the Navy – two huge cylinders, a giant's tabletop of a platform, then a gun tower built on top, brutal and squat despite the height, a badly built boat on fat legs. But it was the Army towers that spoke to me. Built separately then connected by long, narrow walkways (the sea tipping beneath you as you hurried along them), each of these seemed a miracle, the four thin legs converging, a two-storey block of windowed concrete precariously balanced on top. The very fact that it remained there instead of crashing to the floor seemed a proof of futurism. They loomed above the observer like undertakers over an orphaned child. And so smooth! The concrete an answer to an alchemist's riddle, liquid stone.

Despite his many faults, Titfer knew. Whenever the shell was to be ripped back from another section of the structure he would hustle me forward, his sudden urgency a small gift given back to the boy who was making it all possible. I never felt for him as I did for Victor but I was grateful for his attentiveness. And the concrete was incredible. You will just have to believe me on this one.

As for Victor, this was the start of all our problems. He pushed me too far and our relationship never fully recovered. At the time, none of it made sense to me – the new favourite, his coldness, his interest in the forts. Do not misunderstand Me, the sea fort was an excellent idea. An excellent but thoroughly boring idea. I could drone on to you about mines, shipping routes, anti-aircraft guns, innovations in manufacture. Yes, this was the cheapest, most efficient way to protect London against attack from the sea. Yes, it prevented bombers from flying up the estuary beneath our radar. Yes, it was pioneering work in the pre-fabrication of buildings. But so what? What do I care for that? How will it increase your understanding of Me? And, by the same token, what did Victor care? I understood that this was important work for the War Effort, but there was so much important work at that time that I always expected Victor to have at least one other angle on the jobs he chose. It would be many years until my epiphany and through all that time these concrete beasts would itch away at me, looming up on me in my dreams, silent, without reason.

I grow tired of writing of Victor. It upsets Me, frankly. He was quite the oddest person I have ever met. And the more I try to impart of him, the more he eludes Me. Was he fat or thin? Loud or silent? Over the years, the original facts of his existence have been lost to My Messiah legend. To be honest, I would like to downgrade him to, at best, a bit part. But I can't. Even though (or perhaps because) the man has been dead for over thirty years, he is still insisting on playing Gabriel. And I wish he would stop it. I expect you think this is harsh – how harsh you do not yet know. He was, after all, the man who rescued Me from mediocrity, set me on the road to My Messiah status, even put in place many of the tools by which I will achieve My destiny. But I ask you to appreciate how hard it is to be a Messiah, to live in and for One's allotted role, when someone is constantly tapping One on the shoulder and showboating for the crowd. How Jesus dealt with God I will never know. My guess is that it all ties in with his lamb thing and you already know what I think about that.

Enough. Let us talk about Me.

The first of the forts was completed in January 1942. I toured its vast concrete interior with Titfer, our feet slapping out quiet echoes, our two smudged shadows, one lengthening and shrinking above the other, circling round us in sudden quick swoops as we moved from one bulb to the next. It was magnificent – rough-surfaced, huge. As a small child I had become enamoured of the common fantasy that my head was full of tiny people who controlled my every action, from batting my eyelids or masticating up to the act of thought itself. This was not a sinister notion to me but a comforting one, except on the few occasions when I realized that, of course, if tiny people were controlling my thoughts and actions perforce they would make me see this as a comfort. Walking through the dark, concrete labyrinth of Redred's Tower I felt like one of those little people residing in a giant head. I felt a sense of complete control, as I always would in those structures, as if the mind I inhabited and pulled the levers for was not the mind of another ordinary mortal but the mind of God Himself. From that moment I knew that these towers would, somehow, be the womb of my destiny.

Titfer insisted on pointing out this or that feature to me, the engineer's arcana of which he was so proud. I was forced to silence him in the usual way – my index finger passed slowly across my throat. Except for the sinking-bottle gulp he emitted (he loved these jokes), he complied, leaving me to my reverie.

I was with Redred's when it was towed to Tilbury. I stood on the top deck of the fort as water pounded into the dock. It is one of the immutable rules of the world that there is always something stronger than that which you perceive to be the strongest. This lesson came to me as the sea finally built enough around the tower to lift it, the utterly immovable suddenly shifting beneath my feet, the tilt of the world changing slightly to accommodate this new physical reality.

The fitting seemed to drag, my exhortations to the Tilbury workmen becoming ever more frantic, until finally Titfer was called down from London to calm me. He brought me a parcel from Victor – a note instructing me to relax a little, a bottle of very fine brandy and a cosh to replace the one I had broken on the cranium of a particularly hard-headed docker.

At last, one day in February, my mind collapsing in on itself, nails bitten back to cuticles, everything was ready. I and a full complement of sailors were floated out of the dock surrounded by tugs, the sea bristling with people, clear, smooth estuarine water opening up around us, a flat expanse, a page on which the giant we travelled in transcribed his transitory thought. Even with seamen babbling around me I felt a moment of complete calm, the tranquillity of the water lapping up to me, cool and complete. It was only a great effort of will that prevented me from diving in.

Actually, this is not true. That day was much later. I so want to remember that day for you as a tranquil one. In fact, the sky closed around us like a shroud that morning, snow and hail poured across the water and the tugs could not control our leviathan. We hit everything we could find to hit, a lurching, drunken ogre, each crash uprooting men and shivering through every molecule of those on board. And I was sick, a torrent that will never be repeated, way more than my stomach could have held, a biblical flood.

We arrived at 51.53' 40.8" North 1.28' 56.7" East a little later than planned, top men from the Admiralty and War Office positioned to observe on nearby boats, the water ribboned with activity. Once we had been inched into the correct position, the gates on the pontoons were released.

As soon as I felt the roar of the water deep beneath my feet I knew something was wrong. While most of the sailors stood cheering and waving, a garnish of dumb, animal stupidity atop this titan, I turned and marched back to the hatch. I had hardly made it on to the ladder when my instincts were vindicated and the structure began to list, just a touch at first, then a touch more, then further still with no correction. The cheers from above turned to shouts of alarm, soon to be drowned out by the strange screech of concrete in pain. I half slid, half fell to the bottom of the ladder then ran for my target – the control room.

There, in the flickering light, Redred's Tower already angled past the point of no return, I focused myself into the walls around me, felt this cool fake-rock as me, imagined myself as the little man with the lever. Spread out across the floor with no time to remove my clothes, I envisaged myself and the tower as one entity, our powers combined, our fates intertwined. And, lying there, made of concrete myself, I stopped the fall, everything hanging for a moment, the stillness sharp, even the gulls silenced, the Navy and War Office and their various guests spread out across the water, their mouths hanging open. Little by little, every inch hurting every cell in my body, I pulled the fort back and back from disaster, straining through the degrees until finally, maybe a minute later, maybe an hour, it was upright, its water-filled pontoons resting perfectly on the sea bed. I had no idea how I had done it, only that it had exhausted me, only that it was, indubitably, I who had done it. It was the first time I sensed the awesome power within me, as if I were so much bigger inside than out, as if to harness it would be to move planets.

When I saw Titfer later he was laughing uncontrollably, paler even than his usual pallor, utterly intoxicated, I believe, by the prospect of having nearly killed one hundred and twenty-eight men and seen his dream topple like a stroke victim. This was a man a long, long way beyond relief. I decided to forbear from telling him of my part in his rescue. The last thing I wanted from him was any more gratitude.

The Navy lost their nerve and after them the Army. All the other forts were floated into position manned only by civilians. And, of course, me – a special kind of soldier. I sat in the control room of every one of them, in harmony with the concrete and iron, barely there as a separate thing at all. Each building's sentience, I taught them their own importance and with it the imperative of survival.

From: 100001@hotmail.com
To: mandyhart200@hotmail.com

mand - thing is hackings 2 easy. 4 me any way. thats the problem. ur
always going 2 try some thing harder. like drugs in it? u get high so
u do it again & its still a good high but not quite as good. so u do it
again & its less good again. so u do it more till its almost nothing.
so then u try some thing else. & its wicked & the rush is way much
better & ur fingers clatter across the keys faster & faster & ur eyes
flicker back & 4 wuds faster & faster taking all the data in & procesing
it faster & faster until the gap between the thoght & the actions gone
& the gap between u & the machines gone & the gap between ur
thoght & the datas gone. & that moment is it. better than drugs.
exept u dont do drugs do u? not any more. any way its more like
porn but u dont do that ether. hard 2 beleive im your bro sometimes
in it? im just trying 2 explain is all. whatever just write back ok? rob

(Converted from the ASCII)

10

Pete's not exactly asleep when it happens. Not exactly, anyway. He's tensed on the edge of the bed, eyes rolling behind swollen eyelids, a mute exhaustion holding him just beyond consciousness while behind him – and before Martha – Poppy and Gus enact their nightly battle for territory, each moment of sleep a tangle of arms and legs, the two of them slowly turning, the hands on a malfunctioning clock.

So it's not that he doesn't hear his phone's rendition of Patrice LaShuroo's recent No. 1 (an exclusive version of the ringtone played by two-fingered electronic duo Twofinger and available only to panellists from the recent *i-Culture* seminars). It's just that the tune filters gradually so that it is already there, a fact, long before he realises it as such.

Eyes folded together, face dough, he launches himself upward and, with exaggerated caution, picks up his trousers and steps from the room. Grappling the phone from his pocket he can't help but be momentarily impressed by the glow cast by the machine's full-colour, ultra-high-definition screen and ergonomic styling. It's his job, after all, and he's good at it, a natural. He manages to focus himself in on the number, though, a mobile too, and one unfamiliar to the phone's address book. He depresses the relevant button, trying not to feel too good about the satisfying weight of the click, and raises the handset to his ear.

'Hello?'

The personal acoustic hiss – digitally generated – of cellphone silence.

'Hello?'

He looks at the screen again to check the phones are connected, the solid two-way arrow reassuring him.

'Hello?'

The sound gone. Checks again. Call ended.

He knows it's her. It has to be. Peter Jones has drifted through five days of waiting since he delivered his note and has moved, seamlessly and with very little in the way of obvious fuss, from optimism to hope to panic to despair. He has tried to keep himself occupied by being a good father and tidying up a few freelance threads. He even ventured down to Farringdon to make amends with Donald McCracken. Not that the meeting had gone particularly well.

McCracken had been given the Lifestyle desk after having both his legs blown off during a drinking game involving land mines while out in Bosnia. When he realized he had covered his last conflict he'd had a massive nervous breakdown and to this day cannot discuss flavoured vodka.

According to Pete and his fellow Lifestyle professionals this is not his only weakness as an editor in their chosen field. McCracken devotes most of his time to trying to persuade other war correspondents to come and write muscular prose about coffee or sofas. His pages also tend to lean heavily toward camouflage and military chic, which was OK for the couple of seasons when it was (a) fashionable and then (b) fashionably ironic, but now is starting to seem, to say the least, somewhat recherché.

Contemptuous as McCracken is of Lifestyle professionals, he still needs them to fill the spaces – as long as they submit on time. He particularly likes it if they ring the story in. This, combined with the pile of unopened juicer boxes cluttering Peter's office, made for a difficult ten minutes.

None of which is important right now. Right now he needs to talk to her. He brings up the last caller's number and presses to connect. Ringing then a voice.

''Ello?' A male voice.

'Ud, sorry, wrong number.'

When he returns to the bedroom he finds Gus and Poppy have occupied his side of the bed, a gas that expands to fill whatever space is available to it. Quietly, with a certain sense of release, he turns, makes his way to Gus's bed, folds himself in. She's not going to call. He is surprised at how relieved he feels. Sleep comes suddenly, solidly.

Half-light outside, strained through the blue of novelty-patterned curtains. Gus is bouncing astride his hip fuck fuck fuck. She's not going to call. He's not going to be the renowned cultural commentator behind the seminal 'Clearwater' book and TV series. He is going to be just another one among many, just another drone (though admittedly one with better taste). He pulls the boy toward him, feathers the hair at the back of his neck, runs his hand down on to his warm back, kisses the gentle movement of his cheek, carefully heaves him off and stands.

Two hours later, with bit-lip fastidiousness, Peter Jones kneels on his study floor picking at the thick, brown tape, wrapped – with an efficiency bordering on the compulsive – around the packaging of the first juicer. Opens the box, removes the square ruff from its neck, grabs the plastic and pulls it free. Turns it over, tears at the peck of tape, pulls the bag open and finally wrenches it clear.

A sigh. Scuttling from the plastic bag, a plugless cable, the two coloured wires flapping to the floor like an earwig. He rubs at his forehead, reaches for the box and pulls out the compliments slip, a slight ripple of surprise disturbing his features. Barnums don't usually bother with juicers. Major oil spills, corporate malfeasance, the media launch of new weapons systems. And Clearwater. It had to be the people taking care of Clearwater. Twists and pulls the phone from the desk. Taps in the number, his face falling into a repose of sourness.

'Barnums? Can you hold?'

'I . . .' The click and then the music. Peter would be more angry if he weren't so intrigued by the mix of the Patrice LaShuroo tune they're using to hold him. Either they're a very clued-up, very well-connected organization or he's losing touch. It has to be the former, reassuring as it is to both parties.

'Barnums? How can I help you?'

'Could I speak to', checking the paper, 'Alexandria, please?'

'Just putting you through?'

'Alexandria's phone.'

'Could I speak to Alexandria, please?'

'Speaking.'

'Oh. Peter Jones here. I'm doing the juicer piece for the *Abstruser* and you sent me over the', consulting the box, 'Ronoco . . .'

'334 Deluxe. Hi, Peter. Great, isn't it? I've got one at my flat and I'm just juicing the whole time. Have you tried putting some fresh ginger in? It's fabulous . . .'

'Actually, I haven't tried anything because it's not got a plug on it.'

'Uh, so that's problematic . . .?'

'Because I can't plug it in.'

'Yuh, of course. I can see the problem. I don't suppose you have a spare plug anywhere?'

'Nope.'

'Or something you could take the plug off temporarily?'

'You know it's illegal, don't you, to sell electrical goods without a plug attached? There's a European directive. Alexandria?'

'We're not selling it to you, though, are we, Pete?'

'Peter.'

'Peter. I can assure you that the product in the shop in the proper box . . .'

'It's in the proper box.'

'Oh no, that's not the proper box. Those were flown in specially from Korea for reviews. That's the Korean box.'

'It's in English.'

'What is?'

'The box is. The box is in English.'

A pause, Peter feeling victory at hand.

'They always are in Korea.'

'I actually couldn't care less about Korea. I am reviewing in and for the UK and I always review as found. So if you want a review which says something other than that your product fails basic safety standards I suggest you come up with a solution.'

'Uh yuh, right, Peter. Problem understood. Can I call you back? In two minutes? I promise to call you straight back in two minutes.'

Peter stays where he is, by the phone on the floor, enjoying the fact that he has her, proud, relieved he hasn't lost the knack. The phone rings. He lets it until just before he's sure she'll hang up.

'Yes?'

'Peter?' The voice seeming harder, older.

'Ah, Alexandria?'

'No. This is Tina. I'm Alexandria's line manager.'

'So, Tina. Can we get this sorted?'

'I think you'll be OK to review from that. I'm sure you can fit a plug.'

'Tina, I've already explained my position in some detail to Alex-...'

'Let's just have a look shall we? It's Peter Huw with a W Jones, isn't it?' The tap of her fingers sharp across the keyboard. Then a pause. A tap and a pause. Another tap and tap. Pause.

'It seems to me, Peter, that you really need to just get this piece finished.'

'What?'

'You're in arrears on your mortgage aren't you, Peter? Does . . . let me see, *Martha* know? Or are you keeping it from her?'

'That's really none of your business . . .'

'Would you like me to look for anything else? Peter?'

' . . . I . . .'

'Perhaps you should just finish the article, there's a love. I can't wait to hear what you have to say about the Ronoco. I hope it's good.'

' . . .'

'Do we have an understanding?'

' . . .'

'Do we?'

' . . . yes, but . . .'

'Good. That's all then. Enjoy the juicer.'

'This is outrage–'

He's already talking to himself. Sits there, the phone still in his hand, tears of embarrassment flaring in his eyes. He should report her or something. It's absolutely fucking outrageous. That's, well, that's blackmail. That's what that is.

He ought to report her but he already knows he won't. He's scared. How did she know those things? Who told her those things? He can't even ring his bank to complain because she's right and he doesn't want to have to speak to his Personal Finance Adviser until he's got the situation with the arrears under control. No point ring-ing to complain if they're just going to start asking a whole set of questions of their own. That makes sense, surely? That much makes sense.

It's somewhere between three and four in the morning when the phone rings again, as if the caller is a keen student of military psychology and has long ago learnt that this is when the sentries are least alert. It doesn't quite work like that, though. Peter has been waiting for this, has refused to put the previous call down to chance. He has gone to bed clutching his mobile and as it starts to trill he is already in motion, the covers a diagram of his exit, beyond the door before Martha has stirred. The number the same as the night before. He takes a breath, prepares his voice to sound urbane, detached.

'Hello? Hello?' The first a squeak, the second too grand a compensation, a pubescent boy trying to sound like a pipe smoker.

'Hello? If that's . . .' The line dead. 'Fuck. Fuck.'

He doesn't feel like talking to PRs today. He just tries to get on, to get through it, the screwdriver on the desk a constant reminder of retreat. The floor of his office is a hazard of packaging, shining white casings and cables. Peter sits at his desk, scowling through a mouthful of kumquat, not quite ready to begin. The phone shattering his bitter fruit reverie.

'Pete? Don.'

'Ah . . . Donald. How are you?'

'Where's the juicer copy, Pete? Where the fuck is it?'

'There's been a few hold-ups. A few setbacks. You know what PRs are like.'

'Not interested in excuses, Peter. Only interested in copy.'

'Half the machines won't even work and . . .'

'When will I have the copy?'

'End of today? Tomorrow?'

'Which?'

'Tomorrow?'

'Tomorrow. First thing. And today's your lucky day. Got something else for you. Had Johnny Robard lined up for it until they started shooting in Mogadishu. Now he's fucked off and you get it, ya jammy bastard.'

'Uh . . . Great.'

'We're doing a piece on people living in former military installations. Got a guy in a pillbox in Devon, the one who bought the nuclear bunker, a bloke with a sub moored up the Humber. Going to be quite special. Antidote to all that shit about designers' homes and artists' homes and architects' homes and actors' homes and blah fucking blah.'

'That's great, Donald. My only problem . . .'

'You got a guy down in Kent living on one of the seaforts. Setting up a data haven or something. He'll tell you all about it.'

'Great. That really is great. It's just that I might have something that would interest you, a main feature for Living Culture . . .'

'We've exchanged emails and he's up for it. Interesting guy. Unusual. A character. You know anything about data havens?'

'Er, no, but . . .'

'Me either.'

' . . . about the shopping centre. About Clearwater.'

'What about it?'

'That's what I'm working on. That's what I . . .'

'No. Not interested.'

'But you've not even heard what . . .'

'Listen, Pete, do you think no one's ever written about mall culture before? Do you think that just because it's down the road from you and you're you that suddenly it's interesting?'

'I think my angle on it . . .'

' . . . will be a load of reheated bullshit . . .'

'While I don't want to be rude, Donald . . .'

' . . . masquerading as insight.'

'I don't think "People Living In Decommissioned Military Buildings" is exactly . . .'

'And that's why I'm the editor.'

'Well, there are other people interested so I don't know if I'll have time to . . .'

'Do you want to continue working for the *Abstruser*?'

'Yes. Of course.'

'Then you'd better email the mad old fucker and arrange your visit. It's king dot james at vernaland that's victor echo romeo november alpha lima alpha november delta dot com. That's what he calls himself. King James! His Royal fuckin' Highness! Don't tell me you don't have fun working for me. Billy Hibbert's doing the pictures. Two weeks on Monday.'

Once again the phone, the cold scramble, the door. But this time, as he's about to answer, something else - a flutter of darker dark in the dark and a cold drop in his stomach. Was that someone going downstairs? His hand moles out for the light switch as he forces a swallowed word from numb lips.

'Gus?' There is, of course, no response. He notices the phone in his hand, still spouting melody, and silences it. The light now on, he moves to the top of the stairs in time to hear the front door click shut.

Time passes, him standing there balanced on a creaking board, unsure whether his stillness is to listen better or to hide his presence. His skin prickles and twitches with the creaks and tappings of an old house.

It's the children, and in particular the guilty realization that he didn't think of them first, which finally sets Peter moving again. He checks Gus – mangling his covers but asleep, unharmed, untouched; then, at the end of the hall, Poppy, ditto. Unable to think of any suitable armament readily available to him, he returns to Gus, unplugs his table lamp, wraps the flex around his wrist and waves it half-heartedly through the gloom, trying to imagine knocking out a burglar.

First room checked is his study where he is both relieved and disappointed to find his laptop still at his desk beyond the tangle of appliances and packaging. It would have been the perfect excuse for Donald.

Next, he checks the bathroom, also lacking in intruders or signs of intrusion. As he leaves he notices a shining rosette of wet toilet paper in the bowl and automatically flushes, without a thought, as if his mother was pushing his hand down.

Getting downstairs tests him but once he's there and the lights are on his trawl loses any sense of urgency. No one is there and nothing has been touched. It is quite possible he has imagined the whole thing, even likely, it occurs to him.

The back door is unlocked. The key is in its normal place. Peter locks and bolts it, double locks the front and bolts that, too. Retreats to the kitchen, shakily pours himself a swig of whisky and gulps it back. Is he being watched or bugged or something? Is he under surveillance? And why would anyone bother? More likely a burglar has just walked off with one of the many things he bought and forgot he even had. His hand flaps out and pulls the business card lying on the work surface towards his face. He reads it abstractedly as he takes another gulp.

> WANT TO FEEL SAFE?
> For all your security needs,
> both domestic and beyond the home, contact
> LOCKE & HULME
> Experts. Discreet. Safe.
> Call 0800 0212 545
> www.locke&hulme.co.uk

Martha must have picked it up. He should give them a call. Which reminds him of what woke him in the first place. He puts the card down before he has read the smaller print beneath the URL.

Locke & Hulme is a BARNUMS© company

It takes Peter longer than he feels it should have to find the phone on Gus's table where the lamp is meant to be. It then takes him a little longer to return to the kitchen to collect the lamp. It's only after all this that he checks his screen and sees that he has a message waiting.

'Thank you for calling your Ultra Mobile voicemail service. You have, *one*, new message' Machine-portentous emphasis. 'To listen to your messages, press *one* or say *one* after the tone.' One. 'Message received *today*. At three, twenty, *four*, a.*m*.'

Pause and then the background acoustic of a real voice in a real room.

'This is a message for Peter Jones. Got your letter. I'll give it a go. Why not? I'll meet you tomorrow at one o'clock in the lobby of Deep Rest. That's level 5. Get a room and say you're waiting for your wife. Have the key ready when I come in. I'll see you then.'

From: 100001@hotmail.com
To: mandyhart200@hotmail.com

mand - cmon u bitch! im poring my hart out here & u cant even be bothered 2 write back. ur making me feel like a right twat. i cant beleive this. what have u given up? im stranded here. may as well be a ship wreck. i got nothing but this screen in front of me. im not asking 4 much. just a reply. u always did think u was better than me. dunno why u stuck up cow. rob

(Converted from the ASCII)

11

What a beautiful morning! She is sure she can smell the roses as she steps outside, though she is dimly aware (denying it) that this may just be the scent she applied rather too enthusiastically before leaving her humble abode. Whatever the case – and despite the weight she feels in her quivering legs – it is good to be outside, to be *doing something*. She pulls the fur stole a little tighter around her still-beautiful shoulders, moués her mouth and begins a cautious wobble down the path in shoes that have been a challenge to her for the best part of twenty years.

At the gate she stops to rest for a moment, one elegant hand placed uncomfortably on the wrought iron in such a way as to protect her nails and their painstakingly enamelled surfaces, thumb cocked away from extended fingers, a chicken foot. A thin, bright sunshine further emphasizes the translucence of her pale skin, the cool light illuminating its return to dry velvet. The sky is a lovely, delicate blue that reminds her of easier days and more pleasant journeys. It makes her sigh, her lips slackening and losing their carefully maintained shape.

She is, though, and has always been, a trouper. One doesn't get anywhere in this profession, darling, by moping and moaning. Smile for your public. Bring joy and gaiety into their lives. The show must . . .

She pulls herself a little straighter, raises her chin and staggers forward, trying to use every trick she has ever learnt as a performer to keep her mind off the longing she feels, the desperation lodged inside her. Remember who you are, Verna. You have set yourself standards and your public will hold you to them.

Things had been going swimmingly for her until lovely Dr Parlecue had passed away. It had been quite a shock. She had walked into surgery to be greeted with the news of this great, great man's precipitate death and was then immediately ushered into a room containing a young fellow in a creased shirt, the raw and distinctive patina of acne still fading from his bulbous cheeks.

'Hello, erm, Mrs Landor. I'm Dr Watts, I'm here as a locum for now until a replacement for Dr Parlecue can be sorted out. How can I help you?'

'I'm terribly sorry, young man, but I am in shock. Dr Parlecue was not only my physician but a personal friend and confidant. You can't expect me to start giving you my medical history when . . .' She had paused to take in the enormity of the loss. 'And it's *Miss* Landor.'

'I understand completely, Miss Landor. If it's too difficult perhaps you'd like to leave it and book a later appointment?'

Sharp now: 'No. No. It can't wait. Especially not now. Not now of all times. I need a repeat on my prescription.'

The doctor looked down at his notes.

'Which one?'

'My nerve pills.'

'Ah yes. I'd been wanting to talk to you about those. I'm afraid, Miss Landor, I won't be able to give you a prescription for those again.'

This is a new experience for Verna and it takes her a moment to distinguish between idle chit-chat and a refusal.

'I beg your pardon?'

'Put simply, I'm not happy to prescribe Restoril to you again. It's a very strong, potentially addictive drug which the licensing authorities recommend should not be taken for longer than a three-month spell. You, on the other hand, have been taking it in fairly high doses for . . . a little over five years now.'

'It's for my nerves.'

'It's actually for the treatment of insomnia.'

'I don't think you understand. I need it for my nerves.'

'I don't mean to be rude, Miss Landor, but the only thing you need this drug for is to assuage your addiction to it and I am a doctor not a pusher. Now, this could be quite an uncomfortable process in the short term. What I'd like to start by doing is examining you to . . .'

'Do you know who I am? Do you have any idea who I am?'

' . . . to assess what kind of shape you're in physically . . .'

'Does the song "No Man Is An Island" mean nothing to you?'

'And then we can work out the best way to proceed with this . . .'

'Does the War mean nothing to you?'

' . . . and draw up an action plan . . .'

'I may not have fought physically but I fought morally. I fought for morale. Churchill himself . . .'

'I understand this is difficult, Mrs Landor, but I'm afraid our budgets – or for that matter our consciences – don't allow us to just go on and on handing out dangerous drugs on little more than a whim . . .'

'You have absolutely no idea who I am, do you?'

'I may not know you personally, but I make it a matter of principle to read my patients' files very carefully. I try to become as acquainted as I can with your medical history and . . .'

'I am not your patient. I am Miss Verna Landor. And you would do well not to cross me. If it wasn't for the likes of me, people like you would not be living like you do now. Mind you, as you behave like a Nazi anyhow, I don't suppose it would have made much difference to you. I need my prescription.'

'I'm sorry . . .'

'Then good day. I shall be reporting you. I may do worse.'

It had been a bleak walk home – limbs aching, a sticky sweat gumming round her. And, yes, she had cried, something she hadn't done in public since the age of fourteen unless the part demanded it (and even then, grudgingly). When she had finally arrived home, she had been shaking so violently with it all she had been unable to get the keys into the lock. That was where Maeve had found her and, later, taking pity on her, introduced Verna to her nephew.

Barry didn't look much like a Freelance Medical Supplier but that was what his card said and Verna had always been respectful of cards. How was she to know that these days you could get five made up for a pound on a machine up at the station? She placed it carefully in her purse, checked it each time before he arrived, mouthing his name again and again as she trot-staggered down the stairs to let him in.

But this first time, before she knew the wonders he could work? Freelance Medical Supplier? A Mr Whippy of red hair swirled up from his colourless forehead, his cheeks and chin slowly giving themselves up to further ginger stranding. His clothing was – apparently deliberately! – baggy and slightly frayed, one of his front teeth chipped in half, the overwhelming impression being, to Verna, of a tramp. But his card, his manner and his vowels suggested otherwise and anyway, Barry was Maeve's nephew and she was a solid and dependable, if rather boring, individual. She also swore by the pills that Barry supplied to her, admittedly at a cost that left her pension depleted (this perhaps went some way to explaining the extremity of her jutting bones).

He certainly had his bedside manner down pat, taking ten minutes to chat before the issue of medication was even raised. Then he talked symptoms, nodding sympathetically before finally requesting that the last, forlorn and empty pill packet be brought into his presence. It vanished into one of his many (presumably fashionable) pockets and he was gone, the promise that he would be in touch lingering with the pungence of the patchouli.

Barry returned the next day rattling an unmarked tub of yellow capsules at a rattling Verna Landor.

'Not identical to what you had before, but they should do the trick. Not more than one every four hours, OK? And that'll be fifty pounds, please, plus my usual ten-pound sourcing fee.'

Verna just gave him her purse and asked him to get her a glass of water. Soon she felt much better. What a lovely young man, quite charming in his own way.

The only problem was the cost. Occasionally, this worry drifted through the warm haze that held her, usually as a four-hour period was coming to an end, manifesting itself as a sharp feeling of sudden, unfocused tension and a trip to the lavatory. Another tablet and it drifted away. But as Barry visited and revisited the sensation became more frequent and more intense until she finally arrived at the day she couldn't pay him.

Barry was still charming except that he wouldn't hand over what Verna needed.

'I'm terribly sorry, Miss Landor, but it would set a precedent. This medicine is very expensive and incredibly difficult to come by and if I were to hand it over to you just like that without receiving any payment then I might as well just shut my business here and now. Give up.'

The poor boy seemed genuinely pained by this decision but Verna couldn't afford to let up, unleashing tears which felt, even to her, genuine. Barry rubbed at his forehead, scratched at his chin. Appeared to make a decision.

'There's something else I can let you have. On tick. It's the same stuff, basically, just in a slightly less refined form. But it's cheaper for you and my margin's better so I can soak up the occasional late payment without it bankrupting me. Interested?'

Verna nodded through the waterworks as he pulled a crumpled sandwich bag of brown dust from his pocket.

'It will work just fine if you smoke it, but as your consultant and knowing how price-conscious you are, I'd recommend injecting.'

He taught her and this time – and all the times after – all was right with the world.

Don't misunderstand. Verna Landor is no naïf. Although she preferred to refer to it as opium or 'my poppy's heart' she knew exactly what it was she was taking. She liked it. She hated to admit it, but the truth was she was getting old and who would begrudge her – her a war hero – a release from her blasted nerves? So she took it as often as she could afford and revelled in it. She even got Maeve interested and helped her through her aversion to needles and after that her neighbour's visits were much more diverting.

That is, until Barry missed his appointment. He had been late before, up to an hour and a half late. But once the gap between expectation and fulfilment crept beyond three hours, nervousness grew. It was at around this time that they had tried ringing his mobile phone. That first time Maeve got an answering service and had left an old person's message, slow and painstakingly enunciated, as if dictating a telegram. They had continued to leave messages with increasing frequency throughout the night, the careful formality of the first giving way to weepy entreaties, threats and reminiscences of happier days until, at eight thirty in the morning, they were informed that Barry's voicemail was full.

Verna, however, was keeping one piece of information to herself, the reason for this reticence unclear even to her. She knew where Barry lived. Earlier in the year, when they had opened the Sainsbury's they had revamped over on Shaw Street, she had seen Barry up ahead entering a house. She had called out and waved but he had disappeared inside. Knowing it might be useful, scared of forgetting (always scared of this), she had made a note of it there in the street in her largely empty diary, underlining it and starring it and placing the card he had given her in those pages.

So now she totters along, having persuaded Maeve that they should at least *try* to rest for a while, at least give it a *try*, my darling, then returned back downstairs, just throwing on some suitable clothes and tidying up her *maquillage* a little before heading for the exit. It is, though, despite the problems she has had, a lovely day, the blue skies straight from a song.

And, lo, here she is! Standing outside the badly painted but jauntily bright blue door of the house she believes to be Barry's residence. She pulls herself up, shoulders back and, taking her balancing hand from the frame, reaches out with one long finger and pushes the bell. Somewhere inside the house or her head she thinks she hears the distant penumbra of the echo of a ring.

But nothing more.

She waits, her ankles hurting even more than the rest of her, but the house is silent, utterly unmoving, a block of emptiness.

She rings again and this time doesn't even sense the sound of bell or buzzer, a vacuum lurking behind the door. Her mood begins to falter a little, clouds scuttling from over the horizon right on cue, a cigarette-puffing youngster passing her muttering 'stupid old cunt' to his chum. She rings again, weakness coming at her now from all directions and how on earth will she get home?

Verna feels herself pitching forward, the whole thing a terrible mistake, and raises her extended palm for support. Her hand comes to rest – more lightly than she might imagine – on the blue door but rather than stopping there, she finds herself pushing it open.

Beyond is darkness, as empty as it sounded. She calls a half-hearted hello but already knows that there will be no response and she will go in anyway. She is tired, needs to sit, needs to rest awhile. So she goes in, anyway.

Verna has seen how Barry dresses but is still deflated by his interiors. She had secretly hoped that the clothes were some sort of disguise or deliberate distraction and that his house would be the bright and orderly domicile of a gentleman. Instead, it conforms completely – sheets tacked badly over windows, a stringless guitar in the centre of the floor, a profusion of chipped mugs in and around the sink, a couple of stained floor cushions, an aged sofa with a badly tie-dyed sheet thrown over it and then rubbed round into the writhing shape of its last user. Here and there, studding this constellation of junk, full ashtrays in a variety of designs.

Verna picks her way through it, her face set hard against distaste, jaw clenched. She sees it all – the confetti of Rizla pack remains, the blooms of coffee, tea, wine and beer on the formerly beige carpet, the lurid picture of a purple elephant god coming loose from the wall. The details are overwhelming, queasy.

She is tired but loath to sit down here so she stalls with a further weak 'Hello?' and continued exploration. Everywhere the same – as if Barry and/or whoever else lives here has left with little notice, grabbing and chucking as they go. An empty bookshelf with a small pile of books in front of it. A TV remote control in the sink in the toilet. On the stairs, a half-drunk cup of tea and a plate with a single-bitten piece of toast. Verna is a ghost in a world she doesn't understand.

Slowly, with a feeling of regret rather than curiosity or dread, she ascends the uncarpeted steps, the banister wobbling slightly with her weight. The world outside has fled, the only sounds her feet and her blood, both still moving. What is she doing here? She is unsure right now. Only knows that it is somehow important, that her body won't let her stop.

There is a light on in a room off to the right, a polygon of illuminated dust and fluff angling outward from the rip of yellow at the foot of the door. She turns the handle and, as she steps forward into the electric glare, sees his feet.

'Oh, I am sorry. Sorry.'

Steps back again, closes it. Waits a moment. Rummages through her bag. Checks his card again, struggling to see it in the dark. Knocks, her mouth moving.

'Barry?'

The room stays silent, so she waits, out there in the dark, only the edges of her shoes showing. When an intolerable amount of time has passed, she knocks again, waits again. And so on. It is only some time after the repetition of these actions and inactions has become mechanical that his phone rings in the room, the theme from *Mission Impossible* played in a loop. It's only when that stops, too, and she has recovered from the idea that someone else is trying to contact Barry as well, it is only then that she re-enters the room.

She isn't stupid. She knows that Barry will be dead. And so it proves to be. He has his shirt off and is lying back on the mattress, his syringe and works by his side. His belt is still tight round his arm. The top button of his trousers is undone. He doesn't appear to have died in agony. He doesn't look peaceful. He just looks dead. Verna is old. Dead is just dead. She feels for him even less than she thought she would.

Nevertheless, as she moves further into the room she does so quietly, carefully, as though – despite what she knows, despite the cold that seems to be emanating from him – he is just sleeping. She totters through a debris of dirty pants, socks, discarded jeans and disintegrating T-shirts, slowly lowers herself into an uncomfortable and precarious crouch next to him, stretches out fingers not actually as well manicured as she'd like to think and snatches up the bag.

Heading back to the door now, moving as fast as she has done in the best part of a decade, she feels the slight shadowing of a moment of guilt about the ginger-haired man lying upstairs. Such a lovely boy. Then she is back beneath the promise of that clear sky and thinks of nothing but her triumph.

From: 100001@hotmail.com
To: mandyhart200@hotmail.com

mand - sorry. sorry. my bad. all ways my bad in it? i think being surounded by water does funny things 2 ur head. just sea every where. keeps moving but nothing happens. freaks me out. run away 2 sea? u can lose ur self thats 4 sure. i guess its got that going 4 it. but then it aint even like im alone out here. oh no. i got compnay. sort of. when u write back ill tell u about him. my buddy. the reason im out here. rob

(Converted from the ASCII)

12

O is propped against Jimmy's desk, cigarette crouched in the snug of his fingers. The office is smeared amber, every surface sweating tar. Ever since a temp had complained about her working environment, O has made all employees sign a document stating that they actively approve of and choose to work in a smoking office. This has, on occasion, held the company back in recruitment, but for O it is 'a point of principle'. A tight-mouthed smile before continuing. 'My only point of principle.'

'Ah, Jimmy. You decided to join us. Your magnanimity knows no bounds.'

'Don't mention it.'

Jimmy stubs his cigarette into an already full ashtray, carefully lifts the Pyrex crystal and empties the lot, with a miniature explosion of ash, into his bin. He pulls his chair gently from under the desk, occasioning a slight readjustment of O's weight. Sits.

'If you have a moment in your busy schedule for me . . .?'

He sets off toward his glassed-in office, drip lines of brown clearly visible on the panes. Jimmy glances down for just a moment, reanimates his smile, rises and follows.

When he had first met him, O had been everything that Jimmy had ever dreamed of being. Although the elder, Jimmy felt like a child whenever he was near the man. There were simple reasons for this – his suits, his assurance, his well-cut black hair. But more than anything it was the world-weary dryness he displayed – which Jimmy felt to be the very essence of Englishness – and the way that he carried it off so as to make himself more popular rather than less, somehow warmly cynical rather than aloof.

Which was a knack, it would later transpire, rather than a redeeming feature of his character.

'Jimmy. Where to start? You've got your kit?'

'Sorry?'

'Your kit. For the game. This afternoon?'

Jimmy holds the smile, face clear, eyebrows inviting explanation.

'The charity match I said you'd play in.'

'I don't play cricket any more.'

'You don't *often* play cricket any more,' O corrects. 'Which is exactly why they were so keen to get you.'

'My shoulder.'

'Your shoulder will be fine for a few overs. No one expects you to turn it.'

'I would.'

'Jimmy. Do I have to ask you the question again – what exactly do you do here?'

'I'm South East Region Sales Director.'

'Jimmy, be serious. That's your title. I asked you what you did. To which the answer is very little of any great value.'

'Thank you.'

'And when you do actually do something it rarely works out to the benefit of the company. So on what grounds do you have such a good job? Is it your years of experience in retail, your mastery of the art of sales? Or is it the fact that you're a reasonably well-known local cricketer – or should I say *former cricketer* – and are, hence, of some PR value?'

'We both know that's not why I have a job here . . .'

'It might be astute, then, might it not, to keep one's PR value up? Give the odd after-dinner speech, award trophies to schoolboys, go on sponsored walks? Play in the occasional charity match? Act as if – preposterous though it might sound – this creation and mainte-nance of PR value is your job.'

'That isn't really my job, though, is it?'

'Go and sort out some whites in the warehouse. It starts at two. I'll drive you down there.'

'And are you going to sack me if I fail or refuse to maintain my

PR value?'

O just looks at him, his smile brittle.

'Are you?'

'Don't tempt me.'

The first time O had cut him a line of coke he had no idea what he was meant to do or even what it was. A little instruction, some half-hearted snuffling, a sarcastic exhortation to greater nasal exertion and Jimmy was away. Ten minutes later, still trying to hold back the metal slime as it gradually monopolised his throat, Jimmy felt suddenly comfortable with himself, garrulous with others. His conversational skills, usually inhibited by his embarrassment at his accent, became to him polished, easy. His eyes shone, too, he could tell, with an inclusive mischief. He became witty, urbane, as if a man a foot taller than him had unfolded from inside his frame and stood, stretching and smiling, magnificent. He became, in short, O. And he smiled both because he liked this transformation and because he couldn't stop smiling. And everyone, but everyone, smiled back.

Jimmy returns to his desk, sits, lights another cigarette. Sunil looks up and throws him a half-smile. Jimmy draws deep, tosses him back his full grin then lets the smoke sneak out between his teeth.

'What you looking so chirpy about?'

'The usual. The big man calling me in to give me a pay rise and telling me how much the company values me.'

Sunil doesn't know what to make of this, never knows what to make of Jimmy. They've passed each other at tangents for five years now, only their desks touching.

'Oh, and he's kindly given me the afternoon off to play cricket. In fact, he's giving me a lift to the game.'

'You're joking, yes?'

Although Sunil was born here, to Jimmy the boy seems more Indian than him. When he had started at P&G he had invited Jimmy round for food, honoured to nourish such a famous cricketer. His wife had been sweet, the meal excellent and they had had nothing in common. He had been invited again on maybe two or three occasions before Sunil realized that Jimmy wasn't, in fact, always busy. Jimmy sighs.

'No, unfortunately not.'

By the time Jimmy had met O he had been in England for eight years. He had lived in a small flat with his mother, his younger brother and, until she died, his grandmother, trying to be English, surrounded by a very particular Uganda. Long before O had appeared, Jimmy had stopped eating at home, stopped in fact spending any time at home except to sleep. And, in truth, none of them – least of all his mother, who did everything she could to make the small space feel comfortable and familiar – thought of the flat as home. It was just where they had washed up while they waited to go back. To Jimmy it felt more like the sea, with everything around it an island whose interior he couldn't penetrate, eternally cursed to wander the thin strip of beach looking at driftwood before diving back into the cold, rough water to examine once again the corpses of his long-drowned family.

Then from out of the thick woods came O and Jimmy finally realized that it was Crusoe who had been completely dependent on Friday and not the other way around and that, within that, the issue of naming had been unimportant, just something Friday had given Crusoe to make him feel better. And it was when he realized this that he finally stopped fighting his team mates' wishes and began to call himself Jimmy instead of Jaimin. Which was fortunate, because the mutually coked people O introduced him to seemed to struggle with 'Jaimin', which he found upsetting and hence a distraction from his enjoyment of the high.

'Jaimin? It's Hinesh.'

Shit. Jimmy knows, has taught himself, has made it his primary rule and obligation never to answer his phone. His first action upon arriving at his desk is always to turn the ringer off on the fucking thing. Now O has not only forced him to play again, he's got to deal with his brother.

'Hin. Good to hear from you. Listen, I would ask how it's going but I'm about to step into a meeting. I'm going to have to call you back.'

'It can't wait, I'm afraid. I'm sorry. It's gone too far. We need to speak right now.'

Shit. His brother can sometimes be shrugged off. Not today.

'I've got two minutes.'

'I know what you're doing.'

'Sorry?'

'I know what you're doing. I've met him, Jaimin. I talked to him.'

'I have absolutely no idea . . .'

'See? I'm not as stupid, am I? Not as stupid as I look?'

'You're making no sense to me, I'm afraid.'

'Oh come on, don't patronize me. Don't patronize me even more than usual.'

'I'm not patronizing you. I just have no idea what you're talking about.'

'Your spy? The man you sent to keep an eye on me? Your "Peter"? Any flicker of recognition for any of that yet? Got your attention now?'

'I haven't sent anyone to spy on you. Do you think I've nothing better to . . .'

'Of course he hasn't been through since I have rumbled him. I expect you're sending somebody else now. Another of your spies. And he was very complimentary and so I said I wouldn't mention to you that I rumbled him and he said all these good things. But it's been weeks and you haven't called and told me well done and so I began to think . . .'

'Hinesh, I haven't sent a spy.'

'I began to think, what if he only told me he thought the shop was good to get out of the situation? What if he lied to me and told me it was good and then went back to you and said the opposite? But then I thought, no, the shop *is* good. Why would he think otherwise? So then I thought what if he did think the shop was good but was angry because I saw through him and decided to tell you the shop was bad just to take revenge on me? So then

I thought I should call you and sort it out in case he was less honourable than me.'

'I'm sorry to have to say this, but you're acting like a crazy man.
I have not sent anyone to spy on you. I'm really not that interested.
None of us here are that interested.'

'So why did he say you sent him?'

'I'm sorry?'

'Why did he say you sent him?'

'What, this man you spoke to, he said I sent him to spy on you?'

'Yes.'

'Yes?'

'Well, not exactly. He said he was from head office.'

Jimmy decides he has had enough of this conversation. He
never knows what to make of his brother's calls and has long
since stopped regretting getting him the job, let alone listening to
(and even acting upon) his many – without exception – dreadful
ideas. The Clearwater fiasco was entirely of Hinesh's making and
hasn't even had Jimmy's desired effect of irritating O, who, rather
than cursing and screaming and generally ruing having ever met
the Patel family, describes it with a smirk as 'the wild card'.
Which is doubly irritating when you consider his overall philosophy regarding risk, or the preferred lack of it. The torpor that O
had seemed temporarily to have shifted comes sinking down
again, his muscles weakening as he sits there.

'Got to go. I'll look into it, all right? It's honestly nothing to do
with me. I honestly don't think anyone from here cares enough
about the Clearwater shop to pay to have someone check up on
you. But I'll ask. I'll ask O. OK?'

It was with O that he began to go to London and it was in London
(with O's expertise and direction) that he began visiting prostitutes
and this was how he met his wife, so O had good reason to claim
himself the matchmaker. Not that his wife had been a whore. Far
from it. Not Gloria. She had been a cashier. The fact that she had
been a cashier in a brothel was beside the point. They both had
standards, that was what was important.

Jimmy had noticed her the very first time he visited, her hair a single yellow, swirling round into a solid, anachronistic whole. He had smiled at her nervously as she had taken his money and was surprised to be met with neither indifference nor the forced bonhomie usually employed in such circumstances to disguise indifference. Instead, what he was given seemed genuine – not much but real, the tiniest alteration in expression and, as change was passed, the slightest contact of skin on skin. He was surprised by how much this bothered him.

The next time he visited he stopped for a moment and, trying to fix on his face the look which on TV and in films meant *I want to fuck you*, embarrassed himself with a thoroughness which kept O amused for a week.

'So, how long you been working here then?'

'Never you mind. Long enough.'

'Must be interesting, though. Working in a place like this.'

'Yeah, it's all right.'

'Must've seen some crazy stuff.'

'What, you Old Bill or something?'

'God, no. No. Sorry. I didn't mean to startle . . . I'm a cricketer.'

'S'alright, love. I was only winding you up.'

'Oh. Sorry.' Pause. 'You have lovely hair.'

O had cackled, grabbed Jimmy by his overcoat and dragged him on through the doorway.

'We are here to fuck, not fuck about.'

And behind him, quietly, he heard her thank him for his ugly compliment.

He started going there every night he could, turning up for games with iguana eyes, irritated by smoke and lack of sleep. His evenings were mapped out solely in the journey from the cash desk to the bar and back again, the only deviation from this ever thickening black line the trips to the gents to empty bladder and erase white lines.

After three weeks of this he invited Gloria to a game, where he played perhaps the most inept cricket of his now long career. Failing to take this as any kind of omen, he proposed over dinner that night and she accepted. Four weeks later they were married at Gravesend Register Office in a ceremony that didn't stand on ceremony, O – an eyebrow bouncing with over-played bemusement – the witness, alongside someone dragged from the waiting room.

As soon as he puts it down and long before he has had a chance to disconnect it, the phone rings again. Angry now, though knowing it isn't him even as he blurts it.

'The conversation's over, Hin.'

'Actually it's not "Him". Is that Jimmy Patel?'

'Why?' Then remembering himself, 'Yes.'

'Ah, it's an honour. I used to watch Kent a lot in the seventies. You were my favourite player.'

'I'm sorry, who's speaking please?'

'God, no, I'm sorry. Got a little carried away. Mark Lanark. I work for a company called Barnums Futurestat Limited.'

'What can I do for you, Mr Lanark?'

'It's rather delicate, I'm afraid. I was hoping we could meet up and have a chat.'

'I'm not a very delicate man, Mr Lanark. Is this concerning Pleasence & Greene?'

'No. You. You and your playing career. Aspects of it, anyway. In the eighties. I really do think it would be better if we were to meet up. I'm in the area today, as it happens.'

'I don't speak about my playing career. I'm a private individual. I'm not a sportsman any more.'

'I don't mean to be pushy, Mr Patel, but I really do think it would be in your best interest to meet up with me.'

'And discuss my playing career?'

'Well, yes, in a manner of . . .'

'I don't play any more. I am no longer a cricketer.'

'You're playing in a match today.'

'I have nothing to say to you. Goodbye.'

'You'd make it much easier if you'd just . . .'

The receiver returns to its cradle, plastic hugging plastic as Jimmy fumbles his hands behind it, and pulls the cable free.

He sits looking at his unplugged phone for a long time after the conversation has ended. He gets up and walks around the office.

He sits down again and rubs his palms back and forth between his knees and his pockets, once, twice, three times. He stands again. He sits again. He scratches at the back of his head.

Nobody takes any notice. People are used to Jimmy.

From: 100001@hotmail.com
To: mandyhart200@hotmail.com

mand - better than prison any way. least im still net worked here. so many choices. land or sea. prison or fort. angry or sorry. them or me. me or him. do u see what im saying? every thing i do or think or say. all of it comes down 2 that. either or. which is why im binary rob

(Converted from the ASCII)

13

The Yanks have a lot to answer for. Never, at any time in history, have a people rendered faith so banal. That is why false prophets, New Age drivel and the cult of the personality all thrive there. And we, like a senile old lady who knows no better, suckle at our daughter's teat. Not a pretty sight, I hope you will agree. Though one serving a sizeable appetite, if my websearch for 'granny mummy tit suck' is to be taken as an indicator.

What we need, what we all need, is new faith, real faith. Or if not all of us, at least the masses. Our previous religions are all at least a millennium old. Of course they have buckled and warped when met by the forces of unfettered free-market capitalism and technological advance. So-called 'traditionalists' argue for return, as if return is possible, as if it is desirable. I argue for the future. I am the future. I have always been the future.

When the War ended, the war did not end. It merely went underground, which is where we were all waiting. It became ours. And we were quick to make sure it suited our purposes.

Victor could be said to have had a head start when it came to deregulation and privatization as it was always far from clear who we working for in the first place. He was unsurprisingly quick to grasp the new circumstances and much of '47 and '48 were spent discrediting, undermining and blackmailing our rivals, all of which I excelled at. My confidence returned – Verna was just fluff. She was working for Victor now, that much was clear, but only as directed, just a splayed pair of legs and a raised behind in picture after picture, the props between which our victims found themselves caught in my shutters. I was the one who was making things happen through strength of will and cunning alone. I affected a new sneer of condescension when forced to share space with her which she, for her part, reciprocated. I entered a new decade already a god, a malevolent visitor for the forces of Good. It was hard to tell whether my aura alone or the quality of my tailoring silenced people when I entered a room. Either way I was invincible.

So-called peace-time had, in contrast, been cruel to Verna. She had been carried through a few years by the fevered yearnings of squaddies returning from Europe, but the fifties was a harsh decade. Patriotic love songs – still considered her *métier* despite (or because of?) the lusty sensuality she brought to them – became less popular with the record-buying public, as was made heart-breakingly clear by the introduction of sales charts in 1952. She hung on, beloved of the first wave of war nostalgists, but as the decade trundled by, Verna was forced to turn to the stage and, on occasion, film. I never missed one of her performances, drawn to the theatres again and again by a terrible yearning. I think it is fair to say, though, that acting – stage acting, film acting – was not her strength. She was awful. In the moment between her beautiful, damp mouth opening and her line issuing forth, one could feel the whole audience tense up, grimace. So it was with some relief that I – and, I imagine, many, if not all, of her other admirers – watched her gradually slip back beneath the surface of everyday life. It hurt, of course, but it excited me, too. I was winning.

My feelings of triumph were complete when Victor sent me a note summoning me to his house for a 'long-term strategy symposium'. I had never, in the fifteen years I had already worked for him, been to the man's private quarters. In fact, considering that Victor was like a father to me, I had never learnt much about him or been permitted to feel any degree of intimacy with him. Which, thinking about it, was just right for a father figure (this is something that worries me about the internet – its attractiveness as a platform for hysteric psycho-babblers who, even if you start by mocking them, have a way of re-ordering the routes of thought in your brain).

I arrived at Victor's doorstep as close to a-quiver as any thug (for self-knowledge, even after the fact, is a valuable weapon) is likely to get. I felt myself on the brink of enlightenment, an initiate about to become initiator. In some ways I was right.

When Victor's butler led me under the tacky but impressive chandelier and through a doorway, I found Verna staring at me from a sofa at the far end of a gigantic smoking room, an unlit Cuban growing damp in the drenched red of her mouth. Victor's face appeared from behind the seat back of his giant, upholstered throne, his cigar burning brightly. He threw me my own and motioned for me to sit next to my rival, which I did, a feeling of brittleness entering my bones, my fantasies already obsolete. All my fantasies obsolete.

Victor motioned to a gramophone sitting on a small table by his side.

'I've found this little place where you can have your own records cut. You sing into a tube and then they give you a record with your voice on it. It's remarkable. May I?' And without waiting for a response, he lowered the needle into its crackling groove.

> *Two little kiddies who hate each other,*
> *Two little kiddies could be sister and brother,*
> *Two little kiddies consumed with jealousy,*
> *What's a man to do if he's their Daddy?*
>
> *Lock them in their rooms, don't let them roam,*
> *Give them toys to play with in their home,*
> *Put food on the table, wine in their cups,*
> *And if they try to cross you, fuck them up.*
>
> *For when Daddy Fucker fucks with you*
> *Resolves to really fuck with you,*
> *When Daddy Fucker fucks with you*
> *You will stay, yes you'll stay, you will stay fucked up.*

A ribbon of clarinet, slightly flat and the tone too honky, suddenly fell out of silence, fading away into the distance until we were left with crackle and a rhythmic pop.

'Good?'

Jaw set, I looked at my feet and waited for the lecture.

'Ghastly. Absolutely ghastly.'

I confess I actually jumped, though in slow motion, raising myself from my seat perhaps half a foot before gaining enough control to sit again. She had spoken. For the beat before Victor began to chuckle, I could feel my fantasy bloom again. Then wither.

'I am confident that in music, as in so much else, I am merely ahead of my time. But even if it held nothing for you aesthetically surely its lyric carried a certain . . .' He emulated searching for the word. 'Resonance?'

We did not assent. We did not need to. Victor puffed awhile, always the showman, corpulent in a menacingly solid way.

'My two little rats. What am I to do with you? Your talents so complementary, your temperaments so conflicted. I would like to be able to tell you that this is a problem which has exercised my mind for countless sleepless nights, but that would be a lie. Not that I am averse to lying, as you both know. I just don't believe it would best serve my purposes in these particular circumstances. It did, however, ruin my soup course a couple of weeks ago, which was tragedy enough.'

He paused again, either for effect or simply to allow us time to take in both the glistening details and the architectural structure of his speaking style (another debt I owe the man).

'Luckily for both of you, the Beef Wellington that followed is ideal brain food, so a solution was quick to come. I am incorporating a company which will act as our front. It will be called Barnums, in honour of the circus. You two will lead two exceedingly well-separated divisions. The Muscle' (nodding at me, a man who had filled out considerably since my early days at his side) 'will be in charge of Special Ops – security, we might call it, with all that this entails. The Eraser will run Special Services. Prostitution, market research, blackmail, secretarial services. But, most of all, *cleaning*. Ladies' things.' He stopped again, puffing and apparently ruminating. Everything with Victor was, at best, apparent.

'Let me make one thing clear. No one is indispensable either to the fight for freedom and democratic values, or to me.' A wide-pulled smile. 'If you can separate them. I have entrusted you with the future not just of my business, but our Way of Life. I do not expect to find out that you have been undermining one another. I certainly do not expect to find out you have been trying to kill one another. Leave each other alone and we can all gain. Act otherwise and you are dead. Understood? Good. Then let me call for the champagne.'

He imprisoned us there for another two hours, during which time he made us toast each other repeatedly, learn and sing his little ditty in a two-part harmony and sign an oath of complete allegiance to him in our own blood. In short, he tried to teach us the importance of shared ritual as a binding beyond our individual selves. It was a lesson that, at the time, was utterly wasted on us. I hazily remember my discomfort and shame as he made us sing the National Anthem backwards while holding our open left palms over burning candles. It would be many years before the wisdom of Victor's actions finally settled in My head as central to the theology I now espouse.

Finally, exhausted and humiliated, I was escorted from the premises by the butler. Outside, snow had fallen in the square, dampening the already faint sounds of traffic. I walked to the bottom of the steps with an affected swagger, turned sharp left, my footprints half of an incomplete Rorschach Blot across the city, my mind slowly returning to itself.

Listening to the gentle harrumphs of my feet crushing snow, I resolved there and then that I would kill Victor Victor. I like to think that, at that very moment, as Verna Landor found herself crushed once more beneath our master's bulk, the same resolution was reached by her.

I apologize, I have lost My thread. Robert descended on Me to complain about the damp. Again. I can honestly say that I have been tempted to place a special order for a tyre iron over the last few weeks, so that I can cave his head in with it. Ah, the satisfying contrast in tone between the sonorous ringing of the iron and the hollow clonk of the skull. Unfortunately, I am not omnipotent and I need him for the computers – building the network, programming the blasted things, the whole shebang. I am an old man and cannot be blamed for My weakness in this area. Still, it irks Me. The truth remains that without Robert My Project is nothing. Non-existent.

Gone are the days when one could rely on supernatural powers. Or maybe it is as it has always been. As My forebears undoubtedly used conjuring and the tricks of the illusionist so I will rely on main-frames, ultra-broadband cables and superior processing power. The Day of Judgment is almost upon us.

In chastising Myself for digressing I have digressed further – an inexcusable lapse in anyone but a prophet or a deity, so I shall grant Myself absolution. Now I am going, I feel the urge to divest Myself of still more information, though it may make little sense here. Let Me just say this. I have allowed the idea that I am building a data haven to become current, a home for all the information you want to stop your government from seeing, or which you wish to stop your government from stopping other people seeing. It is a well-rehearsed rumour on the internet, where such ideas excite considerable fervour, and has even merited a few column inches in the trade press and beyond. It is, however, a rumour without sub-stance, a cover. Vernaland will not become a virtual home to vast collections of child pornography, laundered e-money, illegally doc-tored tax accounts or the plaintive yelpings of would-be democrats in Saudi Arabia or North Korea. I will leave all that kind of malarkey to the idealists and the crooks, the desperate and the damned.

It will serve My purpose quite magnificently, though, for the idea to be believed. It is dangerous to be a Speaker of Truth in this cor-rupt and sick society. But when the authorities find themselves wondering whether I am in fact the Messiah, they will reach the conclusion that I am not. They will consider this religion lark to be a cover for the astute, quite possibly illegal venture of establishing such an offshore data haven. This is what they would be doing if they were Me and is, hence, a uniquely satisfying explanation for them. And it is so far off the mark, that to think of it makes Me glow with messianic pleasure. We are collecting a huge cache of data, that much is true, but Vernaland is not a safehouse for wrong-doing. Rather it is an instrument of divine justice. Robert is busy using his considerable talents to engineer the kind of spectacular that only comes along once every thousand years or so. I genuinely think that the general populace will be impressed – no mean achievement when you consider what TV-addled dolts most of them are. It will be, if you will allow Me the pun, quite a coup. But if there is one thing I learnt from Victor, it is to keep your true purpose hidden until the very moment you can achieve it.

From: 100001@hotmail.com
To: mandyhart200@hotmail.com

mand - i always thought u under stood me. did u under stand me? what if i was 2 say we need 2 evolve? wud that mean any thing 2 u? that we act like informatoin is here and the worlds here and the 2 can never meet? does that make any sense? does it? what if there were a way 2 bring them 2gether? a way 2 put the world back 2gether? would that even intrest u? can u see how it wud change every thing? i bet u can. u of all people. so we can stop being trapped between the 2. so we can be hole again. binary rob

(Converted from the ASCII)

14

Trundling forward just one more complete rotation of his four wheels, all three lanes clotted with irritable, angry and, very occasionally, blankly philosophical car-users, Peter has ample time to reflect on just how bad an idea this whole expedition is. Seeming to himself to shake and with an undeniable nausea building inside, he spends these sedentary minutes listing and re-listing all the reasons why he shouldn't be doing this, shouldn't even be thinking of doing this.

1. He is meeting with a known employee (he doesn't really know how *known* she is, but he finds his mind adopting the syntax of a police drama) of Clearwater in order to gain information about the company that the company probably doesn't want him to have. This is (a) tantamount to industrial espionage and (b) in breach of known employee's contract.
2. He is meeting the formerly mentioned employee not in a pub in Gravesend or a motorway service station café, or indeed anywhere anonymous and unsuspicious and away from familiar faces, but in the hotel at Clearwater. During her lunch break. With both of them passing, on their respective routes from P&G and car, at least twenty security cameras. At what he considers to be a conservative estimate.
3. He knows nothing about this employee, except that she has an odd, empty face and smokes B&H. She may be (a) a company loyalist leading him into a trap, the Clearwater head of security and ten thugs hiding in the lobby, all buzz cuts, big chins and sneering smiles; (b) she may be a blackmailer (he's not sure quite what the scam would be, but is pretty clear it wouldn't benefit him); (c) she may be a part-time whore, who has misunderstood

his request, with more than merely embarrassing consequences; (d) she may be a lunatic with a grudge who gives him nothing reliable; (e) she may be intensely, corrosively boring and have absolutely nothing to offer him in the way of blinding insight, corporate dirt or tasty aperçu.

4. The whole set-up makes him feel more than a little dirty. He fully understands that this is their cover, that if either of them are recognized going to or from the hotel, the observer will consider it to be an adulterous liaison, not the aforementioned act of industrial espionage. But, even though he knows it isn't a tryst, it makes him uneasy. There will be no cameras, he presumes, in the hotel room and hence no evidence to prove that this isn't exactly what all the circumstantial evidence outside the room points to it being. So, even if he does not have sex with her, objectively, beyond that room-enclosed, private fact, he has committed adultery.

Luckily, he becomes distracted from his squeamishness by the realization that if he stays stuck in traffic for much longer he will be late. And, somehow, the consequences of this seem far worse than any of the minor worries he has listed. On each side of him vehicles trundle forward. He knows that to change lanes is to bate his line into life, but he can't resist the temptation. He flicks the right indicator and, to its tick, watches in his wing mirror as the traffic on that side bunches closer, determined to deny him access. Emitting a slight whine, he looks left, sees a gap and, jerkily, with little thought, pulls out. The sound of the horn accelerates up on him, filling the car and then settling in the centre of his head. His mirror shows the lorry's grille grow exponentially, beyond the confines of this strip of glass, beyond the confines of his back window, even. He feels the horn, the closeness of the massive vehicle, through his whole body. Distractedly, as he and the traffic in front of him slow and that in the lane he vacated begins edging past them, he reaches round and locks the doors.

Twenty minutes later he watches the needle on his speedometer bobbing and bouncing up to ninety, his hands trying to crush the steering wheel, eyes flickering over his mirrors and the road ahead. Peter isn't a speeder, traditionally because the now-scrapped heap of second-hand cars he used to drive were never up to it but, more currently, because it scares him. This is partly a result of a TV documentary he watched for a wry and drily amusing piece on tabloid television. Although he was careful not to let his revulsion show in the article, Peter's dreams had been visited by images from *True Life Horrific Car Accident Victims* for weeks. A combination of alcohol and cheese of an evening can still summon them to this day. And all this before he gets as far as contemplating the excruciating embarrassment of being pulled over by the police. So he prefers to stick to the speed limit on the public grounds that to drive faster is to contribute to congestion and hence national gridlock. Oh, and is also rather crass.

He curves his way back down into the Clearwater car-park with five minutes to spare, quietly and rhythmically cursing. He will have to run, which in a building dedicated to the gentle stroll, designed expressly to enforce the gentle stroll, will not just make him visible but *the most visible*, a source of anxiety to security, an aberration needing to be erased: wrong. He knows all this and so knows he has already fucked it up. But, having parked, he runs anyway.

Everything feels off. The familiarity of the lift is oppressive when he knows some ape up in the control room is watching him heave for breath. He has to press a button he has never pressed before, which gives him a sense of *déjà vu* gone wrong. The smoothness of the fall no longer feels classy and luxurious so much as slow.

He jogs into the lobby and stops, gasping and dishevelled. A man sits at a piano playing what sounds like the eighth hour of an improvised interpretation of the Bond theme, familiar but put together wrong. The walls are covered with photos of all the actors who have played famous spies. Even the look of the lobby and the cocktail bar off to the right appears to be based on a still from a sixties espionage thriller. The barman has a cigarette-holder clamped between his teeth and, though no one is in there, is pouring what Peter immediately assumes is a dry Martini.

Trying to shape his eyebrow to the required level of quizzical detachment, a skill practised in front of the mirror with considerable determination as a teenager, he advances to the desk. He is met by a man in a white dinner-jacket, bald head and monocle.

'Good afternoon, sir. Welcome to the Deep Cover Hotel. How

can I help you?'

'I'd like a room, please.' He jolts. 'Did you say Deep Cover?'

'I did, sir.'

'I thought you were called Deep Rest?'

'Ah, an easy mistake to make, sir. Deep Rest is the other side of the hallway, outside the lifts.'

'There's two hotels down here?'

'Sir has hit the nail on the head. Deep Cover is themed for an exciting, interactive experience, the perfect complement to your shopping experience.'

'Deep Cover? Like in cricket?'

'Deep Cover like undercover,' his face momentarily visited by contempt, his hand sweeping round the wicketless lobby.

'Oh, of course. Yes. And Deep Rest?'

'For the customer who wants luxury in a classic setting.'

Remembering himself, Pete has already turned to leave.

She is coming out of Deep Rest, glancing around while trying to look nonchalant. The anorak has been replaced by some sort of ankle-scraping camel hair. Still a cheap piece of shit, he thinks, but at least she made an effort.

'Darling!' She strolls over, utterly unflustered, and tiptoes up to kiss him on the cheek. Turns him and directs him back toward the lobby, her arm insinuating itself inside his. Peter tries to pull away, surprised by the contact.

'Husband and wife?' she hisses, her smile set. Peter finds himself irritated and a little ashamed to discover that she is better at this than him. Maybe she's done it before?

Before the full implications of this thought have time to take hold of him he is steered to the desk. The woman standing there looks no older than the girl standing next to him and he realizes he had been hoping for a man.

'Sir, Madam, welcome to Deep Rest hotel. How can I help you today?'

'Ah. My wife and I would like a room, please.'

Increased pressure on his arm.

'Where's the Ladies? Just going to freshen up, darling.'

And he is left bereft, facing these new challenges solo.

Overall, he thinks, the next five or ten minutes go pretty well. The mix-up with the cash had been embarrassing, certainly. He would make sure he had enough next time. Instead he had stood there, hearing the edge of desperation in his voice, trying to ascertain where the nearest cashpoint was while the woman serving him had kept insisting he could pay on his card. He had relented, her pen shaking in his hand as he signed, the evidence now obvious, the chance of Martha catching him TV drama certain. But besides that, he feels happy with the air of world-weary insouciance he had, he believes, affected. As if he has done all this one hundred times. As if he really means it and doesn't care.

She re-emerges from the toilet, a new layer of make-up painting her face plastic, surprised. She is wearing heels and her ankles twist in them, as if she's drunk. Or is she just pretending to look drunk, suggesting that they have headed down here on a whim after a boozy lunch, their legs suddenly wrapping each other beneath a thick, white tablecloth? He closes his eyes for a moment, shakes his head slightly. Peter doesn't know her at all. He's scared.

Once she is attached she stays attached. Along three moving walkways until they reach their block and then through a maze of smaller corridors, the electronic signs encouraging them forward: 'Nearly there!' He is suffocating, gagging, fighting a battle to hide his disgust at the liberally applied, undoubtedly market-bought, designer rip-off perfume that clouds up from her. Right until he shuts the door behind them, right until its click, she is far, far too close to him. And then she separates as if it had never happened, moves quickly across the room and huffs down on to the bed, suddenly far, far too far away.

'Gasping for a fag. You mind?' The golden packet already in her hands.

Peter pauses, wondering whether to tell her that this isn't a smoking room or just let go a little, try to relax. But the thought of the exploding shriek of a smoke alarm, running feet padding toward them down thickly carpeted corridors, more confrontation, more interaction (themed or otherwise) stops him. He tries to summon his best goofy shrug, the ultimate apologetic-but-charming wince.

'Sorry . . .'

From: 100001@hotmail.com
To: mandyhart200@hotmail.com

mand - heres what im saying. u remember when we started smoking dope? when dad still left the house now & then? how old was i? 12? that shitty hash. leonis bruv all ways telling u it was red leb! he all ways was a twat. u remember that game we played where wed swim across the carpet? & wed run back through evolutoin? start off as people & then be fish & then wed be bacteria then single cell organizms & then last just atoms? nothing. then forward forward faster & faster atom bacteria fish mammal human. did u ever make the next step? beyond human? body crumbling away every thing crumbling away? i did. i never forgot it. i want 2 feel like that 4 ever. i want 2 be that. binary rob

(Converted from the ASCII)

15

So what took me? My only excuse is that it is all very well deciding to kill someone and quite another thing to do it. To decide requires only anger, hatred and humiliation or orders, instruction and payment. To kill requires a moral rigour which is often at odds with the action's motivating factors. If one's target is a man like Victor Victor, it also requires considerable planning. Not to mention the transcendence of sentimental notions of debt and gratitude and of the continuing sense that in some way the man has fathered one. And then, of course, there was Verna.

They married in 1955, an intimate ceremony for two hundred politicians, movie stars, businessmen and other upstanding members of the community, most of whom we had photos of on file, many of them featuring Verna. My presence was not requested, but I was reliably informed by operatives on the catering staff that the guests laughed when they were supposed to, applauded when they were supposed to and toasted when they were supposed to. Not even the midgets leaping from the cake could discomfort them as they sat under Victor's watchful gaze. Verna performed a few numbers, too, the sound of her voice ghostly, all enunciation gone, out in the cold darkness beyond the marquee.

Rejected, I had thrown myself body and soul into a frenzy of killings, as if in preparation for the ultimate murder. Beatings, shootings, poisonings (administered in every way, from daily cups of tea to a tiny dart in the back of the neck), electrocutions, drownings (both the Thames and a bathtub), knifings, all manner of strangulation, disembowelment and defenestration. I became neutral, driven forward with complete detachment, no method of killing either beyond me or beneath me, whether it was the application of gentle pressure to one of the body's weak spots or the repeated kicking of a head in an alley. Since I was a small boy, I had thought of angels as essentially alien, beyond human, non-moral – operatives for a Higher Power. This was how I saw myself now. I defended a nation and a way of life but I did it with no sense of right or wrong. And it didn't matter to me whether the Higher Power I served was the British Government, the CIA, the Department of Transport (an excellent client for us during their decade-long feud with the Ministry of Agriculture) or just Victor Victor himself. I claim I acted neutrally but – I force myself to admit – there are few more satisfactory releases for pent up tension than a killing (I prefer the term to the morally loaded 'murder') so at times I took pleasure in that. And also in a job well done. And I was clearly excellent at it.

Of course, since I became what I now Am – or at least realized what I always Was – I have eschewed violence. One has to, you know. Although, to be precise, what I have eschewed is violence committed by My own hand, or, even more accurately, violence committed hand to hand (or, involving as it does My considerable presence, should that be Hand to hand?). It seems clear to Me that a Messiah must be concerned with Justice and that Justice requires Punishment. It is, however, considered a little beneath a Divine Being to be going round stabbing or kicking people &c &c. Hence My rule that I can mete out punishment only so long as I do not touch the punished.

One grey area this has thrown up has been firearms. Although their use seems sanctioned by My ruling, I do try to keep the shooting to a bare minimum, solely as a last resort and for immediate protection. One has to have standards, after all. As a whole, I prefer to come up with more ingenious methods of dealing with the Unbeliever. A fine example is the gizmo I had Robert build for Me which allows Me to crash the onboard computers of any aircraft entering the Exclusion Zone I have plotted (somewhat arbitrarily, I am happy to admit) around Vernaland's waters. I look forward with an unbecoming excitement to the day a foreign power tries to take Me out, to the sound of thrashing rotor blades slapping into water, the hiss of steam as recently stalled engines sink beneath the waves. My commitment to the non-violence principle remains, at best, ambiguous, hence an outlet for My impulses is invaluable.

One can, of course, have too much of a good thing. I needed an occasional escape from my blood-letting and it came with my trips out to the forts. I kept a small motorboat in the harbour at Queenborough, a stripped-down, dark-grey military machine bobbing in the slap and gush of the tide between peeling trawlers and the occasional bright-white yacht. The boat was my indulgence, the only aspect of my life that was not completely anonymous. I knew it was a risk and so had taken the necessary steps – or so I thought – to make sure that Victor would never find out about it. As soon as I knew I had a night away from work I would motor down to the coast with a bootful of cigarettes and whisky, load them into my ugly launch and set out. I was well known at five of the forts, an occasional visitor at the rest. There would always be a bunk for me and I would sleep surrounded, once again, by the sighs and snores of my fellow man and, beyond that, the vastness of the ocean.

The sea is never quiet. No matter how clear the night you can feel the force of the water beneath you. It is one thing to skit across the surface of it in a powerboat. It is quite another to lie on top of spindly concrete limbs that the ocean is trying to reject – the fort itself, your room, your bed, each acting as an amplifier of the struggle beneath. It makes you feel infinitesimally tiny, lost. Freed.

Today, all but one of the forts stand derelict. Robert and I bump around the concrete shell of Vernaland, both the final defenders and the pioneers (though, it must be said, Robert rarely leaves his machines, tries to walk as little as possible, seems – despite the impossibilities thrown up by the gap between biology and technology – to want to be one of them instead of one of us). We are brought supplies from the mainland but visitors are rare, the bustle replaced by a damp, decayed grandeur. My last guests were a couple of young girls, twins I think, dressed as boys and pretending to be artists. They wanted to film empty corridors, to march back and forth along them while nothing happened and the nobodies not featured went nowhere. They soon took the hint when I got one of My guns (even unloaded it has a certain symbolic power). Young people are like that – very tough and smart and streetwise until it comes to armaments.

Then in 1956 they closed them. The cunts who supposedly govern us for our own good closed them. Personally, I blame the Cold War. Everyone became obsessed with nukes, the Big Bang, the Last Call, the Final Countdown. As if that was ever going to happen! The subtlety of metaphor, the lone tower in the water – Arthurian if you like – was lost to the (supposed) horror of the mushroom cloud and the flatness that followed it. And something of England was lost with it.

As a matter of fact, Robert worries Me – and I am not a Messiah easily prone to worry. If I ask him (tell him) to write Me an order for exactly what parts he needs, he emails it to Me in binary. As if that transcends humanity! As if I will be baffled, confused, a blubbering wreck before twenty lines of ones and noughts. As if binary is a language invented by machines rather than Leibniz! As if machines can invent *anything!* He has binary tattooed down his right forearm – 100001 – six digits carelessly gouged out with a compass and filled with Bic ink, even his attempt to do a Manson looking childish and ill formed. It is his certainty, this mantle of an obviously false messiah, that worries Me. And yes, I am aware of the irony for non-believers. Fortunately, as the self-appointed Real Thing, that is not something which need trouble Me. They shall repent.

Unfortunately, for reasons I have already partially explicated, I need Robert and, as I don't fully understand exactly what he does, I need to be able to trust him, or at least trust that his fear of Me will ensure his honourable service. But machines do not feel fear, even if they can simulate it. So I am left with the unsettling prospect of believing that machines are built to fulfil a function and that Robert's function is to serve My Purpose. I find the idea that machines are inherently trustworthy both anachronistic and the result of a starry-eyed futurism (I must cancel my subscription to *Wired*) but it is all I have. And so much depends upon it holding true that it behoves Me as a Messiah to expend whatever effort necessary to Make It So. As he wants to be, so shall he be. With all that it implies.

Being who I am is no easy task. I am, by definition, alone. I have no one to confide My hopes and fears to except you. And 'you,' right now, is a computer hard drive (and if I am wrong about the boy, Robert, too). I have My moments of self-doubt. Even those of us who are barely human have those. I sit here and try to get it right. Try to make sure that what is meant to be will come to pass, that from the Sea will come a Man who is more than a Man and that Man will reveal himself a God on this Earth and his Kingdom of Heaven shall be on Earth and, yea, verily, that Kingdom shall be called Vernaland. Or something like that. It is hard to express these things just so in such anachronistic language. What I am trying to convey is that the result of My computer-assisted miracle will not be My immolation or any other such passive-aggressive 'victory' but genuine power – control of the kingdom I find Myself exiled from.

There are only two types of Messiah, so far as I can tell. Those who make loaves and fishes for all and those who rain down locusts on all. I am very much of the latter persuasion – the former are far too eager to please. But locusts are hard to come by in the kind of quantities I need; it would require a fleet of aircraft to drop them and high-strength insect spray is now readily available in almost any corner shop. Luckily, there are other bugs available, cages teeming with them, and a cheap and effective way to distribute them. Praise be, then, to the humble microchip, to internet protocols, to the bright and shining network of our silicon minds!

From: 100001@hotmail.com
To: mandyhart200@hotmail.com

mand - u know i told u how it feels? when im working? like i left my self all most. thats what im after. i been thinking about coming back 2 this body of mine & its making less & less sense. i live in 1 concrete room full of wires & tools & kit & the only time im happy is when im lost in there. or out there or where ever it is i go when im lost. & im starting 2 think im not lost then but found. & data? all this data ive gathered here? this ∞ of bits? it should be free. not free for every 1 all that hippy hacker bull shit. i aint intrested in open access. & i dont mean not costing nothing the script kiddy shit. i mean free. free in its own right. free from the machines. free from any computer but the computer of the hole universe. pure energy. coz thats all infomatoin is. 1 way of storing energy. it & me both. so then the next step is 2 let it go. it & me. 2gether. 2 let that energy go. binary rob

(Converted from the ASCII)

16

When O asks Jimmy exactly what he does here, he really has no idea how complex the answer should be. Jimmy just chooses to keep it simple for O, not least because he has a very strong feeling that his nominal boss (nominal only in Jimmy's eyes) won't fully understand it, won't even see the funny side of it. But Jimmy is kept very busy all day long, mainly in the pursuit of appearing to be busy. And what better way to appear busy than to be busy doing it?

The basic techniques are simple. On as many days as he can justify, he goes out in the field, working his way round his patch shop by shop. He walks up and down aisles as if he cares whether this particular manager chooses to place products together by sport or by function (Bats, Balls, Specialist Shoes, etc.). He engages the managers in lengthy discussions about everything except sales. He even takes the chosen ones – those that have a sense of humour and who never mention the shop – out for long, two-bottle lunches. The truth is he believes, though he tries to keep it a secret from himself, that these visits do some good, that he fosters a kind of carefree elegance of approach that improves the atmosphere in the shops, and so makes them a better retail environment. Though he also has to admit that this is not borne out by comparison of sales figures.

Unfortunately Jimmy can't justify leaving the office every day. It's on the occasions when he has to stay put that his evasions move from being possibly or potentially useful to being work to avoid working. He can barely operate his email system, but he has had it set up so that he can take an hour or so scrolling up and down through his Inbox, highlighting titles according to some sequence which only he or a top mathematician with a week to spare could fully understand. He sometimes picks up his disconnected phone just before Sunil returns to his desk and has an inordinately long, grunted phone conversation with the dead line while he reads the sports pages lying flat in front of him. On occasion, slowly and laboriously, one finger from each hand hovering numbly over the keyboard, he carefully transcribes a random match report from the newspaper, deleting it when he reaches the end.

Right now, he has wandered over to the fax machine with a wad of mainly blank paper randomly gathered from his desk and is busy faxing them to Gloria's office, achieving two purposes at once.

Things hadn't worked out quite as planned with Gloria. They had bought a bungalow just outside Gravesend and both settled in for nuptial bliss. Unfortunately, they had forgotten to discuss what this might be. Jimmy didn't want his wife working at a brothel, or anywhere else, come to think of it. Gloria wanted a job. Instead, she rolled around the tiny house drinking advocaat, snorting tiny lines of speed and dusting (if there was one area Jimmy couldn't criticize her in, it was her commitment to amphetamine-driven housework). He, meanwhile, saw out a benefit year which, despite his length of service to the club, resulted in one of the smallest totals on record. Which was when he went to work for O, saying to anyone who would listen *fuck cricket, fuck fucking cricket*, though somehow, in some way he didn't understand, not really meaning it.

But this wasn't even the root of it, not for Jimmy, anyway. When Gloria and he left the house together, arm in arm, people shook their heads, or tutted, or muttered something as they passed, or just allowed their faces to freeze. There was the one particularly memorable occasion when a man with the face of a skinhead identikit had spat on Gloria and followed them down the road calling her a *fucking Paki-loving slag*. He wasn't sure if it was only him who realized that day that nearly all the anger directed towards them – whenever it happened and whether it was this particular boot boy or a little old lady – was in fact directed towards her. Because she could do something about it.

What was clear was that she did become aware, either before or after that incident, because she did start doing something about it. She became noticeably less keen to walk down the road arm in arm.

She began, it seemed to him, to pull ever further away from him when they were out – side by side not arm in arm – and someone approached. Eventually she decided that she didn't like going out much at all, so they stayed in.

And this irked Jimmy. More than that. Much more. Because although the hatred seemed to be directed at her, it was actually because of him. Hence, it was his hatred. His. Not the yellow-haired woman's. She could just step away from it, stay in the house. It was with him even there. Was she sympathetic or understanding of his plight? Did she stand by her dark-skinned man, as the magazines she read endlessly must surely be telling her? She loved him, she said. She just wouldn't be seen with him.

Gloria was four months pregnant – though she hadn't told him and he would swear he didn't know – when their life together ended. She had called an old friend in London who had informed her (maliciously in Jimmy's version of events, protectively in Gloria's) that her husband was still a regular visitor to the old club.

Jimmy was proud of the way Gloria reacted. She didn't get drunk, scream, cry, hit him. She kept it inside for over a fortnight while she planned and prepared and then suddenly, having purchased Jimmy's favourite fish-and-chip supper from his favourite chippy and sat down with him, her own chicken and small chips going cold in front of her, she announced that she had got a job.

'What?'

'I got a job.'

'Doing what?'

'A secretary. Little company in Gravesend.'

'You can't even type.'

'I've been learning. I'm actually very good.'

'Doesn't matter anyway. I don't want you working.'

'Why?'

'What?'

'Why don't you want me working?'

'Cos if I'd wanted a wife who worked I'd've married someone with a proper job.'

'Well, I've got a proper job now.'

'No, you haven't.'

'How would you describe it, then?'

'You're not doing it so you haven't got a job at all.'

'Really?'

'Really. Not while you're living here.'

Gloria had risen from the table, a slight smile on her face, giving her at that moment, to him, the look of a Mona Lisa (if Mona Lisa had a bad bleach job and used half a can of hairspray every morning, the tang of solvent killing all insect life in their bathroom). She had turned silently and vanished into the bedroom and the living room had been still but for the gentle ring of his cutlery on greasy plate. Before he had noticed, she was by the door, her coat buttoned to her neck, their largest suitcase perched upright alongside her legs.

'I'm not living here. I got a flat. Bye.'

Jimmy sat and watched as she struggled to bump the case out over the threshold on its casters, a forked chip hovering close to his mouth. When he roused himself and ran from the door after her, she was almost at the corner, the case winnowing left and right in her wake. She had ignored his shouted entreaties and apologies right until he touched her arm and pulled her round.

'GET. OFF. ME.'

Gloria's shriek had stilled the air along the road. Movement followed from the street's inhabitants: the lads with the Staffordshire bull terrier opposite turning with more than usual interest, the old lady at number 32 flapping her curtains, the middle-aged man raising himself up from his flowerbeds to shake his head with minute precision, the young mother dragging her daughter, be-triked, across the road and away from them, the little girl's mouth a cartoon zero of surprise. The whole road – his road, his neighbours – seemed to stir themselves for this moment of Jimmy's and Gloria's, waiting to see what he would do. He had let his shoulders drop, stood there as she skittered off, turned and headed for home.

He wasn't sure why he had refused to let her work, anyway. He worried at first that it was some last legacy of his background, that this old-fashioned quirk was a result of the fact that his mother had never had a job until she had to start at the newsagent's when they arrived in England. But he knew that she had worked before his birth and, moreover, if she had succeeded in pairing him with the

Indian nuclear physicist whose parents she had tried to make a match with, there was no way he would have expected the bride to stay away from her particle accelerators. So finally he concluded that it was some part of his new-found Englishness that had compelled him to act this way. Without even knowing that the job wasn't the reason she left.

Their son Martin is fourteen or fifteen now, sandy-haired, Jimmy thinks, sullen and – thankfully – completely uninterested in any cultural heritage from his father's side of the family. Completely uninterested in Jimmy, in fact. He knows this is wrong, a terrible failure on his part. But he doesn't honestly give a fuck. They have never lived together. They don't know each other. They share nothing except DNA and a dull resentment of Gloria. She, for her part, still works for the same company Jimmy thinks she left him for. He likes to block up the fax in her office because it will irritate her and she will know it's him. For him, their relationship today is grounded on such affectionate bating. For her, it's him still trying to fuck up her life, though in such ghostly and ineffectual ways that she almost (only almost, mind) feels sorry for him.

The tenth sheet is juddering through when O returns to destroy Jimmy's delicate reverie.

'Hard at it?'

Jimmy doesn't even bother to move himself to block O's view of the fax machine.

'As ever.'

'Well, I understand how pressing all your work is, but I'd hate you to be late for the game. Got yourself kitted out yet?'

'Was just finishing this.'

'Ah yes,' O counters, glancing with distaste at the chuntering machine. 'Got to get your priorities right. Perhaps you'd like me to come down with you? Remind you what whites look like . . .?'

'Your kindness knows no boundaries. I'll manage.'

Jimmy finds Arvinder outside the fire doors squinting in the brightness, his cigarette smouldering right down in the web between his middle fingers. His presence acknowledged by Arvinder's micro-nod and lack of any attempt to convey the impression of rising,

Jimmy pulls his fags from his own pocket and lowers himself on to the just-warm concrete. Lights up, inhales.

'What you out here for?'

Arvinder inclines his chin quickly up and then back again.

'Gets depressing stuck in there all day.'

'True.'

'The warehouse. It's very dark. Nice to come out and get some sun.'

Jimmy signals assent with an emphatic pull on his cigarette, smoke morphing an intricate strand past his eyes.

'And you?'

'Looking for you.'

'Needed company? Got lonely at your desk?' The sarcasm warm.

'Needed whites, actually.'

'Oh yeah. The comeback. O told me to expect you.'

'How thoughtful of him.'

'Well, you know O. The man is all heart.'

'Oh, I know.'

'I got it all out already. O gave me your sizes.'

'We stock whites for overweight middle-aged men, then?'

'That's almost all we stock.'

Together they finish their cigarettes and flick them away from the door, their parabolas intersecting in the air, a backward-bending cross.

He trudges back up the stairs picking fussily at the corner of the clothes. Arvinder has kitted him from the Pleasence & Greene Vintage range. The trousers are cream, pleated and baggy, the shirt huge-collared, all one hundred per cent cotton. The warehouseman has given him the veteran's clothes. Even though all of Jimmy's career was played out in tight-fitting nylon. He feels a twinge in his shoulder and then the minute motions in the bottom of his stomach he gets before leaving for work. He hasn't even touched a cricket ball for fourteen years. He should just go and tell O he can't do it, but he can't do that either. He turns round on the stairs and goes down again, barges through the lobby's glass doors and is outside, gasping, pursued.

In pride of place, between a copper bedpan and a polished horse-shoe, sits the same photo of him as at his house, only smaller and with a black, felt-tipped scrawl in the right hand corner. It supposedly depicts the run-up to him taking the wicket of Brett Felloner for nought in 1978. This prevented Felloner from completing his fourth consecutive County Championship hundred and was the only time he was bowled for a duck that season. However, while the photo was taken at Canterbury, it could have been any one of a number of no-mark opponents facing him at the other end. It might have been Brett Felloner when he bowled him or it might have been when the fat fucker scored 221 off the team, with Jimmy personally conceding three consecutive sixes in an over that cost him twenty-four runs. Personally he doesn't care as long as it buys him the occasional complimentary drink.

'Usual, Jim?'

He doesn't need to nod.

It's either the second or third pint of lager that spills on to the table as he tries to place it whilst gulping his whisky chaser and sitting down. Shaking his hand free of the yellow liquid, he fails even to try to intercept it before it begins to soak into the cricket clothes piled on the table. Instead, he watches as the fabric sucks the remaining drink from the table top, another grin, this one as close as he gets to genuine, slowly inhabiting his face.

From: 100001@hotmail.com
To: mandyhart200@hotmail.com

mand - what looks like just 1s and 0s to u is beutiful 2 me. is sense.
2 u its un read able. meaning less. imagine if u cud read waves the
same way. if we were surrounded by data. ive been trying 2 work out
what meaning that would have - if waves had meaning. & then the
other way round. if datas like water. got 2 much time 2 my self! i am
going 2 tell u why im out here. but i dont want 2 tell u 2 much 2
soon. binary rob

(Converted from the ASCII)

17

As soon as he had got back into his car, Peter knew he'd overdone it with the Imperial Leather. The generic smell of hotel bathrooms hangs round him, a dark cloud of synthetic guilt.

He raises his hand to his nose for another panicked sniff of non-specific chemical luxury. He hates Imperial Leather as much as any product he can think of – a reminder of Roath and the excruciating, misguided aspirations of his parents and, hence, himself. He blames the aesthetics, says the scent is all wrong, will diatribe with considerable gusto on the way the label stops you from lathering evenly and is eventually left stranded on a nubbin of cracked, discoloured soap. But he knows that none of these is really the problem, that he's ashamed to admit it's social shame. Martha comes from a family so far beyond the need to aspire that she finds the soap quaint, a cause of eyebrow-arching pleasure. But she'll still notice the foreign smell, even if she can't exactly place its source.

On the way back into town he had stopped at a pub for a shandy but once again his over-developed taste antenna had let him down. Instead of smoke seeping into his clothes and hair, gently discolouring his skin, all he found was air-conditioning, light, artfully placed security cameras, not a cigarette burning at the flower-topped tables of the gastropub/designer bar (the two sub-genres at last colliding, he thought, gaining some satisfaction from the prospect of wringing 800 words from this observation).

Which is why he now sits with a cartoon-fish-printed carrier bag in his lap, picking inside at damp grey paper and wafting the invisible grease fumes toward him. Pete has a plan. It may be flawed, it may fail (it may, on the other hand, work better than he could have hoped), but it is a plan. And only a plan can persuade him back through his front door.

The wrapping tearing apart, two steps from papier mâché, a glistening, flaccid lump of thrice-fried reconstituted potato is revealed. Peter, a look of distaste vying with a look of concentration, runs his finger along it and dabs the digit at his neck, head tilted back and to the left, adam's apple bouncing as he gags slightly. Then he bundles the handles of the shapeless bag together and steps from his vehicle, walking a straight line to the door.

It's just ten minutes till he's smiling in the shower, although the smile comes and goes, relief mingled with the realisation that there will be no relief until Martha knows. That not even the Sumatran pumice stone or the guava washing paste will untie the knots tonight.

From the moment he walked through the door to the disharmonised keening of Gus and Poppy, each driving the other to yet more extravagant heights of hysteria, he knew it would work out (today at least, right now).

'I'm home!' The cry hopeless, ignored, as he stood before two wet pillarbox faces, inaudible beyond them. Smiling unconvincingly, with no one to convince, he raised the bag between them.

'Fish and chips.'

His words and actions apparently governed by the laws of a different dimension, the screaming continued unabated. He crossed between them and entered the kitchen, Martha, back turned, listening to Radio 4 loudly, shoulders raised like spurs.

'Hi, darling,' pecking once, fairly randomly, at the back of her head, then as she turned, distraction tugging at her face, again raising the sweating sack. 'I got fish and chips.'

The pause of perfect duration to let him know how insensitive his behaviour was.

'Why?'

'To eat?' Delivered with just enough obviously fake-amiability to rile her.

'I suppose you've already told Gus and Poppy?' Her timing an ideally satisfying confirmation.

'I suppose I have.'

From here the previously existent options were quickly reduced to one. Martha had opened up the oven with a bitter flourish to reveal the healthy vegetable tagine she had spent the last two hours preparing. Peter had coldly observed that the kids wouldn't have eaten it, anyway. Martha had doubted that Peter had any idea what the children did or did not eat. Peter had explained that he had to work hard in order to pay for essentials like a genuine Moroccan tagine dish from Conran's. Martha had told him to fuck off. Peter had grinned and returned the compliment. Martha had hissed at him to refrain from shouting. Peter had expressed indignation at the idea that he was shouting. And so on and so on, through a whole alphabet of unpleasantness until, fish and chips protruding from the top of the bin, Peter had removed himself from the conflict zone and gone to shower. Had actually been sent to shower. Martha, you see, as Peter well knows, hates the smell of fish and chips. Hates it.

He can't stop thinking about her tits. It's unsettling. Her tits had been large, had flopped forward from her bra far too milkily for comfort. He's always prided himself on being too aesthetically sophisticated to become obsessed solely with over-sized mammaries and yet here he his, unable to close his eyes without revisiting that moment, arms behind her back, when they came free. He feels taken out of himself, infantile, the first thrashings of an erection slapping from leg to leg as he tries to recall the moment when they had wiped slowly and gently up his chest.

And *tits*, for God's sake. Even the language fills him with self-loathing. As if his mind has been possessed by a tabloid sub-editor. Next he will be saying *hooters*, sucking his thumb and playing with himself in public. He actually feels more culpable, more dirty, some-how, than your everyday T&A aficionado. He should know better. He has never come up with a satisfactory alternative, though. Mammaries is too technical, bosoms too prudish, breasts ditto and tits is simply *wrong*. The only way he can use any of them is slathered in irony, as if the subject is itself above seriousness (this in itself a problem).

And anyway, he now finds himself hating irony and his reliance on irony even more than the words and things he feels uncomfortable enough about to make him use it. Which makes him more uncomfortable still and so more reliant, the dry twitch of the eyebrow transformed into a desperate blink, the room – whichever room – awash with uncontrolled facial callisthenics.

Peter is not without self-awareness – he has a story about irony which he tells himself for comfort. The story he tells himself is that he has grown out of it. That it was fun at the time but remained an affectation. That, more than anything else, having children has taught him that some things really do matter.

Then there is the truth, which he knows, too. It was great when it was just him and his friends but now it's everybody, everything. And they've ruined it. It's one of those things that works properly only in relative isolation.

Peter is a man born into the perfect time for himself. He doesn't allow the depressing direction of his thoughts to interfere with the matter in hand. He beats out a quick, unaffected rhythm on his dick, without lubrication or showiness. The rub of her thighs on the jutting bones of his pelvis.

He can't believe Martha doesn't know. It already seems to have gone on so long, so many clues forthcoming in the way he talks and moves. She must know something's going on. The shower had been terminated by the jagged panic of Poppy bashing at the door screaming for her potty. Gradually descendent erection tightly smothered beneath thin towel, he had staggered across the room to sudden silence, the door opening to small girl, puddle and tears. The moment had passed as toilet paper rolled into tiny ill-formed crescents over carpet, wet knickers flapped into clothes basket and Poppy, comfortable now on a potty that would remain empty, had monologued incomprehensibly on Darcey Bussell (say what you like about the Swinton-Joneses, but this house a Barbie would never enter).

Suddenly a father again, excused from anything more than rudimentary attempts at comprehension and mopping, Peter had felt for a moment the sweet fug of blamelessness upon him, the complete, bovine involvement of parenthood. Absently, he passed a urine-smeared hand through Poppy's hair, smiled. Then Martha had arrived and his life had started up again.

'What were you doing in there?'

'Where?'

'The shower. You've been up here for ages. Sulking?'

'Cleaning up pee.'

'The pee was because you were in there so long.'

'Trying to purge myself.'

'Of guilt?'

'Of the odour you find so offensive.'

Eyebrows raised toward the little girl: do you want to talk about this in front of her? This being what passes for good-humoured banter between them, Martha smiled at him as she leant forward to wrench Poppy from the potty.

'Saved you some stew.'

'Delicious.'

'It is, actually.'

'I'm sure it is. Did you like the stew, Poppy?'

'"S too red. Don't like red food.'

'Don't start her off again.'

'Red's yucky. Yucky yuck.'

'Sorry . . .'

Which had changed in his mouth now to a completely new word, he found, not just its meaning altered, but its shape and sound suddenly unfamiliar.

'Sorry . . .' He tried the word again, getting to know it all over, as he picked past mother and daughter to the door, right hand holding towel in place.

'Sorry!' he boomed, comedy baritone combined with cod-heroic leap over Martha's legs and out of the room.

'SORRY!' he sang-roared on his way down the hall.

'FUCK SORRY.' Gus's inevitable response flung up the stairs.

Empty retch of prostate the result of his exertions, Peter lifts himself off of her, their skin peeling back from one another's, pore by sweat-filled pore. He falls on to his back, body lost in the darkness, shame crawling across him. His left hand extends to her hair, falls on it

145

palm up, a dyslexic in a library. Wet lips make contact with knuckles, before she sighs, pulls herself up and out of bed and steps from the room.

He has no idea how this has happened. Really. He lies there trying to discern his usual bullshit, but it isn't there, which makes the situation yet more baffling. He thinks Martha initiated the whole thing. Maybe she smelt something on him from earlier, or sensed something, a difference in how he was walking, the self-satisfied swagger of an alpha male? At least he thinks she initiated the whole thing. Perhaps his dick has reawakened and now wanders where it wants, a ghost from a pyramid.

The evening had been unexceptional. He had eaten lukewarm stew, battled the kids to their beds, lain on the sofa flicking diligently through the advance copy of the catalogue to an imminent exhibition of 'found sculpture' by a cultish, reclusive film director. He had put on a CD by the most recent highly credible teen singing sensation and pretended to like it. He had stared absently at ten minutes of the very latest laugh-track-debited fake fly-on-the-wall comedy and had tried to marvel at the daring of it all despite not really finding it funny. Then he had gone to bed, Martha still at her desk pecking out answers to a questionnaire from a post-grad writing a PhD on 'Style and Anti-style In *E-Go* magazine, 1981–1989'. Maybe that was it. Maybe she got off on being the subject of academic enquiry. (She had, after all, been responsible for the ground-breaking cover image of a very thin girl in dark make-up and black shift dress with embroidered skulls which had taken the magazine into the mainstream via the lurid coverage of various middle market tabloids.)

Whatever it was, it couldn't have been ten minutes before she came into the bedroom, twelve before their mouths met loose and wet, thirteen before his hand found itself in the soft, warm skin at the top of her thighs, fifteen before he was out of bed desperately scrabbling through the sock drawer for condoms (his cock rearing up dumbly, desperately, as if trying to point the packet out), sixteen before he found them, seventeen before he noticed they were out of date, seventeen and a half before he decided to chance it and not tell her, twenty before he felt himself inside her, twenty-two before the muted climax. Still, at least this time he'd made it that far. Earlier, he had deposited his semen all over the hotel bedspread. And while it might not have been a day for sexual heroics, it was at least a day for sex. And a man in his position has to be grateful.

Not that he is grateful. Whatever it is that feels a little like guilt has wrapped itself tightly round whatever it is that feels a little like excitement and together they've lodged somewhere deep in his intestine and, very gently, begun writhing. Moments later as, improbably, his phone begins to ring, whatever they are down there prove they were not so much lodged as resting, breaking energetically into a tango. Thick fingers scrabble at trousers, every molecule of him already sure of the cause of the twittering. As expected, her number bathing his face blue.

'I can't talk now.' The whisper forced round a fat tongue, barely comprehensible even to him. She's saying something but the handset has lost contact with his ear, all his attention focused on the soft, well-carpeted sound of Martha drawing nearer.

'No. Sorry. No, no one of that name. Wrong number. Mate.' The words over-enunciated, too loud. He clicks off as she comes through the door.

'Wrong number,' he reiterates. 'Drunk, I think. Or something.' Martha climbs back into bed, bored with him again, too tired.

It's only now, lying in the dark, far from sleep, that the sheer aesthetic dissonance, the absolute tackiness, of finding oneself an adulterer is revealed to him. And while he knows that this too is wrong, that it clearly shows some deficit in his character, he finds himself far more upset by this than by the fact of cheating on his wife. *Cheating on my wife.* He shudders. Imperial Leather, Tits, Cheating On My Wife. His day catalogued by words, phrases, products he hates. His life no longer his own. For this reason and this reason only, the debonair edge to this moral bankruptcy the sole aspect he takes any pleasure in, for this reason and this reason only he resolves to finish it. Unhappy, once again, with his language, he resolves to resolve to end the relationship forthwith. Finally he closes his eyes and reaches out to sleep.

From: 100001@hotmail.com
To: mandyhart200@hotmail.com

mand - i just checked & ive sent u 16 mails now. i been gone
months & ur not replyings ok now. its all right. coz i dont know if
these r even being read & thats no biggy no more. maybe u got a
boyfreind. maybe dads gone 2 & uve got a boyfreind & hes living
with u & while i worry ur snogging on the couch or just stretching out
a little while he pops in2 the kitchen 2 get u another southern comfot
& lemonade. i hope so. i hope thats it. binary rob

(Converted from the ASCII)

18

My life has been bound up with the advances of deregulation, the hysterical, clueless retreat of the state and the unstoppable onward yomp of the corporation. It was Victor who taught me to savour it. He drank of it as of fine claret (greedily). He worshipped its shape, its epic sweep. Of course, he had become rich and powerful as a result of its bounty, but I think he loved it in and of itself. Not opportunity, fairness, nothing as dry as the unfettered functioning of supply and demand. For him these were at best by-products. Chaos. Pure chaos. This was where he found the reflection of himself in it, cackling that, 'economics is the method. The object is to change the soul!' as if this were the best joke he had ever heard. And I laughed, I always laughed, imagining the nationalized ghosts within us being shredded by Market Forces, the shrill squeals these gossamer spirits would emit.

But while I pride Myself on My intuitive grasp of the potentialities of this advance, I must admit that in the case of pirate radio my initial interest was purely emotional. In fact, my initial reaction was primarily one of anger – cold, white, bright anger. The kind habitually washed away in a brief but cleansing burst of murderous violence. Because you know where they were? Of course you know where they were. Out on my towers.

I had developed the habit of weekending occasionally on Cold Mount. Just as I had before, in fact, except now without company or even the semblance of comfort the army provided. No, these days I would arrive with firewood, a camp bed, my army-issue sleeping bag and a selection of high-quality canned goods. And of course my revolver, to ward off any of the local 'fishermen' who without this mild deterrent might be minded to purloin my tethered speedboat. Thievery runs through coastal communities like soil through earthworms.

These were great times. Once I had recovered from my shock at the armed forces' withdrawal I had returned here to learn that it was never the camaraderie that had been important but the place itself. Though the casual sex had been pleasant and the discovery of what you can get from a soldier in exchange for a bottle of whisky certainly educational. First and foremost, I came to understand, was this island, my island. So, ensconced here, alone with my own spirituality, I began to grow again, to dream not just of killing Victor Victor but of supplanting him, whatever the potential cost vis-à-vis Verna (whom I had come to see – as Victor meant me to see her, I believe – as blameless in all this, just a cipher, my symbolic opposite).

Victor, it seemed, was a man who had to be expunged from my system on so many levels that merely to throttle him, or knife him, or shoot him, or push him down some stairs, or break his neck or in any way indulge him with such a banal send-off would be to leave my soul prey to him for ever. For yes, talking of souls, I believed, with shock and disquiet, that I had found mine. Out here, in a concrete and iron shell suspended above the immensity of the sea I had found my own internal place of stillness around which washed crushing tides of appetite and desire. For it to be there at all seemed like a miracle, like something God-given. But the only God I recognized was Victor and it was my soul who said he had to die.

(Re-reading the above after a short break and to avoid any misunderstanding, I think I should make clear, that I do not and did not equate 'soul' with 'conscience'. What a banal and limiting notion, the kind of idea dreamt up by ancient spinsters to make their embroidery seem interesting. This small, hard thing I had found was closer to identity, to self, than conscience and Victor had to die – and die ingeniously, horribly – to leave the space for it to grow. After all, what would be the point of finding self if it did not chime with one's instincts?)

For a long while I became obsessed with the idea of feeding Victor to death, imagining him with head pulled back and food pouring into his gullet, a unique combination of buddha and goose. But my nerve failed me. I pictured him swelling and swelling, my food merely fuelling his physical extravagance, until he filled the room where I held him captive, I myself trapped in a corner, crushed slowly and painfully to my death as he expanded.

I thought of bringing him out here and starving him to death but the logistics defeated me. Just how many months might it take for a man of his proportions to finally expire from hunger? Ideas came and went, plans were hatched and abandoned. And all the while my soul grew, harder and stronger, both my homunculus and me.

So imagine, then, my feelings as I approached the tower that Friday evening, thin summer light bleaching the bones of the structure, to find a human figure, yes definitely a figure up there on the platform, another human figure standing looking in my direction, watching my wake split the water. And there, painted on the side in uneven red blocks, RADIO RANDY.

'Sorry, you're gonna have to move your boat, man. This is private property.'

'This is the property of the War Office.'

'Uh, yuh. It's private.'

'Are you from the War Office, then? Or the Admiralty? Or perhaps a member of Her Majesty's Armed Forces? No, I thought not.'

At which point I reached the top of the ladder and pushed my way past the badly coiffed youth. He was silent now, which was lucky for him, for I had unholstered my revolver and was intent on using it at the first provocation. Even at a hint of provocation.

How is it, then, that within the hour I would find myself in a candlelit bunker deep in the very heart of the tower, masturbating vigorously in a circle of similarly preoccupied men, our shadows juddering across the walls like trees seen from a moving train? Despite my reputation as something of a reactionary, I have never understood the rationale of the prison game in which he who ejaculates first wins. But ejaculate first I most certainly did, splattering the candles with my frustrations and, dramatically, reducing the room to darkness. However, this was not a game, more a ritualized shaking of hands, the acknowledgement of a binding contract.

The honest answer is that I do not know exactly what quelled my murderous impulses. Or, at least, channelled them. Certainly not the music I heard as I entered the tower, a thin yet piercingly noisesome cocktail of thudding, peglegged dancing, animal torture and yodelling that I was soon to learn was 'Elvis'. Certainly not the motley collection of former public-school boys (yes, of course we can spot one another) with slightly too long hair and clothes in which every detail seemed to have been shipped in from an only slightly alternate reality (America, it transpired). Nor could I even say it was down to Andrew 'Randy' Witherington, their leader and guru, though it was certainly true, despite what the world has since learnt of him, that he was the only real charismatic amongst them.

No, when Randy stood in front of me, a slight wobble in his voice as he politely asked me to put down my firearm, nothing I had witnessed since I had entered suggested to me that the operation had any intrinsic value. Finger slack against the trigger, I imagined in loving detail the exact amount of pressure required to transform his sweaty, ginger-flecked cranium into an explosion of shard, glob and splat. I could almost see its desperate pulsations. But then I stopped to think. And I realized that Randy's brain, however feeble, might be more use still housed in its skull.

'Scary isn't it? Stuck out here in the middle of the sea, at the mercy of anyone who passes – rogue fisherfolk, pirates, operatives of Her Majesty's Government, invasion forces from foreign powers, lone psychopaths, even. What you need, my friends,' – and here I lowered my firearm – 'what you need my friends, is protection. Protection and proper investment.'

The deal was sealed in the circle, made concrete in the moment my wasted sperm doused the flames of the candles, our compact signed with the ink from our members, billions of writhing deaths staining the floor.

Persuading Victor of the validity of the operation – and hence of my need to be out there, at sea yet on land, as frequently as possible – was simple. The prospect of broadcast deregulation, of wresting control of communications from the fell hand of the State, that alone would have been enough for him, his lips smacking at the prospect of this fundamental realignment of consciousness. Then there were the profits that we, as chief investors, were certain to accrue. Last, there were certain persons within the BBC and the government of the day who would find our transmissions uncomfortable, a humiliation, an attack upon their very psyche. It is in the nature of a chaotician to be unpredictable. With Victor, it was always wise to have an ancillary motivation ready. And few motivations ranked higher with him than humiliating his enemies.

The staff of Radio Randy were perverts, a term to which I attach no pejorative connotation. Like all people at every time in history in every place they had two sets of needs – spiritual and physical.

'The King' satisfied their spiritual yearnings, their need to believe in something bigger, better, more perfect (less human) than themselves. I am sorry to say that you neither had to be a genius nor wait until the 1970s to know how misguided this belief was. To see that dripping-headed marionette click his groin around in a poor pastiche of sexual action was to witness the final capitulation of our culture. An act more lacking in the sweat (even when he sweated), the spit and (to use a term one happens upon more and more whilst web surfing) the *cum* of real physicality is hard to imagine. Elvis, this 'King', seemed to be nothing more than a machine for separating teenagers from their pocket money. In fact, as both teenagers and pocket money were relatively new concepts and as the three had appeared as one – a trinity of previously non-existent commerce – it was tempting to believe that whole cycle was nothing more than a ruse to separate parents from their money, an excellent way to keep them working while promoting self-disgust, shame and humiliation.

If this was how the denizens of Randy Towers had read the situation I would have had a degree of admiration for them. (I have always believed, even at the times when I was most lost, in the importance of self-disgust, shame and humiliation to the smooth running of a well-ordered society.) But these adults, these renegade entrepreneurs, insisted on seeing it all from the teenagers' point of view, of seeing in this man a veritable King indeed. The ninnies. Their fervour was unbecoming. But then the teenagers (and their younger siblings) were very much the problem at Radio Randy, considering their central role in satisfying the staff's physical needs.

No, this is actually misleading. You only had to meet the men working at the station for a few minutes to know that their physical needs were not often, if ever, satisfied. This didn't stop Randy Witherington's cult of Peter Pan from flourishing out there, but it was very much based on the idea that the Kingdom of Heaven could not be built in a day and that, once the authorities had crumbled and their radiophonic actions were legalized, they would arrive at central London offices as rebel heroes and be showered in young bodies, market share ensured. Which actually goes some way to showing you what a visionary Randy was in his own insipid way.

Day to day, little of this pederastic impulse was allowed to interfere with the smooth running of the station. In some ways it made things easier. The knowledge that the sight of body hair sickened and appalled my colleagues made it much easier to focus during the group masturbation sessions. And while they professed that their inclinations were beautiful, the most natural thing in the world, the threat of these inclinations being made public was usually enough to ensure the upper hand in any dispute. And, if nothing else, I admired their discipline.

This, of course, was down to Randy Witherington, a guru very much of this dawning era, preaching marginally deferred gratification as preparation for a Presleydom of heaven on earth (the 1973 Radio Randy Disco Roadshow being their highpoint, I believe, judging by coverage of the recent convictions). It was he who was the driving force behind the group 'pipe cleaning' as he so coyly put it and in this, at least, he was inspired. If I had ever had occasion to work in an office since those days, the introduction of such a programme would have been amongst my first priorities. It did indeed seem to clear one's mind and fostered the kind of camaraderie only found amongst those who have been intimate and intimately ashamed with one another. It is a feeling, if you will pardon the pun, known only to those who have faced little death together.

I would love to tell you more about Randy, I really would, but I will not. The publicity hungry live in fertile times and Mr Witherington already has three volumes of hagiography, two 'warts-and-all' accounts and an official unauthorized biography, all of which he fully co-operated with. Not to mention reams of newsprint, TV documentaries, docu-dramas and reconstructions. And although it should not be important, damaged pride forces from Me the revelation that in all these thousands of pages, these hundreds of thousands of words, I am mentioned only once, and there not by name and in a footnote: 'It was widely rumoured that Randy had connections to the Secret Service, that a spook with a gun was never far from his side. This seems to be a myth of Witherington's own making. The only mysterious, malevolent presence out at the fort was he himself.' I, who funded, protected and nurtured this half-baked project! I, who am, as it transpires, the One True Great Messiah (in a manner of speaking). Well, there will be some red faces on Grub Street in a month or so, I assure you. Those 'authors' will welcome their death at the hands of a vengeful public. And as for Witherington? I suppose life in prison as a celebrity child molester offers its own unique set of opportunities for moral growth. I forgive him. And he will come to treasure that.

As to what we did out there? We, or rather, they, played records and talked about them in a new language which matched the clothes, as if the richest, most well-bred children our nation could produce had been cross-bred with Americans. And when I say they talked about records, I mean they talked *around* them, an incessant circling, a spiral that never came any closer to expressing what it was about that music that moved them but vastly increased my stock of knowledge of the guitar types, shoes, girlfriends, haircuts and, as the years passed, drug habits of their idols. Yes, it was a tedious, unpleasant job out there. But at least it was out there.

And Victor? Victor was pleased, very pleased. Revenue streams became bank-bursting torrents; all the right people at Whitehall and Westminster were disgusted and horrified and I was the golden boy once more. Or the goose that laid the golden egg, anyway. Excused all other duties, I was left largely to my own devices, undisturbed by anything except the occasional fishing ketch mooring up to deliver bottles of vintage champagne or cigars, all courtesy of my master.

Oh, and the Navy, of course, when they came to shut us down in '67. I'm really not surprised they hushed it up. It was like Chesapeake Bay all over again. Some memories – burning oil on water, frigates colliding, jolly jack tars screeching in terror – are made to be cherished.

And so caught up was I in being there, so warmed was I by Victor's attentiveness, by my own victories, that I allowed myself to try to forget my darling Verna, back there at the office, with her rank upon rank of girls, plotting, always plotting. But while Verna has built a career by helping people to forget, she makes a point of punishing those who have the temerity to forget her.

From: 100001@hotmail.com
To: mandyhart200@hotmail.com

mand - u done me a favor. u were the only thing holding me back. with u gone its easier 4 me. im following u i guess. i dont want 2 be any sort of machine any more. not circits or blood & bone. & u? well even if ur not reading these emails r out there now. an alibi in it? or a confessoin. 4 a moment any way. just 4 a moment. until i decide 2 wipe it all clean. binary rob

(Converted from the ASCII)

19

'You're a fucking idiot. What is your fucking problem?'

O seems to be rehearsing lines, his eyes flicking between the road and the mirror, his tone completely lacking in the irritation that would make it real. Nevertheless, he is irritated. The lack of a joke, one of O's wry observations (Jimmy is sure he thinks of them as wry), establishes this beyond any doubt, despite the apparent dispassion. And the Wagner. The Wagner disturbing the airflow as it gusts from various hidden speakers is a certain giveaway. They have sat in silence amid the disappointingly obvious music of O's anger since he finally discovered Jimmy at the back of the Nag's Head and dragged him to the car. Not for the first time – not even for the fortieth time – Jimmy muses on the fact that O isn't as sophisticated as he likes to think he is. Not for the first time the thought is not one he takes any satisfaction in.

Then, with panic leaping up from inside him, the passenger feels his face contorting, tears over-reaching his eyes, the waterworks beginning again in front of the very worst audience. With a gush of relief, realizes he is laughing, trying to hold it in keeping with O's mood, silent except for the occasional nasal honk, his shoulders shuddering as if driving over pot-holes in a much less expensive car. Water falls from his cheeks and soaks into the yellow-stained kit twisted in his lap. He rocks forward and then back, once, twice, three times, his shoulders quartering the arc. The snorts grow closer together until finally, exhausted by a resistance that only heightens the problem, he opens his mouth and releases his high-pitched cackle.

O turns to him and stares for so long that Jimmy can feel it and laughs harder. Stares so long Jimmy stops laughing and braces a hand against the dashboard.

'The road . . .'

Holds it a moment longer. Gradually returns eyes front.

'You're a cunt, Jim.'

'Yes. I know.'

O's snatch ruptures the foil, a half-hearted glug of creamer making its yellowed mess on the table and his fingers, a curse emitted quietly as serviettes are fanned into it and his hand is dabbed at in a series of agitated pecks.

'I think black would be best.'

'Black fucks my stomach.'

'All the same. I think black would be best.'

Their eyes flicker across each other's. Jimmy redeploys his smile.

'You're the boss.'

He raises the cup of coffee and tips it back, eyes wettening with the heat and the boiled-dry bitterness of it.

'May as well have another.'

O rises as his breath falls away and strolls back towards the counter.

Three more cups before Jimmy finds himself hunched forward with glistening forehead touching door, trousers pushed down on to ankles, shirt unbuttoned to navel by shaking fingers.

The door beyond the door opens and groans shut again. Footsteps approach in a series of mini-splashes. A pause.

'You still in there, Jimmy?'

He leaves his reply as long as seems possible.

'Thought I'd climbed out the window?'

'Thought you might have died.'

'Another underwhelming performance from Jimmy Patel.'

There is silence, his skin flushing with heat again as his guts shape slowly for the next spasm.

'Why are you doing this to yourself, Jim?'

'It's a perfectly natural bodily function.'

'You know what I mean.'

It rolls over him again, his innards contorting.

'Do you find it easier to talk to me when I'm behind a door?'

'Jimmy, we're meant to be friends.'

'We haven't been that for a long time. Not sure we ever were.'

Exasperated now: 'OK, whatever makes you feel better.'

'Do you?'

'What?'

'Find it easier to talk to me behind a door.'

'Yes.'

'Can't face me.'

'When I can see you I want to strangle you.'

He laughs again, another man's snort, feels his throat tightening. The sudden recollection of O slumped over the steering wheel, air coming in high, gulped groans that time they'd driven back down from London to Canterbury and had spent half an hour in a lay-by trying to pull themselves together after they lost it. He can't remember (never could) what had set them off, only the face-aching hysterics, the mutual hilarity and uneasy attempts to be the first to recover.

The warmth cracks on his suspicion before it can be articulated. *When I can see you I want to strangle you.* The joke is contrived, O's syntax mangled by the effort of the lie. The whole conversation feels stage-managed, scripted, even. Far too close, certainly, to the icy science of the American TV dramas he watches, where every word, every pause, each almost imperceptible facial twitch seems perfectly calibrated to encourage either laughter or sadness. He feels, with a melancholy all his own, the depths of manipulation he is being subjected to. Feels it. O knew he would get drunk, gave him the room to do it, his humiliation this afternoon all part of the plan to finally break him so completely that there can be no recovery. Even his anger in the car a ruse, a dance of words and gestures to beguile Jimmy with the fantasy that somehow, on some level, he's still in charge.

And this point he has reached right now is where his life diverges from the script of those dramas, where, upon realizing he was being used, Jimmy would sober up, grit his teeth, march out on to the pitch and bowl the best cricket of his life, rediscover his self respect, be carried from the field by his strapping son and reunited with Gloria at the tearful finale. It won't happen, mainly because Jimmy can't be bothered to make it happen, would prefer another drink, actually, and because this would be O's victory anyway – his performing dog doing his tricks for the committee of Bigots Village CC. For O, every situation is a win-win, a no-risk gamble. The bookmaker's art. He has expounded upon the subject at length, has joked about writing a risk-management guide for small business-men, where he would advise them to buy off anyone buyable ('and that's everyone, by the way'). There is no way to beat him. You may as well follow the easiest route and lose with a rueful smile.

'All right?'

'Yeah. Great.'

A pause filled by the gush of urinal rinse, a party of bloated cigarette ends and blue air-fresheners jiggling their unseen dance in the flow.

'Lovely in here, actually. Thinking of moving in.'

'Thought you already had.'

Jimmy doesn't have a great deal of friends, old or new. In truth, he has exactly one and he is just outside the door and that he hates him, that he feels manipulated by him is, in a way he doesn't fully understand, beside the point. He is all there is, the sum total, and while this may be a bleak thought it's also reassuring. Whatever plan this man might have for him, it's his plan, too.

'Nearly done. Go and pay for the coffee.'

'It's OK – I'll wait for you.'

'There's only one way out.'

'All the same. I'll wait.'

'Worried I'm going to flush myself away?'

'Oh, a washed-up comedian as well as a washed-up cricketer.'

'So hurtful . . . Get the cuffs ready, I'm coming out.'

He rises carefully, knees still bent, torso angled along the line from seat to doortop. Paper wadded into a loose carnation, pats tentatively at buttocks and anus, grimacing, refusing to look down. Pulls yesterday's pants and yesterday's trousers back into position, begins to fasten his belt.

'Seriously . . .'

'Surely not . . .?'

'You do understand what you did to me, don't you?'

'I understand what you think I did to you.'

He shapes to punch the door, already knowing he's not going to, returns to trying to buckle his belt, the graffiti about where to stick it swaying in front of his face. A pantomime with no audience.

* * *

'Do you remember that girl who – how shall we put this? – who shit herself while she was sucking your balls?'

Jimmy finds himself, hovering just above oblivion, being pulled back to a leather seat, rolling skull, O's car. A line runs from exactly three centimetres above his left eye, one centimetre left of the pupil, back for six centimetres. Along the line, a chiselling pain.

'No.'

'Poor girl. You must.'

'I don't.'

'Your performance reminded me, I suppose.'

'I don't need reminding.'

'So you do remember, then.'

'No. I just don't need reminding.'

He tilts his head carefully round to the constant stutter of green beyond the window. O continues, his tone absent-minded, pleasant, pitch perfect for a conversation about the weather.

'I guess in normal circumstances she probably would've given it a miss. Yes? Just gone home. She must have known something was going on down there. And I only raise it because your recollection is so hazy, but you were rather insistent. So I suppose you only had yourself to blame.' The words drift off, finally punctuated by a snorted chuckle.

'Is there a point to this?'

'Point? Just reminiscing. It's what friends do. Remember the good times.'

'And some girl shitting in my lap is the good times, is it?'

'She had her head in your lap, so short of being a contortionist she could hardly shit there. You really don't remember, do you?'

'Whatever.'

'It was fucking funny, though.'

'If you expect me to bowl without making a complete fucking idiot of myself then I need to sleep.'

'"I've 'ad a accident!" I suppose it wasn't so funny when she started crying.'

Jimmy shuts his eyes, tries to close down consciousness, the headache, frankly, the least of his worries.

If Jimmy dreams, his dreams are private, even to him. So when he wakes it's from nothing, a sudden tear of light and noise, something tugging at his sleeve, his jolt upwards terminating in solid contact and sudden pain, his eyes extremely open. And there, filling this new world, is O's face, moving back now, his eyes glossed, pupils forcing out irises, those black holes Jim's rest receding.

'Always were a good sleeper. A talent. Of sorts.'

They are stopped in a lay-by, a scattering of broken glass and a semi-shredded tyre for company.

'We there?'

'Thought you might need a pick-me-up first.'

Just saying it enough to send index finger rubbing horizontally across nostrils, his hand animal, all habit and no thought. It flutters down and alights on the mirror on the dashboard, raises it with infinite care and guides it, glinting in a patch of dusty sunlight, to Jimmy's knee. A generous, wobbly line of powder bisects the glass, the slight granular debris caused by its journey reflected round it.

Hunching his shoulders, the mirror held delicately between thumb and second finger (index finger raised above it, an exclamation), he angles himself anxiously round to check the rear view, trying to keep the hand steady and below potential sight-lines. A long stretch of concrete culminating in a burger shack, a man standing in front of it biting into something in a serviette, from this distance a flamboyantly cuffed hand-chewer. Reassured, Jimmy returns eyes front, takes the proffered roll of note, leans forward.

'Do you remember when your mother disowned you and I had to act as your – how shall we put it? – as your ambassador?'

He can't feel any difference yet but knows that he can. Already, honestly, the world's tauter, snappier, as if long-loosened strings on a guitar have been tightened and brought back to pitch. But he's just the same in it.

'No.'

'Oh, don't start that again. I know you remember.'

'I'm not in the mood for reminiscence.'

'But you do remember, then.'

'No, I don't remember anything.' Enjoying it now, in spite of himself.

'Let me remind you, then.'

'I'd rather you didn't.'

'I'm doing you a service. Perhaps you drink to remember.'

'Ha ha.'

The world beyond the membrane of the car seems impossibly sharp, defined, leaves stopping exactly where sky starts, the piece of grit kicked up by the wheels utterly distinct from the road. O is driving faster, it feels, but more smoothly, as if the road is a conveyor belt and all he need do is sit there, constantly pulled forward.

'I went to your mother's flat to plead your case. We sat, we talked. She made me some disgusting tea which I of course drank. We chatted some more . . .'

'I'm not listening . . .'

' . . . you obviously are or you wouldn't know not to. So we chatted some more, not about you now, but about the weather, England, the rudeness of the people, the impossibility of finding good food. At that time. The situation is much better now, as you'd know if you ever cooked. Anyway, we chatted and then when I took my leave she stopped me at the door and said that she wished I were her son. I assured her that she didn't and left. And the very next day you were reconciled.'

'The point being?'

'Admittedly it wasn't exactly the longest reconciliation, but . . .'

'The point of the anecdote. What's the point of your anecdote?'

'Like you said, reminiscence. I think you forget – friendship has a point in itself. There's no grand plan.'

'I wouldn't know.'

'No. I don't suppose you would.' There is another silence, the whole collection from the years they've known each other seeming to Jimmy to have run to months. What if they'd just stopped talking fifteen years ago? Would they be sitting there relaxed, smiling unaffectedly at one another?

'You seem to be feeling better, anyway.'

'Oh yeah, I feel fucking great.' Irritated by his own peevishness.

'Well that's something. I'm sure the trustees will be very pleased.'

'. . .?'

'Of the charity? It's a charity match? Remember?' Sighing. 'Let's not start this again. Just try to smile, chuck a couple of balls down, smile some more, try not to insult anyone and we'll get out of here.'

Swinging round into the drive, the Geiger-click rush of gravel beneath.

From: 100001@hotmail.com
To: mandyhart200@hotmail.com

i tell u what mand. i cant beleive p&g still dont do there accounts on computer. what fucking years this? but i know ur still there coz i checked at clear water. remember the disc i gave u with the pics of mum? remember? i said id digitized them 2 keep them fresh. take them 2 work i said. mr patel wont mind u looking on his machine. just mischeif at the time but it got me on the system. my little trapdoor. cos clear water was hard man! thats proper security. no messing. i needed a break on that 1 so thanks 4 looking at the pics! they were nice tho in it? nice pics. now im gonna look 4 u on the cameras. i didnt wanna have 2 go on the clear water system again. long story. why im out here in it. the only reason im out here. but i want 2 see u. i can may be even get the camera 2 nod at u & u wont even know its me in there! a lost little wave but beutiful i think ;-) binary rob

(Converted from the ASCII)

20

Verna leans back on the pink clam of the headboard, so light she barely dents the quilting. Under her left hand lies the silver box, fine-patterned, *gorgeous*, a present from an admirer originally, probably her husband, but who cares about provenance, frankly, after all these years? In her right hand is the remote control, sharp-edged and boxy, futuristic over a decade ago. Her arm moving toward the television at the foot of her bed like stop-motion plantlife, she presses PLAY.

And there she is again on the screen, her solicitous gaze directed toward the chest of drawers, her skin a fraction tighter, her lips fuller, her hair the same beacon of hope, all lit with the flat harshness of Golden Age television.

Q: So, in our first interview we talked about your early days on the stage and the war years. Today I'd like to focus on your career in the post-war period.
A: That seems logical . . .
Q: In particular your move away from performance. Was that a deliberate decision or just due to circumstance?

On the bed her shoulders drop a little, the remote falls on to the covers, a hazy smile breaks on her face. She cannot understand for the life of her why the documentary was never finished. It would have been dynamite, showbiz dynamite. She imagines the phone clattering with the queued entreaties of agents, the flowers piling up on the doorstep, the tiny, numberless attentions of a personal assistant.

A: Can I just say first, dear, that I will always, *always* be first and foremost a performer. The rush. When the lights come up. And you sense this . . . raw . . . mass of people just beyond them, huddled there in the dark. It's I suppose it is primal. A primal thing. Like cave paintings. Or dancing to the tribal drum. I feel, one feels, like a priestess, the high priestess. The exhilaration. Quite wonderful. An irreplaceable sensation. Or so I felt.

Q: But you came to feel otherwise?

A: To a degree and to an extent, yes. The war came and it changed us. It changed us all. It changed one's sense of priorities. The things we had all seen, the things we had gone through. One couldn't put it back in a box and pretend it had never happened. It wasn't something you could pack away and hide in the attic. God knows, my life would have been easier if it were. But something had been awakened in me.

Without taking her eyes from herself, she flips open the lid of the chest and begins laying out its contents on the bed beside her, each move slow and deliberate, fingers lingering on the textures. Nods gently to herself – understanding, encouraging.

Q: And what was that something?

A: (*smiling wryly*) I suppose you could call it Duty. Love. Patriotism. A sense that there was something bigger than any of us. Something that was worth fighting for. England.

Q: You mention love. It was around this time that you got married, was it not? Was that a factor in your career change, your change of direction?

A: Perhaps. My husband is a great facilitator. A great man, in point of fact. But a remarkable facilitator. And a great scout for talent. He can sniff out something in a person that they never knew was there. That's certainly what he did for me. When we met I was stuck. I felt my life was over. He showed me the way out.

Q: He offered you a job.

A: Not straight away, no. But he helped me to understand that I could be more than a star. That I could use my power to inspire in other fields.

She pulls a silver statuette from her bedside table, the weight surprising her, just as it always does. It represents her as Britannia, the outline of a Union Jack still clearly visible on her tarnished shield. She makes sure the base is flush with the bed then pulls back the figure's helmet, the flame sizzling up, blue and bright, from the miniaturized representation of her ever-perfect coiffure.

Q: And so . . .?

A: And so I set up Barnums Secretarial Services. It seems so ordinary now. I suppose that is my greatest achievement. It's hard to imagine, but at the time the idea of temporary secretarial services, of a truly flexible workforce able to respond at a moment's notice, unencumbered by the shall we say somewhat archaic attitude to employment at that time – well, it was unheard of. Outrageous.

Q: But it worked?

A: It worked. (*She looks down and then slowly up.*) Efficiency. Flexibility. Discretion. The willingness to go the extra mile. Those were our watchwords. And our girls were the best. The best in the business.

The camera cuts away to the interviewer, smiling encouragingly as he delivers his next prompt. She is momentarily distracted from what she's doing, nearly spilling it as she lunges for the remote control and locates the PAUSE just in time to hold him there, his forehead gashing out across to the edge of the screen in a continuous spectrum shiver. What a lovely boy he had been. So attentive. And handsome. She can't recall his name but remembers the light touch of his hand on her shoulder as he had steered her, his face looming in so close she could smell the young man's smell on him. Whatever had happened to him? Where had he gone? She thinks she knows but has no idea of the answer. Knows she used to know. Thinks she did anyway. Trying to locate it again and again will just exhaust her. PLAY.

Q: And where did your staff, your girls, come from? How did you persuade secretaries to leave secure employment, jobs for life, for what must have seemed at the time a pretty crackpot idea?

A: Oh no. No. We didn't persuade anyone to leave any job for life. Oh no. That was not the idea at all. We trained them all ourselves. Not one of them had ever typed before in her life. Not one. No, our girls came, I suppose you could say, from a much older profession.

Q: I'm not sure I follow . . .

A: A lot of girls had to do things they didn't want to during the war. There are needs during wartime, economic needs. Steel, for instance. Armaments. Soldiers. And soldiers have needs, too, if they are to perform in battle. It was their duty, *our* duty, as Englishwomen. And they did their duty just as much there as in a munitions factory or in front of a camera. But after the war we were left with excess capacity. In all kinds of sectors within the economy. But, yes, particularly this one. Particularly when the GIs went home. And we were to discover that the girls who had excelled in this line of work, well, they tended to be the ones who excelled at secretarial work, too.

She has to take her eyes from herself now, if she's to get this bit right and waste nothing. And the eradication of waste is important to her. But they disobey her, flicking between the two in a morse code of distraction. She keeps returning to it in spite of her efforts. What had happened to the man who had interviewed her? What had happened to that lovely boy? For some reason the question makes her think of her husband but she is wiped clean of cause, her entire life effect.

Q: If I understand correctly you seem to be saying that you used, erm, I believe the term would be ladies of ill . . .

A: Oh, come now, darling. Don't look so shocked. Have you never indulged? Most men have. Even those as good-looking as you. No ties? Do as you please and then go? Surely you understand the appeal?

Q: Fortunately we're not here to talk about me.

A: No. More's the pity.

Standards, standards. Her mind stuck in the loop of his absence, she takes the Hermès silk scarf from the night-stand, its corner between her thumb and finger as she scythes it through the air, catching it at its thinnest and wrapping it quickly into position. She loves the feel of it cutting into her skin, even if she does have to use her teeth to get it tight.

Q: Tell me a little more, if you would, about your husband and about Barnums.

A: My husband? Oh, I see. How coy. As I said, he is a great man. A truly great man. If Barnums were to trade publicly we would be amongst the leading stock-market performers. And my husband has built it from nothing. Our core business is insurance. But my husband understands this as risk management and, with his approach, what we practise externally we must practise internally. So the company spreads its risks across a number of ventures, some large, some small. This diversification becomes a constant evolution, even within divisions. It's not really a company any more in any traditional sense. It's a *modular organism*. It's very much in our interest to compete selectively within the organization.

Q: So how do we know if we're dealing with a Barnums company?

A: You don't. That's the beauty of it. Some of the companies don't even know they're Barnums companies. Competition and evolution. This is what makes us so successful. For instance, I can give you an exclusive here. We are moving out of temporary secretarial work and retraining our staff.

Q: But you've just been extolling to me the virtues . . .

A: Yes, of course there are virtues *now*. But in twenty years time? We've been using computers to model the future. Prediction, you see, is the core of our business. And we have noticed how quickly the size of the processor is diminishing. Which has led us to . . . (*she pauses, reaching for the words of the statement, the only fault in her whole performance*) . . . *postulate* that there will come a time soon where every office worker will have their own personal computer, for writing letters and reports and the like. At which point the secretary will gradually become redundant.

Q: And so?

A: And so we are moving into public relations. We see it as the next wave.

She is always bored by the next part, a little embarrassed by the stiltedness, her failure to imbue the remains of the interview with any light or grace. So she sets it running forward, her screen head jerking dementedly, then settles back to puncture her skin.

And it's as the warmth spreads out from her stomach, the whole world sucked inside her comforting embrace, it's just as it hits that she remembers. Remembers even where they buried him, wrapped in bin liners and Sellotape, the whole terrible misunderstanding. Unless that was just a film she saw, or something on the television. It gets so hard to separate it all out. Her finger makes one last heavy contact with the remote control and the video-player clunks back to normal.

Q: . . . pleasure, an absolute pleasure talking to you. There is just one more thing if I may? I'm sorry to backtrack a little, you said earlier that Barnums' main business was insurance?

A: Yes, that's right.

Q: Well, this may be somewhat sensitive, but I have good evidence that the company was actually founded as some offshoot or front for the intelligence agencies . . .

A: I beg your pardon?

Q: The intelligence agencies . . .

A: The intelligence agencies?

Q: Yes, I have a signed . . .

A: Where were you educated, young man?

Q: If we could just . . .

A: Darling, we'll get to your question in just a moment. Where?

Q: Christ's College, Cambridge.

A: And did you enjoy Cambridge?

Q: Yes, very much so, but, if . . .

A: And the girls?

Q: I really don't see where . . .

A: So you preferred boys? I had my . . .

Q: I most certainly did not. I. Can we? May I . . . return to the question.

A: Of course, darling. I am sorry. Sometimes I just let my imagination run away with me. It's the performer in me, I suppose. Ask away.

Q: . . .

A: Ask anything.

Q: . . .

A: Go on. Do. You were about to ask me something? You can ask me anything, my dear. Anything.

Q: I. I seem to have forgotten.

A: Is it in your notes?

Q: I . . . It . . . The thing is . . .

A: They do look a little messy, I must say. Just take a moment.

Q: It . . . No, I'm sorry it's completely gone. I'm not usually so. I'm usually very. It seems to happen to me a lot with you.

A: You're not the first to say it, darling.

The screen returns to black. The room is silent. Verna Landor lies very still on the bed, her eyes closed, something seeping from beneath her dress. Her unseeing pupils have dilated even beyond the bounds of her irises, her eyes blank, black glass. The effect will last for ever and then for ever, a constant absence, a continuing mystery, until exactly the moment her lids are pulled back.

From: 100001@hotmail.com
To: mandyhart200@hotmail.com

mand - i saw u. only 4 a moment then i got scared. just a couple of iregallurities but it felt like some1 was watching me. u was standing behind the counter & it looked like u was frozen there looking strait up at me. i guess u was just staring in2 space. a nice moment 4 me. i didnt fuck with moving the camera. my nerves gone in it! but they must be after me. how ever good u r if ur on a net work some 1 can find u. so it stands 2 reason there on 2 me. u aint got a clue what im talking about. i will explain i promise. just give me time. binary rob

(Converted from the ASCII)

21

Of course, resolving to do something and actually doing it are very different things, as Peter knows all too well from, for instance, giving up smoking. He still remembers the way his friends, their own addiction already dealt with, had stared glassily past him as he stood in the pub, his plastic cigarette substitute in one hand, Marlboro Light in the other. Up to this point he had justified his continuing combustions as an aesthetic preference, but there was no aesthetic merit in a piece of plastic tubing, nothing iconic in the images it formed. He had re-thought his position, returning from exile an addictive personality, obliquely likening his plight to Art Pepper kicking skag.

This, though, is casual sex with a shop girl. With a source. It has to stop. Every action sharpened by faked-up permanently midday light, he takes the tape out of his dictaphone and examines it half-heartedly, his hands moving a little too fast, his eyes finding their own way, again and again, back to the bed.

It hadn't stopped the last time he saw her. Not exactly. Which is why he wants to be sure that the tape is definitely right back to the very start.

In retrospect, it probably hadn't been so clever to buy her the jacket. It hadn't been anything he'd planned, obviously. He had just happened to be at the Balanga sample sale and had seen it and thought of her excruciating outerwear and of the torment of being seen with her in it, in fact even of just being in the same room as it. And it had just so happened that only minutes earlier he'd been to the cashpoint and taken out a hundred quid, which was just enough, so on a whim and as a sign of good faith relating to the imminent re-establishment of their relationship on a strictly professional basis, he had bought it. It wasn't a pre-meditated thing, obviously, and he certainly didn't think about how such a gift could be misconstrued until much too late. Until it had already been misconstrued.

And perhaps it hadn't been so clever to decide to conduct the interview with both of them perched on the end of the emperor-size double bed, only the dictaphone separating them and an expanse of perfectly fluffed duvet rolling out behind them. Once again, Peter knows his motives were good. All he had wanted was to set her at ease, to allow a poorly educated young woman to feel as though she were partaking in a casual conversation rather than being interviewed for a groundbreaking critique of shopping culture. He had hoped merely to tease insight from her, to facilitate her critique and celebration of her own everyday existence. He hadn't thought it through.

Which is why the dictaphone is this time positioned on the edge of the small bureau and she, when she arrives, will sit on the florally upholstered chair that goes with it while he, sensitive to the nuance of his every action, will pace or lean against the sink, or perch at the far end of the bureau.

And yet, despite his precautions, his body seems intent on betraying him. His dick rolls round his pants demanding contact; he has the shaky ultra-sensitivity of someone who's just about to get it, objects looming large in his fingers, the very fact of being in a hotel room an odd kind of come-on. In fact, his mind also seems intent on betraying him.

Peter has never been an avid consumer of pornography. The mainstream of tits and ass and crotch shots and cum shots has largely passed him by. The reason is simply that he finds his titillation relies as much on the production values of a photograph or film as it does on the content of the image – in particular the lighting, the heaviness of the make-up on the woman's face, the level of airbrushing, these and one hundred other indicators signal that the vast bulk of this material is not for him. And he is forced to admit that his taste here verges on the middlebrow. As a teenager, a friend had showed him what amounted to a catalogue of closely cropped images of female genitals, the missing legs pulled back as far as they could go, the flash gun glittering on them. He had to admit there was something *Goldinesque* to them, but they upset him.

But once, almost twenty years ago now, he had been utterly captured. A student with a large overdraft and an urge to connect with real people (by which he meant working-class people), Peter had taken a summer job at a small warehouse in South London in preference to returning back home to mum and dad. It was a family-owned business, only eight full-time workers, a manager and a woman who came in just to cook breakfast for them. The staff were well looked after, a spare room put aside for them to take breaks in, a small pool table supplied, the baize scuffed and dirty, a couple of tired armchairs and a huge cache of soft-porn magazines. Peter had no idea where they had come from, had never dared ask. But there they were, piles and piles of them – a mountain from which he tried to keep his eyes averted.

Impossible. At every break all the other men would pick up a stack of their chosen literature and, while playing pool or waiting to play pool, begin a detailed commentary, replete with exclamations and obscenities. He himself would be invited to contribute, to add to the conversational thread, to pass judgement, his failure to find the requisite gusto, let alone employ the correct jargon, marking him more clearly every day as, at best a student, at worse *gay*. Neither assumption should have bothered him, he knew, but both did. So he began avoiding the recreation room. It was summer, after all, and the quest for a tan seemed a reasonable cover, even if the industrial estate didn't exactly offer picturesque sunbathing locations.

Peter could probably have made it through the next few weeks without incident if it hadn't rained. But rain it did, sweat clouds coalescing into downpour, forcing him to scuttle back inside and, with a feeling of dread, climb the stairs to the staff room.

One of the younger guys whose name Peter can't remember now – and who, now he came to think of it, worked there with his father, sat and discussed the tits on that with his father! – was playing darts. His target was a picture of a naked woman. What else would it have been?

'Whatcha fink, Taff?' (Despite his mother making sure nothing of the Principality showed in his accent, a quick question about origins had undone six years of voice coaching.)

'Very nice,' he replied non-committally as another arrow thudded into the girl's cheek. But his gaze soon returned there, a series of furtive blinks establishing that his initial fascination wasn't misplaced. He tried not to look but, face whitening, blobs of red flashing in and out on his cheeks, he couldn't keep his eyes away, not even as an erection formed, which only the timely deployment of his copy of the *Guardian* kept from public scrutiny.

The next week was a rare misery. His body constantly buzzing with frustration, he would invent excuses to leave the warehouse floor and find himself standing in front of the increasingly pock-marked picture. He wanted to take it, carefully to fold and hide it in his bag, but was too scared of being caught. He wanted to masturbate every time he went into the toilet cubicle but was too scared of being heard. So he drifted through the days, paralysed, gulping for air, until, without announcement or explanation, the picture disappeared, an absence, her shape inaccurately represented by the pinpricks in the wall. And, gradually, the fever passed, as though a spell had been lifted and he had found himself again.

He has had cause to wonder since what it was that obsessed him in that one image. The girl's pose was porn-standard – her buttocks raised up high and pushed toward the camera, her arms slightly bent so that her nipples almost touched the floor, her head craned round over her left shoulder. Maybe it was because her pubic hair was so much longer than was standard, or because her breasts were a little smaller than the norm, or because the stockings rolled halfway down her thighs looked loose and dishevelled. Or maybe it was because she seemed utterly unaware of the camera, her eyes looking past it, as if it was invisible to her. Then again, perhaps it was nothing to do with the picture itself and it was just that the image represented the moment where his supposedly refined sensibilities cracked apart to show something else underneath.

Whatever the case, when this other girl – Mandy, his girl – had rolled over and pulled herself away when they finished that first time, he had suddenly remembered that summer and that picture and maybe somehow (though he knew it was pathetic to justify it this way, as beyond his control, pathetic and demeaning) something of that spell or curse or madness had been reawakened. And now when he thinks of the picture, it's Mandy and has always been Mandy and when he thinks of Mandy it's with her arse shoved up into his face, even though he has never seen her like that and even though she is far, far, far too young to have been in that picture all those years ago (this thought once again sending his stomach bouncing and stumbling with guilt and self-loathing).

Which is all another way of Peter explaining to himself that resolving to end it and actually ending it are two very different things.

And then, of course, he's fond of reminding himself, is it only down to him to start it or end it? Doesn't Mandy have a part to play in that decision? Does she want it to end? All the evidence suggests, preposterously, that she doesn't. Which Peter knows is crazy. She is half his age, so while his motivation isn't hard to fathom, hers is impossibly obscure. When they finish it's her who pulls away, affectionately but firmly, as if she's the man of the world and he a needy teenager. She seems to want nothing from him. And it is just this extent to which her behaviour conforms to a middle-aged man's fantasy that disturbs him the most. Is this his life or badly made pornography? Which brings his thoughts back to the picture and starts it off all over again.

Peter checks the tape one more time, pressing rewind and feeling the chunter of the motor pulling against the empty spool. Lowers himself gingerly into the chair, checking his watch. She's late. Or perhaps she's not coming. This thought bothers him. Not so much that he won't be seeing her but that she might be the one to finish it. It's not that he wants her to need him, obviously. It's just a little humiliating this way. Theoretically.

It's more likely she's just lost. The hotel is huge, the room numbers are confusing. He already has the phone hooked under his chin and is about to press 9 for reception when he decides his voice won't come out right and replaces the receiver. Which is when his mobile rings, his hand flipping the receiver loose again so it falls and hangs swinging, him chasing it like an overgrown kitten while simultaneously trying to pull his own handset from his pocket.

'Hello?'

'Don here.'

'Donald! Hi! Hi. How are you?' Peter pitching higher as his morale sinks.

'How am I? Where's my fucking piece?' Even though Peter knows Donald lays the Scots nutter thing on when he wants something sorted he is taken aback by his ferocity.

'Piece? Your piece . . .?'

'You know which fucking piece. "You're In The Army Now". Former military fucking living spaces. The old fucker on the tower. Which fucking piece! King James? Lives on a sea fort? Ring any fucking bells? The fucking piece I commissioned from you how long ago? Two weeks ago? Would you like me to check how fucking long ago?'

'Ah yeah, that, Donald. The former military living spaces . . . Yeah, very exciting. Very, er, current.'

'And . . .?'

'Yeah, I am looking forward to . . .'

'When?'

'The truth is it's proving quite difficult to contact him and . . .'

'I had a fucking email from him this morning asking when the fuck you'd be getting in touch.'

'Ah, so his email's back up, is it?' Back in the groove, working like a true pro now. Donald actually splutters, momentarily silenced by Peter's defensive certainty.

'I need to talk to you about it. There's been developments.'

'I've got this book proposal I'm working on, actually, Donald. I have to meet with my agent and . . .'

'I need to talk to you about it. Face to face.'

' . . . I think you'll be really interested in the book actually . . .'

'Jesus Christ, man, this is important! It's not some fucking book on interior fucking decor! He says we can bring Verna Landor out with us! Verna Landor! He used to know her. She can be in the fucking shoot. The whole fucking piece has suddenly . . .' The silence more shocking than what preceded it, Donald suddenly overcome by an incomprehensible significance. Peter takes his chance.

'I appreciate the point you're making, Donald, I really do. But . . .'

'Did you hear what I said?' Donald too good, the consummate commissioning pro.

'Of course, Donald. I . . .'

'Verna. Landor.'

' . . . yeah.'

'Do you have any idea who the fuck I'm talking about?'

'She's the, erm . . .'

'Oh, for fuck's sake! I'm not going to call again. When can you come and see me?'

'Early next week? I haven't got my diary on me . . .'

'Call me tomorrow. Arrange a time. Or that's it. You can fucking forget it.'

Pete drops the phone down on to the desk, cheered for a moment by the heavy thud of its workmanship. He looks absently at the dictaphone, tapping it with his index finger, glances toward the door, his watch, presses PLAY.

The tape has been worrying him all week. More accurately, the possible – though admittedly highly unlikely – confluence of the tape and Martha has been worrying him all week. It seemed far too risky to keep it on his person, so he had secreted it down the side of his filing cabinet, having to use the ergonomically efficient carbon-alloy backscratcher he had reviewed a year or so ago every time he needed to retrieve it. He knows, of course that it would make more sense to have wiped it, but he finds himself gripped by an awful fascination, his tertiary hand, metal scraping on cabinet's metal, retrieving it from its hiding place at least once a day so that, shoulders raised and eyes fixed on the door knob, he can listen on an earpiece, something in his throat making it impossible to swallow. He has played it so many times he knows exactly how it all happens. Once more, then, before he starts again – re-records history and makes the world clean.

First, the loud internal click and roar of ambience before the microphone adjusts, then a low hum with whispers of movement. Then his voice, metallic and nasal, all the rhythm and assurance he feels when words come from him removed now as they reel out from plastic.

'So I thought we'd start today, if you're happy to, with the . . . oh, I forgot, actually. I got you a present. Well, not a present, really. More of a . . . Here.'

A rush as the jacket is pulled out, her intake of breath as it registers.

'Oh, wicked.' The intonation London-perfect. 'That's wicked. Oh, cheers. Fanks.'

'It's no big deal. I was at a sa–' She kisses him.

Now, for a couple of minutes, just the occasional rustle, the odd sharp exhalation of breath and, if he really concentrates, perhaps just the suggestion of their mouths losing and finding suction, their tongues lapping spastically around each other. Then a sudden looming of movement, a thud whose volume is pulled down just too late and a clattering as the dictaphone falls to the floor. Peter listening tries to put a piece of clothing to each sound as the movement becomes frantic, his muttering inaudible, the only clear words when she says, 'It's all right, s'alright, I got it.'

And then he starts up. Just him. She remains silent but for a single exclamation which is still a good few revolutions away. No, it's just him, unobtrusively at first, as if he is quietly mourning something, then gradually, with increasing rhythm, volume and intensity, each emission pitiful, somehow, isolated.

Of course, this is where the knock comes, Peter immediately back on his feet, his right fist clenching round the player, his scrabbled attempt to hit STOP ending on FF, sending his high-velocity, pink and perky tape-self speeding toward climax.

Dictaphone promptly stopped and thrown on the bed, he opens the door and there she is, smiling emptily, just the same but for the jacket.

'Hi. Hi. Was wondering if you were coming. Did you want to sit over . . . Ah. On the bed. OK. I was just listening through to some of our previous . . . Let me just get a new tape out of my bag and . . . file the one in here away nice and safely . . . and then we can begin . . . Should I? should I just squeeze . . . in . . . here . . . next to . . .? That's cosy . . . God, it's good to see you.'

From: 100001@hotmail.com
To: mandyhart200@hotmail.com

mand – ok. so here it is. why im here & not at home with u. i found
some thing at clear water. a wicked thing. & i kinda took it. thats how
it started. not a thing really. some thing on the system. code - a way
2 tell a computer 2 do some thing. a way of making some thing. & i
made it out here. made him.

it was when i 1st got in there. on the clear water system. when i took
it. stole it i guess. i was just looking 4 u. like the other day. looking at
there camera configs how there controled all that. how they were
doing it all. & i suddenly saw it. it aint security at all. there not tracking
shop lifters. there tracking customers. the pictures the credit card
trails the car they came in. the hole thing set up 2 follow how &
where there spending. 2 work out what therell spend next. 2 lead
them 2 where therell spend next. but thats not even the point. it was
intresting & every thing but it aint the point. not 4 me. the point was
the code.

the code made life. its the only way i can describe it. it was doing a
better job than it was meant 2. the way the cameras moved. the
jumps. it was like it was guessing. just a flicker really. but a flicker of
a mind. u heard of a.i.? machine intelligence? it was there & i dont
think they even knew. & if they didnt know then they wudnt mind if i
had a little look at how they did it wud they? i was doing them a
favor when u think about it. & why wud they mind me doing them a
favor? binary rob

(Converted from the ASCII)

22

It was his final betrayal, as it turned out, and it wasn't even of me. But I found that out many years later and by then I didn't care so much.

In the spring of 1972, Victor summoned me to meet him in a nondescript and shabby public-house in Gillingham. Here, over one of the worst lunches I had ever eaten in his company, the great man gave me detailed plans for the conversion of the lower floor of the central tower at Cold Mount into an impregnable strong room. My first task was to dispose of the architect, then hire the relevant contractors, making sure that they, too, vanished once work was complete (and believe me, it was a challenge to find unattached builders in those days). No one at the station was to know. I was to report only to him. I was to consider eliminating anyone who even suggested an interest in the project.

So far, so Victor, nothing in the commands themselves out of the ordinary. Over the years many nosy parkers had come to learn the error of their ways in quite the most Old Testament of fashions. Except that since our symposium all those years before, the cover-up – the *cleaning*, as Victor like to put it – was Verna's job, this woman's unique touch considered superior to my force.

This alone would have been enough to alert me that something unusual was afoot. But in addition there was Victor Victor, the supposed colossus. It was the first time I had ever seen him shifty, the sweat not that of a fat man who did not care, but reeking quite distinctively of fear (yes, I can tell the difference – few people have smelt more fear than me). Even his legendary physique, his height, bulk, enormous girth, all seemed reduced, as if he had turned in on himself. Still, I knew better than to question him, better than to complain about the food, better certainly than to twitch or turn as his eyes flickered past me to the door again and again. I remained – in many ways I remain still – his loyal lieutenant.

And so the months passed, the gigantic safe was built to his specification and I forgot about my mentor's unsettling demeanour on that day. After all, who could Victor Victor be afraid of, I reasoned, and what could he have done – especially without my knowledge, if not direct involvement – that could possibly be so much more malign, illegal and dangerous than the countless acts he had committed before? I threw myself into the work to the extent of laying the reinforced concrete of the floor myself and if it was not as smooth as I would have liked, well, I would have bought a drink for the professional who could do better with four dead builders to cover.

This being the early seventies, we didn't have a telephone out there, just an already old short-wave radio transmitter manned by an already old radio operator, Ronnie, both of whom looked like they had been out here since the end of the War. I was outside that morning, the sun unseasonably warm on the side of my face, my gaze travelling north-east into that unimaginable expanse of water, thinking of the ends of the earth and how, if there were an end, this place would probably be as good for it as any. Then Ronnie's voice sounded behind me, dissipating the mixture of elation and melancholy that this momentary fantasy had engendered in me.

'Got a Code Red for you, sir.' Ronnie always called me sir. It was the only thing I liked about him. I turned to face him, pulling a couple of cigarettes from my pack and dropping them into his shirt pocket.

'You stay here and smoke for me. I'll go and talk. I don't want you accidentally overhearing. What with your ears being so sensitive . . .'

Skipping down the steps, I barricaded myself into the radio room, settled into Ronnie's still-warm seat, raised the cobra head of the microphone to my mouth.

'King, over.'

'Hello, James. Victor asked me to contact you, over.'

Even through the thick burr of static I could recognize her voice, imagine her caressing the handset, the silk of her stocking tops rubbing gently upon each other. Verna.

'How can I help you? Over.'

'I'm afraid he's pulling you off. All of you. The Broadcasting Bill's been enacted. Over.'

'What are you talking about? I don't understand. Over.'

'We are to be granted one of the first commercial radio licences. We're legal. There's no point being out at sea. And we need to get set up quickly. Competitive advantage, I'm to tell you. I'm sorry, James, truly I am. I know it was important to you. Over.'

I was gasping, unable to fathom the depths of this treachery, the beautiful intricacy of its construction. She was to force me from my fort, my only home. Her. Which meant he knew not just how I felt about the tower, but how I felt about Verna, too. Eventually I squeezed out a constricted reply.

'Message received. Over and out.'

But before I could flip the switch and weep, her voice inveigled its way back in, fluting, seeming to hover in the air in front of me. Her voice talking to me, *just me*.

'Oh, James. James. I'm so sorry. But I'm still glad. At last we get to speak after all this time. Over.'

I could think of nothing, find no way out of this fragrant corner.

'James? Do you understand me? I've been longing to talk to you since we first met. Over.'

'I . . .'

'Victor thinks he's beaten us both here. Using me like this to crush you. But you know, darling? I don't think he has. I don't think he has at all. Has he, James? Over.'

'What do you mean, crush me? Over.'

'I love him but sometimes. Sometimes I wish he were gone. I think we all do, don't we, all of us who work for him? I think we all wish sometimes he were gone. Do you, James? Do you? Think of the conversations we could have then . . . Do you understand James? Over.'

'I . . . understand . . . Over.'

'Soon then. Soon, James. Over and out.'

I sat for a moment in that unquiet room on an unquiet sea, the cool damp in the concrete released into my bones, while the hardened kernel of self inside me suddenly exploded out with the force of desert weeds sensing moisture in the ground. The scent from the flowers was horrible, but I always knew it would be.

If Victor did not look surprised to see me, he did show a flicker of something a little like fear, a half-glance over my shoulder for the heavies he had positioned to protect him. I had to smile – though he had chosen the best he had available, they were poor copies of me myself, blurred in detail, lacking in contrast, quite clearly not the genuine article. I had trained them personally and almost felt a glimmer of regret or fellow feeling as I broke their necks. So much for the bodyguards. It seemed that Victor's security had become lax while I was all at sea.

'Ah, how nice of you to visit,' Victor deadpanned. 'Come in.'

The house was darker than I remembered from my previous visit, less grand, diminished, Victor already dead and this a reprise in a minor key. The chandelier was no more than a few strands of badly cut glass around a dim bulb, illuminating only the flurries of dust from our steps.

'Sorry about the mess, old man. Haven't been here too much recently.'

One thing you probably ought to know. Death is almost always, almost without fail, banal. It is not only that it is an essentially meaningless event. It is that it sucks meaning from everything around it. Not as some dramatic, astrophysical occurrence. Pathetically, like a long, barely audible whine.

'Sorry about the mess, old man. Haven't been here too much recently.'

These, then, were the last words that Victor Victor – My saviour, My mentor, My only father – spoke to me. I suppose, thinking about it, they were the last words he spoke full stop. But I hope that, just this once, you will allow Me a degree of solipsism that I Myself would decry in other circumstances.

As he shuffled across the room in threadbare carpet slippers I dipped slightly and pulled the generously dimensioned marble ashtray with me, hefting it in my hand for a moment as I rejoiced that here at least was something as I remembered it, something real.

Gleefully, now, I swung the ashtray round above my head and, as Victor half turned – his left eye swivelling up like a cow's as the receptacle continued its journey – brought it down on his newly exposed temple. The crack as stone met bone sent a shiver through my privates, a cool string of my own spittle slapping on to my cheek.

Victor, to the last, confounded the clichés. He neither span off and down, crashing through furniture, nor continued as if nothing had happened for a moment before crumpling up. He moved from vertical to horizontal quietly and without showiness, as if he had lowered himself there, his only flamboyance the way he turned himself as he went down so that he faced me from the carpet, his right arm raised towards me, wrist uppermost, fist clenched. The ashtray, on the other hand, cracked in half – another shoddy fake.

I fell on to Victor, resentment and love exploding in my mind, and dug my thumbs hard into his Adam's apple, fingers tightening on his lapels so that, as I throttled him, his head could be beaten rhythmically on the floor. His eyes still seemed to be moving, following me without judgement, as his head clonked up and down. I took this as an encouragement, I suppose. I carried on long after his concentration drifted, eventually shifting back to the half-ashtray, pummelling him till his face was not just unrecognizable as his, but barely recognizable as a face; till his skull was rendered rhomboid, I, a cubist failing his practical.

Even then I was not satisfied. In my yearning for a greater meaning, for some symbolism, I grabbed at the humidor and began stuffing unlit cigars into the sad, swollen, tiny mouth perched on that monstrous head. The results were grotesque, the blood that welled from his throat and covered both him and me also quickly turned the Cubans faecal, giving him the appearance of a man gorging on his own waste matter. It took me years to recover from that moment, years in which I saw shit wherever I looked, everyday life one giant toilet pan.

This sobered me. I removed the offending objects, straightened his tie, even took his giant smoking-jacket from a chair and covered him with it. Thinking again, I resolved to disappear the body, leaving a convenient couple of corpses in his stead. It was very much the done thing in the early seventies.

The rest of the house was empty, though. Not empty in the way a house is when its occupants move out. There was no cracked paint, no clean wall or floor where furniture had stood. Every room was bright, white, perfect and clear, so that it felt that I was walking through a set for a dream sequence in a film. The light itself seemed to come from all over the ceilings rather than any discernible fitting, washing you with the intensity of a spring morning, though none of its warmth. Eventually, disorientated and sick, I found my way back to the corridor and from there to the old living room, even darker and dirtier, now, to the twin pinpoints of my eyes.

A search of the room revealed nothing, but search it I did, like an animal in a zoo, operating by instinct. The drawers were all empty, ditto the floor safe. Victor had never lived here, had left me nothing. I wanted to believe he had planned all this, right down to the instrument I had used to batter his head in, and that he would leave me some sign. Without that, what sense did it make? What sense did any of it make?

We all of us need to believe in something bigger, better and more beautiful than ourselves, even spooks, blackmailers and contract killers. It sounds trite but there you are. Life is trite. I am yet to find any evidence to contradict this assertion and, believe me, I have searched. It is not merely that we want to believe in that something but that we need to, and if this is trite too, so is what we actually find to believe in. If I had at least proved that Victor was not immortal I still wanted to believe he was omniscient. So I searched not just for money or files or letters but for meaning – meaning in the angle of a chair, meaning in that bright white empty house and that grubby, reduced front room. And I found none. Once again I thought that this, finally, must be his last act of treachery.

I had given up, given up everything, abandoned myself, when I saw the glint coming from his clenched hand, the one he had raised toward me. The tiniest hint of a chain protruded from the fat of his fist, a sign, a sign so blatant that I began to laugh and cry, both elated and ashamed of my doubt. With considerably more squeamishness than I had brought to Victor's murder, I broke his dead hand open.

The two keys were still warm, tiny and delicate, a buttery gold. I knew immediately which door they were for. How could I not? I myself had installed the locks out at sea only a month before. I myself had delivered these twin solutions to him. I kissed the tips of his mangled fingers, rocking with my devotions.

Then I left. After thirty years of meticulously covering my trail, disposing of evidence, manufacturing false leads, obfuscating, obscuring, complicating, I staggered through the front door dragging Victor's almost weightless corpse behind me, covered in his blood, red smears spiking my hair, sweat writing messages down my face. A middle-aged man – suit, glasses and fulsome moustache, every bit the respectable paterfamilias – crossed the road muttering disgust in my general direction. I think he took us for the hippies he had heard so much about. Beyond him, the way was empty, the yellow of the street lights dyeing Victor's juices almost black as I squeezed him into his Rolls and began the journey to Kent, thinking only of escape, just escape, the lights flashing across my face again and again, all movement looped.

I had almost reached my mooring before it finally registered that I had nowhere to go. Returning to the fort would be suicidal. Verna knew where I would go and I had no reason to believe that the cream of Barnums' security would not be waiting for me there. I set light to the car and rolled it over the edge of an unused dry dock, Victor finally leaving me, suitably, in a descending fireball (his resting place celebrated now by a colossal shopping centre, his ghost walking their brightly coloured galleries, his ashes folded into their walls, this Clearwater nothing but a temple to him). And then I was alone. Anchorless, I stole a new vehicle and returned to London to be lost.

Even back then, the biblical resonance was clear to me – washing blood from my hands surrounded by whores. Or was it Shakespeare? It hardly mattered. In the end, both were just words, while this was reality, the sink running red under the harsh light of the unsheathed bulb, the bedclothes still contorted from the previous occupancy. Shakily (a new sensation to me), I made my way back to the desk where I had been told I could use the telephone. A pound note was enough to ensure a little privacy, the door crone shuffling off to fix herself another drink, leaving a silence of muffled, distant moaning, the building slowly expiring with pleasure. And in this dark, damp corridor I finally, from memory, dialled her number, the digits an engraving across the inside of my skull.

'Yes?'

'It's me. It's done.'

A pause.

'James? I'm sorry, you woke me. It's late. What's the problem?'

'No problem. It's done. Dealt with.'

A pause, this time with her palm making a vacuum over the receiver, the ambience of the room closed out for one, two, three, four, five, six seconds.

'I'm sorry, James. What's dealt with?'

'Victor. Victor is dealt with.'

'Dealt with . . .? Dealt. Oh . . . my. My . . . G–'

Another pause, another slight squelch as her room was extinguished.

'I'm sorry, James. I'm sorry. This is so. I'm going to have to take this in another room. It's very. Do you want me to call you back? Can I call you back? Where are you? What . . .?'

I wanted to trust her, an odd, milky feeling bubbling up inside, but one that lapped harmlessly against the hard bulwark of all those years of caution.

'No locations. We speak now or not at all.'

'But James, I'm. This is. I'm *with* someone . . .'

'I don't care.' (But of course I did, the thought of her there with another human causing water to prickle in my eyes, nausea to sweep through me, my plan already crumbling.)

'. . .' She seemed to gather himself for a moment. Or give the impression of gathering herself for a moment. 'Where did you . . . I mean how? Where did you *deal* with it?'

'The house.'

'Which *house*? What do you mean *the house*?'

'The house. Where you live?'

'I'm sorry?'

'The house where you live. Lived. Where we met him that time?'

'Oh, Archley Square? Do you mean Archley Square? We never lived there.'

'Where he lived, then.'

'No. No, he never lived there . . .'

'I really cannot be bothered to debate it with you. That's where I did it.'

'All right, James. I'm sorry. It's just. I'm trying. Let's keep calm. It's important we all keep calm. Keep calm, darling. We. Where is he?'

'Kent. With the car. All tidied up.'

'OK. OK, my darling. You. You stay where you are. You must. We can. I'm sure. I'll get one of the girls to check things out and we can. We can work out the best way to. Proceed. OK? You just stay put. OK? I'll. Give me an hour and then call me. Call me at the office. I'm going to go there. I'll go there. Then call me. It will. Call me in an hour. We'll smooth this all over. OK, James?'

I suppose I knew what would follow – there was only one possible outcome, fated both by our natural mindsets and the way we had honed them in pursuit of our profession. I sat in that room smoking cigarettes as if each was my last, the light from the window an unchanging flash of red neon. If you had blocked my nose, I might have believed that I was on the set of a film. Unfortunately, I could smell all too vividly the damp in the walls, the sweat soaked into the bed, the decay. I went back to the lobby and requested the whore who should have arrived with the room, returned, smoked yet another cigarette.

She tapped her way in, her eyes impenetrable in darkest dark glasses, her hair, despite her youth, styled in the classic manner, a mould used after twenty-five years' neglect. She walked carefully, hands caressing the air with little wrist flicks, until her feet shuffled into contact with the bed, at which point she lowered a fulsome *derrière*, its shape stretching at the thin nylon gown in just the way intended.

'And what is it to be, my dahling?' The voice perfect, a cracked, tremulous received pronunciation with just the slightest edge of a less salubrious London upbringing echoing through. 'Fuck, suck or hand job?'

The dissonance between voice and words sent a spasm through my groin.

'I don't really do that. I have some time to kill. I thought we could chat.'

'You've got me all wrong, dahling. I don't chat. Chat doesn't pay the bills. We are not at a tea dance. Fuck, suck or hand job?' All the while examining something up in the corner of the room, her face never turned to me. My erection painful now, held out from me at an angle in a knot of underpants, I gasped to maintain my position.

'I'd really rather just chat . . .'

'A song, then. How about a song . . .? Yes, I think I know what would appeal. Close your eyes, my sweetheart. That's it, close your eyes and lie back.'

I did as I was told. What else was there to do? I knew, somehow, what was coming, felt it as she cleared her throat and then, reedily but with the slur I had so missed, launched into the tune.

> No *man is an island*
> *Oh yes, that's for sure*
> No *man is an island*
> *In times of war* . . .

It was not Verna, of course. The woman was too young, her face – despite the hair and the carefully applied make-up – all wrong. But as I lay there with my eyes screwed shut, my trousers and under-wear being gently pulled down, that voice enveloping me, her perfume mixing perfectly with her hair spray, it was. It really was. And, as I let her name, disguised in a groan, escape from my mouth, I felt cold thighs pressing hard on my pelvis, the warm, almost painful slide into her. I whimpered, hitting the high note at the close of the reprise.

'Verna,' writhing, a suffocating fish.

'I can feel the power in you. I can feel the power,' my genitals seemingly being pulled from my body.

'VERNA!' My hand reaching up to the wrong face, feeling her lips, her cheek and, beneath the glasses, the lid of her right eye.

'Oh, I can *feel* the power. I can *feel* it.'

And then it was over. As my legs went rigid and my toes splayed there was a hammering at the door, so that at the moment I released my load I also sat bolt upright, my hand accidentally hooking her shades and sending them clattering across the room. I do not know how long we stayed like that, face to face, her eyes spiralling wildly, independently, unseeing, her hands two crabs foraging over bed-clothes for specs. Not long I suppose, though in My mind it is an eternity.

'Call for you, sir.'

I left her, hair tilting slightly, crawling across the floor, her hand sweeping in front of her again and again and yet, somehow, her dignity still intact.

'James?' Verna's composure regained, she the caller now, I the called. 'Oh, James. You didn't tell me it was such a mess. What were you thinking of . . .?'

'It was complicated.'

'What do you expect me to say?' The sigh a rush of static on the line. 'We can't sweep this under the carpet. What possessed you? We can't pretend nothing has happened. We don't want to have to cut you loose, darling. We really don't. But we will have to. We all have to do what we have to do for the good of Barnums. You are no longer a part of the organization. We will . . .'

The words fading away as, with infinite care, I soundlessly lowered the receiver to the desk and retreated from the front door. I wanted to protest, to explain, to remind her who had led me to this, who had told me to do it, but my survival instincts counselled otherwise.

As the first sledgehammer blow sounded (exactly at the moment I had expected, the moment I had trained them to choose) I was already shutting the door of the room opposite and walking quickly past the couple on the bed. He, balding and coated in a gloss of sweat, stared at me, jowls quivering. She – dark glasses, hair similar, singing another show tune I knew the chorus to – continued to grind uninhibitedly (or unaware?) as I pulled back the curtain, lifted the sash and made my exit.

Why? you may be wondering. Why name this Divine Kingdom *Verna*land? Why give her a central role in a theology I could have made however I wished? Why so much love and veneration for the woman who betrayed Me? And let us be clear – she took me from

193

My home when I was removed from the fort and then tempted Me to kill My father so that she could exile Me from My family. Why, I repeat, *Verna*land?

These are the kind of questions common in modern, liberal religious debate and as such they have no purpose here. It is not for you to understand Me. You do not psychoanalyse your Messiah. We have seen where this kind of nonsense leads – the Twentieth Century. And no one wants to go back.

However, it happens that the question interests Me, so I will elucidate, though only to the extent and in the way that I see fit. Do not imagine that this sets a precedent of any sort, unless that precedent is simply that I do as I please and you go along with it.

So. First, there are excellent theological reasons for Verna's importance in all of this. As I have said, I am not a leading authority on world religions but they all seem to involve a female character of some sort who can be used to add a different emphasis, a sashay of femininity to the laying down of Law. It is a minor role, no doubt, but an important one. And yes, I am aware of My occasional prolix nature. It is the direct corollary of My years of isolation. It will be good to have a cool, soap-perfumed hand to touch Me on the shoulder now and then should the rhetoric become too fierce.

In addition, if Hollywood has taught us anything it is of the importance of the arc of a story. There has to be something to overcome, a challenge for the protagonist, pain and heartache and then transcendence. It goes back as far as Moses. Without it, the audience is lost. But throw in repentance and reconciliation and, in the words of King Vidor or some other ghastly man, that spells box office. And Verna will repent.

Then there are the more personal reasons. Verna is a truly unique creature. She is not like other women (and I mean this quite literally). She belongs to an era where people accepted the truly magical without question, where, for instance, a woman copulating with a wingéd bull would be offered understanding without question instead of being signed up by a newspaper in terminal circulation haemorrhage. She is an original, physically unique. She can have been put on this earth only to take part in myth, to play a role in creating Great Religion. It is absurd to imagine that the sum of her life would be a couple of wartime anthems, a number of years as a successful madam and a pioneering role in increasing labour-market mobility.

Furthermore, I believe that it was not her intention to betray Me, or to the extent that it was, it was done regretfully, with a woman's feeling for (but lack of understanding of) the Higher Purpose to come. It is possible that her aim was simply to test Me. And, if so, I have passed the test quite magnificently. I am, I must admit, even beginning to regret using the term 'betrayal'. Please try to remember the profession we two were engaged in, how high the stakes were. If anything, that was the moment when my feelings for her truly deepened, respect and admiration burnishing my lust.

And so we come to the most delicate reason of all. The most difficult one for Me to directly address. I love her. Absolutely. I believe our atoms to have come from the same experiment, or that we are one being halved, or that I am a shoe with sand in and she is the beach, or that when we finally copulate it will be like two black holes turning in on each other. If I could have continued photographing her having intercourse with important strangers until the end of My days, well then, perhaps none of this would have been necessary. Perhaps I would have died a contented man. Which, incidentally, I intend to do anyway.

So is this all we have, then? Another love story? No. Because when love and desire become so strong, in utter isolation from their subject, they transcend themselves and turn into something Other. There is no name for it any more. We used to call it Duty.

I am sure there were other reasons but they escape Me right now. Oh Verna, My Verna, come to Me here. The future demands it. And so do I.

From: 100001@hotmail.com
To: mandyhart200@hotmail.com

mand - so like i said i took this code from the security system at clear water. & i wanted 2 find out about this code. so i searched it. looked into it. had a rootle around. all the security system at clear water is from this company called barnums. & i found out all kindsa stuff about barnums. not good people 2 mess with. really not good. but i had 2 go & mess with them any way in it? coz that code was so beutiful. some people think the seas beutiful or girls. 4 me its code. & i cudnt keep my hands off of it. had 2 take it & pull it apart & play round with it. i had 2 make it in2 some thing else. just coz i cud. i know thats hard 4 u 2 understand. but its what i said 2 u be4. u just have 2. but i knew thered be after me. coz thats that kinda people. barnums people are that kinda people. very hot on protecting there property. 2 me whats code is every 1s. but not 2 them. so im waiting for them 2 make a move. may be therell offer me a job! binary rob

(Converted from the ASCII)

23

Peter Jones sits, washed in the blue light of his computer's Start Up screen, a supplicant. He watches with impatience, as he has done many times before – how can something so quick be so slow? Somehow he finds it in himself to be understanding. Icons pop up out of nowhere, stars in a darkening sky, and the machine settles into a steady whirr.

He goes straight to his email, rising from his chair to exit the room before the manic twittering and scrawl of static begins. He is infuriated by still being dial-up, uncomfortably aware that the failure to install broadband is due to the rapidly accelerating decline in his income. Leaving, he hears the data scream settle into a loop and, his shoulders effacing themselves, every last muscle in his body drooping, turns back.

'Fucking thing.'

Peter Jones is having a bad day, a bad week, in fact. A bad fortnight, actually.

First, there was the business with the car. Every time he went to Clearwater, he would be guided down and down to the lowest level and parked next to a defective lift which, without fail, would deposit him outside McDonald's on Aztec. All attempts to get the lift down to the hotel level ended in failure, a crowd of impatient shoppers gathering as smoothly as film extras, eventually forcing him to abandon and walk the best part of a mile through the busiest part of the whole centre to another elevator with less against him.

He sits down, waits for the beep, wearily reads the incomprehensible error message, reaches behind the machine with a long, wasted groan, flicks the modem on and off, begins again. Except this time he is going nowhere until the connection is right. Email is a compulsion rather than a service. He checks as often as he can, always hoping that this time his Inbox will contain an urgent, life-changing missive nestled between the offers of Viagra, kiddy porn, animal porn, bigger penis, unsecured loan. He has to wait and make sure the connection's right.

Next, there was the Sex Incident. Peter had been feeling guilty at his somewhat perfunctory performances in the various rooms of the Deep Rest Hotel, which, when he actually analysed it, could best be described as stick-it-in-and-come. So this time he had elected to end the relationship after having sex instead of before, which hadn't worked anyway. But not just any old sex. Peter planned to indulge her in sex at a higher level, to throw himself into lengthy foreplay, to take her to the Ten Realms of Clitoral Ecstasy (though he would never dream of admitting it, Peter is an avid consumer of women's magazines), to leave her gasping, sated, almost deranged with pleasure, lying on the devastated bed almost unable to speak and just grateful to have ever known him. And the plan had gone well, she seeming more animated, more lost in it (and certainly noisier, he distracted momentarily by the thought of a neighbour complaining, hotel staff hammering at the door). Until, that is, having finally locked genitals – she straddling him, head thrown back and in the last whimpering moments before coming – Peter found his body convulsing, his hips shooting upward in a huge, inappropriate thrust, she, her weight all wrong, beginning to topple and them both hitting the floor. Or rather, she hitting the floor and he landing on top of her, his testicles choosing that very moment to discharge. Which might have all been very funny if she hadn't clipped her head on the edge of the bedside table as she fell, if her eyes hadn't rolled round to reveal two expanses of bloodshot emptiness, if her hand, when he released it, hadn't flapped back to the floor like a steak dropped on to a butcher's board.

He thought he had killed her, was sure he had killed her. And in those brief moments before her eyelids flickered and her eyes refocused, he lay on her, paralysed, his tongue bigger and wetter than his dick, this lump of dead muscle blocking his throat, as below, the other organ shrank and slipped from her. Then that flutter and with it the thoughts of scandal, misunderstanding, trial, even prison, all of them coming rushing in. He had leapt from her, burnt. Ducked falteringly and, with an unforeseen degree of difficulty, manoeuvred her on to the bed, covering her at last as the direction came back into the flickering eyes.

'What happened?'

And here is the incomprehensible part, the part of the whole thing that really haunts him, even more than the fact that she's been a little more vacant ever since, a little distant. Although, yes, this bothers him, too, and he suspects they may be related, even if the small, private smile she wears suggests not. But nowhere near as much as remembering his response when, without hesitation, without thought almost, he had told her that she had passed out, had a fit of some sort, and fallen down unconscious. And she had believed him, or seemed to anyway. She had no reason not to. Seemed to find the whole incident amusing, or smiled a lot, at least, though with eyes narrowed by the pain tracing lines forward from the back of her skull.

This time the machine catches the other machine, they converse in their strange, speeded-up gibberish, come to an understanding and deign to let Peter in, patronizing him with a small message to that effect. He is grateful and irritated all at once, the awareness of the proximity of these two emotions creating a background hum of unease. The amount of time he spends working on computers has bred familiarity with this particular package of feelings, but no let-up in its strength. He clicks his Get Mail icon and heads to the kitchen for more tea.

Then, most recently, there was the little problem at reception. Peter had been making his furtive way back to the lift when a call of 'Mr Jones!' had caught him and twirled him before he had time to think. Carrying out a thorough internal chastisement, Peter had forced together a hastily assembled smile for the dark-suited man whose name tag, gently pushed forward by him himself, identified him as

Ed Sullivan – Security Manager, Barnums *for* Clearwater.

'Do you have a moment, sir? Would you mind stepping this way?' The questions purely rhetorical, like examples from a video for foreign-language students.

Peter had found himself sitting at a formica table in a bare room, the light as bright and unnaturally natural as ever, Mr Sullivan, no please, call me Ed, opposite him, his hands locked in the aleph of some secret sign language.

After a moment for quiet contemplation, Ed had begun.

'Before we commence this interview I must inform you that we tape all interviews for monitoring purposes. These tapes are used to ensure the quality of service we offer you, the Customer, during your time with us and may also be utilized in training to guarantee the future excellence of our services to you and all other Customers. The tapes are starting' – he had raised a finger above his head, held it a moment, then flicked it forward as if cueing in the string section – 'now.'

'Let me start by saying that we all hope you have enjoyed your Experience here today in our hotel and that you have enjoyed your previous Experiences here with us. There is, however, a discrepancy which we need to clear up.

'Could you confirm, for the record, that your name is Peter Huw with a W Jones?'

'Er, yes, it is.'

'And you are the registered owner of a silver 2000 Volkswagen Beetle, registration number W332 TXR?'

'Yes. And I can actually explain . . .'

The security manager's silently raised hand brooked no further argument.

'Do you have on your person any identification that might establish beyond reasonable doubt that you are who you say you are?'

'I assure you, this is all a misunderstanding . . .'

'I'm very sorry to have to hurry you, sir, but we here at Clearwater deal with over 200,000 individual Experiences a day. Do you have on your person any identification that might establish beyond reasonable doubt that you are who you say you are? We value your custom and want to, as far as possible, prevent this from becoming a police matter.'

His hands shaking, Peter had slid his driving licence over the table top, watched Ed scrutinize it – affably but thoroughly – then look up, wearing the same detached, satisfied smile as her.

'That all seems to be in order. With your permission, we would like to take a copy for our files in order to prevent any future misunderstanding.'

Peter barely nodded in reply, certainly didn't look up, before another suited minion removed the document. He and Ed just sat in silence, one watching the other feign an examination of the table's surface.

'This is something to do with the accident, isn't it? It was just an accident. No one was even hurt.'

Ed sat opposite him, that slight smile, his expression quizzical.

'Please, you have to understand . . .' his words stopped again by the man's raised hand.

'Mr Jones, Clearwater are outcome neutral concerning your activities in your hotel room. I assure you there's nothing you can do in there that hasn't been done before and very little that won't work out to our commercial advantage. But we like to know who our customers are. You have been signing into our hotel for weeks now as Mr Smith, for the most part paying in cash, yet driving on to our premises in a car registered to Peter H. Jones. Now, I could tell you that we are concerned about terrorism, which of course we are, but I can see you're not a terrorist, just an intelligent man. A journalist, perhaps?' He allowed himself a laugh, no humour in it, but no malice either. 'Of course, I already knew that. Which is my point. We like to know all about who our customers are. The more we know about you, the easier it is to serve you, to enrich your Experience with us, to remove what you don't want and add more of what you do want. Knowledge is the power to serve you better. Do I make myself clear?'

Behind Peter, the door clicked, a hand sliding his licence back on to the table, Ed nudging it toward him.

'So now that everyone is clear about the situation – who we are, what we're all trying to do – we can carry on as if nothing has happened. You can sign into the hotel under whatever name you like, Mr Jones. Nothing incriminating will show up on our invoicing system or hotel records. As long as we know, everyone is happy.'

It's there, just beneath the mail from his mother. Peter hardly dares click on it.

Name: Leah Barley
Subject: Re: Book Proposal.

Peter feels ill, just a little ill.

He despises himself for contacting Leah Barley. He has known her – known of her – since college, when the two of them had found themselves sharing a tutorial on Women in 19th-Century English Literature and the don had been exasperated in equal measure by the half-read lumps of post-Structuralist theory Peter vomited out and the whimsical potted biographies Leah had offered in place of textual analysis. They both ended up with thirds. Peter's result was, in his own mind at least, either a reflection of the effort expended on his glamorous extra-curricular activities or his principled refusal to bow to the traditionalist conservative orthodoxy prevalent amongst his markers. Leah's result was, in Peter's own mind at least, because she was as thick as pigshit.

She got a job at a suitably stodgy publisher, where she fell into an editorial position and caused outrage by commissioning their best-selling 'Where's My Willy?' range. Bought out by a major conglomerate, Leah was promoted to an executive role where she showed a talent for sacking excess staff and drove the list relent-lessly downmarket, in the process turning a profit for the first time in a decade.

Then, just as her reputation was becoming a cliché, she had quit to become an agent, signing as her first client a heavyweight novel-ist who had just moved to New York and discovered that his teeth were repulsive to Americans. Still a great believer in the biographi-cal reading of literature, she had counselled the author to channel these experiences into his new book, *Dentifrice*, which she promptly sold for a cool million, so that when the writer smiled his new, triumphant grin on collecting his Booker, the nearest audience members reported being subject to a temporary blindness.

Newspapers now, as a matter of course, preface her name with the words 'über agent' but when Peter had rung he had been put straight through; she remembered him, knew his writing and couldn't wait to see his proposal, no, no, don't pitch it to me now, I want to be surprised. Then two weeks of silence, his email checks taking on a renewed urgency. Until now. He double-clicks on the name.

'Daddy?' Gus nudges into the doorway. 'Can you come and play?'

He is cured. Miraculously. After all the expensive therapies and guilt-shadowed consultations, he had chosen, for no clear reason and under no compunction, to return to speech. The word – his *word* – gone now, replaced by a torrent of others, the questions coming in thick clumps, the stories he tells Poppy stringing along to fill the available space, spilling over, bubbling out. Peter has told no one, has tried to keep it even from himself: he misses him, the warm reassurance of his singular vocabulary.

'Sorry Gus. I'm working right now. After tea, OK?'

The boy stays in the door way, not quite ready to give it up.

'Dad . . .?'

'Yes, love?'

'Why aren't there dragons any more?'

'I don't know. I don't think there ever were.'

'There were.'

'Well, I think they're just something in stories . . .'

'They're not.'

'Then why ask? If you already know? I'm sorry, but I really do have to get on now.'

With a huff he turns and retreats to his own bedroom, whatever he had planned trailing behind him.

Hi Peter –
Thank you so much for letting me take a look at your proposal. It's beautifully written and insightful and I am sure it would have been a really fantastic, important book.

Unfortunately, I have to be the one to tell you that Scripture are publishing *Glaucous Gleam* by Daniel Mercurine next month, which uses the Clearwater shopping centre as a central strand in its narrative and which touches on many of the themes you have laid out in your proposal.

I am not of the belief that the market can support two such titles, so I am afraid I will have to pass at this time. I do hope you have not expended too much time and effort on the proposal. Please feel free to call me if you need any further clarification.

Leah

Peter can't move. He's suffocating. His eyes flip back and back over the text searching for a clue that it's a joke, desperate for any ambiguity. It is beautifully, deadeningly closed. He knows of Daniel Mercurine, has seen him in the culture section of the paper he writes for, an academic in trainers. The cunt. The cunt has stolen his idea.

'Hi, Peter.' The voice cold, evasive. 'I didn't expect to hear from you so quickly.'

'Well, I just wanted to clarify a few of the themes from my proposal. Set it out a little more clearly. If you have a moment?'

'You have had my email, Peter . . .?'

'Oh, that? Yeah, thanks for that. I just wanted to say that, I mean obviously Daniel's work is great and I'm an admirer and everything, but I think you'll find what I'm proposing is a little less theoretical, a little less highbrow. It's really going to be driven by the story rather than dry critical theory . . .'

'Sorry, Peter, I've read Daniel's book and it's certainly not dry. Any theory in it comes from the story. It's like a *Longitude* of shopping.'

'Well, it's almost like he's stolen my idea somehow. I mean, how else . . .'

'He was there nine years ago when they started the excavations. The book opens with this terrifying description of descending into the darkness in this . . . cage filled with ex-miners. All UDM members, too. No NUM allowed. It's scintillating – like Orwell crossed with Barthes and Bill Bryson.'

'This isn't an idea I just dreamt up, you know. I have been thinking about this, talking to people about this for years. Practically since I left college . . .'

'Well, I'd think very hard before throwing around accusations of plagiarism, Peter. I have to say, I'm amazed you haven't heard about it. He was in *Esquire* back in January in their Dr Feelgood feature on sexy academics and he talked all about it. I do hope something hasn't fed through to you subliminally. Are you sure you didn't see it? It's got Clover McMurty on the cover in that new Alexander McQueen lingerie.'

'You're his agent, aren't you?'

'I always strive to give the best representation to the best.'

'Thank you, Leah. I'll let you go now.'

He lets the phone fall heavily into its cradle and turns, weighted with fear, to the pile of magazines stacked by his desk.

There is always a large-breasted starlet ready to promote her latest self-referential horror flick, even in a territory as insignificant as the UK. Still, he doesn't have to dig deep to find the particular harbinger of this new nightmare, her nipples taped out rather than down, the airbrushing more vivid than reality. He checks the index and flicks through to the relevant page. It shows all the smudged signs of being read, the picture now the one he thought he'd seen in the paper, the text suddenly familiar. The magazine flaps and flips to the ground like a dead bird, its final flight ended amid the unopened envelopes of the bills and statements and final demands Martha knows nothing about.

He has to end it. He has to finish with the girl now.

From: 100001@hotmail.com
To: mandyhart200@hotmail.com

mand - & thanks 2 all that 2 all that stuff i told u theres him. king james! man friday more like. i think he thinks im his man friday. but hes my man friday. hes a bit back wud like that. i mean hes a miracle when u think about it. that he thinks at all. but a bit back wud. binary rob.

(Converted from the ASCII)

24

'I'll get a lager, please. And a whisky. With ice. A double.'

The boy just looks at him, taut with discomfort, his long, stooping frame a collection of tent poles put together wrong.

'We've only got tea,' he finally manages. 'Or Pimms.'

'Pimms then, please. In a pint glass. No bits.' As jovially as he can, turning back towards the recently introduced head of some committee or other. 'Never could stand all the bits.'

O deploys his most natural, relaxed laugh and focuses in on their host.

'You'll have to excuse Jim. His sense of humour is somewhat eccentric.'

'It's a pleasure to have him.' Turning. 'You're something of a hero of mine. Spin it a little myself. That 5 for 32 you took at the Oval. I was there. Marvellous stuff.'

'Can I smoke in here?'

'Of course. May I introduce you to my wife and the rest of the board?'

Jimmy inhales deeply, all the sound into the room being sucked into the crackle of tobacco.

'I need to prepare for the match. After. We can talk after. Pleasure. Where's that Pimms?'

He sits in his pants feeling drained by his perfunctory warm-up, another cigarette dangling from his mouth, and examines himself in the smudged mirror opposite. The thick black hair which used to cover his legs has gone from his ankles, the skin left looking shiny and stretched. He has a couple of ugly-looking, blistery spots where his irregularly washed trousers rub on the inside of his upper thighs. His arms look blotchy. His stomach rings him in a layer of self that isn't there in his mind. His silver chain nestles now in silver hair, squeezed into a trickle between the meat of his breasts.

Unleashing the cloud of smoke stored deep in his lungs, he pulls on the shirt and buttons, straightening up and working his right shoulder in small circles. Reaches down, hooks the trousers over his feet and tugs them up in a series of twitches. Totters upward and pulls as he moves foot to foot. Zips and buttons, the waistband cutting into him till he pushes it down under his belly. Right sock, left sock, right boot, left boot, it has always been this way, the rhythm of it surprisingly easy to recapture. Perhaps the smell in here helps – he'd never realized he had missed the smell. All the same, there is no need to be over eager. He is not on trial. He has nothing to prove. He leans back against the breezeblock wall, his clothes scattered around him, his bright white presence stretched out before him, and lights another cigarette.

'So what we thought was that the rest of the team could take the field, the batsmen could come out, they can play the first ten overs and then we would announce you on the public-address system and you could run out, give the crowd a wave and bowl your overs. How does that seem? We don't expect you to field . . .'

Jimmy has the cricket ball in his hand, is feeling the weight of it, its satisfying heaviness, the way the seam locks with his fingerprints, how it feels as he pops it from between his fingers with a twist, how it lands again, gently grazing his palm. He repeats and repeats, feeling the beat of it returning first to his hand, warming his arm, heading to his stomach.

'So, er, how does that seem?'

Trying to keep it there, to keep it growing.

'Fine. Fine. Whatever you think's best.'

'OK, Jim?' O's voice, just behind him, no real question in his tone.

Just keeping the ball turning, feeling for it.

He can't decide whether the applause is hesitant because he looks like shit or because nobody has any idea who he is. He opts to ignore the question. Elects, too, to avoid jogging, just trundles out smiling with a half-wave aimed up at the sky back beyond the pavilion. His new team mates do that special kind of cricket applause, elbows jutting, faces intent with the effort of making each contact as loud as possible, that desperate attempt to feel truly involved, part of the team. Jimmy smacks his hands together once, rubs them hard and fast against one another (a villain dreaming of his victim's riches), wipes each fastidiously down their side of his trousers, then raises both them and his eyebrows in request for the ball.

Despite machines, no two cricket balls are exactly the same, Jimmy thinks, especially once they've been hit. As he rolls up to the stumps and begins pacing back, still nodding good-humouredly at his new team mates, he tosses the ball around in his hand, runs his finger gently along the seam, holds it and shakes his wrist, searching for its differences, for the differences that will help him. He turns and allows himself to examine the batsman – another child, much like the one who had served him Pimms, or more accurately like the one who bullies the one who served him Pimms. The cocky fuck taps hard earth then pulls the bat up behind his head like it's baseball, taps and up, again and again, seeing Jimmy looking and sending him a stare with no recognition in it. It will be a pleasure to bowl him.

When it comes to it, though, he remembers that he is a professional – even now, when he isn't being paid. So he stands there, at the end of his run-up, silent and still, after the umpire's arm drops, emptying thought from his head, focusing solely on the hard globe of leather linking his hands. This is the best moment – all possibilities open, every delivery perfect. Up on to the balls of his feet, he hangs for a moment, then leans slightly forward, starting his gentle run as he begins to fall. As he takes the five curving, half-jogged steps back to the stumps he finalizes the grip of his right hand on the ball, the left shielding it like the answers to a test. And as his arm goes back and then over, he realizes that he has decided to show this over-muscled teen, in fact to show all of them, to show O in particular, that he is worthy of respect. He finds himself, teeth suddenly gritted, trying to fizz the ball from between his fingers, to send it down there spinning like a gyroscope. To show them what class means.

And inevitably, horribly, it slips loose from digits grown weak, loops off at entirely the wrong trajectory, covering the distance between wickets too slowly, painfully sailing past the kid's left shoulder, his bat whistling through the air beneath its path, before flopping, momentum spent, at the feet of the wicket-keeper. Jimmy stands, hands on hips, shoulders lowered and feels himself sink into the silence around him. Somewhere, maybe miles away, a bird is singing, probably to some purpose.

'Balluck!' One of his team tries, over-enthusiastically, to rescue the situation, his rising intonation almost strangled by his lack of conviction. Jimmy stands absolutely still and looks at the ground for a moment, a true pro going through the agony moves. It would never do to look as if he didn't care. And the truth is he does care.

Trudging back to his mark he realizes he forgot to make a mark. Feeling very tired, he turns, receives the ball, returns to the wicket and paces out his run-up once more. This time he strips it down to absolute basics, pushed through faster, a difficult length to play, straight on the off stump. It's a coward's choice, he knows, particularly by his own long-abandoned standards, but he's not feeling too clever, the coffee bubbling with the Pimms in the cauldron of his stomach, his right eyelid twitching out suggestive semaphore and the dull inner ache in his shoulder already starting to tear out to his skin and down his ribs. The kid surprises him by patting it down guardedly.

His team and the crowd applaud too loud, as if they're more relieved than he is. Which is when the full humiliation of that first ball reaches him – a message from a distant galaxy where his guts seem momentarily to wish to return. Then it's time to throw down the next – a looser, slightly distracted version of the last which just drifts slightly at the last so that the youngster's imagined sweet, hard drive turns into a scuffed, messy swipe, the ball trundling out to a fielder who gathers it clumsily and returns it girlishly. The next ball – still more banal – he is not so lucky and the kid runs through for a single. Which is when he sees him, facing him from the crease.

Except for the small matter of skin and hair colour, it could be Jim himself staring back – a sweating, overweight disaster of a man, still breathing hard from the thigh-chafing scuttle between wickets, thin grey hair running in rivulets from his crown, his face swollen and blotchy with drink-ooze from the night before. It's one thing to be hit by a kid who doesn't know any better and quite another to be hit by a middle-aged drunk who in twenty-five years of playing has never made it out of the pub team. Authority now has to be asserted.

So Jimmy waits a moment longer before shambling in, picturing the ball coming from his fingers as hot and fast as a planet, until his mind is as empty as space. He skips the few steps suddenly unaware of his weight, his wasted muscle, and twists it, the ball looping up high, slow, perfect, the seam a blurred band of solid colour. He smiles as he watches its slight ascent, the way it seems to sit a moment, its unreadable descent.

Then sees the drunk's speeded shuffle forward, his bat coming down and then up in a wild, uncontrolled arc, making contact with his beautiful ball and smashing it up and away, the steep curve left of its path all there is for Jim to see of his artistry. If he looked up, that is. He stands transfixed at the moment of contact by the batsman's face – a grimace of teeth and wet eyes creased shut. Roused by vigorous applause, the spinner retreats past the umpire's double point heavenward, defeated. Behind him the batsmen come together, their sausage-fingered fists bumping in a show of respect which, to Jimmy as he turns, has everything to do with everything but each other.

It finishes there. He bowls the next ball and then, after a break out on a distant boundary, another over. He gives away some runs, takes the wicket of the drunk (more thanks to his opponent's incompetence than anything he did) and would have had the kid, too, if the wicket-keeper were consistently capable of catching the ball. But it doesn't matter. He had found himself momentarily seduced, lost in it again, but now it's shut off for ever – a series of meaningless, pointless, unnatural actions of no worth. He feels light, still, but hollow, eggshell brittle. He comes off smiling, absent from the applause, beyond interaction, heading straight for the bar.

'A lager, please. And a whisky. A double.' This time they serve him.

Spirits drained, beer splashing cool and sticky on to his hand, Jimmy semi-limps toward the dressing room, pushing through the door with pluming cigarette hand, the smell of his acrid sweat hitting and then mingling with the years of bodily excretion that have gone before, as if large rodents have been urinating on piles of already damp straw. He slumps down to a bench, placing the pint beside him so that he can peck impatiently and ineffectively at his laces, eventually abandoning the effort to devote his attentions to finishing the cigarette.

There's a noise like a knock at the door and a head pokes through, smiling and nervy.

'May I come in?'

'Not doing autographs yet . . .'

'Ah, wasn't actually . . .' His voice trailing away without the rest of him following. The rest of him, in fact, still very much there and demanding a response.

'Can't stop you, can I?'

Slacks and a shirt, a little too tucked in to look comfortable, hair thinning on top of the round, well-shaven face. He smiles like they all do and offers his hand.

'Good to see you out there again. Been too long.'

Jimmy can genuinely think of nothing to say to this, not even anything dismissive, so he just shakes the hand without enthusiasm and blows smoke through his nostrils, blank.

'It's Mark Lanark.' Another name for Jim to ignore. 'We spoke this morning.' Still nothing. 'I work for Barnums Futurestat Limited.'

Jim coughs a clouded laugh. 'Wasted your day.'

'Not wasted. I got to see you play again. And I really think we need to talk.'

'Doubt it.'

'I'm trying to help you here, Jimmy. Can I call you Jimmy?'

'Nothing to stop you.'

'I'm an admirer of yours. There are certain issues, quite sensitive issues. If you'll just hear me out I think you'll be interested. I think you'll be very interested.'

'I'm not interested.'

'Jimmy, please believe me. I'm not trying to set you up. Far from it. I'm not trying to be funny. All I'm saying is that I need to talk to you. And when you've heard what I've got to tell you, I'm willing to bet you'll want to talk to me.'

'Why do you mention betting?'

'I'm sorry?'

'Why betting?'

'It's a figure of speech. It's just a figure of speech, Jimmy.'

Jim leans his head back against the cool wall and, reaching his lips forward for the sticky fizz, lifts his pint. Replacing the glass with studied care in the ring it left, he raises his eyes to the guy, whoever he is, now sitting on the bench opposite, feet apart, elbows to knees, his eyes flickering between Jimmy and the door. He looks down at his briefcase, side on next to him on the bench, glances up at Jim, back down at it. Adjusts its position slightly.

'Go on then. Better be good now.'

The other man leans back smiling. Still keen to make sure they're alone, though.

'Why do you think you never played for England?'

Jimmy's shoulders bounce into a tired laugh. 'I thought I just had to listen and then decide whether I was interested?'

'That was a little misleading. Why do you think, though?'

'Maybe I wasn't good enough.'

'C'mon, Jim. If I'm not being too familiar? Neither of us believe that, do we? The year you became eligible you were third in the averages and way ahead of any other spinner. And you could bat a bit. Why do you think you weren't picked?'

'This isn't really what you want to talk about, is it? Why don't you just tell me what you're really here to talk about?'

'This *is* what I'm really here to talk about. What else would I be here to talk about? As I said, I've always been an admirer of yours as a player. And it always frustrated me that you weren't picked for England. Now I have a much clearer idea of exactly why.'

'What do you need me for, then?'

He manages to look disappointed, but eager to get on. Jimmy, by contrast, just tries to keep his face still, tries to keep the fear hidden.

'Jimmy, one last time, I'm not here to stitch you up. I think I know why you were never selected for England. If you're looking for the stitch-up, you should try Jonathan Greenacre.'

'What's he said?'

'He's not said anything now. It's what he did say.'

'What did he say?'

'I got the minutes from the selection committee for the '86 Ashes tour. They were thinking about you. Seriously thinking. So they asked your captain, your old friend Jonathan . . .'

'He was never my friend . . .'

'They asked him and he strongly advised, that's a direct quote, strongly advised against your inclusion on the grounds of suspect character. And that's another direct quote.'

'So there you go then. There's your answer. What do you need me for?'

'Well, it seems a little odd as a statement, don't you think?'

'You know what you want – why don't you just say it?'

'I want to know if you think he had any reason to impugn your good character.'

'Yes, he had reason. We knew each other for years. No one's perfect.' He raises his pint, bobbing it in the direction of his interrogator. 'Now, if that's it, I'd like to get changed.'

'I'm afraid that's not it, though, Jimmy. Is it?'

'If you haven't got anything else to tell me, I'd rather you just went.'

'That's only just the start of it, isn't it? I'm meeting with Greenacre tomorrow. I'm sure he'll be happy to put his side of the story.'

'Oh, I'm sure he will.'

'I'm really not trying to stitch you up. Quite the opposite. But you have to help me to help you.'

'Just go.'

'I can't see what you've got to lose . . .'

'Do you know what Jonathan used to do . . .?'

'I don't really know very much at all about Greenacre. But I do know you were both throwing matches at the time. And not just the two of you, either.'

'I'm sorry?' The best Jimmy can manage.

'You were throwing matches. For money, I presume.'

'And what is this . . . this story based on?'

'Like I said, I'm a cricket fan. But I work for a company called Barnums Futurestat Limited. We specialize in database analysis and forecasts – crime trends, shopping patterns, that sort of thing. We were approached to tender for work with the ICC's Anti-Corruption & Security Unit. They were meant to be investigating match-fixing. But that just meant pressuring the very few cricketers who admitted to anything to shop their team mates. It's just a lot of bullying for very little result. So we were brought in to provide an information-technology edge to proceedings.'

'I've got no idea . . .' The other's hand finishing the sentence.

'So we built a database from *Wisden*. Or rather I did. It's perfect for this sort of thing – a closed system, detailed statistical records. And once I'd put everything in, I began to notice these incredibly strong player patterns. Much steadier than you would imagine. A really beautiful discovery in its own way – as if there's some internal rhythm to how a person plays the game.' A mock-wistful pause for effect. 'Except for the aberrations.' His voice assumes the scripted surprise of a continuity announcer. 'Inexplicable. Just something to mess up the graph. Imagine my disappointment. Until I compared them with matches which it had been alleged were thrown.'

'Anyone can have a bad day.'

'True. But it's surprisingly rare to find more than three players having one of these aberrant days. And you find at least three in every game which is known to have been thrown. So I went through the County Cricket records for the eighties, when people believe this kind of thing might have been going on and whaddaya-know, Jimmy, you and Greenacre and the rest popped up . . .'

'It doesn't prove anything. Cricket's an unpredictable game.'

'Not as unpredictable as you might think. Try not to worry, though . . .'

The door clicks and O appears wearing his hard smile, his voice crackling with deliberately half-suppressed irritation.

'Everything OK, Jim? This gentleman bothering you?'

'This gentleman is from the ICC. Or works for them, anyway. He's trying to help me,' the sarcasm coming wrong, sounding desperate.

'Oh, what an honour, Jim. Still, a man has a right to get changed in peace, doesn't he?'

'I really . . .'

O raises a hand to silence him. 'I think you and I should go and get a drink while Jim gets cleaned up, don't you?'

'Well,' the boffin trying to catch Jimmy's downturned eyes, 'I'm sure that would be a pleasure. And you are?'

'I suppose I'm sort of an informal manager, aren't I, Jim? Do you have a card? And what, as the saying goes, is your poison?'

'Jimmy? If I could have a moment more? I think it might be sensible . . .?'

Jim keeps his eyes on the floor, leans right forward and keeps his eyes on the floor there. Lanark sits for a moment. Rises, his briefcase held at a slant and, with O's hand on his shoulder, makes his way to the door, the antagonism amiable. Obviously for Jim's benefit, cut free from any other possible meaning. He devotes himself to finishing his drink, then, gripped by a desperate tiredness, reties his laces, rises and follows them out.

They are at the bar, drinks already in hand like props in a photo shoot, their faces working through an unreadable series of meanings from an urbane private language. The air around Jim feels fragile so he moves through it towards them as unassumingly as he can. They see his approach, turn in concert, O's hand outstretched with a double. The noise in the room breaks over him as he takes the glass, downs it. He almost shouts above it.

'Left something in the car. Can I get the keys?'

O treats him to another glance from his repertoire – a second take sublimated into an enquiry – but is perhaps too concerned by what a direct question may elicit actually to ask it. Instead, he reaches into his pocket, his eyes holding absolutely firm on Jim as the latter's in turn dip to follow the hand.

The car moves more sharply than he had expected, the sudden leap forward nearly terminating the journey on a bollard. But Jim spins the wheel, pushes hard on the accelerator, sweeps through the gateway and away, away down to the road.

From: 100001@hotmail.com
To: mandyhart200@hotmail.com

mand - i dont intend to leave any thing of mine behind. least of all him. maybe now its time to reach for the off switch. do u see what im saying? coz i aint expecting any thing good from barnums. not really. i dont think therell be offering me a job. i dont think thats there style. i think its more like ending up back in court. & we both know what that means. & thats probaly at best. so id prefer to really get lost. i mean really lost. gone. binary rob

(Converted from the ASCII)

25

The secret to a successful, long-term disappearance is to see it not as an effacement of one's personality but a chance to invent a new one, unburdened by history and coincidence. It is, in effect, to become a superior being, whose every thought and action is chosen, rather than the only possible outcome of the set of circumstances known as one's life. It is to transcend, to fly.

This is what I told myself as I headed north. Whatever it was that had grown up inside me wanted to come out now. Victor had always prohibited facial hair. As my first, tiny, conscious act of defiance, I elected to grow a moustache. A big one, a curly, Victorian affair, all wax and gumption, an unignorable affront to public taste. To deliberately refuse to hide was the best way to hide, to stand out in a crowd. And so I continued north until I reached Edinburgh, where I stopped.

This was unplanned, part of no strategy. It just felt right. Not the town itself, a horrible, dour little hole, mile upon mile of shit-brown stone laid out glistening beneath a rain-heavy sky. Certainly not the people who inhabited the town, a cavalcade of rotting teeth leering from misshapen heads, nary a smile between them. No, only in terms of my flight from those I knew would pursue me did it meet my requirements. The agents that Barnums despatched to find me would head to Kent first and by the time they thought to try anywhere else I would have changed reality so thoroughly that, in a very real sense, I would no longer exist. I won't lie to you, have in fact promised not to lie to you. That is not quite how it worked.

I made for the newest estate in the newest suburb I could find. Don't ask me for its name. On leaving – a lifetime later it seemed – I vowed to forget that particular grouping of letters, to delete them completely from my memory – their size, their shape, the way they felt in my mouth. Above all, of course, I wanted to escape the dread and self-loathing that I believe the place engendered not just in me but in all the inhabitants of that strip of land between the grey and the green. But the feelings clung to me, like the smell of the place in my clothes, right up until the very moment of my Messianic Epiphany, when I was washed afresh, rendered as a newborn babe, brought unto Myself as I truly Was. All that malarkey. But once again, I get ahead of Myself, time and the demands of linearity barely able to contain My divine force.

(This is a problem in general, frankly. The sooner I have a proper retinue of disciples to take care of the manifold details of My Coming, the better. I am so run off My feet organizing the delivery of this or that, arranging press interviews, translating the increasingly demented ASCII-encoded emails Robert insists on sending Me plus one hundred other seemingly insignificant tasks that sometimes it is hard to focus on the big picture. Which, I am sure you will agree, is more than just problematic when one's aim is to free this island people from the tedious detail of everyday life and show them once more that selfsame big picture one is struggling to keep in mind.)

I walked into a library to find a wife. I needed cover and I thought that here I could source myself a nice, mousy, tweedy, short-sighted spinster who would be bowled over by my dashing looks and authoritarian manner. Instead I found Janey. She was young enough to make me nervous, all blue jeans and cheesecloth, her hair deliberately teased into a haystack motif. I had neither the time nor inclination to assess whether she was wearing a bra, but as a lady whom I would discover to be of a startlingly literal nature, I suspect that she might actually have burnt it. And, like most idealistic young people, she was not very clever. Sensing that I was 'not her type' I quickly concocted a story about being a fugitive Yippie on the run from the FBI. Though in reality I was too old and certainly too English to be any such thing, the poor girl bought into this improvised fantasy with such gusto that for weeks after she would leave the house only in dark glasses and, from that day forward, besuited men flicking idly through the Crime section were given the kind of welcome previously reserved for the type of elderly gent with a penchant for the children's corner and cutting holes in the bottom of his trouser pockets. That is to say that, brilliantly, with barely a thought, I found the hole in her life and filled it – snugly, perfectly – with a simple lie. It was meant to be.

Her house, like all the others, was like all the others, its basic sameness highlighted by the half-hearted attempts at individuation. As I walked through her door, grimly fending off her thoughts and theories on feminism and the counter-culture, I felt a dread sliver of despair chill me. I had been betrayed and this was where it had led me. I sank to the ground and buried my face in the patterns of the carpet. I was soon to find out that this was a ritual of the Hopi Indians upon entering a friendly dwelling. Janey was suitably impressed.

And so my new life – my un-life – began. Janey would wake me daily to the thick, sweet smell of incense, guaranteed to send me staggering gagging to the bathroom. We would breakfast on some kind of compacted cereal product that she travelled to central Edinburgh to buy at the city's sole wholefood store. Only after she had left the house could I return the Barleycup to the cupboard and, carefully removing a jar of instant from its hiding place, make myself coffee. How did this apparent exotic end up here, in a modern house on a modern estate in Edinburgh's newest annexe? All fads start and end in the suburbs, however radical they may appear. Janey's parents, it transpired, had bought the house for themselves, just weeks before dying of food poisoning on their very first foreign holiday, the odds of coming across a radical separatist Basque chef on the day he finally cracked stretching credibility beyond its limit.

Janey, with no other family, few friends and certainly no connection to the political and cultural underground she was so fond of reading about, had just stayed. And she loved to read! Her hunger for the printed word was, I would say, one of the few genuine, unaffected aspects of her character (which placed her a step above the vast majority of humanity). Even when not reading, her right hand would always be attached to a book, her index finger squashed between the pages as a bookmark, so ever present it came to look less like a book and more like an accessorizable deformity. Yes, it was degenerate and self-pleasuring and, frankly, boring, but at least she had an interest. Which left her less time to irritate me.

Gradually, with the kind of careful attention to detail that I would previously have lavished only on death threats, I began changing her. I pointed out again and again that we were too conspicuous, our Alternative Lifestyle bound to bring the forces of the State Oppression to the door, that her insistence on eating health food and wearing ethnic prints directly jeopardized my continuing liberty. Soon steak was back on the menu. A tweed suit was worked into her wardrobe, then given primacy. A warning that I was sure I was being followed encouraged a new, severe, pulled-back hairstyle. The final blow was struck with the news, delivered *sotto voce* on a park bench one lunchtime, that her house was being bugged. All the prating was finally expunged and my life regained a semblance of normality. It is worth noting here that it was the belief that she was being watched rather than any actual watching which was alone enough to alter Janey's behaviour completely. She coped well with the changes, grew into her new role. If the truth be known, I think she was looking for someone to rescue her from the times she found herself in and her own weakness in succumbing to their idiocies. We were married two months later.

And so my life dragged on. I needed to earn a living so I demeaned myself around the council estates of Craigmillar and Muirhead, collecting money for local thugs. Unsurprisingly, I excelled at the work and, if it had not been for my need to maintain a low profile of sorts I would have been running their operations within a matter of months. (It is a complicated science, this business of conspicuous inconspicuousness and inconspicuous conspicuousness. Perhaps after My Accession I will devote some time to a study of the field.) As it was, I soon found I had to devote more time to not collecting money than to collecting it. My moustachioed features were rightly feared in those mean, terraced streets and the sight of me promenading down any particular turning was enough to bring even those with no debt rushing furtively from their doorways to force upon me whatever cash they could muster.

Maybe that was the problem. If I had lived in greater fear of being caught by Barnums' agents or whoever Verna was working for, if it had been less easy to find an alternative arena for my unique range of professional skills, if my wife had proved less malleable, if even one of these were the case, perhaps my thoughts would never have turned to siring a dynasty. There is no such thing as good luck – only bad luck and bad luck waiting to happen.

I have already written of the many disappointments, disillusionments and embarrassments visited upon me by my son. What I have not yet imparted is how they started at his birth. Summoned to the hospital the day after his arrival, I informed my wife and a passing nurse that his name would be James. The nurse, her face collapsing inward in the Scots way from too many sweets, struck a smile of sorts.

'Oh, Jamie, is it? That's a lovely name for a little boy. Hello, Jamie.'

She did not know what she had done, of course, but when I looked down, it was no longer my James that I saw in my arms, but *Jamie* – a flighty, diffident child, already prone to introspection and singularly lacking in co-ordination. *Jamie*. Not Jimmy, as you would have imagined, which though vulgar, at least has a certain virile roguishness to it. *Jamie*. And Jamie it stayed – from his mother, his mother's colleagues, the staff at his crèche, to his teachers, his snot-nosed friends, his social worker and on and on, no doubt, to his probation officer, his drug dealer, his therapist and his hairdresser. I, meanwhile, continued to call him James – his true name, the name I gave him. But somehow my voice was never heard in the tumult started back at the hospital and so the boy was lost. To me and to the world. How could I even register this terrible mistake? I commissioned a fake birth certificate from an associate, adding my own omission to his erasure.

Never imagine for a moment, then, that a name should be chosen lightly. Scientists trumpet their double-helix discovery, the unalterable blueprint of each human life. But were any of the men behind this supposed breakthrough called Quincey Zander? Of course not. This would have constituted greater proof than all the blood in Iceland.

The only binding between us, father and son, was our opposition. James did not look like me when he was born and grew to look less like me. I even wondered, with my rudimentary grasp of the mechanics of reproduction and my wife's hidden but not extinguished interest in the politics of free love, whether the boy was mine at all. And I could see from the glances we received when out in the neighbourhood that I was not alone in entertaining such a possibility, the looks turning heavy with the suspicion of child abduction where I was not known. Mind you, some of this might have been due to the moustache, or at least perceptions of the moustache. Edinburgh was a very conservative place in the seventies. I suspect it still is now.

Even in conflict, James was my opposite, refusing from an early age to answer my ferocious wit with anything but bovine passivity, this refusal to engage the most vicious engagement of all. As I battered him with truths from on high, as I expounded upon the degenerate culture he had been born into and seemed destined to exemplify, as I raised my oratory again and again until the spit flew from my mouth and it felt as if the heavens would open with the thunderous applause of angels, James would follow his mother soundlessly from room to room, or distractedly play with a train, or efface himself in the thin light from the television set. If he had attacked me with a knife it would have hurt less. Much less, come to think of it, for I would have sensed the blade being driven down toward my back and, in one long fluid motion, turned, catching him by the wrist and, using his momentum and my own, taken his arm right through its arc and onward, smooth and sharp, right up behind his back, where intense pain would cause him to drop the weapon just a moment before the cartilage in his elbow began to rip and pop like a cheap firework.

But I could not win against dumb insolence. Not in an obvious, clear-cut style, anyway, though my revenges were many and sweet, and he is dead to me now. I raise the subject only to impress upon you that even prophets suffer setbacks on the long road they travel. My mistake, perhaps, was to set my sights too low, to attempt merely to father a son, rather than a people, a belief system, a way of life. I will not commit the same error twice.

Mind you, I look at (more accurately, I observe, as he rarely leaves his room) Robert and I do wonder. His behaviour so closely matches James' – the exaggerated diffidence, the refusal to engage except when he wants something from me, the deeply held belief that he (he, of all people!) somehow stands at the centre of the earth – that I find Myself concerned that it is I who have somehow engendered it. But then I move from the worries of the father to the worries of the Father and I can see that in this once great land this is how all the young are. Lost without the sense that they even *are* lost, too afraid to look for meaning in their lives, too afraid certainly to let it in when it comes battering at their doors. And I cry for them, great rivers wetting the coarse fur of My lion cheeks. Or is it lamb cheeks? The animal element always seems to me to obscure as much as it illuminates.

The important thing is to get the Plague and the Miracle finished and ready to go and then most of the chatter will become redundant. Robert is an expert in the writing of programs called *worms*, his being more elegant and surreptitious, I believe, than any that have come before, so that every day there is an exponential increase in the hard drives its many clones have entered and the trickle of data returning to us becomes a flood and then the flood itself is flooded. And when I have all the major data sources for the whole nation backed up out here at sea, Robert will send out the signal to his seemingly benign information gatherers and they, in turn, will command their machines to wipe their memories and shut down. And the country will be Mine.

Do you grasp the significance of this? Can you begin to see what I am suggesting? Perhaps as little as twenty years ago it would have made no difference whether the computers were running or not. We would have gone back to our files, to our triplicates, to the tiresome baggage of centuries. But the paper trail has gone. We've spent our time since destroying it – burning it, shredding it, burying it. Without our little machines we lose not only our banks but the money in them, not just our television but our electricity, not just our credit cards, but our very identities. Do you understand? No one will truly know who they are. They will crawl through cold darkness and they will not even have selfhood to fall back upon.

And with the nation in this weakened state, the government collapsed, law and order breaking down, a country full of lost souls – souls anchored to nothing but anonymous dying flesh – a leader who can put right the wrongs, return people to themselves in the way he sees fit, a benevolent engineer such as Myself, such a Leader can retune society until it sings in clear, pure notes of worship.

Of course, all we can do is store the data here. Robert has explained to me that there is so much of it that we have no processing power left to do anything with it and why would he lie? But as Janey's story amply illustrates, the sensation of being watched over will be enough to convince all but the most anti-social elements in society that obeisance is the best, the only course. The all-seeing eye. All that matters is that people know you are watching, that people know that you know them, not what you do with it.

So get on with it, Robert! Do you think I am so unworldly that I do not even suspect you of reading My work? Do you not think that I keep endless versions hidden away in My mind, all different, some by a letter or two, others sharing only a few words? I do, Robert, and even if you find them all, only I know which one is the right one. Stop wasting your time and focus.

From: 100001@hotmail.com
To: mandyhart200@hotmail.com

mand - im feeling nervous about it. squeemy. never expected 2 be squeemy about him. i cud do it right now end it all. kill the king & dissapear. but i dont. i keep not doing it right now. coz i guess i want barnums 2 know. coz i dont think they know what they got there. & if im honest coz i want them 2 reconnize what i done out here. coz its never been done before. & althogh im always saying i dont want 2 be part of all this theres an other part of me that wants every1 to know. coz this is like the greatest thing. & it shud be me thats on the magazines. even tho i aint ment 2 care. but when i send u these mails i sound so confused and lost in all the wrong ways. & i aint. im clever. im really much cleverer than i let even u know & some times im tired of hiding it. tired of thinking about every word i write of making sure it sounds just rite. tired of the pretending.
& then all so coz i just wanna see a little bit more. thats the real truth. i wanna see what hes gonna do next. all ways just a little bit more. u dont even know who he is! im not sure i know my self.
binary rob

(Converted from the ASCII)

227

26

The Facts, Myths And Legends of Clearwater, Related By Her To Him May – July 2001

1. Clearwater is the largest underground retail complex any-where in the world. It is the largest retail complex of any sort anywhere in Europe. It is the third-largest retail complex of any sort anywhere in the world. The biggest is in Ohio and has its own airport, flying shoppers in from all over the country.

2. Clearwater is a purpose-built, privately funded, government-backed research project aimed at finding ways to transform the UK into an international retail powerhouse.

3. The first baby to be born in Clearwater was the progeny of a fifteen-year-old Saturday girl called Claire, who gave birth in one of the changing rooms in Next when she should have been on her tea break. She left the baby under a rack of trouser suits, went home and killed herself by overdosing on her mother's sleeping pills.

4. Someone who ate a chilli burger from a Mullah Burger franchise on the Pashtun floor got food poisoning. When his blood was tested he was found to have three strains of bacteria never before found in the British Isles.

5. The manager of Top Shop fucked one of till girls and then sacked her when she was late in the next day.

6. There are no unions in Clearwater. This is not because of

any objection to them on the part of management, management have been anxious to stress. It is due in part to the excellence of the centre as a place of work, they emphasize, and in part to a dispute between the unions themselves as to whether Clearwater employees are shopworkers or miners.

7. The communal staff smoking area is filmed on CCTV and Clearwater Security send an email to your boss at the end of each day detailing exactly how long you spent in there and when, plus estimates of how long it must have taken to get there and back. They even highlight emails concerning individuals they judge to be taking Far Too Long (as opposed to merely Too Long).

8. There is no truth in 7, but it suits Clearwater and the management of all shops for the staff to believe it is true. It is they who propagate this rumour. Why else should the cameras in the Smoking Area be so much bigger and more obvious than anywhere else in the complex?

9. There are another two whole levels beneath the hotels, one devoted to the mechanics of keeping Clearwater running, the other to Clearwater administration and security staff. The security staff beat shoplifters with hosepipes in the special cells they have down there.

10. The underground transmitters which mean customers and staff can send and receive mobile phone calls and text messages also mean that all such communications can be monitored by Clearwater.

11. The Head of Security at Clearwater is ex-MI5.

12. A new member of staff got lost in the staff corridors when she went on break and it took her four hours to find her way back. She was sacked on the spot and has since been unable to find employment in the retail industry anywhere in Kent.

13. Because of the distances beneath the earth and the quality of the sealing, Clearwater depends entirely on its bleeding-edge

air-conditioning system for the flow of oxygen. Fresh air is pumped in from above ground, mingled with pure oxygen and a tiny measure of the smell of fresh grass clippings, and then disseminated through the complex. In a scientific study of rats it was found that people enjoy their shopping experience more in an oxygen-rich environment and so spend more money.

14. There is a group of old ladies who come to Clearwater every day on the special bus and never, ever buy anything. They call themselves the Clearwater Club and pride themselves on their lack of expenditure. Their ringleader was a ninety-year-old anarcho-syndicalist who nursed in the Spanish Civil War. She has stopped coming and their numbers are dwindling. Nobody knows if security is picking them off one by one or they're just dying.

15. If you stand at the top of Escalator 92C in Aztec at peak time on a Saturday, in excess of 12,000 people will pass you in an hour. As long as you are not moved on by security.

16. Clearwater, having been planned and built during the internet boom, is an Experience Shopping Centre, where the emphasis is placed firmly on the Value Added of the Experience Itself, rather than the retail purchase. For instance, the centre is a great place to meet a single member of the opposite sex, as Clearwater buses them in. They used to use RomEOs (Romantic Experience Operatives – mainly women, despite their title) until concerns were raised about the possible public-relations and legal issues surrounding the practice. Instead, Clearwater now acts as an aggregator for every dating agency in the South East, organizing mass away-days with vouchers for romantic meals thrown in and it is a well-known fact that (unless you are staff) if you meet and marry your partner at the centre, Clearwater will cover all your wedding costs and even pay for your honeymoon in exchange for image rights and the placing of interviews with you, the happy couple, in journals of their choice. And,

when this fails to attract sufficient quantities of singles, the management have been known to fly in young women from the Philippines, Thailand and Russia on temporary visas, who can often be seen wandering beneath the cathedral-like ceilings, skirts short and faces slack with awe.

17. The Clearwater Media Division generates a considerable amount of revenue through the sale of security-camera footage to television shows around the world. If anyone ever read the closely typed sheets outside the lifts, they would know that they forfeited all rights over said images hereafter entrance into or conveyance therein the elevationary transportation of Clearwater (hereafter known as 'The Lifts'). But no one ever does, for some reason, not even the old men in oddly-shaped cream jackets who always stop to read everything.

18. The only graffiti ever to be seen in Clearwater has so far appeared in somewhere between ten and fifteen locations. It is always written small with some kind of permanent fibre-tip pen and always in very open spaces (which constitutes about 90 per cent of Clearwater). It always consists of the same word, 'BEG', written not in the stylized, swooping capitals usually favoured, but simple block letters. Those who know about these things claim that 'BEG' is the writer's tag, though they are made nervous by its deliberate lack of aesthetic conformity and so secretly entertain the less fashionable idea that it is meant as an instruction and hence contains some kind of threat. Certainly, the locations that the graffiti appears in seem impossibly difficult to deface without attracting some kind of attention. And even if you managed to get something up on a wall, all security would need to do on being informed of its existence is watch the previous 24 hours' worth of security tapes. Which tends to lead to the rarely fully articulated idea that the author is somehow supernatural.

19. As soon as your car is filmed by Clearwater's cameras it and you are categorized by class and, hence, taste and, hence possible spending patterns. You are then routed to a specific

car-park and a place in that car-park near to a specific lift. Every lift in Clearwater is programmed to stop first at a certain floor and it takes a concerted effort then to get it to go the floor you originally requested. Most people just get out. A database follows your credit-card purchase trail so that your entrance point can be confirmed or revised for future visits. There are twenty-four possible entrance points to the shop floors rated from highest to lowest and most customers are only ever moved one or two steps either way from their initial Automobile Analysis. Failure to leave any credit-card trail, though, automatically defaults you to the lowest step.

20. Following on from 19, unique socio/psychodemographic software is used to build up a Consumer Profile on every customer in the centre. Utilizing social indicators including car type, home address (information gleaned from the DVLA) and credit-card type, plus an ever extending list of purchases, the software then uses Clearwater's next-level, instantly reactive electronic advertising boards to blur the distinction, so to speak, between prediction and marketing.

21. Unit 348 on Medieval is thought to be cursed. Despite an excellent location in relation to food franchises and elevators and both a low Passing Customer Fatigue Ratio and a high Feng Shui Consumption Aura, no one has managed to sustain a business in there for more than a month or two. While the cash tills on either side burst with takings, each increasingly flustered manager/owner at 348 tries the same set of failsafe tactics to halt decline and continues to decline none-the-less. Clearwater never has empty or boarded-up units, though, and there is always a new entrepreneur eager to show he has read a particular American business manual that the others know nothing about.

22. Clearwater prefers to persuade whole families to work in the centre. There is a small clause hidden away in the contract you sign on taking employment which entitles the employer summarily to sack any relatives employed if any member of a

family group should be in breach of said contract. It is held by management that family-group pressure is a powerful deterrent against wrongdoing.

23. Clearwater offers a crèche facility for the babies of employees at highly competitive rates. Although it is run by an outside agency (a company called Barnums), it devotes a high proportion of its time to showing the children Clearwater promotional cartoons, using flash cards to develop their brand awareness, teaching them the basics of their rights as shoppers and generally equipping them 'in a unique and innovative manner for the challenges of this, the Consumer Age'. Due to its pricing, the quality and newness of its equipment plus an excellent teacher/pupil ratio (as well as the fact it is open from an hour before the centre opens until an hour after it closes), there is always a lengthy waiting list. This despite the fact that savings gained by using it are more than offset by purchases made to momentarily silence these well-drilled mini-consumers.

24. All the other girls at P&G are slags who think they are better than you just because they are shagging some petty criminal or other from Margate who is too thick to stay out of prison long enough even to go to the abortion clinic with them.

25. The extra-glazed-looking woman with the odd, deformed face who used to work in Knox Perfumiers was a former Miss Kent. She squandered her chance at Miss England, though, due to her liberal use of a high-strength hairspray, from which she graduated to a full range of solvent abuse, eventually passing out in a puddle of Super Glue and ripping half her face off when jerking up in surprise as her husband slammed the door on returning from work a few hours later.

26. It has been claimed privately and reported to her by Mr Patel that the Clearwater computer network is unhackable which is patently bollocks. As her brother had once explained to her, the endemic insecurity of any system cannot, at the end of the day, be overcome by better machines, stronger firewalls,

quicker and more responsive virus checkers, but only by the elimination from the system of human beings, of human error, human folly and human greed. Of human love, even.

27. The unique Sunlite Ambient Glare©™ lighting system used throughout Clearwater was originally developed by the CIA for use during interrogations. It is thought that prolonged exposure to the light can cause a variety of skin cancers and partial blindness.

28. Despite Clearwater's status as an Experience, customers are not allowed to take photographs in the centre. If you wish for a record of your visit you can hire a photographer to shadow you taking candid snaps. The edited highlights of your shopping expedition will then be posted to your home within three working days. If this approach is too expensive, there are stands scattered around the centre where you can have a single portrait shot and instantly printed. But, most exclusive of all, you can be tagged on entering the centre and receive (also within three working days) a DVD of the complete CCTV footage of your day out. Rumour has it that people are using the service to enact elaborate silent movies but most people you see sporting the plastic bracelet just seem to walk round stiffly, a tight smile slashing their face.

29. Clearwater was built across two abandoned dry docks and the adjacent waste ground. Only one resident needed to be moved, David Smithers, who lived in the unsanitary, damp, three-room cottage he had been born in seventy-two years earlier. The management offered him a generous pay off and a place in a care home with a waiting list so long that most potential residents died before they got there. But Smithers, inspired by the roads protests he squinted at on his black-and-white telly every night, refused the deal, opting instead to resist. He dug a network of tunnels and chained himself in. When the time came he was quickly and efficiently removed, emerging, blinded by the light, to just one local reporter who filed a story of the 'rescue by contractors of an eccentric "Mole Man" living in a

complex of squalid tunnels'. There is a happy ending, though. Clearwater honoured its offer to place Smithers at the Happy Gramps Home and made him a guest of honour at the opening of the centre. He is a regular visitor now, often to be found sitting on a bench, sometimes with his teeth in, smiling and arching his hands back and forth through the clean, bright, permanently fresh space where once the only tunnels were his own.

30. Clearwater is officially considered to be in the top ten of the highest security risks for a terrorist attack in the UK.

31. In the event of a cut in power from the National Grid, Clearwater's first reserve generator will be brought online within five seconds. In the unlikely event of a malfunction or failure of the second generator, a third will be brought online within a further fifteen seconds. In the almost impossible event of this generator failing, a computerized system operating on its own battery (replaced and recharged every twenty-four hours) will relay an SOS message to the emergency services. Depending on the amount of people present at that moment, air within the centre will be 'good' for up to four hours.

32. At the deepest, deepest level of Clearwater, one level deeper than the centre is even supposed to go, so far down you feel you might burst out the other side of the planet at any minute, right down there, is a room with a twelve-inch-thick reinforced-steel door and nobody, but nobody seems to know what's in there. But it has to be something important, doesn't it, or else why all the secrecy?

33. If you work somewhere like this long enough and talk to enough people and if you're inclined, anyway, to like a bit of a goss, then eventually you'll hear everything it's possible to hear about the place. And some of it will be true and most of it will be bullshit, but the day will pass a little quicker either way. And it's not that it don't mean nothing. It's just that's all it means.

From: 100001@hotmail.com
To: mandyhart200@hotmail.com

mand - truth is i want barnums 2 come. i want them 2 come 4 there property. i want them 2 come 2 get me. coz i aint going back 2 jail & 1nce i know theres no other choice i think ill have the strength 2 switch it all off. switch my self off and king james off 2. maybe thats really why i took the code in the 1st place. so that they wud come & make it so i had no choice. make finishing it easier. may be i need 2 be trapped before ill have the strength 2 escape. i dunno. thats how it feels today any way. but hes boring my only so called freind. i never thoght hed be so boring. i thoght the barnums stuff wud at least give us some thing 2 discuss. i thoght he might even be some help. thats why i fed it all in. every thing. every scrap of data i cud find on barnums. all of it. i gave it all 2 him. more fool me. hes no help 2 no1. just him & his own thing. its all he talks about but its just his own thing. every thing he learns just becomes part of his own thing. his own imaginry little world. binary rob

(Converted from the ASCII)

27

At some stage in our lives, we all feel trapped, trapped by the routines and relations which make up our daily existence, stuck in our own web. We know we want to escape, but our imagination is smothered. What other possible way could there be to live except wriggling hopelessly in this particular predicament right here and right now? Our days stretch out in front and behind us, uniform, bright, a tunnel with one exit. We know exactly where we are and are lost. There is another exit, of course, always an exit, but we have to be brave to see it. The exit is marked FAITH. I know. I have been trapped in that tunnel. The only difference between you and I is also our greatest similarity. I had to have faith in Myself and you have to have faith in Me.

I stayed a long time in Scotland. Much longer than I needed in order to be sure that I was safe from pursuit. The truth is that I had no idea what to do with myself. I couldn't return to London and continue with my career. My skills, as I have stated before, were specialized. I had only one boss from the age of sixteen and I was now about to turn sixty. But more than that, a fog seemed to have descended on me, a narrowing of my imaginative reach. I had let myself down – in reinventing myself I had created a paper doll. I had imbued myself with an emptiness which I found utterly compelling, comfortably awful, terrifying to let go of. And in this state a short stay turned into a decade, time both speeding up and slowing down, each day, each week, each month an unendurable grind and then suddenly, unexpectedly, another year gone.

I wanted to forget, tried to cocoon myself with music, to short-circuit this strange momentum. I would sit in my study for long hours listening to the same 78, Verna's unreliable voice hobbling jauntily over the steps of the tune, every pop and crackle memorized, the arm on my automatic returning again and again to the start until, gradually, out of the collision of bathetic libretto, badly recorded, under-rehearsed dance band and Verna's own unique, wet delivery something magnificent would begin to emerge, something luminous. And I would rise up out of myself and float for a moment before it passed and I returned to the emptiness that was me.

Until the night the sensation became concrete. Oh My. I am about to describe to you an 'out of body experience', as if Janey and the hordes of crystallographers, halo-diviners and pisspool re-birthers who haunt the World Wide Web had all conspired to take up residence in My brain. And yet that is what it was. I am powerless before the truth.

There was no reason to expect anything from this particular evening, no sign. Yet as the arm returned to the start, time after time as it had done time after time before, I found the familiar feeling beginning to transcend itself, the correct state of mind or spirit now a gateway to a new reality, my eyes telling me that I was indeed floating, was indeed hanging just beneath the ceiling, was indeed staring down at my physical self. It was magical, entrancing and, as night slowly slipped into morning, I was still there, each time managing to hold it for a moment longer, each ensuing descent more sickening and depressing than the last. Until, as dawn darkened the bulb-lit room, I stayed up there, bobbing slightly, looking down at my ageing but still impressive form. And as I watched, mute and ethereal, my body suddenly roused itself and, with considerable purpose, marched to the door. Like a balloon attached to my own belt buckle by a length of string, I bounced along behind, devoid of agency, a shadow with no grasp of physics.

Out of the house myself and I marched, over to the car, into the vehicle and away in a rush of gravel, I silently assenting above the back seat, amazed almost to the exclusion of all else by how odd the close-shaved back of my head looked. But slowly, as the roads I took became less familiar, my attention was drawn away from my Other to where my body and my spirit were going.

We had never been here before, at least not while I here in the back had been inhabiting myself up front. The roads turned to lanes, the lanes to tracks, briars slapping and scraping at the car, the pace never slackening. My body drove completely without fear, not just as if it had made the journey one hundred times before but as if it knew that there would be nothing around the corner, just this ever narrowing, living tunnel, darkening by increment without end. And it seemed without end, ever endless, all movement gone, just me and me, thorns scraping over the shell of this singular, shared momentum.

Then I was out, out into a sudden brittle whiteness – space – and the first smell I had noticed since my bifurcation. The sea. Which was when it started to make sense and I smiled my invisible smile.

My body stopped the car sharply, staggered down through a multitude of stones, rotting seaweed, twisted driftwood, bright flashes of plastic, and began removing my clothes. A couple of minutes later and they were a neat pile beside a patch of tar, shoes aligning instep to instep, my physical self hobbling determinedly to water's edge. I had but a moment to consider why it should be hobbling if I, the conscious self, was out here – and to ponder whether my body's ability to feel discomfort without me was a sign that some other consciousness was inhabiting my flesh – before I noticed that I was gaining ground. As my feet touched the water we became one again and I continued my escape.

The icy embrace of the sea pushed the air from my lungs, turned my hands to talons, my legs prosthetic. A current caught me and dragged me outward, the clear water turning suddenly black, impossibly deep. I was never a natural swimmer, but with the cold inside me, my bones shrieking with the pain of it, all rhythm deserted me, my attempts to stay on the lip of that abyss increasingly desperate. I slowly rotated in the flow, gulping and spitting brine, my breath coming like morse code, hopelessness pulling me down. I was dead. I was dead. Story over.

Dead.

The sea relented, the moon moved, the tide turned. With the same speed and purpose with which I had been swept out to my end I was washed in again, a full stop transformed into an opening letter, still sinking, always still sinking and every time bobbing up again, my life a scrap of paper in a sealed bottle.

A Samaritan came wading through kelp from the shore to rescue me, fully dressed, shouting for me to stay calm. What he was doing there, all alone on a cold Scottish beach, I will never know. But all the same, this complete stranger, this fool to himself, came to my rescue and his arms closed round me with a father's unbreakable grip. Perhaps every beach has one – a self-appointed lifeguard. Or perhaps he was positioned there solely for me. Either way, my response may have surprised him. I tried to strike at him with my frozen stumps, to force his head beneath the surface, but he was too strong, the rescue an assault. The pair of us spluttering in our terrible clinch, he dragged me back to land, pulled me through the pebbles until he fell and we lay, entwined. His own chest was heaving now, heaving as if his whole body was inflating and deflating, heaving as his eyes widened and widened further. Then the heaving stopped, he gurgled, our roles reversed, he the baby, a thread of spittle connecting his mouth to my cheek.

We continued to lie for a while, my strength returning, the warmth from his corpse transferring to me, my muscles loosening. Until, carefully, I rose to my feet – still racked with muscle spasms but suddenly clean now, reborn – and began searching for his wallet. I forget his name now, though his driving licence was the first thing I plucked from its leathery nook. It may have begun with a W, though it matters not a bit. A passerby fortunate enough to give his life in the cause of something bigger than his comprehension is a fortunate passerby indeed. I was more interested, I am happy to admit, in the two hundred pounds folded in there and the keys to his Bentley back up beyond the beach. In the boot was a complete change of golfing clothes, soft, beautifully laundered (like me), a perfect fit. In the glove box was an electric razor with a fitting to make it run off the car's cigarette-lighter. The moustache I had cultivated for a decade was gone in seconds, a pale shadow all that remained. Yes, this was fate, an alignment so perfect, a set of circumstances so far beyond coincidence, that who could question me for following? I started south. Everything was in place. I knew exactly where I was going.

You know, too, of course, don't you? Even you know, Robert, and you barely exist in the physical world, always reducing your vision of yourself and your surroundings to data. Where else would I have been heading, after all? I made the skipper cut his engine two hundred yards out and row me in, I on one knee in the bow watching those giant henges grow dark above me, a monstrous hum building in my ears, the structures flickering like ancient film, buzzing with welcomes.

Up here, alone, finally alone, I carefully took the two tiny keys from the chain around my neck, the keys that Victor had held out to me in his bloodied fist all that time before. I slipped them into their locks and turned, one clockwise, one anti-clockwise. And, despite the years of dampness and salt accretions, the time they had lain dormant, they unlocked as if they had been oiled every day, the door rolling back with the stately, ominous rumble of a tomb. I stepped into the room beyond and found myself inside a kind of shrine, Victor's shrine to me. Or if not *to* me, for there was nothing of me in there, then *for* me. The purpose he had given me. A shrine only I would have understood correctly.

You want to know what was in there. Of course you do. And I, of course, am not going to tell you. Even though what is in there has paid for this entire project and much more besides. But, still, I am not about to tell. Only the highest, the very highest of the acolytes will enter. One has to keep offering treats or even the most committed disciple can become bored. Suffice to say here that what I saw in there left me in no doubt of my destiny or of Victor's part in unleashing it. It was in there that I became Me, the Messiah, the One And Only. I finally emerged, a veil of tears soaking My two cheeks, a choir whistling unlikely musics in My ears, the walls of the fort contracting to the laboured, gristly beating of My swollen heart. Reaching the roof, My legs like lead, I sank to My knees, laughing and crying. And at that moment, the heavens opened, the violence of the downpour awe-inspiring, the rain turning to mist as it pounded into warm concrete, the brown darkness thick with violence. The thing which had started growing inside Me all those years before, which had shrunk and shrivelled again during My long sojourn in Scotland, sprouted a precipitate lifetime, bulged for a moment, burst. Finally burst. I raised My arms from My sides, the sharp stings rousing Me from Myself so that, without warning, I realized that beyond the edge of the fort there was nothing but sunshine and clear waters, rainbows arching up and away to each of the four points of the compass. I had brought Myself here and called upon Myself to save Myself and with Me the Chosen People of the Heaven on Earth which would be known forthwith as Vernaland. It was time to answer that Call.

It really did happen something like this. I promised you honesty and I have tried to deliver. It happened something like this. Not exactly like this but near enough. It is not every day you realize you are the Messiah. It is bound to be a big event.

Do you understand that, Robert? It is not enough to declare yourself Messiah or Prophet. One needs a Sign or Signs, an objective hint that the universe understands one in the same way one understands oneself. That one is, in effect, that universe. A miracle. Nothing less will do. That is the proof (as if proof is needed yet again, yet again, this depressing, repetitive Age of ours). A further example? I want Verna here to launch My reign, to witness it, to be debased and exalted in My presence. But how to find her without alerting Barnums? How to tempt her out here alone? I am emailing the (Scots!) newspaperman who wants to send a team to photograph My dwellings and interview Me. I am regaling said hack with tales of the War and mention My acquaintance with Verna. He nearly faints, his hurried email back a model of febrile excitement. If he can find Miss Landor, would I consent to have her brought here to Me? Would I consent to be photographed here with her? Would I be happy to have the images so created printed upon the very cover of a national magazine? As long as it can be a surprise for her, I say. As long as she does not know whom she is coming to meet. We will have a party, I say. Be sure to send your best man to cover it. It will be quite an occasion, I promise him.

It is almost as if I had planned it, somewhere deep in the labyrinth of My infinite mind. Together, you and I and Verna will give the Unbelievers the Sign they are not yet aware they have been waiting for. We will free them and enslave them once more. Be clear, Robert – when my One enters her Nought the world will shake.

I have to hold My eagerness in check. It has been a long time coming and as the day draws close My patience begins to unravel, revealing behind it the raw anger of the Godhead. And I have been so patient. So many would-be religious leaders throw themselves straight into recruitment at the first hint of a vision. They proceed piecemeal as if they are Jesus Jesussed until he has not even a loaf or fishes. They underestimate the need of the masses for Spectacle-As-Proof. Think of Moses. That's more like it. Muhammad. My doctrine, My First Commandment if you like (though is it My third? I don't have time to check back, so this is one for the disciples to straighten out), is simple – One should not do anything until One can do everything.

I purchased a large television set and a satellite dish and began educating myself about the society I planned to rescue. Long, depressing days were spent munching on specially imported junk food and studying, in alphabetical order, the arcane genres of the format: chat, comedy sketch, comedy drama, current affairs (documentary), current affairs (news), drama (series), drama (single play), game, magazine, quiz, sitcom, soap, sport. I tried to avoid the obvious *clues*, so clearly signposted they could only be deliberate diversions – the upbeat, the downbeat, the sensational. Instead, I looked for answers in the details. The way an actor angled his head as he delivered his lines. The ball's gentle curve mysteriously straightening out during the crucial end of a championship match of lawn bowls. The revelation that not even the people in documentaries who were meant to be happy appeared to be happy. The quiet desperation of the smiling quizmaster. The 'and finally . . .' stories about talking pets. Through these and a thousand other moments I built a picture of a society in decline, a society losing touch with its traditions and values, where individuals drifted, lost in a world of surfaces, anchored only by their database selves, where people were scared of the unknown and also fascinated by it, filling it with ramshackle thievings from worlds where life, death, family, honour all still meant something. In short, I saw a society which was ripe for My Coming, the kind of conditions that many of My forerunners could only have dreamt of. It was being given – I was giving it – to Me on a plate. And one man more than any other was making it happen.

In killing Victor, through some occult process I appeared to have unleashed him, as if he had willed Me to destroy his physical form so that he could take root everywhere, a virus in human relations. His presence was felt across the land, from earthquakes in the coalfields of the north to plagues in Wapping. Every Jehovah needs his Satan, his fell messenger to prepare the material conditions. As I had been to Victor so was he now to Me. There is a unique, sickly sweet pleasure in becoming your boss's boss.

All I had to do was wait. Occupy My time with television and the development of My theology as the ground was prepared for My Ascension. Stay vigilant, searching, until the method for the enactment of My Miracles was placed in My lap. Or laptop, as it turned out.

Oh, I have been patient, Robert. It was years before the World Wide Web caught My attention, years more before it ripened to a point where it was of use to Me, years again until I lured you from your father's fetid semi-d and harnessed you to My higher purpose. Not to mention supplying you with the kind of kit you could previously only dream of. You have no idea. If your latest demands are not met within a day you stamp your feet with the quick, staccato rage of a toddler. I was in My prime. I am old now, older already than you will ever be, and yet I am barely beginning. Your need for immediate gratification scars your whole generation.

The hour is nearly upon us. But don't become too excited. There is still time for a parable before battle commences. Yes, a parable. While I feel that the elucidation of My life contained herein goes further than most religious texts in accurately expounding and reflecting upon My theology, I am eager not to leave gaps in My repertoire for naysayers to focus upon. And the only lacuna is in the parable department.

In the very centre of a grey, bare plain stood a dark tree, leafless, impossibly tall, twigs pushing up like the dislocated fingers of old people begging for mercy. And in amongst its branches, the scribbled nests of rooks hung, a network of static. The rooks had no recollection of when they arrived here, only that their fathers had hatched in these same nests and their fathers before them and their fathers before that and so on and so on back and back, faster and faster until the whole became a blur. Nor did they know where the other trees had gone, though there were garbled stories of the sky being full of them and of other 'colours', though none of the rooks knew what that meant. So most of them believed that this was where you went when you died, that God was all the things that made no sense.

There was little pleasure to be had in the lives of these rooks. Not much else survived out there, so every moment of daylight was spent flipping stones searching for the tiniest bug, the slightest hint of movement in the dirt enough to bring down a frenzy of pecking. Then, the moment past, stillness, the head up and tilting, swivelling, a machine for choosing another random rock from the countless thankless options.

There were only two rules to this endless, thankless foraging. First, never criticize another rook's system for choosing the next stone. Last and most importantly, whichever rook flips a stone owns all life beneath it. This was the code that made life bearable.

Unsurprisingly, rooks being living creatures, after all, it was broken. Two young friends argued bitterly, damaging their relationship irreparably. Let's call them, for the sake of ease, Morecambe and Wise. The basis of their argument is lost to us, but Wise claimed Morecambe criticized his method of collection, something the latter denied. Wise vowed revenge, agitated against his former friend, refused to let the matter go. So when, only days later, Morecambe found the slug, the outcome was inevitable.

What a slug. He had turned over the rock to discover it reclining there, three inches long, almost an inch thick, a lazy squeeze of glistening black flesh. Perhaps it was the majesty of the find, the sheer beauty of this unexpected bounty, but Morecambe hesitated before stabbing down his sharp black beak. And in that moment the slug was gone, borne aloft in the maw of his enemy, Wise, who, as his wings flapped their ragged ascent, tipped back his head and, without even savouring this feast, swallowed it.

The next week, Morecambe crept into Wise's nest and ate the smallest of his female's new hatchlings, an honour traditionally reserved for the father. And with this, the feud took wing. At great personal risk, Wise picked up a scorpion he had found and dropped it into Morecambe's nest, where it killed three of his brothers. Morecambe retaliated by nudging four fledglings from the nest of Wise's sister while the tatty fox waited below, its dry tongue tumbling sleepily from its mouth. And now the feud spread. Every bird in the rookery was related to one or other of the protagonists, some even to both, and there was no room for remaining neutral. The circle became a spiral, ever widening, sucking bystanders into a whirlpool of violence until the tree was consumed with intrigue, with attack and counter-attack, with ambushes and traps. The generations accelerated, Morecambe and Wise dying horribly, their sons following, their sons following them. With the fighting and the fornicating to make more fighters, there was less time for scavenging, but there were also fewer rooks and so food seemed easier to come by. So a new kind of equilibrium was established, one with no code, only violence, treachery and hatred. Life was good now.

Then came the Runt. The bastard son of one of the rapes that were endemic by this point, in the normal course of events he would have been eaten while he was still a yolk. But his mother, unhinged, hid the egg until the day he hatched, when his pitiful squeaks alerted both sides of the feud. She knew what to expect and succeeded in hiding the baby before the two camps combined to peck her to death. Unnamed he survived and nameless he thrived as, one by one, the main protagonists in his mother's murder dropped dead and the legend of the ill luck he generated grew round him like armour.

And so the Runt was allowed to live and grow on the margins, no nest, no friends, avoided by all those around him, a study in hopelessness, the lowest in a landscape of lows. And he existed like that for eternities, until he was fully grown in fact, when he decided just to fly, to fly as far as he could in the direction of the rising sun and die or escape or die escaping. He flew all day until the sun was sinking behind him and his wings felt as if they would break and fall to the ground like two jagged stones. And there he found the bush.

It was a dirty green, but dazzling to his eyes, unbelievable, a visitor from another planet. Coating its branches, heavy with them, were red berries, berries that seemed to talk to him, demanding to be eaten. And as soon as one slipped down his gullet, he crumpled to the ground, asleep.

He dreamt he was back at the tree, only this time he stood on the highest branch and his dark wingspan cast a shadow on all the earth beneath him and down there in the gloom and dust, tiny, crawled the other rooks, his subjects, scraping their broken beaks through the dirt in homage to him, chanting his name in ragged croaks, fear in every blink of their glossy black eyes. And if he moved they cowered and if he stayed still they cowered and the flap of his wings was like thunder and he felt as if he had arrived, finally arrived at something that had been meant to be all along.

The Runt woke at sunrise, tore the largest, most berry-laden branch he could carry from the bush and started the long, painful journey back. He arrived at sunset the next day, his flight path like giant stitches through the sky. And this time he did not go unnoticed and before the branch had hit the ground, a black swarm of birds fell toward it and the frenzy of their stabbing beaks was horrible for him to behold, circling above thinking of Dear Lost Mummy whom he never even knew. From then on their dreams were the only place they would see, because the Runt scuttled and flapped from sleeping tangle of feather to sleeping tangle of feather and peck peck pecked out their eyes, every last one of them. And when they awoke they acknowledged him King.

For a while, anyway. When they rebelled, he took a stone and smashed their beaks. When they tried to fly away, he broke their wings. After that, as in his vision, they crawled in the dirt, feathers dropping from them like dead leaves. The Runt took their eggs for himself and hatched a new generation to heed his teachings and they rebuilt the nests that had fallen into disrepair and began work on a series of canals to channel what little rain there was to the seedlings that grew everywhere – nourished first by blood – from the berry-rich faeces of the eyeless masses. Only the Runt ate the berries, surrounded by his most trusted Fledglings. And in his dreams he began to see some calamity awaiting him, undefined however hard he searched for it, so that his berry-fuelled reveries grew longer and more frequent. And when it at last revealed itself, clarity came too late, for the calamity was already taking shape and the Runt could not escape from sleep as, down below him, one of his own children struck the flints together and sparked the plantation of bushes and the tree in the middle.

Which was how they came to live in ashes, killing one another and killing one another and perhaps this is not a parable at all, just a story, though a very good story, that could keep going on and on, page after page after page. Try as I might, it will not resolve. It will offer neither moral nor meaning. And I so wanted it all to make sense.

From: 100001@hotmail.com
To: mandyhart200@hotmail.com

mand - i dont understand it. ive left them clues every where. every where. there aint 1 hard drive at barnums i aint fiddled with. evry web browsers homepage replaced with vernaland.com & theres some pretty bad stuff about barnums up on there. i mean theres like my finger prints every where. & it aint like i tried to hide where i was coming from. & still no1s showed. i got 2 email my co ordinates? i cud wait 4 fucking ever. but i cant wait. i dont want 2 care about any thing any more. i just want 2 start. binary rob

(Converted from the ASCII)

28

He stands, hunched over in the drizzle, cool water seeping down his collar to mingle with the warm sweat blotting across the back of his T-shirt. Close to his chest, the manilla envelope, already turning plantlike at its corners, inside which he carries his soul, his all-new soul. And if it isn't improved exactly, if it isn't original, or outstanding, or incisive or lyrical or in any way profound, well, at least it's measurable, quantifiable. At least it's here, beneath his arm, at least something is here.

And he needs something at moments like this, his finger an extension of a distant bell, the rain smearing its way through another English summer, the streets thick with old folk in transparent plastic macs, thick indeed with death, the slip and slither of mortality. He has had to abandon the consolation of genius. Even of genius thwarted. He is ordinary. There will be no arts programme dedicated to him. He will not be presented prestigious awards at expensive dinners. Glamorous female novelists will not recognize him across the room at his publisher's parties. Their lips will not be wet with his presence.

He feels what remains of the crispness in the envelope and, squinting into precipitate, looks up at the building, trying to guess her window. The residents, to a man (and mainly woman), expected to die ten or twenty years ago. Their savings are gone, service charges have been paid late, then not paid, then abolished in a popular vote. The bricks are rotting and crumbling from salt water, doused in trickles of soot. Paint cracks back from window frames, a microscope's view of human skin. Beneath it, blood-clot rust bubbles up. The guttering is home to a unique microclimate of plant life, the water displaced by the vegetation jagging down in a heavy-weather line and splattering across his raised forehead.

'All right there, love?'

He turns, reassesses the empty space he finds, looks down into the irrigated face below, focusing on the raindrops solidifying the spectacles, eyes lost underneath.

'You all right? Who you after?'

'I . . . er . . . I'm here to see Mrs Landor? Eighteen, I think.'

'Intercom don't work, love. Best to go up and knock on her door.'

Unlocks and heave-limps through then turns with a pink smile to welcome him into the gloom, the whole sky making mirrors of her glasses, he a silhouette at their centre.

Peter Jones is scared. He is scared of his house being repossessed during a period of unprecedented economic prosperity. He is scared of Martha finding the smashed dictaphone tape, which he hasn't yet smashed, or his itemized mobile bill, or his credit-card bill (the last two even though he knows it would be impossible right now). He is scared of his own normality, his lack of distinguishing features. He is scared of how he will pass the time now he has no affair, no book, no fantasy of uniqueness, nothing but this ordinary, bog-standard self. He is scared of dying, scared of being forgotten (but then we all are, all of us declining and scared to decline). But most of all, Peter is scared of Donald. He pulls his soul close to him, tries to derive a little warmth from it as he starts up the stairs.

Excellent on pots and trinkets, less hot on theology, Peter feels he has been through three circles of Hell without knowing how many more there are. Mapless, he wanders on, lost, with only where he's been to guide him. He revisits the first circle again and again, searching it for some clue, a hint of where he's headed.

''Ello?'

'Hi. Hi, it's Peter.'

'I know. All right?'

'Yeah. Well, no, not really. Not really, no.'

'Right.'

'Can you talk?'

'Yeah.'

'You sure?'

'Yeah.'

'You sound distracted.'

' . . . no.'

'It's just I need you to listen.'

'I am.'

'You at work?'

'On my break.'

'OK.' Unsure of the best way to approach this. 'OK.' Still desperately trying, somehow, for a formulation that didn't match him. Failing.

'I'm married. I've got kids. You know that. So you have to understand, it's nothing to do with you in a way. I mean obviously the result's to do with you. The result's very much to do with you. But not the reason . . .'

'You wanna cool it a bit, then?'

'Not so much cool it. More . . .'

'Finish it? What I meant. That's cool. Weren't anything serious, was it?'

'Uh, no. No. No, I guess not. I'm sorry.'

' . . . worry about it . . .'

'You're really not upset?' – concern beginning to warp into irritation.

'Just saying don't worry about it. 'S fine. You're married. You got kids.'

'I mean, I really, I've really had a good time. It's been really . . . special.'

'Honest, it's fine. What about the book?'

'The book? I just, I mean, having researched it and everything, I just don't know if there's enough there really, to . . .' He sighed, tried to shape it. 'I got an offer for another proposal I was working on.'

'Wicked. What's it about?'

'It, I, it's . . . It's complicated. I'll send you a copy when it's done.'

'If you like. Listen, I gotta go.'

'And you're really OK?'

'I'm fine.'

'I mean, maybe we could meet up now and again? Maybe I could call you?'

'You're married. I think you're right. Best just to leave it. See ya, Pete.'

' . . . er, OK. Bye. All the best with . . .' The phone suddenly just some metal in his hand.

He could tell she was devastated, whatever she said. And he was pleased. Peter found himself blaming her, even though he knew it wasn't her fault. If only they'd spent less time fucking and more time working. Even though it would have made no difference.

He is trying to let go of these feelings, but is still glad to have hurt her. And yet, and yet. He returns over and over to the thought which had dropped like a pebble into a pond as he had drifted from wakefulness on the night he had finished it – that in some way it was her who had dumped him.

The second circle. Unable to admit his adultery, fearful of waking alone in a bedsit, suddenly tearily affectionate for the gruff sound of Gus's demands for his time, Poppy's damp sheets and nightie, the groan and huff of Martha's rise, nauseous with guilt, gagging on it, Peter had decided to own up to a lesser crime. After all, some sort of confession and penance, however limited, is surely better than none? Surely?

Martha had ruined it, of course, that morning in the park, the wind cold, when he had revealed the financial pit he had been assiduously digging, when he had shown her the baroque complexity and depth of the structure, the unique secondary chambers, the decorative walkways, the absolute grandeur of this negative edifice. She had refused to forgive him. Refused to admit that there was anything to forgive. Taken the blame as her own, in fact, castigating herself for leaving him to cope with it all, her deliberate blindness. She had known he had been distracted, she now admitted, and hadn't dared to ask him what was wrong. Feared that she knew his answer – that he no longer loved her, that he was leaving her, that there was *someone else*. Her relief now a gush of homily, of their strength as a team, of the unimportance of money. Her reassertion again and again of his specialness, of his unique attributes as a writer and thinker. Her belief that this was not a problem but an opportunity, a chance to reassess the direction of their life together, to leave the city, move, unmortgaged, to the country where he could truly fulfil his potential and she could make jam from brambled berries. Most of all, she had emphasized that *it'll be all right*, her hand rubbing round and round his back as he had sat hunched forward, his hands hiding the look of despair, not shame, which had settled round his eyes.

The third. Donald had insisted on meeting at his home, a ground floor flat in Hampstead, the whole street an indictment of every career choice Peter had ever made, even the sun appearing wealthier (though understated) when dappling this brickwork. Donald's flat not at all as he expected, either, all light and airy and minimal and yes, much more tasteful than Peter's own. Even Donald looking less ravaged in this context, dapper in his olive drabs, the brushed chrome of his wheelchair glowing.

'So, Pete. I've never liked you, you know that, don't you?'

'Well, I didn't realize it was quite as . . .'

'I was going to take you off this. I really was. But when we spoke yesterday I detected, how can I put it, I felt there was something different in your tone of voice. A certain resolution. You sounded . . . more manly, I suppose, which I expect will offend you, but . . .'

'Thanks. I . . .'

'So I thought, fuck it, give him a chance. Take a risk. And I was lunching with Tina from Barnums and she mentioned how good she thought your juicer piece was. Very complimentary. And so her judgement, which I have the utmost fucking respect for, reinforced my own. Which is how you got the biggest assignment of your life.'

'I . . .'

'Whisky? I won't ask if you want ice or water. You'll drink it straight like it's supposed to be drunk. And tell me what you know about Verna Landor.'

'Oh, right, OK. Erm, Verna Landor was an actress, dancer and singer who made her reputation during the Second World War with popular hits such as 'Keep Smiling, Keep Fighting' and her most well-known song, 'No Man Is An Island'. A minor figure compared to . . .'

'I'm going to stop you there, Peter, before you offend me. A minor figure? Minor? Sounds like you've spent too much time on fucking Vera Lynn fansites and not enough time using your fucking ears. Minor? The woman was a fucking genius!' He took a moment thinking through a decision. Or gave the impression of taking a moment to think through a decision.

'Come into my war room.'

With alarming speed, Donald span his chair and launched forward, Peter left perched at the edge of the sofa, noticing for the first time the size of Donald's hands, the strength in his fingers as he gripped his wheel rims. Then up and after him, through the door he was holding open, panic controlling Pete's limbs, so that it was only as he heard the door click behind him and the music start up that he remembered his bag (and inside that an envelope and inside that, his soul) still sitting on the Chesterfield in the empty room behind him.

'Listen to the tone of her voice . . .'

No man is an island

A slow arc round, his mouth too slack to make an O . . .

' . . . the slight hesitancy in the delivery at first . . .'

Oh yes, that's for sure

The sandbags, uniformed dummies, the rack of rifles, the shell casings.

' . . . then the slowly building confidence . . .'

No man is an island

And the pictures, blown up to the height of the wall, the figure in them almost life size, her edges softened by the grain, but undoubtedly, again and again, Verna Landor.

' . . . until she hits the end of the verse with the kind of certainty a squaddie needs to hear.'

In times of war . . .

The music stopped, Donald allowing a quiet moment for contemplation, his head angled down. Peter, at a loss, completely elsewhere for the length of the silence, standing there without an idea even of his name, much less his purpose there.

'Genius. True genius. It's the music I heard when I came round after they blew my fucking legs off.' Pretending to listen, he had nodded a faked approval, no rhythm to it, as his life came back into focus. 'I suppose you could say it was the – how do they put these things? – the soundtrack to my recovery.

'You're very quiet, Peter. Is there a problem?'

'No, Donald. No. Not a problem at all. More of a thought, really. More of a thought than a problem.' The room suddenly very quiet, distinctly cool, Pete caught in a shiver. 'It's just. It's just I always thought that people . . . people in . . . your line of work would be, I don't know, sort of anti-war?'

Donald began to laugh, so Peter began to laugh, too. Donald

opened his arms ape-wide, so Peter did, too. Donald's far-stretched hands beckoned Peter in, so Peter allowed himself to be beckoned in. And then snap, he had found himself with his chin pressed down on to Don's shoulder, that knotty, muscular right hand hard on the nape of his neck, clamping him there, beard bristling at his ear.

'I'm a soldier, Peter. War's a fact. What matters is how you get through it. Do I make myself clear?'

Pete managed to nod-nuzzle his consent.

'Good. Now, if you can get me Verna Landor out on that tower I'll make it the cover feature. Fifteen hundred words. This is important to me, Peter. Personally. Do it well and you'll never want for work again. I look after my troops, Peter. I'm fucking renowned for it. But I need that story.'

He released, pushed Peter – breathless, embarrassed – up and away from him.

'Fuck it up, though, sonny, and you may as well forget it. You'll never work again. Not just the *Abstruser*. Fucking anywhere. I'm surprisingly well connected.'

Fourth. Peter knocks again, silence from behind the door at the end of the silent corridor, silence all round, just the spyholes to hold his attention. Hopeless. Pointless. He taps the envelope against his leg and tries to focus. Knocks again, wrist loose and knuckles out of line, the unsatisfying, high-pitched nature of the noise created suggesting the door is made of, what, plywood? Reaches for his phone, nervous and relieved.

'What?'

'Donald?'

'What?'

'Peter.'

'What, Peter?'

'She's not here, Donald.'

'Course she's there.'

'I've been knocking for, I don't know, half an hour?'

'Have you been in?'

'In?'

'In the flat.'

'Like I say, I don't think she's . . .'

'Have you tried the door?'

'Donald, I hardly think . . .'

'You're a fuckin' hack! Try the fucking door.'

Peter glances at the corridor, two lines of identical, singular beady eyes, the phone hot against his ear. He pushes at the door with his fingers.

'It's locked.'

'Give it a fucking push, man!'

Peter pushes a little harder.

'It's definitely locked.'

'There'll be a key. Try the top of the door frame.'

'Someone's going to see me.' A hint of desperation pulling his voice up now.

'They will if you keep fucking around.'

Phone clamped between ear and shoulder, he drags his fingertips through dirt, a scrawl of fluff fluttering down into his undercut hair.

'Nothing.'

'Use your fucking initiative, Peter. Is there anything near to the door? Some sort of pot plant, perhaps?'

'Yes, a yucca I . . .'

'I can honestly say I have no interest in its fucking genus. Have a look under the pot.'

Peter crouches, places his phone on the floor and tilts the terracotta. Lowers it back down. Cradles his forehead between his index finger and thumb. Mouths a silent curse. Carefully raises it again and grabs the key. Picks up his phone, sick with his own thought: has Donald been here before?

'Got it.'

'Good. Now get the fuck on with it.'

Fifth. How many more can there be? Peter finds himself in a dark hallway or anteroom, the walls lined with picture frames, black rectangles reflecting the line of light beneath the door in front. A vase of dead lilies sits on some sort of occasional table, its cloth almost luminously white in the gloom. Quiet. He stands, soaking up the stillness for a moment, trying to ignore the thick smell welling up round him. As he moves it gets worse, as if he's wading through a pool of heavy particles and stirring them up.

'Hello?' His voice already an echo of a voice, tremulous, unlikely.

Taking a deep breath he reaches for the handle and opens the door.

Sixth. The light throws him, the brightness dissolving the room in front of him. Then, between blinks, it re-forms – a velvet sofa, chair and chaise longue, all worn, a highly polished cherrywood table, a mass of ornaments cluttering a dresser and an armoire, an upright piano and, next to it, an old gramophone emitting a fast heart beat as it skips again and again through the record's final locked groove. The smell markedly stronger in here, Peter half retching, unable to resist the urge to open a window. A single bluebottle launches itself into somnolent flight.

'Hello?'

The continual thud from the record-player unnerving him, he tries to lift the stylus, instead sending it screeching across the black rink. His hands jump back and forward after it, catch it, bundle it home. He waits for the someone to come and investigate, but the room remains silent.

Peter looks up at the framed photographs which black out the white of the wall above the gramophone, an infestation of silver gelatin prints. She went to a lot parties, it seems, met a lot of people. Churchill he spots easily, Cary Grant, too, then a whole crowd of half-familiar faces (was that Terry-Thomas?) and an even larger mob of strangers, many of them in uniforms decorated with a spectrum of ribbons. And at the centre of them all, her. A handsome woman, beautiful, even, though with the slightly bulky, upholstered look of a Marx Brothers dame. Eyes straight down the lens, teeth never showing, just the slightest pout. Around her, drunken men and women constantly miss their cues, are looking off stage right or stage left or at an interesting patch on the ceiling, have allowed their hair to be or become dishevelled, have their mouths half open, or a sheen of drink or dribble on their chins. Verna Landor is the epitome of composure throughout, as if they had wheeled in a cardboard cut-out, seemingly oblivious to everything around her but the camera – the noise, the conversation, the man groping her.

Seven. Controlled by some other force, robotic, Peter looks at the doorway by the photographs, steps forward and begins to walk down the corridor, unperturbed as the stench works its way inside him. Dragged onward, his movement eerily smooth, as if he is floating rather than walking. More of the flies eddy round him, black glitches in a computer-generated reality, gaps more than insects. The smell already everywhere – on his skin, in his hair, scratching at his eyes and ears. He turns into the room, his whole body wheeling round, a battleship, chin and eyes staying straight ahead.

Eight. A clot of flies buzz lazily up from the bed, the drapes turning the sunlight outside a deep brown, the television opposite casting a cold, grey emptiness. No warning, just Peter marching forward to the edge of the bed, his legs bending too high at the knee, somehow.

She appears to have been dead for some time. Her colour is all wrong, even in this light, her flesh swollen. The flies return to their resting places – mainly around her groin. He stands and stares for a moment, unable to take it in. His brain just ticking over, his chain slipped.

It registers in his stomach first, the sudden rush up. For some reason he tries to hold it in, his mouth a medicine ball, bile shooting up his nostrils, the sick squirting out between his teeth, the pressure spraying it across the wall in a fine film. He releases the rest as he bends over, the remains slapping down round his fraying trainers.

Peter turns and runs. Runs through the door, back down the corridor, into the sitting room and out into the dark anteroom. Has his fingers on the handle of the front door when a treble realization descends upon him, crushing even his urge for flight. He is implicated. His vomit is in the room. Police forensic experts can no doubt do remarkable things with vomit. He is obliged. If he runs, Donald will hold him to account. He will never work again. A whimper escapes him. Surely this is the last circle? Surely this is it? He hesitates, looking longingly at the door handle, his shadow cast across it. But he has dropped his envelope in there, too, so he has to go back. Has no choice. He returns to the living room and arms himself with handfuls of pastel tissues from her box.

She is lying on her back, her face looking straight up at the ceiling, her arms spread at right-angles to her body, palms up. A syringe sticks from her elephant arm like a pin in a cartoon balloon. A blackened spoon, a silver box, a dirty sandwich bag, a remote control, a silver figurine of some sort, all sown across the bedspread beneath her upturned hand, the fingers tensed, rheumatoid, around an imaginary cricket ball. Peter finds his eyes drawn back again and again, though, to her hair, a yellow glow emanating from it, each strand perfectly in place, as if she had just been teasing it in front of the mirror before lying down for a moment, an old-fashioned cut, yes, but executed just so, the living, Technicolor original for all those photos out there. He is sick again.

Recovering, the unused tissues clamped over his mouth and nose, he looks round for his soul, hardly daring to breath. Sees it, its brown now dotted with greasy blots of sick. Bends to pick it up. And then the unthinkable, noise from the bed, a cough or exclamation, sudden movement, his own balance gone so that it seems that he's pulling the corpse upward as he falls back. Rolling from his heels on to his arse while in front of him, the bony body and the skull on top, snap up – toothless, rictus-grinning, the hair left lying on the bed.

He surprises himself by not shrieking, his throat squashed flat, his only exuberance the wild flail of his arms which sends his soul spinning upward toward the ceiling, the damaged envelope seeming to split apart as it turns, disgorging its contents, letters from bailiffs, court summons, final demands, the complete history of his failure, so that as he sits, trying to scream, the papers flap and flutter down around him.

The mouth shuts, the eyes roll, gradually focus in on him, eyelids narrow.

'Well, hello . . .' That 'o' extended, dropping, the pit he's falling into.

Nine.

From: 100001@hotmail.com
To: mandyhart200@hotmail.com

mand - i tried 2 make it as obvous as possible. all the cameras at clear water pointing this way. the same up at metro centre. simple triangalation - where lines cross is x marks the spot. when they still dint come i did it every where else. every single 1 barnums run security 4. & if this aint a come & get me i dont know what is. the shires bull ring palissades pleasence the vales meadow hall white rose west quay east orchard crown gate merry hill wharf side friery lake side corn mill - the lot. all those cameras pointing here. every camera barnums controls. all pointing out 2 this tower in the sea. & the people at each 1 was just the same. me watching the cameras all these cameras sweep round over them & there all just the same. empty. a head of me some how. still a head of me. not for long. therell come 2 get me now. & when they get here ill be gone. binary rob

(Converted from the ASCII)

29

The sea gently rearranges the pebbles on the beach – a mother absentmindedly smoothing her child's hair, one world-weary, world-size sigh after another. There's no wind, the sea in front just gently fucking with what's laid out in the sky above it, playing a game of some sort, a kind of solitaire with infinitely complex rules. And at the intersection point between stone, water and air stands a naked man, the grey hairs on his back picked out by moonlight, the soles of his feet remoulded by pebbles, the salt water from his eyes rejoining itself in the sea at his feet.

This is the situation Jimmy Patel finds himself in, crying naked on a pebble beach, suddenly sober, his cricket whites – two banks of pebbles back – folded more neatly than any of his clothes at home, as if someone else has led him into this, brought him here, taken his hand and gently helped him to this point and then vanished. He looks along the shore line to the left and then the right.

It's all going to come out now and Jimmy doesn't care. Or rather, does care, but for all the wrong reasons. The ethics man has uncovered a truth of some sort, or, if not exactly a truth, certainly a story. If he goes and winds up Jonathan Greenacre then Jimmy's former captain will do whatever he has to do to protect himself. And you can rest assured that when he begins telling tales about Jimmy and O and brown envelopes rigid with blocks of banknotes being slipped into kitbags, about the tiny margins at the very top of the game between a win and a loss, of the gambling rings in the Far East for whom Kent versus Sussex being rained off is a million-dollar disaster rather than, well, rather than nothing, a cause for complete national indifference, you can rest assured that when it all comes pouring out of him, somehow, despite all the evidence to the contrary, Greenacre will emerge from it clean. Cleaner, even – purged and purging. And, in the final analysis, Jimmy is glad, about as gleeful as you can get when you're standing naked at the sea's edge building yourself up for suicide.

Jimmy's considered killing himself for so long now, has dreamt of his obliteration, of some sort of peace, that it seems as much a part of him as his face in the mirror. But there's something old-fashioned in Jim's character, something decorous. To kill yourself for no reason? Just because you can't bear to go on? It seems so indulgent, self-serving. He has lived, he feels, a pathetic life and does not wish to cap it by dying pathetically.

But to kill yourself as a matter of honour, to die of shame? Well, that's more like it, even if it isn't quite true. And if, in the process, you make investigation of events ten or fifteen years ago even more likely and, hence, fuck up O's life as well, could there be a better way to go? Because O is at the root of all this, not just the business with the brown envelopes but all of it – all the dirt in his life, the long days, the despair – and if he's going to end it here, he wants to end O, too.

O, for God's sake! Like he's a character in a Bond movie! When in fact he's just a bookmaker's runner and his name is Omprakash. And if they were back in India (that 'back', even! Only one of them is from there and it ain't Jim) he would be slopping out Jimmy's shit, not sliding round in his tailored suits pretending to be some kind of dark-skinned aristocrat.

He takes a few steps forward, the water surprisingly, painfully cold, sliding screes of pebbles reducing him to a shuffle, robbing him once again of his sense of purpose. As the water reaches his knees he's desperate to piss, his bladder suddenly filled through his feet. It feels ridiculous to stand there holding it, directing the flow away from his imminently washed-forever skin, but, however full, he finds he can't go without the reassurance of his right hand round it. So he stands there, laugh-crying at the absurdity, feeling the tingle of spray bouncing back on to his lower thighs, momentarily childish again, as he whips the silver line into a sine wave.

Anyway, he reasons now, he doesn't necessarily actually have to die. He can just swim out a little way, follow the coast along, drag himself ashore and make off to start all over again. Again.

Back when they'd left the camp and found the flat, he had become obsessed with a certain sitcom showing on the TV he bought with his first cheque. Not the programme itself, actually, but the introductory credits, where muted horn fanfares heralded a neatly folded pile of clothes on a beach, shined shoes next to them and the impossibly pallid back of the man who had owned them striding out into the waves. The sequence excited him, made him think, titillated him again and again with the possibility of an escape from this family, this flat, this life. It was like magic, how good it made him feel. He bought a Betamax – state of the art – and began recording all the episodes, then, late at night, when even Hinesh had been persuaded to bed, he would watch that sequence again and again on SLOW, the painfully retarded scrape of tape over heads shooting lines of static across the pebbles and almost scientific piling of suit.

When sleep finally came, Jim would find himself by the river beneath the dam. Or not himself exactly (this being the point of the dream), but his eye as a camera sweeping back from the water along the miles of path, past Coronation Park and up towards the temple, all in one endless tracking shot, angled down from about ten metres up, the bright green to each side of the track chequered by an infinity of neat little piles of clothing, each individual and many, so many, known to him. There was mother's, then Uncle Muljibhai's; over there was his friend Amit's sister's, Upendra, Praful's father. His cousins, teachers from school, boys he had once played cricket with, the first girl who had let him kiss her, shopkeepers, lawyers who had come to dinner, doctors who had treated him, tennis partners, his brother's friends, his mother's circle, people his father talked of over breakfast, somehow the anonymous heaps of discarded clothing revealed themselves, one by one, the husks of people. And Jimmy would travel faster and faster above the path until the identities began to blur and overlap and then he was falling, always falling, wakefulness coming suddenly, a sharp inhalation just as he splattered into the rapid ascent of ground.

Jimmy hated the dream, felt it belittled the odd lightness he experienced during his nocturnal slow-motion binges. But, more than that, he wanted to keep the two countries separate, unattached, to enjoy his new fascinations as new, as choices. He would abstain for a week, maybe a fortnight, as his unease dissipated, then find himself right back in it again, helpless, hopeless.

Piss spent, he acknowledges to himself that really, if he intends to disappear, a little planning might have been in order. What's he going to do? Climb out of the water naked, walk into the nearest town naked and withdraw money from a cashpoint naked with the card currently still behind the bar in the last boozer he visited? And imagine failing to disappear, imagine the look of complete victory on O's face when he finally catches sight of Jimmy shaking inside a rough blanket in the corner of what passes for a drunk tank in some rural police station. He shivers, a sudden breeze catching him, and turns toward the beach.

As Jimmy shows his back to the sea, the headlights of O's BMW, back up beyond the pebbles, suddenly snap on, the glare illuminating the wedge of grey stones tumbling down towards him in the water. At least he thinks they snap on. Maybe they were already on and he just didn't notice.

Jimmy isn't sure whether he left the door wide open and the keys in the ignition as a gesture aimed at increasing the mystery of the situation or whether he was just too drunk to care. Either way, it doesn't seem so clever now. There is someone in the car – perhaps O, or a policeman or a thief or a drunken thug rolling back from the pub. Whatever the case, it can't be good, cannot possibly be an improvement on the previous situation. He is no longer alone out here. He can't really judge where the beam from the headlights ends. Can whoever it is see him standing here? He leans forward, trying to squint through the halogen to make out a silhouette behind the invisible wheel. As quickly as he can, his feet still squeamish on the stones, he turns and strides out, his blinks planting bright red echoes of the bulbs throughout the darkness.

He seems to be in some kind of pond. Mud squelches between

his toes, he pulls his knees up in pony steps again and again but the sea gets no deeper. How can he kill himself in a foot of water? How can he hide himself in a giant paddling pool? The no-horse dressage feels ridiculous but he begins to stumble when he tries to walk more normally. Gradually, though, he notices a change. As the stones become fewer in number and his feet find only silt, so the water finally creeps on to his thighs, then touches his retreating privates, washes through his pubic hair, fills his belly button and, at last, covers his chest. He doesn't stop until it reaches his neck. And then he stands again, the slight swell taking his weight then dropping him, taking his weight then dropping him, gradually, incrementally, dragging him out to sea. Behind him, the headlights are suddenly distant, the faintest message from another world.

Even if he knew anyone who he could talk to about it and then wanted to talk about it, Jimmy couldn't explain why he wants it all to end. All he could say is that he needs it to stop, that it hurts and keeps on hurting, that he can't see why it should ever change. Which takes him exactly nowhere, naked in a cell, dreaming of new identities. He bobs his head beneath the surface, imagines inhaling liquid, feels his hair mushroom out and comes up again.

Jimmy knows now exactly what his problem is, has always known. He hasn't got the bottle. He is perfectly aware of what he wants to do but can't do it. It's always been this way and it always will be. Even in suicide he lacks that killer instinct. He may as well give himself up to O completely, become a sniggering sidekick. Except he doesn't have the nerve to do that either.

He remembers, with an evasive queasiness, how, aged around twelve, his closest friend, Sanjay, had come to Jaimin to tell him that the other boys in his class had taken against him and were planning to humiliate him by leaving him hanging in and by just his underpants from a changing-room peg. He went straight to the ringleader and persuaded him that Sanjay was a better target, without thinking, really, consumed by a kind of numb panic. The fact that the boys didn't act on his advice barely lifted the shame that fell on him that summer. Jim knows he can never justify his actions that day but has tried, has tried so hard. He was young. His father was already drifting. School is a duplicitous and cruel place. Through it all, though, all the fog of excuse, Jimmy knows that, however he puts it, however he tries to look at it, that one incident tells him something fundamental about himself. Perhaps the fundamental something about himself. Which is another excellent reason to at least try to overcome himself and finally stop it all right now. At least to try.

So he will just swim. Swim out and keep swimming until his arms and legs lock and, like a statue washed from the deck of a pitching galleon, he sinks slowly, rolling over and over, to the ocean floor. Swim until the decision is taken from him. He kicks his feet out of the mud and pulls himself into a steady crawl, his legs straight but loose, his arms coming over and cutting down into the water perfectly, his head rolling out for air flush with the surface. Jimmy is a good swimmer despite the shoulder, loved it as much as cricket as a teenager. Had a thing about the sister of Nikesh Mehta and went every day one summer to impress her with lengths, cruising up and down their pool looking up to her window at the turn, until Nikesh asked her what she thought of him and she said, 'What, the goldfish? Must be wrong in the head to just do that up and down up and down for so long.'

Now, the length of his stroke perfect, a blankness coming over him, the memory of that girl at the window (she did look, she always looked), he decides to swim back to Uganda, to keep going away and away from the headlights with his poor mother, grandmother, Great Uncle Roochi, Maniben, Deepa, Premal, even Sanjay, dear Sanjay too, and all the other exiled dead falling in around him from the dark as the water gets warmer. Some will choose breast stroke, others butterfly, many will try to match the rhythm of his crawl or lag behind with doggy paddle, a great mass of the already-drowned swimming with complete dedication up the ever narrowing Nile, five thousand miles of it, and finally walking dripping on to the shore to find their clothes still waiting, the folds as perfect as origami.

From: 100001@hotmail.com
To: mandyhart200@hotmail.com

mand - i can all ways trust him 4 a larf. better than telly. hes got
some woman coming out he thinks is a old flame! verna lander. a
real old lady! & he thinks he knows her. if he can get thru this then
eat ur turing test hart out! but beleive me it gets better. shes
barnums. or at least shes some thing 2 do with barnums. so there
on there way now 2. 4 sure. binary rob

(Converted from the ASCII)

30

What a nice young man. How very sweet of him. She smiles across at him. Three hundred and fifty pounds for one day's work! That should keep her going. She knows it isn't that much, but also, deep, deep in her blood, understands the proper functioning of the market, the rules of supply and demand. Her stock is low, her need for liquidity high. She would have done it for fifty. So she floats out here, happy, knowing that the money he gave her up front has bought more than enough to keep her going until she hits land again.

The poor boy looks a little unwell. His chin is slumped forward into his bright yellow lifejacket, the reflected glow from the material giving him a cartoonishly queasy aspect. And he's barely a boy at all, when you look at him closely, when you bother to look beyond his teenager's outfit, those trousers practically falling off of him. The skin of his face has unmoored from the bones beneath, his eyes are two thumb-smears of purple, worry lines gash him like a broken window, his teeth huddle in closer and closer together, petals after dark. And his hairline? Well, she only met him this morning and she can tell it's not where it used to be. And isn't about to stop now. Still, very sweet. Imagine offering to buy her a lifejacket! Most chivalrous. Although of course he had already purchased his own. And she would not be seen in public wearing yellow. Hadn't worn yellow since she was in the chorus line. Never again. Twenty girls dressed as daffodils and that old cow booming out her tunes. Some things best forgotten.

The poor fellow does look ill, his papers in a plastic wallet now, its plastic zip shut, attached to his buoyancy aid by bright yellow string but still gripped tight.

'Are you suffering, dear? I am afraid I have forgotten your name again.'

'Peter. I'm not too good with boats.'

'Peter. Well, they take the most unlikely people that way.'

'Not too good with the sea, actually. Not too good with water. Anything bigger than a bath and I come over all funny . . .'

'I remember, it must have been, oh fifty years ago now, though it seems like only yesterday. It's true you see, darling, what they say. I've forgotten your name again already but. I'm sorry, where was I?'

'You were reminiscing.'

'Yes, of course. During the War – I hope you're making a note of this because I may forget to mention it later and I'm sure it will be good for your story. During the War I came out here to watch one of these towers being sunk or put in place or whatever or however they called it. It was when I met my husband, actually. I think so anyway. I am sure, at least that he was there. Although that's irrelevent in this context. Am I boring you?'

'No. No. Not at all. Though I am feeling rather nauseous so I hope you'll excuse me if I have to . . .'

'Well, you see, this was the point of the story, my dear, if I can just make myself get to the point. This was exactly the point. I had some very good friends at the Admiralty and they invited me to come and do that thing where you break the bottle. On the blessed tower if you can believe it. For the newsreels. Morale booster. Only the weather was so bad we couldn't get near enough to do it so the whole expedition was a complete waste of time. Except for meeting Victor. My husband. If that was when I met him. Oh dear, I've done it again, haven't I? The point. The point. Yes. The admiral who had invited me was sick as a dog. All the way there and all the way back. Wretched. Great torrents of foul-smelling vomit. All over the deck, all over my shoes, my job to smile of course, so there I am, smiling while . . . Oh dear. Are you . . .? Can I get you anything?'

Peter manages to shake his head, though hanging over the gun-whale, so that it translates to Verna as the slightest wiggle of his raised behind.

She can hear the captain, his name stuck in her head just short of articulation, cursing and laughing and telling her companion not to get any on his boat. As if it won't wash off! And he had seemed quite the gallant when she had boarded, kissing her hand and so forth, though in retrospect the scrape of his stubble on her velveteen skin should have acted as a warning. She pulls a handkerchief from her bag to pass to the poor boy – the poor man – then notices what looks like blood on it, a succession of brown spots of varying size and shade, running at a diagonal across most of its off-white surface. She is about to re-bag when she sees him turn back to her, the afternoon sunlight glistening in the slick on his chin, gulls already swooping down to feed on the trail behind him.

'Here. It's clean, dear. I know it doesn't look it. Came out of the wash this morning.'

'I don't suppose you've got a bottle of water?'

'No, dear. Sorry.'

'Perhaps I'll go and ask Tom.'

'Who?'

'Tom. The guy who owns the boat . . .'

'Oh yes. Our skipper. Yes, of course.' She watches him grope his way down the very middle of the craft, trying to keep as much of his body as near to the deck as possible.

'I'm not as forgetful as I pretend, you know. Nowhere near as forgetful. Sometimes it just suits me not to remember.'

Verna's mind is like a computer. She knows this, she studied them. Thinks she may have done. Everything is in there, ones and zeros, impossible to delete. There are only two types of data, Verna feels. The few bits she files which she hopes to retrieve. And the rest, clogging up the dark corners of her hard drive. There is so much she has chosen to forget.

Her childhood. The shadow from the railway line above engulfing the tiny house so that it was always cold, the yard damp regardless of season. The name they had forced on her, the ugly, throaty words which attached to her. Her brothers, her sisters, not a father in common amongst them, each enjoying a short time of favouritism till daddy moved on, each battered and bullied and made to pay and pay after he'd gone. The constant hunger, like someone slowly wringing moisture from your intestines. The clumsily made, brutal clothes. The slate-wet streets. The dirt. The lost lost lostness of not being what she already knew she was. Being in the world completely wrong. Endlessly.

Verna has decided that she will tell the reporter, the old-young man, that the story of her life is the story of love – of the search for love, of loving, of being loved, of losing love. It's the story she's been telling, mainly to herself, for fifty years. In fact, she knows, the real story of her life is a story of survival. Of how the change that should have changed everything changed nothing. Of the beautiful dresses bought for her by other men. Of the accommodation they paid for, the elocution lessons they lavished on her, the musicals they funded, the records they cut, the film they exposed. Of their John Thomases, a multiplicity of them, the range of sizes, shapes and shading constantly surprising her, forests of them, the faces forgotten while they still juddered behind her eyelids, a mute rememberance. Of the orifices, crevasses and indentations into and against which they poked and rubbed and tore, their shining, purple dinasoid heads printing smudges of their colour all over her. Of the smell of sperm coating her, just rolling over on the bed or table or floor or wherever they left her, just turning her head, even, enough to release another waft of its sweet staleness, her own unique perfume. More than anything, of the repetition, the repetition and the repeated repetition, the sameness quickly smothering any attempt at novelty, the weight as if every one of them had stayed on top of her, her face crushed down into the pillow.

And the way to survive this survival? She long ago forgot that this is what it is. Forgetting, surviving the survival. Forgetting, her gift from dear, sweet Victor, who trained her to forget. Or helped her to develop her talent. To be a forgetting machine, for her own sake, for his sake, for the organization, the country. For a Greater Good she has no recollection of, Verna forgot whatever she was asked to, a human shredder, information trails deleted, connections removed, her speciality the links between two events, the world reduced to discrete segments, no one even recalling a time without the gaps. A what? I'm sorry, you've lost me.

He's returned smiling, winningly sheepish, she thinks he thinks. A little more flesh in his face.

'Feeling better, dear?'

'Better out than in.' An ingratiating shrug.

'The colour has returned to your cheeks. You'll make a seaman yet!'

'Oh, I think there's a long way to go before that. Wouldn't even go on the boating pond when I was little.'

'Quite the intrepid reporter, aren't we?' He mugs a half-wince. 'I'm sorry. That sounded much more harsh than it was meant to.'

'That's fine. No offence taken.' He waits what he feels to be the appropriate length of time. 'The truth is I'm not, really. A reporter. Never mind intrepid.'

Sharply concerned about the status of her fee, Verna almost snaps.

'I hope you haven't brought me out here under false pretences, young man.'

'Oh God, sorry, I didn't mean . . . I do work for the *Abstruser*. This is for a commissioned piece. I just meant that I'm not so much a reporter as . . . as a, well, I suppose you'd say a cultural commentator.'

Her eyes narrow.

'A critic?'

'No, not a critic, as such. More like a, like a. More like. A cartographer?'

'As long as you're not a critic. Frightful little men.' She smooths down her skirt, lifts her right leg a little and, pointing her toes, examines the silk of her stocking. Her legs, she thinks, are still beautiful. 'And what, my dear, does this cartography entail?'

He tries to laugh again, to shrug it away. 'I think I've been pretentious enough already.'

'Oh dear.'

'What?'

'Oh dear.'

'Is something the matter?'

'I have given my time to listen. It's insulting to just shrug me off. Am I beneath you? Do you fear it's too complex for me to understand?'

'Oh God, I'm sorry, I didn't mean . . . It was a reflection on me, not on . . .'

He tries to look thoughtful. Just looks tired. Tired of himself.

'I map culture. And we inhabit culture, in a very literal sense. It's where we live. So I suppose I try to help people navigate their lives.' The words trundled out, bumping into one another, rickety.

'And so I suppose you yourself are good at navigating life?'

He leaves it just the right amount of time but when he says it he's blank, as if someone just behind him is talking.

'No. Not very.'

They sit for a moment, the engine rumbling through them, the sky rolling above them.

'Have you said all that before?'

He nods.

'Even the part about not being good at it yourself?'

'Especially that part. Only usually I laugh. Usually I find it funny.'

'To me?'

'Sorry?'

'Have you said it all to me before?'

'Er, no. Not as far as I'm aware. No.'

She pulls her head up.

'I thought not. Always best to be sure.'

She feels sorry for him, she thinks, though she's not sure why. She doesn't do sympathy as a whole, empathy she associates only with those blessed flower tinctures, the never-ceasing quest to dilute. All the same, she feels sorry for him. She is sure that's what this sensa-tion is. She becomes distracted trying to remember the last time she felt sorry for someone, a hopeless task, she knows, but somehow more alluring for that. And preferable to this unsettling emotion. She knows, or senses or perhaps just decides, that he's in no way worthy of her pity (and you see what she's done here, how quickly she's moved on, unaware of her own mind's speed). He is begging her for it, *begging*, head all bowed, eyes like to two wet dinner plates, these self-deprecating shrugs and blinks, these self-effacing smirks and flicks, this grotesque panto of faked self-doubt. The self the self the self, the self-loathing that infatuates him so.

And she pities him because he knows no better. How could he know better? Who has he ever met but himself? What has he ever done but himself? Where has he ever been but himself? She doesn't need to ask him for a biography, she can work it out, prefers to keep it brief, frankly. She knows a Chosen Specialized Subject when she comes across one. They all have them. And most of them are the same.

But still the pity will not shift. Poor boy never had a chance. How could it have turned out any other way? He just keeps on looking at her, waiting for an opportunity to hold forth or, even better, for an opportunity to deny himself an opportunity to hold forth. She has long since pushed from her mind the small kindnesses he did her back at her flat when she had woken, toothless and wigless, her own ones and twos dried to her. Not so much that he helped to get her to the bathroom and made her tea, but more that he had done it all without allowing the disgust he must have felt to show. It hadn't shown at all.

She sharpens up, a jolt straightening her from cranium to coccyx.

'Where's the photographer?'

'I'm sorry?'

'The photographer. I'm sure you said there would be photographs.'

'I did go through this with you. Tom'll bring the photographer out tomorrow. Our host invited us to come out tonight and have dinner and stay the night to give me more time for background . . .'

'Tonight? Out for the night? You said a day. I distinctly remember you said a day.'

'Well, it is less that twenty-four hours . . .'

'No, I'm sorry. I can't do a day and a night for how much was it you were paying me?'

'We agreed three hundred and fifty . . .'

'Do you have any idea who I am? A day and a night for three hundred and . . . You seem like a nice enough young fellow, but really this is too much . . .'

'We did discuss it. You did agree to this. I haven't tried to mislead you.'

'Turn the ship around! I refuse to proceed with this charade! This is piracy!'

'I'm sure we can sort this out if you'll just . . .'

'Where is the captain? Is he party to this abduction? This *villainy*?'

'Please. Really. I'm really no good at this sort of . . .'

'Five hundred.'

'Sorry?'

'Five hundred is the minimum acceptable.'

There are no words left for him, his face trying to shape these blanks.

'Five hundred or we can turn the ship around and you can use your powers of persuasion with a police detective. Abducting an old lady!'

'. . .

'. . .

'I'll need to get some sort of receipt from you . . . Now. Straight away. I think we need an agreement on paper. Something we can both refer back to in the event of any more . . . problems.'

He flicks through the contents of his precious envelope carefully, solicitously, his fingertips resting too long on certain pages, until at last he selects a final demand for outstanding hire-purchase payments on his car, failure to make good the outstanding balance in full plus outstanding interest plus legal costs resulting in immediate repossession, etc., etc. Stroking the paper out lovingly on the plastic envelope, a gauzy look comes over him, a contented smile slowly forming, his movements smoothing themselves out.

'Why don't we make it six hundred, Miss Landor?'

She immediately suspicious. 'Why?'

'Why not?'

'Because why?'

'You've earnt it. There is no piece without you. Humour me.'

Laboriously, in clotted ballpoint, he writes out their compact.

I, Peter Hugo Johnson, promise to pay

'I'm sorry, I don't know your name.'

'Are you trying to be amusing? It's Verna Landor.'

'I mean I know your stage name. Your real name. I don't know your real name.'

'That is my real name.'

'It surely can't be. No one uses their . . .'

'That is my real name. I'll hear no more about it.'

I, Peter Hugo Johnson (hereafter known as The Writer), promise to pay the artiste professionally known as Verna Landor (hereafter known as The Artiste) the fee of six hundred pounds (£600) (hereafter known as The Fee) for accompanying me to the former military installation Cold Mount (hereafter known as The Trip) as part of the Sunday Abstruser *feature provisionally entitled 'Oh What A Beautiful War!' (hereafter known as The Feature). All copyright in The Feature will rest with The Writer. The Artiste will have no right to make further claim in relation to The Trip or The Feature, or any work or revenue generated by The Trip or The Feature. All personal expenses etc generated by The Artiste in relation to The Trip will be recompensed from The Fee. The Artiste acknowledges that she has taken fifty pounds (£50) as an advance against the balance of The Fee.*

He staggers across the deck, his legs splayed and knees bent as if he has soiled himself, she thinks. He lowers himself next to her, proffers the sheet of paper, still resting on the waterproof document case, still attached to his buoyancy aid by a short length of string, so that he has to lean right forward, his head uncomfortably close to her cleavage.

'I think that should suffice. But read it and be sure you're happy.'

Leaning back as far as she can, she pulls her spectacles from her handbag, uncases them and holds them in front of her eyes. They have never sat on the bridge of her nose. She has seen the damage that spectacles can do to the nose.

'Something seems odd.' She knows she has no idea what. Perhaps it's just that she has never liked contracts.

'Really?' The man angling his head round and looking at his writing with a certain scholarly intensity. 'It . . . seems . . . OK. Can you be more specific?'

'It's your name, I think.'

'Ugly, isn't it?'

'I thought it. I seem to remember. It. Are you sure that's your name?'

'Am I . . .?' He chuckles good-naturedly, looks a little concerned, then gradually, his hand drawing a jagged graph through the air, touches her shoulder. 'Are you feeling all right? It's hard sometimes, isn't it? So much to remember. If that was the only problem, maybe you could . . .?' And he inveigles the biro into her hand, holding it gently there as he looks up at her.

'My signature alone is probably worth more than that.' But she signs, anyway, and, despite the tremors generated by her years, the muscle wastage, the lack of practice, despite all this it loops out magnificent, the work of a star.

He looks up, expectant.

'We're there.'

What a nice young man. How very sweet of him. She smiles at him. Six hundred pounds for a day's work!

From: 100001@hotmail.com
To: mandyhart200@hotmail.com

mand - every things ready. im taking 1 last moment 2 say my
goodbys. my goodby. then i can sit back & wait 4 barnums. i know
therell be coming. ill be sorry 2 leave i think. leave it & this place. my
bunker. the smell of always damp concrete the salt blooms stepping
out side 4 that moment i allow my self 2 the fog or the brightness the
water so sluggish it looks like sirup. or the wind when it batters u.
the best fucking moment when it suddenly gos straight thru u & ur
just a ghost hanging there 60 foot above miles of water all of it
sucking out & down the whole choppy mess of it cursing coz ur
nothing & nothings no good 2 it. i want 2 be part of this world. a
proper part. i never have. binary rob

(Converted from the ASCII)

31

And so we reach the end of this, the First Testament of King James of Vernaland, your Messiah, Holiest of Holies. Verna is coming! The scribe who is to accompany her emailed me from an internet café in Markham. Tom, my trusty fisherman/acolyte type, has the boat made ready. A great banquet awaits her. Some may feel that being reliant solely on dried and tinned goods might limit My ability to mount such a feast, but anyone who lived through the War will salivate at the thought of fried corned beef and rehydrated potato granules. And when the banquet is finished, Verna and I will become One in what I believe is referred to as the biblical sense. This union, postponed for six decades, will unleash the power and resolve in Me to see through My plan. And so, Heaven will be on Earth. Robert will do all the mechanical computer stuff I am tired of having to elucidate – the Crash, the Darkness and later, once I have seized control, the Bringing of the Light Again. I will be crowned God and Emperor. The future Vernalanders have never been very good at the separation of Church and State and this will make things considerably simpler for them.

As you are reading this, you will probably have been one of the first to recognize and embrace the One True Way and The Light, hence guaranteeing yourself a pretty cushy position from the off. I will not be able to be too choosy at first. But try to remember that the quality of candidates will be rising all the time, so I encourage you to learn the lessons contained herein. Be ruthless.

Allow Me a moment's weakness. I will not have time for them after today. I am trying (for it is part of My job, part of what I am) to imagine what your feelings would be if you were to reach the end of My Testament only to discover that I am not a messiah. That I am only a lonely old man, driven mad by My background, My line of work, by seclusion, by unrequited love. I suppose the very fact of your reading means that this is not so. But humour Me, however painful you may find it. I am trying to imagine the unimaginable. Imagine with me – I am not the Messiah (a blasphemy probably punishable by death by the time you get this far. But then the fact that you have got this far means you are part of the elite who get to blaspheme as a matter of course. And to slaughter lesser blasphemers. What a jolly life!).

I am not the Messiah. I may not even exist. I am only these words dripping down this page.

Let Me tell you, even if this were so, I would console you. If I am not the Messiah, the Messiah is near. I can feel it. If it were not Me, for whatever reason, then I would advise you to look close by, to trace My place in a web of impossible coincidences. To acknowledge, indeed, that the coincidences within My story remain too great to be coincidences and so can be the consequences only of the actions of a Higher Power. If I am not the conclusion of those consequences there cannot be many steps left beyond Me. The gap between prophet and messiah is tiny, the thrust to the line in a hundred-yard dash.

Have you begun to think it through? Have you looked beyond the obvious candidates, searching for a Divine Twist? Have you thought for a moment that perhaps it is you? That this whole Testament was nothing but a preparation for you? Of course you have. All of you have.

Oh, it is woeful indeed to be genuinely unique in a time and a place where everyone believes themselves genuinely unique. Call it a thought experiment, one that you have just failed. I will give you one last chance to atone (and I intend to say this again before dawn). Get down on your hands and knees and think only of Me.

From: 100001@hotmail.com
To: mandyhart200@hotmail.com

mand - as 4 him 4 what he is 4 the so called king james who cares? does it matter wether he bought me out here like he says or i bought him out here like i say? not 2 u. what diffrence does it make? if hes what he says he is then the only thing that proves he exists is his tired old body. & if he turns out 2 be nothing more than some code i stole & improved & pumped full of data from every machine in england? what if he turns out to be that? an intelligent machine making up stories 2 fill the gaps? just code making an other kind of code? well the result will be the same. i got it all set up. when i go of course he goes. & the question of exactly what kind of processers hes built of is redundunt. sorry if that seems harsh. it is harsh. the worlds harsh. it dont change how i feel about u. dont change that i luv u sis. but u never replied. not 1nce. & i cudnt wait 4 ever. binary rob

(Converted from the ASCII)

32

Can it really be just a coincidence that at the precise moment the sun finally rises from the sea, biting down into the horizon so that it looks as if all the water will pour into the gap, at the exact moment the dark expanse of wave on wave turns golden, can it really be a coincidence that this is the moment at which Jimmy chooses to live? If you could reach down now and bring yourself near enough to Jimmy's ear to whisper the question, as he screw kicks and spits water, a clockwork frog on its winder's last rotation, if you could reach down to ask, if Jimmy had the strength left to answer, he would tell you, yes, it really is. Just another fucking coincidence. Or fate, maybe. Maybe fate. Because all Jimmy has done, as far as he is concerned, is give up on giving up. Today, anyway, for now. And it's typical of Fate or whichever malicious God looks over Jimmy to give such grand notice of his failure to die. *Fuck you,* thinks Jim. *Fuck you all.*

It had started well enough. The last of the tide had caught him and pulled him out into a dark current, the current had carried him further, an easy graduation from force to greater force that made swimming almost unnecessary. Glancing over his shoulder at the increasingly tiny lights on the shore, Jimmy was surprised at how quickly there seemed no possibility of going back. And out there in the dark, just the rhythm of his strokes and the sound of the water multiplying into a deep murmur, Jim began to anticipate oblivion.

But oblivion, it seemed, was always just a little further on. Jimmy kept swimming, easily, without fatigue. In no hurry, knowing that the end would come. How could he be sure of the exact moment when it occurred to him that his limbs, his whole body in fact, had opted for mutiny? At some point on his journey, as he swam on and on, his body implacable, never faltering, as the minutes turned to hours and the moon plotted its slow course across the sky, he began to feel like a brain in a box strapped to the back of a turtle, his commands going nowhere. Perhaps no one even knew he was in there.

Regardless, his legs kept on flapping and his arms pumping. When they felt themselves cramping to the point where their performance was in serious danger of suffering, they switched to a gentle breast stroke, all seemingly without Jimmy's input.

It was then that the fear came. First of his own body trundling forward without him through the night. Then of the depth of the black water beneath him, of what waited all that way below. Last, of where he was being taken. And the more scared he became, the more urgently he seemed to pull himself through the water, an autopilot with no plane. It was only the absurdity of a suicide caring about these things, the absurdity, in fact, of a suicide caring about anything, that finally ripped him free. A spasm of high-pitched laughter rippled through him, his mouth dipped into brine and, for the first and last time that night, he inhaled water, his limbs all immediately conspiring to lift his shoulders above the surface, his neck extending, as he spluttered the few drops – less than it would take to fill an egg cup – back out again.

He knew, of course, that it was impossible, that he couldn't be trapped in a body that didn't want to die, that the compulsion must be his, somehow. So, as time slowly passed out there on the black surface of this wet existence, his arms and legs finding their rhythm again, he tried to isolate the thing he already knew would make life worth living. Or if not worth living, then an obligation he couldn't shirk.

He thought first of his son, of how upset the boy would be, of the epilepsis of flashbulbs as he left his house, of the taunts at school. He tried to think beyond all this to the boy himself – how he looked, the last words they had said to one another, something sentimental, even. But nothing came back. Not even his face. Already wearying of the task, he turned his attention to the mother, Gloria, who he knew loved him still, had to. Or, at the very least, pitied him. Or perhaps gave him the impression of loving him just enough to stop him moving on or doing anything else with his life. His brother? A debt he had repaid again and again, a man whose main purpose in life seemed to have been to make Jaimin appear well adjusted. His family? The family name? His mother was dead and his father, reputedly, blew half his face off with a shotgun back in Jinja, so there was no huge reservoir of family honour left to drain. And you know what? Now he thought about it, he couldn't even honestly say that his father wouldn't have done it anyway, regardless of what happened out there, regardless of the big history. In which case, nothing in Jimmy's life – not one from the multitude of complaints he has attributed to it – could be blamed on the expulsion, either. He has brought it on himself. The thought gives him some kind of grim satisfaction, hours after it first occurred.

And so, having dismissed duty, nobility, honour, Jim turned to the smaller, more personal reasons for existing. The first cigarette of the morning, the smoke's hot trail through his innards. Les Dawson at the piano. Those all too rare moments when the trajectory of the ball in your hand exactly follows the trajectory of the ball in your mind. Abba's 'Waterloo' played loud to a room of drunken sportsmen. His grandmother's cooking. That part at the back of a woman's legs where a thigh becomes a buttock. Cold beer on a hot day. He's not deep, never claimed to be, but all these things carry weight.

A perfect cup of tea, the same brown as the back of his hand three or four weeks into the season. Beans on thin white toast for breakfast on a sunny morning. Good whisky, the proper stuff, drank neat without distractions. The feel of a cricket ball hitting your hand. Coming (with such force it feels like your prostate has been ripped out) just as the coke really kicks in. The marzipan picked off a piece of Christmas cake. 'Born To Run' by Bruce Springsteen. Lying down on recently cut grass.

They kept coming, a trickle turning to a flood, Jimmy struggling to keep up with his mind. Watching clouds on a windy day. Swimming, the rediscovered pleasure of swimming. Clean bowling a batsman who you know doesn't rate you. Those purplish flowers that remind him of the jacaranda in their garden in Uganda. Morecambe and Wise. The second, third, fourth, fifth cigarette of the day, etc. Blocking in the driver of the newer sports car behind you. The complete works of Tom Sharpe. Pornography of the 'beautiful pictures of beautiful women' variety. Marilyn Monroe. Alfred Hitchcock films. *The Man With No Name*. That moment when, after being on your feet all day, you finally sit down, stretch out your legs and sigh. *Emmanuelle*. The sensation in your wrists when the ball hits the sweet spot of the bat. One of Gloria's back rubs after a long day's play. Black fruit gums. Guava so ripe it's just about to turn. Not having to be anywhere. Honey eaten straight from the jar on a spoon, or even better, a finger. That armchair that O used to have that felt like it was hugging you. Okra. Chinese spare ribs. Walking in a crowd, invisible. The moment when you let go of something you know both that you should do and that you aren't going to do. The chime of the clock that got lost when they left. The way sparrows tilt their heads. Women's tennis, not for the tennis. Humming at the exact pitch that makes your head buzz. Walking down an empty street at dawn. The smell of linseed oil. The mingled aroma of chips, vinegar and the sea. A clean cottonwool bud scraping wax from inside your ear. A deep, hot bath on a cold night.

The first few mouthfuls of Frosties before the milk starts to strip away the sugar coating. The moment when a swallow glides. Anything by Isaac Asimov. The smell of creosote newly painted on a fence. Walking into a supermarket on a hot day. Eating outside. Proper coffee. Clean sheets. Having your cock in someone's mouth. Taking a catch behind you as you fall back through the air. *Dad's Army*. Being mistaken for Sunil Gavaskar at charity cricket events. Having a really good shit. Sharing candyfloss. Champagne drunk from the bottle in a communal bath. Winning. Popcorn in a cinema. Proper striptease from a girl who knows what she's doing. Finally dislodging that dry lump of snot from your nostril. Those donuts that flop straight from the fat into sugar. A clean home you haven't had to tidy. First class travel on any form of transport. The towels in good hotels. A fridge full of miniatures. 'White Christmas'. Walking in a crowd all walking in the same direction, invisible.

Jimmy rejected them all, first individually then collectively. Phlegmatically, with a certain pride, even. But as the ideas came, so his limbs moved and when one was behind him there was always another in front such that, despite himself, he found himself dragged forward in this summer fog of sentiment, this haze of good feeling. Jimmy fought it, though, turning each stroke into spadework for his grave, resisting the temptation to choose to live, mocking the banality of his own choices, laughing without humour at himself. Tried to regain control of his swimming body.

He failed only in the last. His reasons melted under his derision, were made grotesque, questionable. But his body didn't care, didn't want a debate, just kept on going, its strength drawn from some hidden power source, Jim still at its mercy despite all the attempts at analysing the problem. So he swam on, a head bobbing on the surface of this vastness, the hair washed back now from the brown crown of skin, the dull shine from it soon lost in the swarm of reflections running from it.

His official surrender, then – long a formality – comes at dawn. He knows now, with a certainty he hasn't felt about anything for years, that he won't die today. However long he keeps going. However clear his intention. Today just isn't going to be his day. Sometimes, he reasons, it's better to be realistic about your limitations. And it's at this moment, the sun in his eyes, the taste of defeat mingling with salt in his mouth, that his strength leaves him. He feels it drip out of his arms and then his legs, feels his torso go slack, his momentum evaporate, the cold suddenly deep inside him, his brain shivering. He rolls with the waves, barely able to keep himself above the surface. But it doesn't matter. He knows now he won't die.

He had seen them first in the light before sunrise – black grids above the water, tripods with ugly, bulbous heads, a gang of gods clustered up ahead of him waiting to mock his retreat. Now he's nearer and everything has changed, the towers a smear of piss yellow and rust brown, ragged, eyes wild and smashed and staring, mouths spouting twists of ruptured metal, all sense of scale warped by those four long legs, the blocks above constantly about to topple, small factories someone's played a joke on. He's lived in Kent for thirty years and he's never heard of the sea forts. Not that he cares. All Jimmy cares about is keeping his arms and legs going long enough that he can get there and, somehow, with the last of himself, drag his corpse from the water.

Jimmy Patel has chosen life.

mand - barnums are coming. they must be. shes here. this verna lander biddy. she was meant 2 come & now she has. it cant be 2 long 2 go. & i want u 2 know that what im gone do aint revenge. thats important 2 me. its just my idea of a send off. a send off 4 my self. try 2 imagine it. every hard drive in england blank. every computer crashed. all the data in england stored just out here. all that data being set free turned in2 energy me being set free turned in2 energy. so that my matter becomes part of all that matter & all of it becomes part of the data of this bit of england. this water. all free. like the firework when mum died. only hopefuly itll work ;-) u remember? u wouldnt let me go & pick it up till next morning. & it was raining! uve always been over cauitous. thats why ur still working in the shopping centre. theres an other man here. just looked in & tried 2 talk 2 me. i gotta be quick. i aint got long. mand i know i aint 1 2 talk but theres more 2 life than the shop surely? & i know its a good job but ur better than that. u cud be i dont know what a secretry or some thing! work in a office. wear 1 of those suits with a skirt. actually put ur specs on 4 once. shag the district manager u cud be running things in 6 months! i dunno. just not that fucking shop 4 ever. u got 2 have dreams? i have & im making mine real. thats it i guess. running out of time. got 2 finish this &. & any way no more 2 say. u know i love u. & i wish that cud be enough. but it aint. see u. ur little bro rob xx

(Converted from the ASCII)

33

32.

The two witnesses stand side by side in the lift, facing the door and looking up in mutually copied abstraction. His badly made suit is slightly too big, hers slightly too small. He pulls at his collar, she smooths her tie. Both suck, with the occasional slurp of lost traction, at boiled sweets.

'Bloody 'ell. Dying for that coffee. Took ages.'

'Yeah. Yeah. It did.'

'You all right?'

'Yeah. Yeah fine . . .'

'But . . .?'

'Well . . . nothing.'

'No, go on.'

'Well . . . I was just wondering. Where were the guns? On the submarine thingy?'

'Guns?'

'Yeah, the guns. For them to fire at the target. The sea thing. The army thing in the sea. Whatever it was. The thing we're attacking.'

'. . .'

'Oh.'

'What?'

'I see.'

'What?'

'The submarine thing. That kind of *is* the gun.'

'What?'

'The front of it's a warhead. You just point it at the target and . . . boom.'

'. . .
'Blimey.'
'Yeah . . .'
'. . .
'But what about. What about the girls . . .?'
'. . .
'Dunno.'
Their eyes suddenly lose their carefully maintained stillness, flutter
about like dreamers', meet for a moment and, just as quickly, drop to
their badly chosen shoes. Both of them begin sucking harder.

●

'Hello?
'I'm sorry, I can't see you.
'Yes, I can hear you, but where are you . . .?
'I'm not *supposed* to see you?
'Well. Well, this is most, I was going to say "foolish", but I will
content myself with "irregular". This really is most irregular.
'So be it. I'm not sure a gentleman would . . .
'So be it. Most irregular. Miss Verna Landor. Delighted to *meet*
you.'

31.

Up the ladder, rust gnawing at his palms, Peter begins the penultimate
stage of his ascension. He never looks back, refuses to look down,
keeps his head absolutely level, his eyes flickering up to the next rung
with whichever hand and panning back down to horizontal as he pulls
through on it, flicking up, panning back down. He seems to have been
here for ever, in this stilted tomb above the sea. He has explored every
option, taken every passage, waited endlessly for the pay-off and now,
her groans, the echo of that song bouncing round at him from strange
angles, now he just needs to get some air. Some daylight.

●

'And whom do I have the pleasure of meeting?

'Oh.

'Oh yes.

'Of course I remember you, darling.

'Of course I do.

'Of course I remember you.

'Of course.

'Of course I do.

'Yes. Yes, *James*. I was about to say it. You worked for my husband.

'I'm sure I would have got it quicker if I could have at least seen you.'

30.

It had started with the winch, Peter sure he would be sick again as he watched the old lady corkscrew one way and then the other, moving round more than up, it seemed, the strange harness holding her arms out at right-angles from her, her skirt billowing up and away from her straight legs, the last of the evening's sun turning her hair coppery. Up and slowly up toward the oblong block of darkness in the tower's side.

Peter doesn't like heights much. It's not a phobia as such, just a strong aversion to being suspended a considerable distance above a huge expanse of water and a pitching tub of a boat captained by – if the messy explosion of his facial capillaries is anything to go by – a career drunk. But he is learning to live with doing things he doesn't like, is even developing a certain pained relish for it.

He had asked Tom to strap him in and been refused, forced to make the journey upward unattached, his hands slipping with sudden moisture, his legs twined round themselves and the footstraps, Norman Wisdom impersonating ivy, his eyes unseeing beneath the tight-scrunched folds of his lids' flesh.

●

'Oh and what are these, darling?

'What? No, what are these.

'What's it? What's what?

'Oh, I see. My, you have gone to a lot of trouble.'

There was no welcoming party. No welcoming individual, in point of fact. A long, dark, concrete corridor irregularly bulb-lit, the patches of 40-watt gloom serving only to illuminate the walls' pollocked filth. And in front of him – as he stood there, leaning, searching for breath, caught between cowering away from the bright drop behind him and what lay ahead – a Lidl bag, an envelope sellotaped to its top. The word 'Scribe' written in wobbly copperplate. Could no one use his fucking name today?

My Dearest Scribe,

Thank you for your attendance. I am sorry that I am not available to, so to speak, usher you in. It causes Me great pain to be forced to miss your arrival. However, Miss Landor and I are old acquaintances (more than acquaintances, if truth be told) and we need some time to ourselves. We have a considerable amount of catching up to do.

I hope you will forgive Me the inconvenience, in fact feel sure you will. By tomorrow you will have a much bigger story than My interior décor. A much bigger story than you have ever had before. A much bigger story than it would actually be possible for you to have had before. You may think that I am over-emphasizing the point but if so, you are wrong. An understandable mistake.

So please try to be patient. We will play a game between us where we pretend your purpose here is exactly as it was originally set out (and here I quote from your charming editor's email): 'to look at the use of military space in a civilian setting, to understand how [My] environment impacts on [Me] and how [I] have impacted upon it'. I place My entire property, this perfectly proportioned Kingdom of Mine, at your disposal. Go where you will, look at what you like. Investigate, explore, theorize. Only two doors are locked. Please do not touch any computer equipment.

On your travels you will most probably meet My assistant, Robert. I have informed him of your presence but would advise against wasting too much effort on conversation. He only really interfaces with machines.

In the bag to which this letter was attached you will find some provisions. Nothing too fancy – just solid, unpretentious vittals. Also a blanket. Tomorrow will be a busy day. I would advise you to get some sleep.

I look forward to meeting you, young man.

Your humble Master,

King James of Vernaland

•

'Are you going to join me or am I to eat dinner alone?
    'Just your voice for company?
    'Could you turn it up? Or come and sit with me?
    'You want what?
    'No. No, I won't command you to.
    'No, I won't. Most certainly not.'

28.

Two bags of own-brand crisps and what looked like an own-brand Twix sitting on top of a very thin tartan dog blanket apparently custom made for a chihuahua. Peter pulled himself up again, sighed as if he wanted to expel all air from his body, crumple down like discarded packaging and be blown away. Wheeled slowly round to the now darkening rectangle of outside but failed to persuade his body to step back towards it. Took out his mobile and summoned Donald's number from his address book, though he knew he daren't call it. Finally, with a smaller, less self-dramatizing huff and the almost human exclamation of his zip, removed his lifejacket, unclipped his document folder and added it to the contents of the carrier before lifting the bag and stepping forward. The logo scuffed and scratched, the handles with the stretched, translucent, human-skin quality of a disposable item already over-used.

•

'Have you been out here on this fort, this thing for long?

'Ever since the . . .?

'Ever since . . .?

'No? Scotland? Lovely, darling. Lovely.

'No? Well, the views are good, I suppose.

'No, the views here. It seems. It seems quite . . . roomy.

'Oh, I should like that. I should like that. But later, perhaps. I am not as young as I used to be, darling. The journey . . .

'I beg your pardon? A shrine, you say? How very interesting. Yes, but later.'

27.

Initially he had roamed with caution, a character from a first-person shoot-'em-up, the concrete, the darkness and dirt, the occasional flutter from the bulbs, all scraping at his composure. The first corner had been the hardest of all, his eyes drawn back unbidden to the rectangle of the entrance, now a deep, velvety, sensuous sort of blue. A false symbol of hope, of course, just water and sky out there, and the gap between them. He had forced himself onward by composing an opening line for the piece, finally abandoning *If you were to search for a (literally) concrete embodiment of the slasher aesthetic* . . . in favour of the more pragmatic, *If the location scouts for* Scream 28 *(or whatever number they're up to by now) are running out of ideas, they could do worse than charter a fishing boat out to* . . . With which he had finally left the outside world behind.

●

'You named it after me?

'Oh.

'Oh. I suppose that's flattering. Whatever next?

'Oh.

'Oh. The whole country.

'Yes, I suppose that would be flattering.

'I'm sorry, I really am struggling to hear you. Despite what?'

26.

Neo-modernist brutalism. Inside the Leviathan. After a while, Peter had begun to enjoy himself. *The council block foyer of Middle England's nightmares. Erno Goldfinger with David Cronenberg decor.* The ideas kept coming, each whispered into his dictaphone, flirtations with himself.

As he had approached the tower in the boat he had realized it was less a pillbox on stilts than a warehouse on legs, as if Orson Welles had been busy adding the finishing touches to his radio hoax. Inside, walking corridor after corridor, glancing through doors at room after abandoned room, the place had grown yet again, the building sprouting up and out round him. Lost in it, happy to be lost in it. In his element.

•

'My *actions?* Despite my actions?

'I'm afraid if you wish me to have any idea what you're talking about you are going to have to be a little more clear. My *actions?*

'You know, I've always said that I love to be teased, but there are ways and there are ways.'

25.

The bones in Jimmy's arms and legs seem to have warped now with cold and damp. His hands each try to tickle their own wrist, his legs feel so twisted he could walk backwards. If he were on dry land he could walk backwards. Out here all he can do is whine, a continuing, desperate survival whine. The towers, which seemed so close when he made this decision, seem no closer still, another trick of the sea and his body, their intimate conspiracy, this game they're playing. All the same, like a puppy in a kiddy flick, he paddles on.

•

'Why should I know you were in Scotland?

'What?

'Why should I even care, for that matter? You are an exceedingly bumptious fellow.

'I can assure you I had more important matters to deal with after Victor's death than where you were holidaying.

'I should imagine.'

24.

Wherever he went he was followed by Verna talking, her voice looping calmly and slowly through a conversation in which the replies registered only as hot, wheezing breath. At first the effect was, he felt, a little tacky, as if his conscience was punishing him for taking advantage of the senile old crone with his deliberately worthless contract, his decision to pay her nothing more (when in fact, if anyone had been trying to manipulate the situation to his or her advantage, he felt, it was her). As a way of lessening the guilt he obsessed on the mechanics, imagining a rudimentary communication system of pipes and mouth holes networking the whole tower. The hygiene implications of such a network slowly transforming interest into an uneasy repulsion, a vision of rats spluttering out germs, the structure's nervous system their nest. But gradually, as he stopped listening to what she was saying and adjusted to the well-modulated, soothing quality of her voice, he had begun to enjoy the disembodied murmurs as the place's own ambience.

•

'You think I'm running Barnums? That I got rid of you so that I could take over?

'Would it make you feel better if I did?

'My recollection is that Victor double-crossed me. I don't think he even owned it.

'The Americans, I would imagine. Who else? All I got was a flat in Markham.

'You did better out of it than me.'

23.

He found a room with a rusted bedframe in it and, on the floor, one burgundy rubberized glove, the plastic applied to the fabric so thick and noduled that it held its sausagey, cartoon-hand shape. A room with the word BEG whitewashed on the wall. A room packed almost to the door with (presumably) broken, black-encased audio equipment, a confusion of white tide lines texturing the surfaces. A room with a dead animal of some sort (he didn't look too closely). A room with the floor carefully covered with newspaper, yellowed and matted together. A room with a military cot-bed, the blankets neatly tucked in and the floor swept. A room with a congregation of pots of paint, their lids encrusted with openings and closings. A kitchen. A room with an Elvis poster on the wall. An empty room, the dust lying even, undisturbed bar Peter's footprints. A room that wasn't there, the metal door swinging back to reveal smooth, clean concrete. A room with a desk and a computer. A room full of thick yellow wires and dirty beige boxes, screens here and there clattering out row after row of numbers, the whole emitting a low hum, the atmosphere warm and dry. Another room almost identical to the one before. Another. And another. So many rooms, minutes turning to hours as he mapped them with quotable insights. A room with Robert in.

•

'As I said I was as much a victim as you. More, perhaps.

'Maybe it was a trap he set for us. That would certainly make sense.

'Oh, he was dying anyway.

'Cancer, I think. Something terminal, anyway. I thought that was what killed him.

'Yes.

'Yes. Yes, I know I was married to him, but does that have to mean that we shared everything?

'So, no, I don't suppose he was too upset. Are you sure you killed him?'

22.

With lift in continual ascent, the second witness reaches for something in his pocket, the hairs on his hand just feathering the first witness' hip. A scared rodent, it's pulled out of the way, hidden, while they cough and puff out their cheeks and the first witness checks her watch.

'Do you think it's there yet?'

'What?'

'The sub– . . . the missile thing.'

'There at the target?'

'Yeah.'

'Probably not. Nearly, probably. Nearly but not quite.'

Their two bodies imperceptibly swaying with the lift's microscopic lateral roll, their shoulders momentarily touch.

'I mean, it moves fast and everything. But no, I wouldn't think it's quite there yet.'

•

'Speak for yourself, darling.

'No. No.

'No, I suppose it's a reasonable point.

'No, you probably wouldn't forget killing someone.

'Least of all Victor.

'But then again, personally speaking, I forget the most unlikely things.'

21.

Peter presumed it was Robert, anyway. A young man sitting at a keyboard, his shoulders puppet spikes, the short hair on the back of his head a nondescript, uniform brown, his long, thin right arm, apparently tattooed down the inside, suspended precariously between shoulder and desk, his index and middle finger tapping out an unending polyrhythmic line on the two keys they rested above. This the only sound in the room, this steady crackling, except for Verna's words, harsher here, more metallic, generated by circuits. And, on the screen partially obscured by his left shoulder, the face that had bobbed in front of Peter on the boat, a greenish tint to it, the folds of skin around her eyes brought into greater relief by the complete darkness at their centre, the one candle in view flaring so bright on the screen as to register as a lack of information.

●

'Did you resent me awfully? I think Victor said you resented me awfully.

'I seem to remember I quite liked it. Being resented. I think that's why Victor told me.

'So did you?'

20.

Peter had seeped into the room, the couple of steps necessary transformed into a stuttering choreography, his eyes on Verna's image more than the boy, the intent, almost cross-eyed concentration, her head tipped forward to register the croaks.

'Uh, hi.'

The response minimal, in fact non-existent, not even an aberration in the keyboard's patter. A strangled attempt at a stage cough then, louder, 'Hi. Hi there.'

The typing stopped. The only sound another probable question or declarative statement hissing from the speakers. The slow turn.

Peter had seen the expression before, of course. Or rather, the non-expression – the same unusually relaxed facial muscles, the same seemingly careful lack of animation, the same eyes, like a cow's or a coma patient's. The same *blankness*. The shock of recognition so great that he immediately got a flash of Mandy's face as he, dribbling and quietly keening, had spluttered semen into her. The recollection causing him to blush, the blush further discomfiting him, so that he could meet the other's silence only with another, 'Hi. Hi. Peter. You must be Robert.'

The face – Mandy's face, unmistakeably her face, sewn on to the head of this boy's body – continued its uninterested appraisal of him, saturating him in emptiness, before, slowly, returning to the screen.

The fingers resuming their private duet and Peter left standing there, his feet hot, swollen-feeling, however he distributed the weight.

It was only moments later, as, with renewed hesitancy, he turned and left the boy to himself, the look he had seen on his face now always overlapping with Mandy's face, only then that it struck him. Perhaps this was how all young people looked? Perhaps they were all like this and he just hadn't noticed until he'd got to her. Had been too busy with things, with objects, too enamoured with *the semiotics of historically specific timeless style* to notice. Too busy getting old. No, this was too easy. The truth was he didn't really care about the aesthetics. It just seemed preferable to admitting that he didn't care about anything, that life passed him like something viewed through glass. And that not even this fact could be made to matter.

He had stopped, raised a palm to the sticky wall and tried to imagine Gus's and Poppy's faces like that, the terrible stillness. Imagined going home tomorrow to find them like that.

•

'Oh darling, I'm sorry. I am.

'You want it all to add up, don't you? You want some grand conspiracy to make sense of it all.

'Life isn't like that, I'm afraid. All there is is incompetence and greed and random error.

'That's all there is, my darling. Especially here. Especially in England. It's our forte.

'I'd like to be able to say we were world leaders, but it's in the nature of incompetence that there's bound to be someone even better at it. Though I forget who.

'Are you lost for words? Has it taken you all this time . . .?

'And it's never even occurred to you?

'Well, I'm sorry to be the bearer of bad tidings but that's all there is to it.'

19.

01110100011010000110010101110010011001100101011100110010000000110000101101110001000000011011110111011101000110100001100101011100100110010101110010011001010101110010011001100101011000010110100001100101011100100110010100000011011010101100001011011100010000001101000011001010101110010010010010010011001001

299

0010011100010000000110101001110101010111001101110100000100000011101100
0110111101101101111011010101101100101001100100001000000110100101011101110
0010000000100110001000000111010001110010011010010101100101011001100
0010000000110010001000000111010001100001011011100011010101100100000
0011001000100000000110110101100101001011110001000000110100100100000
0110011101101101111011110100011101000011000010010000001100010010011001
00100000001110001011101010101010100101011000110110101011001011100010000
0110100100100000000110000101101010010101101111001110100000100000011001111
0110111101101101100000010000001101100011011101110110111100110011001011
He has to get this done. Rob has to finish this email now. He's disappointed in himself, of course, the neediness, the hint of desire. He tries to focus back in on the rhythm of his typing, to ignore what he's writing, to forget even that he's writing. But still he has to get this done. There's no denying that time is running out. Everything points to it.

•

'What's that . . .

'What's that snuffling noise . . .?

'You're not weeping, are you?

'Surely you're not weeping?

'Or . . .? Oh gosh, really, darling. I mean, *really.* Oh.

'Perhaps I should leave you to it . . . wherever it is that you are.'

18.

Down at the bottom, at the very bottom, a pale, shoddy-looking fish noses at the piece of yellowish weed which has managed to force its way through a silted geometry of discarded bicycles, sofas, tins, smashed TVs, old turntables, cracked bathroom suites, broken bottles – all the cast-offs and rejects that have crawled here to die. The fish, its eyes bred ten-pence large for a chance to see through the brown gloom, is tentatively, unenthusiastically reaching forward to eat the weed, obviously lacking in both nutritional value and flavour, when it stops. Flickers its head side to side. Tenses. Dives into a hole between a backless sideboard and a holed watering-can. Stays there.

Then there is stillness. Then more stillness. A little more, the quivering in the water still imperceptible. Then a gentle hum. Then a louder hum. Then a sudden bubbling roar through the water as, directly above the fish, a vicious black monster swoops over, its long nose glinting despite the gloom, each of the three eyes visible on its side containing the head of an illuminated blonde, each of those blondes smiling (though if the fish weren't so busy hiding, he would see that g-force is playing havoc with the definition). Gone almost before it has arrived, the absence of the monster pulls three-legged chairs and halved tables and cracked bowls and squashed cans and mud and weed and even the fish dancing and winnowing along in its wake. And as the fish flips and flips over, rolling round laterally, backward, up into the thing's passing, it's too disorientated to appreciate the novelty of the moment, this unique event in its clouded existence. It just wants to go home.

•

'Is there a powder room, darling? Not that I am expecting much in the way of facilities. I can tell that only men live out here. Nevertheless, nature calls.

'I do hope you at least mopped the floor. You knew I was coming.'

17.

Peter had staggered down corridor after corridor pursued by Mandy's face, retching. Poor kid. Had admitted it now. Poor kid. The unique stillness of her features had aged her, the make-up, too, but there was no excuse. Poor kid. His skin not seeming to fit right. His legs heavy, unfamiliar. He would like to be able to claim that he had been rotting, fermenting in his own cynicism, but he knew it wasn't cynicism, that even this would require some engagement or act of disengagement. His eyes bleary with excess liquid. That what really drew him to her, that kept drawing him back to her again and again, despite his resolutions to the contrary, despite his clever words, despite the supposed refinement of his taste, was the blankness of her face. The perfect, unanswerable, concrete reflection of his own mind.

•

'Do you really think so?

'It seems a little outlandish, if you don't mind me saying so.

'It sounds as if your planning processes may have benefited a little from an outside input or opinion.

'Do you think anyone will care? Even if you are what you say you are? Even if you had parted oceans or created life or some such?

'People nowadays are very hard to impress.

'Do you think anyone would care?'

16.

0110101001110101011100110111011010000100000011011100110111101110100
0010000001110100011010000110000101110100001000000110011001110101
0110001101101010110110100101011011100110011100100000011100110110101000
0110111101110000001000000110100001000000110010101011101100110010010
0111001000101110001000000111010100100000011001110110111101110100
0010000001100100000010011010000101110110010100100100000
0110010001110011001000010110101100010101101011100110011111110100100000
0110100100100000110100001100001011101100100100100100000010011010
0010000001101001011011010010000011011010101100001011010101011010100
0110111100110011100100000011011010101010010010110111100110010010010000
011100100100100101011000010110110000101110

Even as he tries to drift away from all this, from his worldly concerns, even as he tries to fix himself on the pleasing patterns of lines and circles he is sending scrolling down his window, even then Rob's eyes refuse to be part of the machine, stay firmly on the old lady's face filling the screen. It's not her as a human being, or even her as an icon. It's just this. He wants to see what will happen. Even though he knows it will inevitably disappoint.

•

'And am I part of this plan? Have you been trying to lure me out here for years?

'No? Well, you certainly know how to flatter a lady, darling.

'Oh, it's part of the *divine* plan. Of course it is. How foolish of me.'

15.

Peter's legs had followed their own course. Not looking for escape. That would be stupid. But the next best thing. A compromise. So that as he devoted his mental energy to the pleasures of shame – implying, as it did, a definite commitment to the world – his legs shuffled back and forth down corridors to dead ends, almost running, seeking staircases to bound up, ladders to propel his weight up, following, at last, a clear-cut imperative. Up.

●

'Are you sure this is really what this is all about?

'Really?

'Did he still sleep with you after I came along?

'I apologize for the euphemism. Did he still fuck you?

'Occasionally? Was that occasionally occasionally or occasionally never?

'The latter? As I thought. He was a surprisingly bad liar. I'm sure I would have known. I'm sure I would recall *that*.'

14.

Even a witness knows when to change the subject.

'So what you doing tonight?'

'Dunno. Nothing. Nothing, I don't think.'

'Really?'

'Yeah.'

'I thought you were a party animal.'

'Well, maybe not tonight.'

'Whassup? Not feeling well?'

'Whassup, eh?

'*Wazzurp . . .?*'

●

'You like it when I talk dirty, don't you?

'Yes you do. I can tell.

'I can picture you blushing.

'Surely we're getting a little old for all this nonsense? I know what you want.

'Do you have money?

'Really? *Bullion*? Here? How much?

'Well, I never. Victor . . .?

'And you are the one feeling hard done by. Well, let's get on with it then. I'm awfully tired.

'Here on the table? Oh, *elsewhere*. Do you have another surprise for me, darling? Will you be there waiting for me?'

13.

Jimmy is in amongst them now and indulging a final perversity, a last choice, though it may be due to nothing more than the currents beneath him, dragging him back and forward like a piece on a board. There you are, that's how it is, why stop at the first, anyway, when you can splutter and whimper through the water to the tower at the centre, the nexus? It's not as if he can ship more liquid, his pores closed over litres of it, his stomach barrelling with brine, the dribble escaping his desperate, contorted mouth indubitably saline. It may be the salt that is keeping him fresh, in fact, his arms a blotched, deathly blue. But something about the layout looks like a wicket with a fan of slip catchers and, in Jim's mind, perhaps, compels him to go for the stumps. One last shy at the stumps.

●

'I hope it's not too far. I really am quite tired.

'Left here? Left?

'I thought you said left.

'Have you ever thought of putting some pictures up?

'Just something to brighten the place up a little?

'Which door? Which? The *far* door. Of course. It would have to be the *far* door.'

12.

0110101001000000110101101101110011011110111011101110010000001101001
0010000001101100011011110111011001100100101000000011101010010101110
0010000001001100010000000110100100100000001110111011010100101110011
0110100000100000011101000110100001100001011101000000011000011
0111010101100100000100000011000100111001001001000000011001010110111
0110111110111010101100111101101000000101110001000000110001001110101
0111010000100000011010010111010000010000000110000101101001001101011
0111010000101110000100000011100110110100101011001010010010000000111010
0010011100010000000111010101011001001000001101100011010010111010100
0111010001101100011001010010000001100010011100100110111100100100000
0111001001101110111011100010001000000111100001111000

She's vanished. Rob has switched between cameras and followed her progress, knowing already exactly where she is going, his every cut anticipating her next turn. He has seen her gradually grow larger as she slowly, so slowly, approaches another corner then suddenly turn tiny again as he flicks her on to the next. He has watched the door roll smoothly open before her, the light flood out. He has seen her face, illuminant, as she steps in and so out of view. It's obvious to him now that he should have fitted a camera in there. It made sense at the time and now it's too late. All he has to go by is the sound of her drawn-breath exclamation, her words.

•

'Oh My. Oh. My goodness.
'Yes I see. I see what you mean.
'The pictures are . . . They're very. Very. They're me, I presume?
'Yes, very close up. Very . . . explicit.
'And here's the. Heavens. How much did you say there was?
'Oh, I should think so. At least.
'How about I put one in my handbag now as insurance and you give me the other after? My, they're heavy aren't they?
'Will you be joining me?'

11.

Peter pushes the hatch back, the sudden light an alien abduction, his eyes blind with clean white. But not pulling away, blinking up sightless, seduced by the novelty. It seems like he's been down in the dark for years. A cold waft of salted air coats his face. The sea suddenly smells good to him, a comfort. His eyes adjust and, at last, he can see the rungs again, is ready to emerge.

•

'So how do you want me? Robed, disrobed or semi-robed?
'Disrobed? As you wish, darling. Anything else?
'Well, you of all people should know it isn't going to work like that. You claim to have photographed me enough times.
'Are you trying to pretend to have forgotten or have you never seen anyone naked except me? I never go on top. Never. It would be

possible, just about, I grant you. But so undignified.

'Does that mean you're going to put in an appearance?

'Oh, on top of all *that*. Not you. Of course.'

10.

The sky so sky blue it becomes a copy of itself, endlessly reproduces itself, overlays itself until the intensity's that beautiful it's vulgar. Peter feels surrounded by it, by sky, which seems to run not just through heaven but beneath the island of concrete he finds himself crouched on, his hands flat to the floor, warmth entering them. Carefully, as if the ground might tip, he unfolds himself, stands, the sea suddenly rising with him, a band of darker blue, a sediment. To his left and his right a scribbled line divides the two shades, so he takes his step forward, away from the open trapdoor, to where the sketching meets.

•

'You knew, though, didn't you? Of course you knew.

'What is it, darling? Didn't you understand?

'I must say I can't help but feel rather pleased. Why? Why what?

'Why this in particular? Darling, it's been so very long I'm not sure I can remember.

'What?

'No, I'm not bored. I sighed because it's hard to explain. I suppose the truth is that we very few of us are happy with the body we find ourselves in. With who we are, physically. There are degrees of it, I would think. Mine, I seem to remember, was a particularly large degree. I wanted to turn right around. And then I suppose there was conscription.

'Well, we couldn't all rely on Victor, could we? Some of us hadn't met him yet.'

09.

0111000001110011001011100010000001101001011001100010000001110101
0010000001100100011011110110110111001110100001000000110110001101001
0110101101100101001000000111010001101000001100101001000000110001
0110111001100100010000010000001101001011011010010000001110011011011111

0111001001110010011110010010100000011000100111010101110100001000000
0110100101110100001000000011101110110000101110011001000000011011110
0110010101011011100110010101110010001000001011010011001010110000I
0110111001110100001000000011001000100000000111000001101100011001001
0110000101110011011001010010000011101010010011100010000000011101111
0110100001100001011101000010000001110111011010010100000011001101
0110010101000010110010001010110011010110110111101110011011011010100
0010000001100100001010010101110011011011101000111001001101011110111001
0111001100100000011101010101110011001001011100010000000111010001101001
0110110101011001010010000000110010001000000011100110110110100011011111
0111000000100000011000100110010101100101011010010110111001100100000
0111001101011000010110100001011100100110010101100100001011110

He has rejected inner turmoil, the conflict of desires, but they have not rejected him. Robbie wants to see the room. He loves his sister. He needs to evolve. Wants to be free of wanting. Curdles with fear. Has refused involvement but is still involved. He's finished his last message but still has to stay where he is, be ready when the moment comes. Be ready for his own plan, for the attack he has anticipated with such longing. For escape. But, then again, there's the room he decided to leave to them, something he needs to free himself of. He goes to stand and his legs quiver under him. How long has it been, he wonders, since he left this desk?

●

'Oh for heaven's sake . . .

'No, not you . . .

'It's just these buttons. Or my fingers. I would have worn some-thing else if I'd known I was going to strip.

'I *am* taking my time.

'You might at least have turned the heating up.'

08.

Pete doesn't know why he does it, what he wants from it, what it means, even. He just pulls his phone from his pocket, squints at the bar representing a weak signal, smiles. Beds the phone down in his hand and begins poking his thumb at the keys. Any signal at all is a minor miracle and, in his sun-fuzzed head, he thinks he should man-ifest his gratitude through use.

Sorry about everything That's happened. I love you. Call me.

He knows her number, of course, in a moment it's gone and he does-n't stop, even now, to analyse his motivation, its meanings, the multiple ambiguities. He is happy. He has no idea how or why. He pulls his lifejacket from the carrier bag and starts hitching it round his shoulders as he takes a tentative step closer to the edge.

•

'And you're sure you're up to this?

'I don't want to be responsible for you dropping dead or some-thing. Not after you've waited so long. Mind you, what a way to go, eh?

'Darling?

'I beg your pardon?

'You just worry about yourself.

'Are you going to come and join me?

'At least come and sit in the room. I really don't mind what you do with yourself.'

07.

All three of the girls feel the angle of the machine change, the sud-den tilting upwards of the nose, its eagerness to break the surface and fly – air replacing water – the last metres to its target. So, by the bright glow from their own hair, the glint of their resplendent teeth, they clear their throats and prepare to sing. There is only one song it can be, the company song, the first they learnt and have since sung every day, each morning from their discovery, wrapped in swad-dling, snuggled in a cardboard box, resting in an Asda bag, in the waiting room of a Barnums hospital, under a bush in a Barnums park, on the steps of a Barnums orphanage, the offspring of an eleven year old, a teenage prostitute, an illegal immigrant. They have sung the song, with increasing gusto, the comfort of the words enfolding them, in Barnums nurseries, Barnums schools, Barnums universities, Barnums offices, Barnums brothels, Barnums laborato-ries, Barnums salons. Most of all in Barnums salons, their hair never before this perfect, pristine, immune to gravity, to human error, to fashion, never before so bright.

•

'And you want me just . . . so. And nothing I say can persuade you to join me?

'No? Well, then, anything else?

'Oh God, really? You're making this very difficult for me.

'It's just rather. Rather tacky, don't you think? A little unimaginative. I mean, of all the songs . . .

'Still, as you wish . . .'

06.

Above and in front of the three girls, coughing and spluttering, lashed by jellyfish, nibbled at by herring, Jimmy half-floats below another ladder, at last all animal. It's simple now. There are laws for how long a human can survive in the sea and he's broken them. He has to get out.

A final lunge up, a last spasm of effort, his legs thrashing beneath the surface, and his fist, Jimmy's once work-hardened right fist, the calluses long ago turned translucent and soft, Jimmy's old, English right fist clamps tight round the lowest rung, trigger finger squashed by thumb. His torso hangs quivering beneath, his legs coming and going, coming and going, with the swell of the waves.

•

> *No man is an island*
> *Oh yes, that's for sure*
> *No man is an island*
> *In times of war . . .*

05.

So it's just as Robbie has finally arisen, determined to see the room, certain now that this is the right path, that he can't leave without it, it's just at this moment that the alarm goes. The tower is under attack. There is a foreign body on the ladder from the sea. The moment he's been waiting for has arrived. As he slumps back at his desk he allows himself to enjoy his relief. His defences have worked, he is still at his post, he will never have to make another decision again. He stretches back, flexes his hands against each other, savours the anticipation of his last moment.

Then the alarm stops.

●

> *No island can be one man*
> *No island can*
> *We must all stick together*
> *And fighting we will stand.*

04.

Jimmy falls through water, the palm of his right hand ripped, bubbles fizzing round him, the whole of the sea taking refuge in his head. Every hair on his body comes alive, tries to float away from him. The world seems very small.

There's no sense of panic, no shock, just determination. He waits until he stops sinking and then, as the remaining air inside him starts to drag him up, he begins to swim. Leaves the water diving in reverse, his two hands raised high above his upturned face, flying up as if he will never stop, up, up, until his open hands, left and right, collide with metal and latch there. And, before momentum finally deserts him, the next seconds a tangle of desperation, his leg is hitched up, too. Safe.

●

> *The man needs a lady*
> *The island needs a port*
> *We both need each other*
> *We'll together win this war.*

03.

Robbie's first thought is that they've bypassed his security somehow. Then, when his tests come up clear, that it was a seagull perching for a moment. When his computations suggest a different weight ratio, that it's a malfunction. Finally, with this ruled out, the cold, hollow feeling that he's been hacked. The relief, then, when the alarm starts up again, is like a perfect line of code.

Slowly, deliberately, single-fingered now, he taps out the thirty-two ones and noughts he randomly generated and learnt, as he has done every night for a month now, before he went to sleep. Slower still, enjoying his last sensual impressions, he brushes his hand across from the number pad to his main keyboard. Runs his finger slowly down the stained plastic nubs, each one carrying the penumbra of a former owner's prints. F9 Tries to picture the huge oceans of data he has stored here. ± Imagines it all compressed to the size of an atom, compressed until it bursts. } Thinks of computer screens going blank, all of them going blank, that grey, hollow glow, everything stopping. | Traces his finger gently around the last key's unusual shape, a capital L flipped upside down, stubby. Tries to concentrate on picturing everything stopping. Looks at the faded lettering. RETURN

He's too caught up now in his personal moment, the feel of this key alone beneath his index finger, to notice the dot on the radar moving rapidly towards the centre of the screen. Why, after all, would he notice? He is the only person on the tower expecting an attack and as far as he's concerned he already has it, already has everything he has ever needed.

•

> *We are a mighty island*
> *Of islands mighty strong*
> *We strive together ceaselessly*
> *That we may stay as one.*
> *We strive together ceaselessly*
> *That we may stay as one.*

02.

Peter stops about a metre from the edge, hot already, goofy with it, the trickle of sweat on his neck perfect, a caress. He looks round with a nervousness he's faked for himself to make it all more funny. Quickly unzips and fumbles his dick from his pants – bursting – and feels it gush through his internal pipes. The main thread of urine clears the side, but its flow's contractions and the usual spray between them begin to spot the concrete black.

As he pisses, Peter shuffles forward. Just a little bit. Then a little bit more, then further. Until finally his toes lie flush with the very edge and he can watch every permutation in the stream, every kink, all the way down to the water.

Begins to laugh. It's all so beautiful he begins to laugh, the light like a strobe running fast enough you can barely see the gaps, each drop utterly distinct, shining, falling but suspended somehow, too. He thinks he will never forget this, the way it looks, the sun, the juxtaposition of the yellow liquid falling to the green. He's right. Just keeps smiling and for some reason there are tears in his eyes.

Does he notice anything unusual in those last seconds? Does he see the machine, this missile or submarine or aeroplane, finally break from the water one hundred metres in front of him? Does he see the spume froth up as it shatters the surface of the waves, its body angled directly towards the concrete beneath his feet, so that all that shows is its glistening tip? Does he hear the noise of its rockets suddenly crashing through the sound of all that water moving, the gulls, a distant aeroplane? Does he feel the very air change when confronted with this force ripping into it, so close now to its target, its carefully chosen and final destination?

And if he does?

He will not, however sharp his eyes, have time to notice the picture of a young Verna Landor painted on its side, her limbs wrapping it. He will not have a chance to make out the white and red words running alongside her. Nor will he see the faces of the three girls in the small round windows, their smiling mouths closing as they hold the last note of a song passionately but now definitively sung. He won't, however sharp his mind, have time to ponder the painting's significance (the one thing his life has equipped him for). No allowance will be made for him to reflect on how much like the girl in the painting the young women look. He will not have time to make the connections between that painting, the old lady, a company or companies called Barnums and the man who has apparently invited him here. Or, alternatively, to wonder whether any such connections really exist. With certainty we can say he will not have time to reflect on the meaning or non-meaning of there being or not being any such connections. Even if he has seen it – especially if he has seen it – these concerns will not exercise his imagination. And even if he could stop time for a moment to work it all out, why would he bother? But all the same, does he see it?

There is no way of knowing. No way to ask. No time even to articulate the question. In a moment he will be falling upward, always falling up, and all his certainties and all his uncertainties will be gone. It would be better to leave him. Leave him exactly as he is now, watching the wobbly, imperfect descent of his piss, laughing, happy. Intact.

●

'. . .are we done then?

'Is that the lot, darling?

'. . .

'Darling?'

01.

There's no grey area. Decide. It's either/or. It's all either/or.

The time has come to shut it all down. Time to stop imagining. Robbie's finger presses the thirty-third key.

RETURN

●

00.

The witnesses don't seem to realize that the lift has stopped, that the doors remain closed. They just suck and stare, he brushing at a snag in his trousers, she examining her nails.

'I'm gobsmacked.'

'What?'

'All of it. It doesn't make any sense.'

'In what sense?'

'Why blow it all up? Waste all that money? And the girls, too. I mean . . .'

The first witness heaves a long, wisdom-thick puff.

'At the end of the day it's economics, isn't it? I guess? What I'm saying is. If you see. The market's beyond meaning. Isn't that what they say? In Induction? Something like that . . .'

'What the . . .? Wha–? What the fuck happened to the lights?'

'. . .'

'. . .'

'. . .'

'. . .'

'. . .'

'Bloody dark, innit?'

'. . .

'Yeah . . .'

'. . .'

'. . .'

'. . .'

'. . .'

'You ever, y'know? In a lift?

'*Done* it?'

After

Mandy leans back against the thin strip of wall between P&G and the shop next door, looks up towards the sun-bright ceiling and watches the slow swoop of the two nearest cameras as, like spotlights in a theatre, they come to settle on her. She stares straight up at them and smiles her best smile. Mandy has, she knows, roughly three minutes before Security arrive and ask her to move on. Her right hand keeps reaching for the space in her pocket where her fags should be. It's been nearly two weeks and she thought her hands, at least, would be used to it by now. Instead, it's like they think that, if only they can find one, they can sneak it into her mouth and light it without her noticing. But she likes it, likes not smoking, even if her body doesn't.

Take this, for instance – standing here watching people trundle past her, working out the routes designed for them, waiting for Security to come and nudge her to her next spot. On her first break Clearwater is still filling, the flow of people irregular, leisurely. You can pick out a shopper, usually a woman, and follow her all the way from one end of the galleria to the other, plot out her steps in front of her like a dance instruction manual. At lunch, there's so many more, moving so much faster that it's easier to let your eyes glaze and just enjoy the patterns the movement makes. By mid-afternoon, the volume's the same but the speed of movement has fallen, so now you can catch a face in the crowd and then wait for its appearance at the end of the route you've planned, like a stick appearing from under a bridge.

Until she stopped, Mandy had spent all her breaks, every one of them, down in the Smoking Room with Clea, or Tina or Mandy 2 or Mary From Marks, or Lisa or Marissa or whoever was there, cackling and coughing in the haze. And it's cool and everything, but it's nice to have a change, to watch all these people moving through this space designed for them to move through instead of always always always discussing boyfriends you haven't got, make-up you can't afford, clothes that make you look fat. It's all good and everything, but it feels nice to have a change. And she thought she'd really miss them, her mates, at school with some of them. But she hasn't. She really hasn't.

Mandy pulls the jacket more closely round her, trying to hide as much as possible of the horrible *costume* Mr Patel has the cheek to call her uniform. Not that it's his fault. Poor guy spends most of his day out the back weeping. Mind you, if he got a grip and just occasionally bought something for them to sell that wasn't complete crap, then maybe he wouldn't be crying in the first place, the Norman. Mandy likes to look on the positive, though. She's in charge for the morning. He had woken her at half five begging her to come in, sobbing on the phone, some story about his brother going missing, a stolen car, the involvement of the police. She's in charge. How many of the other girls working here can take a half-hour fag break at nine o'clock in the morning when they don't even smoke? Even if it should be her day off. Even if really she should still be in bed. She has met the brother – works up at head office, got her manager the job they say, wet-eyed and bearded when he came through, the sick smell of drink wafting round him. She smiles as she pictures him sitting in a stolen car somewhere smoking crack while her Mr Patel wrings his hands and pleads with the police, his cheeks, as ever, slick. Mandy pulls the coat round her again, this time for the feel of it, the material soft as anything. It's a lovely jacket.

The first time Mandy took him to the hotel, he had asked her to tell him all about herself. So Mandy had. How her mother had left them when she was six and Robbie was four, left them to go off and live in St Lucia with a millionaire and them stuck in a council house and with holes in their shoes. How Dad started drinking and lost his job and then, when she got older, started interfering with her. Really interfering, her lying in bed every night with her sheets wrapped tight round her, hoping it would stay just that black, that no parallelogram of landing light would perform geometrics across her floor as he came creeping in, curled – humiliated, humiliating – forward.

None of it was true. Not strictly true, anyway. Mum had died when she was twelve (cancer's a horrible thing, prefers not to think of it, prefers to imagine her in St Lucia with a millionaire's servant rubbing sun-cream on her back). And then Dad had got so drunk that he couldn't have interfered with her if he'd wanted to. Got drunk and stayed that way.

But there was something about the way he looked at her that made Mandy feel he wanted more drama than that. He was a journalist, after all. And that particular story, the one she told him, has a funny effect on older men. Mind you, being young and having a good pair of tits has a funny effect on older men. Being young and having a pair of tits, even. So while it's clear that he sat down on the bed and put his arms round her to comfort her as she wept for extra effect, she's less sure of what may have prompted his tongue in her ear. No complaints, though. No complaints. Would be good to know, though. Future reference.

Here they come – Little and Large. Little's actually larger, but seems smaller, about the same age as Mandy but still acts like a kid, flushes when he talks, has co-ordination problems. Large? Well, it's all in the gut. Security are, Mandy thinks, a law to themselves. Everyone else in here is contractually obliged to dress in keeping with the era and geography of their zone at all times, from managers to cleaners who work only when the centre's closed. Security march round in black uniforms with silver buttons and red lapels – every bit the Sally Army if it weren't for handcuffs, truncheon and stun-gun dangling from belt. Watching the approach of these two unlikely enforcers, Mand coughs back a giggle. They look stupider than she does. Almost.

'Hi, guys.'

'Morning, Mandy.' Large does the talking as usual, Little compulsively extending and retracting his neck, his chin describing a series of perfect ellipses.

'And how can I help you this morning?'

'You know how, Mandy.'

'Ooh, officer.' With a faked flick of her hair which doubles the speed of Little's chickening.

'Very funny. We need you to move, young lady. Same as every day.' He sighs and puffs the smile from his face. 'And I'm going to have to report you this time. I don't have any choice.'

Mandy pouts a little, lets her jacket fall open and, clasping her hands over her fanny, pushes her tits up toward him as unsubtly as she dares. The dirty old fucker stares straight at them, mesmerized. While he's occupied she uses his name badge to remind herself.

'Oh, Malcolm? Do you have to? I just forgot again. Promise I'll try harder?'

'You know the rules, Mandy.' (Malcolm loves using her name, like they're friends).

'I'll get fired.'

He makes as if he's thinking it through, though they all know he's already decided, had in fact decided even before he marched up, and is just using the time for one last, longing, hungry look at the place he wants to suckle.

'Go on then. Get going quick before I change my mind. You owe me.' Yeah yeah. Says that every day. Too chickenshit to collect.

'Thanks, Malc . . .'

Then she's moving, threading between people, determined to throw off the equation of anyone who thinks they've got her course plotted. Though, as she always goes to the same place she knows it's pretty futile, the electronic board opposite P&G still flashing the image of her favourite steaming hot beverage.

Another advantage with stopping smoking – you can afford a Choco-Deluxe with whipped cream and marshmallows as often as you want it. She sits at her usual table, where she'd sat that first time when she'd come here with him. Not because she's thinking of him, but because you get a really good view of all the other tables and you can see the staff looking pissed off behind their stainless-steel counter. Mandy is a firm believer that, if you spend your whole day serving other people, you should make the most of it when it's others suffering. She tries always to be rude, never tips. The boy she likes is working today – she flicked the change on to the metal so that 20p clattered off on to the floor and she got a good eyeful of his skinny arse when he bent over. Still smiled at her, though. Still keeps glancing at her now.

Mandy takes the long, thin teaspoon supplied and pushes one of the mini-marshmallows down through the whipped cream and into the hot liquid below. Holds it there for a moment and then a moment longer until she can imagine it just starting to dissolve, fishes it back out through its snow hole, pops it in her mouth. Repeats the process. The little bastard has only put five on there. The median is six, the mean higher still. She's had as many as nine in one cup. She'd like to believe he'd done it to get her back for being rude but she guesses that the truth is just that he's a boy – too busy thinking about his prick to even count. She shoots him a dirty look and he notices, gives her a bashful half-smile, like a puppy entering a sack race to the riverbed. Bored of him, she finishes off the marshmallows. Not enough about him.

Approximately a quarter of the tables round her are in use. Nearby, an old fella struggles with a tube of sugar above his tea, the label attached to the bag's string floating on the surface, strange to him, a newfangled garnish. A tanned man in a suit and loafers, no socks, smoking and drinking a huge cappuccino, tries to look Italian rather than the assistant manager of a mid-price menswear chainstore just back from a week in Ibiza. A woman and a little girl face off, the child kicking rhythmically at the table as the level in her fizzy pop drops, while her mother hisses again and again to *pack it in fuckin' pack it in*. Another woman reads a glossy magazine, her right index finger tappety-tapping on the corner of the page as it waits eagerly to turn it. A fat old couple squeezed in next to each other on one side of the table hold hands beneath the blond wood surface. A child abductor straight off the TV is grooming a sandy-haired boy with a plate of cream cakes (probably just his divorcee dad, she admits).

She's just settling down to try and eavesdrop on the mother and teen daughter at the next table, who seem to be involved in a far-reaching consumer report into the merits of various brands of thong, when she feels her phone buzz in her pocket.

You have a new message.

Read.

She clicks on his name.

Sorry about everything That's happened. I love you. Call me.

Options.
Erase.
Erase message? OK.

It's not really that she's got anything against him, it's just that it's over and she thinks that's for the best, was trying to find a way to end it, in fact, when he'd done the dirty work for her. Not that he wasn't sweet. He really was. And quite good-looking, even if he did dress a bit funny for an Older Man. She likes designer clothes and trainers and everything but what was he, forty-five? Fifty? There's a point where they start to look, what's the word? Preposterous. Preposterous and maybe a little forlorn.

But she's being hard on him. He hadn't gone that far. He looked all right. Maybe she's secretly just a little bit pissed off he finished with her, even though she wanted to finish it. No one likes being dumped, do they? No, if she's honest, he looked alright. She wasn't embarrassed to be seen with him. Not that embarrassed. And he was sweet and quite good in bed. Not great, but he was gentle and took it slowly and seemed to care about whether she was enjoying herself. Most of the boys she's been with know about foreplay, approach it mechanically like they've read the moves in a wank mag, then get bored, stick it in and pump. At least he was interested.

And, she knows, she's been lonely since Robbie left. Just her and the old man, usually too drunk to talk long before she gets home. Telly and a TV dinner, him drooling long threads of brown Guinness spittle. Mind you, it was like that when Robbie was there, but there was something, dunno, comforting about knowing he was up in his room fiddling around with his computer, his occasional grunts from the doorway as he went to the fridge for more Coke. Something steady. And it's not even like he hasn't been gone before. But at least that time she could visit him. At least that time she always knew exactly where he was.

This time he just fucked off. No note, no warning, just his stinking room, pizza boxes mixed with underwear and CDs. She would have thought he'd evaporated into the ether or dived into his screen if his bag and his laptop and a couple of his favourite T-shirts (including his Microsatan shirt with the red-horned Bill Gates) hadn't gone, too. Oh, and if his main machine wasn't completely dismantled and packed in boxes scrawled with the words 2 THE FEDS – ULL NEVER CATCH ME & IF U DO ULL NEVER PROOVE IT! Which had kind of put her off reporting him missing.

Actually, he probably had left a note of sorts. There was a three-and-a-half-inch floppy disk taped to Mandy's door that morning with 'MAND' written on in her own lippy. She had ripped it off, a flake of gloss on the sellotape, thrown it on top of a speaker and charged across the landing to scream at him for messing up her paintwork. Which was when she found him gone, the boxes. It was the next day when she remembered it, put it in her bag, took it to work, waited for five clear minutes to sneak it into Mr Patel's computer. Nothing. A blank disk. Blank now, anyway, after twenty-four hours demagnetizing.

At lunch she'd tried it at the internet café and, having found it empty yet again, checked her email. And it had fallen in as if from space – five lines of static translated into random symbols. Meaningless now, but definitely from Robbie.

It's been months and still they come. Mandy tried half-heartedly to decipher that first time, failed. Now she checks, opens, sits and stares, making up messages from her lost brother. Sometimes she imagines him in a tax haven doing that thing where you take 1p from everyone's bank account and become a billionaire. Other times he's working for a top-secret government programme. She even pictures him cackling and wringing his hands, deputy to a Bond villain. Then again, maybe he's crouched on a bed in a YMCA somewhere, plugged into their phone line, helpless. Part of her believes he's ceased to exist in any material form, that he's become an information organism, an endless stream of ones and noughts. She wonders whether he felt under-appreciated, whether she should have made more of an effort to let him know how grateful she was. But all their utility bills keep coming through with nothing to pay and the cable's still on, so he can't be that upset. She's pissed off with him, yeah, but hopes, sincerely hopes, he's happy. For some reason, she's never thought to hit REPLY.

One thing's for sure, *he* was never any replacement for Robbie, just a bit of fun. Not even that. Just a way to move her story forward.

It wasn't the last time they had sex, officially, but it feels like it was the last time – the last time they did properly. The only time. He was really trying to make it good, anyway. And it was, really good, and she felt it building, her muscles tightening, every one of them, her movements being taken beyond her control, her hips dancing to their own tune. Concerned he was going too soon she had leant right back and got her hand down there, tipping her head away from him and looking straight up into the white *lite* of a summer's day.

So when that whiteness flooded down on her, quickly, so quickly, it took her a moment to realize she wasn't shagging in a hotel room any more but was somewhere else altogether. This whiteness, this blankness, this perfect nothingness, like the place she had imagined for irrational numbers to exist in. Just like that, no warning, there. And though it was nothing like water, Mandy had begun to swim, as if you could move forward through nothingness, as if you could pull on abstraction. But all the same she swam, unthinking, unable to stop, her muscles aching like she always had. And it went on for days, the whiteness, the swimming, the clean blankness of her existence until she thought, *I'm dead, I must be fucking dead.*

Which was when she found herself in the study, like something from a film, books everywhere, worn brown patterned carpets, a leather armchair and a woman, a woman there in the room, always just at the edge of her vision, like those microbe echoes on your eyes, jumping away in seahorse loops when you try to look at them. And this woman was saying something again and again, just three words, but no sound was coming out and when Mandy tried to focus on her lips the woman had moved again and when Mandy said *I don't understand, I can't hear you*, no sound came out and the room was silent, too. Not silent like a silent room, silent like Mandy had been born with no ears, no auditory canal, no nerves, nothing, silent like a pin dropping in a vacuum. *I can't hear, I can't hear anything. I can't hear anything.*

And then the woman was directly in front of Mand, only Mand didn't look at her face or really watch her mouth moving now that she could. No, Mandy watched the woman's right hand, flat palm toward her, swing round in a perfect half-circle – machine-tooled smooth – and disappear from her line of sight moments before exploding on the back of her head.

The pain a flash of the whiteness, everything around her gone, all gone, just this ice-pick pain to say she was still there. And then, as she felt herself lying somewhere, lying in a bed with covers over her, the cotton sharp beneath her fingers, a voice, her voice saying *I am Chosen*. Like that, just like that, *I am Chosen*, capitals and everything.

Which was when the sound returned, his voice asking *Are you OK? Mandy, are you OK?* The only time she can remember him using her name, actually.

I am Chosen.

Like that.

When Mandy was little, her nan gave her a stone egg, polished, a seaweed green colour, which she had bought on a special old folks' pilgrimage to Iona. Mandy had convinced herself that if she kept it warm a dragon would hatch from it, so carried it everywhere, carefully swaddled, one hand or the other always wrapped round it. For months. Seemed like months. Never told anyone.

She has two eggs now. One slowly sinking into the back of her head, as if the woman had put something inside her when she hit her. The other the words, her words and that woman's, too, held tight to her, kept warm: *I am Chosen.*

Mandy's not sure what it means yet, not exactly. She's always felt she's not fulfilling her potential, that she must be great at something, *special*. She has had the feeling since she was small, looking through magazines at famous people, watching their smiles on telly. She has always known she is unique. Not like we're all supposed to be. Like only the special few. She's just never known how to express it, how to show it to the world. Now it's all being revealed, it's all coming true. She spends her evenings flicking through the Discovery, History and Life channels looking for religion and finding it in everything.

She knows it's not going to be any kind of thing where she has to wash anyone's feet, because for one thing, feet are gross, and for another, you don't go to the bother of being Chosen to be someone's lackey. She's been someone or other's lackey for long enough, she thinks. So, right now, she picks and chooses the best bits and hopes it'll turn out something like that when she receives her next Sign. A bit like warming up before a race, shaking out her legs for the hundred-metre sprint. Sometimes she sniggers to herself at the thought of the clothes she might have to wear. Then she remembers her *uniform*. Mandy is Chosen, even if she doesn't really know how or for what. What need has she got for worrying? Or for him? What does it matter if it's true?

She can feel it, though, feel this crackling power in her, the movement of the sea beyond the walls. It's always been there, churning in the darkness of her stomach. Her nerves so alive the table top feels like an island. She swills down the last of her chocolate cold, a tendril of mallow and milk clotted up the side of the cup, checks her watch. Better get back. Rises, the chair and floor screeching, then stops, her hands still on the table, smiles.

Fucking silly. Silly idea.

But then again, why not?

Mandy closes her eyes and pictures the blankness of her vision, tries to will herself back there. Breathes deeply, imagines the world around her disappearing. Then flicks them open.

She's met by a shudder of brown, the lights fading for a moment then stuttering up again, the world re-forming.

She thinks there's something wrong with her till she hears the boy at the counter (*'What the fuck . . .?'*), sees the faces at the tables, the fear deferred, people sitting down again. Numbers the gap in her head. One, two, three, four, five, six, seven, eight, nine, ten. Closes her eyes. Holds it there.

When Mandy looks again she sees the lights along the great hall go out one by one, each panel diminishing to a central spot and a smaller central spot, sucked out until there's nothing there at all. The lights in the cafeteria follow. The lights in the shops. The shops' signs. The emergency exit trails embedded in the floor. Every light gone. The world reducing. A whole world vanishing. And last, blackness. At last there's only blackness, so thorough that Mandy begins forgetting everything that was there before. There are no stars to navigate by, no constellations to interpret, nothing in the sky but concrete and earth.

In the moment before the screaming starts, before panic roars through Clearwater like a fire, Mandy hears, hears this time, a complete silence – music, coffee machines, tills, phones, electric doors, air-conditioning, the hum of computer fans, even people, all stilled. Frozen, so that for an instant there is nothing to see and nothing to hear, just phantom touch transmitted by phantom limbs to the gap where her head should be.

And so it is that she closes her eyes. And so it is that she pulls herself up. And so it is that she steps forward. And so it is that she walks. And let it be said that she sees nothing yet walks as if she sees. And let it be said that nothing stands in her path. And so it is that those around her cease their fearful cries at her approach. And so it is they step toward her (blind, all blind). And so it is that, like her mouth, their mouths curve upward, all their smiles, each one, invisible in the dark. And so it is that they are unsettled by their own sense of calm, this tranquillity they feel. And let it be said that they follow her unseeing through this long, unending night. And let it be said that she gathers them about her. And so it is. And so it is. And let it be said.

Imagine it – there are people here who wish they had never come shopping. Mothers, fathers, brothers, sisters, sons and daughters all. Huddling, groping, each history reduced to this. Regretting now the angry words snapped over breakfast cereal, the urgency with which the kids were despatched to school, the middle finger to fellow traveller who blocked the motorway's outer lane. Regretting the phone call that wasn't made last night, the bustle, the torpor, the uneasy watching of cookery programmes and makeover shows, the ready meal, the marriage, the drink, the hours at art galleries or theatres reaching for the pretence of understanding. Regretting ever trying crack, regretting never trying crack, regretting giving up smoking, regretting starting, regretting reading the wrong books, regretting reading the right, regretting those hours on the running machine and those hours off it. Regrets clumping together for warmth, a comfort in these difficult times. Regretting coming here to satisfy a need that has vanished with the light. Regrets mush-room-cultivated here in the damp of each mind. Regretting, most of all, not buying that key-ring with the torch built in.

Her moment has arrived, her moment of destiny, we could say, though it makes us blush a little. What does it matter if she knows where she's taking them? Somehow the cameras will keep running. Somehow they will record it all, each aura, the heat flaring from their armpits. This is their nation, after all, these people. It's their right to be filmed. You just have to believe. All you have to do is believe.

Acknowledgements

Special thanks for advice, encouragement and/or patience to Nick Midgley, Simon Skevington, Matthew Shapland, Adam Wishart, Patrick Walsh and Lee Brackstone.

Extra special thanks for all of the above and more to Leila Baker and to Miriam and Saul.

In 1981, Margaret Thatcher quoted Victor Victor's sentiment that 'economics is the method; the object is to change the soul,' but it's probable she meant it more piously than its originator.